Praise for Ben Marcus's

THE FLAME ALPHABET

"In the guise of a horror novel (albeit one written by a supremely intelligent literary novelist), Marcus has delivered a subtle meditation on the necessity as well as the drawbacks of human communication . . . in searing, sometimes hallucinatory prose."

—*Richmond Times-Dispatch*

"Thrilling, boasting an erudition and an obsessiveness that smacks both of Jorge Luis Borges and of Darren Aronofsky."

—*The Boston Globe*

"As I read *The Flame Alphabet*, late into the night, feverishly turning the pages, I felt myself, increasingly, in the presence of the classic."

—Michael Chabon

"Marcus succeeds in creating a parallel universe that mirrors a side of human social life that might be more comfortably concealed."

—*The Columbus Dispatch*

"An apocalyptic nightmare. Its vision is eerie, droll and heartbreaking, both lavishly written and haunting to behold. . . . [Marcus's] use of language could hardly be more vibrant." —*Portland Press Herald*

"Some of the most thoughtful and moving writing I've ever read about family life." —Michael Jauchen, *The Rumpus*

"Disturbing and remarkable." —*LA Review of Books*

"This novel will cause many mouths to open. Dialogue will ensue. People will have something to say." —*The Plain Dealer*

"A mystery, a compulsive page-turner." —*Salon*

"*The Flame Alphabet* has the force of a nightmare, a testament to Marcus's skill."

—NPR

"Ben Marcus is the rarest kind of writer: a necessary one."
—Jonathan Safran Foer

"*The Flame Alphabet* is less about linguistics than the decay of relationships, the fracturing of familial loyalties, and the everyday heartbreak of human estrangement." —*The Millions*

"Ben Marcus is a genius, one of the most daring, funny, morally engaged and brilliant writers, someone whose work truly makes a difference in the world." —George Saunders

"A brutal, wonderful book, streaked with the sickly brown and gray hues of Philip K. Dick and David Cronenberg."
—"The A.V. Club," *The Onion*

"A truly strange, original vision of a post-linguistic world."
—*Slant Magazine*

"Freakishly sad and incredibly good." —*Bookforum*

"An authentic meditation on the sacred cruelty of communication that will leave his readers speechless." —*San Francisco Chronicle*

"You will not read too many books like this in your life."
—*Financial Times*

"For all its surreal touches, it packs an emotional wallop." —*Wired*

BEN MARCUS

THE FLAME ALPHABET

Ben Marcus is the author of three books of fiction: *Notable American Women*, *The Father Costume*, and *The Age of Wire and String*, and he is the editor of *The Anchor Book of New American Short Stories.* His stories, essays, and reviews have appeared in *Harper's*, *The New Yorker*, *The Paris Review*, *McSweeney's*, *The Believer*, *The New York Times*, *Salon*, and *Time*. He is the recipient of a Whiting Writers' Award, a National Endowment for the Arts Fellowship in fiction, three Pushcart Prizes, and awards from the Creative Capital Foundation and the American Academy of Arts and Letters. He lives in New York City and Maine.

ALSO BY BEN MARCUS

The Age of Wire and String

Notable American Women

THE FLAME ALPHABET

THE FLAME ALPHABET

BEN MARCUS

Vintage Contemporaries
Vintage Books
A Division of Random House, Inc.
New York

FIRST VINTAGE CONTEMPORARIES EDITION, NOVEMBER 2012

The Cataloging-in-Publication Data is on file at the Library of Congress.

Vintage ISBN: 978-0-307-73997-1

Book design by Soonyoung Kwon

www.vintagebooks.com

Printed in the United States of America
10 9 8 7 6 5 4 3 2 1

To my family—Heidi, Delia, and Solomon

1

1

We left on a school day, so Esther wouldn't see us. In my personal bag, packed when my wife, Claire, had finally collapsed in sleep against the double-bolted bedroom door as it was getting light out, I stashed field glasses, sound abatement fabrics, and enough rolled foam to conceal two adults. On top of these I crammed a raw stash of anti-comprehension pills, a child's radio retrofitted as a toxicity screen, an unopened bit of gear called a Dräger Aerotest breathing kit, and my symptom charts.

This was the obvious equipment, medical gear I could use on the fly, from the car, at night. That is, if I even got the chance.

I did not bring LeBov's needle. I had tried the needle and the needle did not work.

My secondary supplies consisted of medical salts and a portable burner, a copper powder for phonic salting, plus some rubber bulbs and a bootful of felt. Eye masks and earplugs and the throat box that was functioning as the white noisery, to spew a barrier of hissing sound over me.

Tucked into the outside pouch, for quick access, I placed a personal noise dosimeter, hacked to measure children's speech. I wanted to be able to hear them coming.

In my pocket I carried the facial calipers, even if by now finer measurements weren't required. You could perform the diagnostic just by looking.

Murphy scoffed at this gear, called it salt on the wound. He called it things worse than that, said I was fooling with toys. Medicine, said Murphy, was a vain decoration inside of your body. Invisible war paint, ritual and superstition, typical Jewish smallwork.

Murphy had other plans. Murphy was arming from LeBov's list and LeBov's orders came straight from Rochester, where reports on the speech fever had first collected and the cautions were so total now, it was a wonder people weren't burying themselves alive.

Of course I have no evidence that they were not.

Finally in foil shielding I packed the volatile artifacts themselves: some samples of our daughter Esther's speech, recorded and written. A language archive of the girl. Paper and tapes, a broad syllabus of topics, a spectrum of moods. Our viral girl, fourteen years old, singing, laughing, yelling, whispering, arguing, speaking sotto voce, making up words. Reciting letters, numbers, crying out in pain. Even some foreign language statements, which I had instructed Esther to recite phonetically.

These I sealed in the woolen dossier because I could not look at the writing anymore without feeling what I could only call the crushing.

Pain is too soft a word for the reaction. *Crushing* was more accurate, an intolerable squeezing in the chest and the hips, though I didn't have measurements to support the claim. The Marshall Symptom appliance, bolted to the sidewalk outside the medical center on Fifth Street and visited by a procession of gray-faced neighbors, was meant to detect just how slushed our insides were from too much speech, how blighted we'd become from the language toxin. But the needle was pegging on every sniffle and pain, the appliance red-lighting nearly everyone it tested as overdosed, scorched, past the point of help.

So far the crushing was a personal observation, as with most of the symptoms we'd heard about, and as such it might as well be dismissed.

This bag of gear, as heavy as a small child, would go into the car last.

Claire and I weren't the only parents to ditch our houses and, in some cases, *other items of value*. The command went out in early December, issued in a final radio report before the stations went mute, and everyone was leaving. But there was altogether no eye contact from the other men and women likewise packing their cars. The conferring, the hand-wringing, the coolly delivered expertise some of us had to endure from the defensive, uninformed types—that had come and gone, leaving only stupefaction in its place. A disbelief walled off by illness. The know-it-alls are always the last to know. Everyone's a diagnostician, and everyone's wrong.

In cities, in towns, in the rural deposits, along the ledge that dropped off into outer Rochester, and in the middle field beyond the swale that some still called the Monastery, quarantines of children clustered up, overtaking neighborhoods, fields, forests, any venue that could be roughly bound by fencing. Loudspeakers lashed to trees, broadcasting the vocal repellent. Fairy tales blasting into the woods, convulsing any adult who came near. Loved ones telephoned each other to exchange dead air, a language of sighs, because to do any more, to build any speech into that heavy breathing, would bring them to their knees.

Which is where some of us belonged.

Today our leaving was blessed by a sheer wall of privacy. The body language on our street could have been studied for its gesture-perfect evasions. Just weeks before, Rabbi Burke, speaking by cable to our Jewish hut, called it defended semaphore, the gestures of a body craving disappearance. How many ways can you say *Stay the fuck away from me* without speaking? It was a well-crafted public solitude. We were all artfully alone out there, a condition we had better get used to.

After we were sure Esther was gone, I helped Claire downstairs and tried to get her to eat. I pushed some eggs at her, even though I knew that soon I'd be scraping those eggs into the trash. I gave her the sippy cup of juice and forced her hand around a piece of bread. She did not fight my attentions. I pulled her over to the sink and cleaned off what I could. A yolk stain at the corner of her mouth resisted my rough scrubbing, until I realized it was no stain, but jaundice blooming under her skin. Later I could examine her with the lamp, but now it was time to get her out to the car.

Claire's sole task, given her condition, was to sit in the passenger seat and keep watch. Any sign of Esther walking up the street, a girl with an overstuffed book bag, or so it would seem, and we'd be gone.

It's not that Esther would be allowed near us. The foam-clad officials, barricaded from what the children sprayed, had taken care of that. It was that we chose not to see our daughter captured as we drove away. We wished to avoid such a sight becoming our last image of Esther. Trapped in a net, twitching from a jolt they fired at her. If I policed

Claire on this task, holding her to my small request, I would be viewed as endorsing and even relishing what we were doing. I'd like to call that a small price to pay, but it wasn't. It was a steep, nasty price. Blame no longer hovered over this whole enterprise. It had landed badly, breaking into pieces inside me, and I was making it welcome.

Even before the quarantine was announced, we knew we had to leave. We talked it through as much as Claire could endure, and she had agreed, or, at least, she had assented silently, before wandering back to her soundproofed room, that our exit would be undertaken without the *complication* of Esther's presence. We would not so much as let ourselves see her.

She hated how I verbally rehearsed everything.

I hated it, too.

Once just days before we left, when she was eating candy with a corpse-like lethargy, her hand a cold, blue paw tucking sweets beneath her hospital mask, I showed Claire the timeline I thought we should follow and she held the paper away as if it were an old diaper, heaving an ugly laugh.

Claire had just accommodated a long needle in her hip and she remained perfectly quiet, the stoic patient submitting to her treatment. Now she was rewarding herself with a bowl of candy. My timing was not fine.

"You actually wrote this down," she finally said, her voice hollowed out through the mask.

A statement and not a question. Some essential marital weaponry from the arsenal of not giving an inch. Verbalize someone's actions back to them. Menace them with language, the language mirror. Death by feedback.

"It's a suggestion," I said, in the bedside voice I'd adopted as her caretaker.

Of course it wasn't a suggestion. It was the plan and it was what we had to do. Otherwise there'd be chalk marks around us in days. We had tripped our Esther threshold weeks ago, and our medicine—the comprehension blockers, the agents of estrangement, the treated smoke that left a sick chill to our faces—was only making us worse. There was nowhere safe to send Esther, so it was we who had to depart. The children would remain.

How the children would conduct themselves now that they were the only ones not sickened by speech, that was their business.

If you were smart, if you wanted to buy yourself a few more days, you wouldn't speak at all. Perhaps you already couldn't. The symptoms swallowed some people faster, circled others more slowly, allowing false strength to set in. But for most of us the face was hardening. The lips were pulling back. Inside the mouth was turning tough, numb, and the tongue was docking. Denial had lost its blissful appeal as Claire turned into a paper-skinned creature, sloughing each time she disrobed, too tired to cough. I could live without all the pretense we poured into discussions where the issue had already been decided, where the issue left us no choice. So much ceremony around caring what the other person thought. We'd rub our faces in etiquette, obsess over manners, and fail to notice that we were on the floor and the light was gone and it was no longer possible to breathe.

Claire gave the timeline back to me and turned away.

"Unbelievable," she whispered. "I hope you're enjoying yourself."

"Oh, I am, Claire," I said. "The time of my life."

2

The day my wife and I drove away, the electric should have failed. The phone should have died. The water should have thickened in our pipes.

When the Esther toxicity was in high flower, when it was no longer viable to endure proximity to our daughter, given the retching, the speech fever, the yellow tide beneath my wife's skin, to say nothing of the bruising around my mouth, that day should have been darker, altogether blackened by fire.

That day should have been visibly stained at the deepest levels of air, broken open, sucking people into oblivion. The neighborhood should have been vacuum-sealed, with people reduced to crawling figures, wheezing on their hands and knees, expiring in heaps.

A seizure of cold brown smoke should have spilled over the house.

What are the operative motifs from mythology when parents take leave of a child? Is there not some standard departure imagery offered by the fables?

The day we finally left, birds should have frozen midflight in the winter air as they cruised the neighborhood. Birds locked up with ice, their wings too heavy to hold them aloft. Birds fallen to the ground and piled at our feet, eyes staring up at the sky.

In the street, cars should have quit and rolled to a stop and the road should have buckled, with gases leaking forth, with water foaming out, with perhaps an unclothed man clawing his way from under the asphalt to stalk the neighborhood.

The yard where we played and sometimes picnicked, where Esther and I once staged father-daughter pretend fights, with fake angry faces, to confuse the passing motorists—*Is that a man fistfighting his young daughter?*—or where we argued in earnest, with calm faces that belied our true feelings, Esther asserting, no doubt correctly, that there was something I didn't *understand*—this yard might have functioned as a massive sinkhole. The yard, a throbbing pit in its center, should have exerted a steady pull on anyone in range.

From above, through the brown smoke, you should have seen people and dogs and the smaller trees getting dragged into the collapsing grass.

The day we left there should have been mourners in the street, a parade of weeping parents walking from their homes. Or not weeping. Past that. Devoid of all signs of feeling in the face. Just walking with calm expressions because their faces had finally failed to signal what they felt.

There should have been music pouring from a loudspeaker on the roof of an emergency vehicle. Or perhaps no music, no sound whatsoever. Instead, an emergency vehicle broadcasting a heavy coating of white noise so that even the leaves rustled silently. A plague of deafness, as if an unseen bunting smothered everything, drinking noise, so we could hear nothing.

Making mimes out of all of us. So that we couldn't hear ourselves breathe. So that our shared language would have been suddenly snuffed out.

What a fine bit of foreshadowing that all would have been.

But our neighborhood was failing to foreshadow.

What is it called when features of the landscape mirror the condition of the poor fucks who live in it?

Whatever it is, it was not in effect.

This was, instead, a plain day in the neighborhood, save for the shielded officials of the quarantine, lurking under trees until an enforcement was needed.

If you took the Sedgling exit off 38 and hugged the access road until the Beth Elohim Synagogue reared up, and from there you veered right, keeping the highway at your back, you would pass the ring of bread and coffee shops, and the town square with its deafening fountain, before entering our not-so-gated community of houses just new enough to be nothing special at all.

Perhaps the first thing you'd see that was curious as you circled up Montrier Hill, in the shadow of the electrical tower, which on a clear day dropped a net of darkness over the houses, yards, and roads, was a clottage of ungaraged cars, skewered hastily against curbs, up and down the street with their trunks and doors open, bags spilling out, and men and women who, if you examined them closely, looked more medically defeated than frantic.

And you would have seen, no matter how hard you looked, even if you checked the houses from closet to attic to cellar, precisely no children, least of all those blasting language from their not-so-innocent faces.

Adults only. Cars, suitcases, tears.

A masking silence probably would have been noticed. The neighborhood language-free.

There'd be coatracks flashing across lawns, strung up with intravenous pouches fashioned from sandwich baggies, toppling over into the grass, with people scrambling to leave.

Everyone ill from something no one could explain. What the news first had called hysteria, which everyone wished was true. If only it were that.

And finally, at the dark, water-soaked end of Wilderleigh Street, an area of limited sun penetration, there'd be the anemic figures of my wife, Claire, and me, shuffling from the house to the car, carrying one item at a time, loading up for a getaway, with Esther, our only child, thank you God, nowhere in sight.

Do the math on that.

3

In the months before our departure, most of what sickened us came from our sweet daughter's mouth. Some of it she said, and some of it she whispered, and some of it she shouted. She scribbled and wrote it and then read it aloud. She found it in books and in the mail and she made it up in her head. It was soaked into the cursive script she perfected at school, letters ballooning with heart-dotted *i*'s. Vowels defaced into animal drawings. Each piece of the alphabet that she wrote looked like a fat molecule engorged on air, ready to burst. How so very dear.

The sickness washed over us when we saw it, when we heard it, when we thought of it later. We feasted on the putrid material because our daughter made it. We gorged on it and inside us it steamed, rotted, turned rank.

Esther sang as she walked through the house. Her voice was toneless, from the throat, in a frequency high in warding power. A voice with a significant half-life, a noxious mineral content, that is, if it could be frozen and crystallized, something then beyond our means or imagination. If her voice could have been made into a smoke, we would have known. If you heard it you were thoroughly repelled. She muttered in her sleep and awake. She spoke to us and to others, into the phone, out the window, into a bag. It didn't matter. Nice things, mean things, dumb things, just a teenager's chatter, like a tour guide to nothing, stalking us from room to room. Blame and self-congratulation and a constant narration of this, that, and the other thing, in low-functioning if common rhetorical modes, in occasions of speech designed not particularly to communicate but to alter the domestic acoustics, because she seemed to go dull if she wasn't speaking or reading or serving somehow as a great filter of words.

She did it without thinking, and she did it to herself, and it was we alone who were sickened.

But of course we'd find out it was others, too. Others and others and others.

What she said was bitter, and we sipped at it and sipped at it, her mother and I, just ever so politely sipped at it until we were sick, because this was the going air inside our house, our daughter talking and singing and shouting and writing.

Whatever we thought we wanted, to hug or kiss our daughter, to sit near her, it was our bodies that recoiled first. We cowered and leaned away from her words, we kept our distance, but Esther was a gap closer, bringing it all right up to our faces. Some sort of magnet was in effect. A father magnet. A mother magnet. As we fled, Esther gave chase. We covered our ears and she talked louder. Our daughter seemed not to care who was listening, and we were ready at hand, ready to service her needs. We stood up to it and took it like parents, because doesn't the famous phrase say: *shit on me, oh my children, and I will never fail to love you*?

We'd heard this at the forest synagogue from Thompson during an intermission, when Rabbi Burke allowed his staff access to the radio transmission, and we'd sat in the hut nodding our abstract consent to such a promise. Yes, of course we would love our daughter no matter what. How ridiculous to think otherwise. *Ridiculous*. It was so easy to agree to what did not test us.

The sickness rode in on my name. Loaded and weaponized. Samuel, which Esther was old enough, her mother and I thought, to call me. A little grace note of parenting, which seemed to work for other people, and which we proudly took up as though we had invented it. But Esther wasn't impressed by this privilege. She barked my name until it became an insult, said it louder, softer, coughed it up and spat it at me.

We had missed the warnings on this one, phrases transmitted to our synagogue, the rabbi's droning cautions. *And they were killed with their own names*. From the Psalms. *Beware your name, for it is the first venom.*

Revelations. These warnings had always seemed like metaphors, the wishful equations of some ancient person's mind. Little comfort, in the end, and it wasn't my name alone that was toxic, but all of them.

It came in hello and good-bye and any little thing she said. Except Esther didn't much say hello. When she didn't use my name she said *Hey* and *Daddy*. She said *Ciao* and *Okeydokey* on her way out, language she shared with some of the gender-neutral underlings, incapable of eye contact, she prowled around with, and with fingers I dragged my mouth to smile, even though it fell slack again when I dropped my hand.

The reasoning, when reasoning seemed possible, was simple. Better to stand up to those happy moments, if that's what they were, and give Esther a father who wasn't such a spoiler, who didn't turn pale on the occasion of even the most basic speech. But my face leaked force each time. A daughter was someone to pretend to be healthy for. A daughter shouldn't see such sickness. *Your child will be the end of you*, Rabbi Burke had not yet said. I could speak back to her, and I could hear, technically I could. I could ask about school, or the feuds that consumed her, the massive injustices, often by omission, perpetrated by her friends, but the words felt foreign, like they were built of wood. A punishment to my mouth just to extract them, like pulling bones from my head.

That this poison flowed from Jewish children alone, at least at first, we had no reason to think. That suffering would find us in ever more novel ways, we had probably always suspected.

4

At first we thought we were bitten. Something had landed on our backs and sucked on us. Now we would perish. It was September, and the air was still soaked in heat, a nasty fried smell in the yard. Claire and I traced our lethargy, the buzzing limbs and bodies that we dragged around like sacks, to a trip to the ocean, where we succumbed to ill-considered napping atop a crispy lattice of seaweed and sand gnats that left us helplessly scratching ourselves for days.

If we looked closely, a spatter of red marks spread across our backs. Map fragments, like an unfinished tattoo. Not freckles or moles. Possibly the welters from a bite, some rodent eating us while we slept.

Claire spread out on her belly and I straddled her for the examination, but this was the wrong, sad view of her. Her bottom flattened beneath me, as if relieved of its bones, and the generous skin of her back pooled onto the bed.

Esther walked in, looked at us with disappointment. I waved her away, mouthing some scold, hoping Claire wouldn't notice that she'd been exposed in this position.

"Really?" Esther said, louder than necessary. "I mean you couldn't even close the door?"

One should not look too closely at a spouse's back, should not pin her this way to a bed. This was ill-advised scrutiny. I didn't know what I was looking for anyway. Claire squirmed under me, tried to hide from Esther's sight.

"Mom's not feeling well," I said, climbing down.

"Then maybe you should leave her alone, Dad."

"I'm trying to help."

"Hm," said Esther, using her face to freely show what she thought of that.

Hadn't Esther, her skin unspoiled, still tauntingly clear, napped on the same tangled nest? We'd set up camp on burnt sand, waiting our turn in line to splash in the fenced-in patch of ocean. The three of us ripped through a bag of salted candies, then fell into one of those blissful afternoon beach comas, sleeping in the sun, our limbs fat with heat.

Claire had an explanation. The old, the tired, the ruined, got done in by bites. Turned into leaking sacks of mush. Whereas the young, they swigged venom to the lees and it supercharged their bodies. They could not be stopped.

Conversations from the museum of the uninformed. It troubled us that our common sense had so little medical traction. There were doctors, and there were armchair doctors, and then there were people like us, crawling in the mud, deploying childish diagnostics, hoping that through sheer tone of voice, through the posturing of authority, we would exact some definitive change of reality. Perhaps we thought the world we lived in could be hacked into pleasing shapes simply by what we said. Maybe we still believed that.

The medical tests, when we sought counsel, came back clear, the numbers low and dull. The doctors shooed us out. We had not been bitten. We would shake it off when the weather broke and the cold air came in. When the understaffed apparatus of our immune systems decided to take notice and erect a defense.

Who even said anymore that fresh air was supposed to help anything?

Drs. Meriwit and Borger did. Dr. Levinson did. Dr. Harris did. Nurses did, and interns at the clinic did, and the evening advisories did, as long as your doctor did.

This was hobby diagnostics. This was troubleshooting by the blind. The hindsight on this isn't just twenty-twenty. It sees straight through walls.

As Murphy would later say: *We are in a high season of error*.

The early diagnostics were sad and random, experts holding forth confidently on the unknown, using their final months as language users to be spectacularly wrong. We have unverified complaints, moaned the news.

In Wisconsin the trouble was pinned to dogs. Animals took the blame up and down the coast. From Banff, from almost everywhere, came the question of pollutants, which wasn't so wrong. Something in the air, something in the ground, a menacing particulate in the water. *Something from the child's mouth*, it took them too long to realize. Drink less water, drink more. Use this filter. Put this filter in your fucking throat. Stop breathing and cease listening for a little while. Victims were dried out and saltless. Salt played a role. Of course it did. Streaking dunes of salt collecting first in the Midwest, sweeping to the south. Drifts and ridges and swells. Attractive in the landscape, if you didn't know what it meant. Children themselves, their noxious oral product, were not yet being blamed, unless you counted the outskirt finger-wagging of LeBov, which too few of us did. But people were noticing that among the ill numbered no children. No one cared to connect the line from Lamentations that declares, *And not one child fell to the plague*. A university silo in Arizona published the theory that the impact of speech can be measured, with high dosages producing symptoms of the little death, the evening coma, a rictus in the legs. That would have been someone from LeBov's staff, operating under a fake name, floating the notion.

Before all names were fake. Before all notions had floated so far off, you could no longer see them.

No one important was really looking into history yet, uncovering precedent, so much of it that the foreshadowing was embarrassing. It was not yet discussed that from Pliny comes the idea of the child who speaks the poisonous word, who uses certain mouth shapes to spread pestilence. In our reading of Galen we had not yet connected several mentions of disease originating in the child's mouth. Herschel's cone, termed by Vesalius, describes the spray radius of speech, a contact perimeter for exposure, and this we did not know. Nor did we know that an acoustical rupture is observed in Herschel's cone by Paracelsus. Or that 1854 sees a medical exhibit in Philadelphia featuring the child-free detoxification hut, a prototype only, never adopted. Or that in the end Pliny had shielding nailed to his walls and sought immortality by banning children from his presence, dying only days later.

Our symptoms at first were too vague to name, too easily linked to how we always felt: a bit of sludge in our systems so that we dragged around the house and slept long and looked away from our food. Pushed our plates to the side. Caught ourselves staring into space, drool flooding from our mouths. Friends smirked. The childless ones, underexposed so far. The old loners. The selfish mates who perfected hobbies and tended their own interests instead of turning over their lives to what Claire called a stewardship of the small and crazy. For a while they were fine. Just for a while.

In retaliation we limited our evening drinking, took aggressive walks, performed the recommended stretches and bodywork. But our joints were hardening and our muscles were tight, and when I bent over I could no longer easily breathe. At night we filled ourselves with water and slept more deliberately, with silencing and darkening gear, when we weren't waking up to dry heave. But we were every day stiffening, growing sicker, paler, more exhausted with what Esther could not stop doing.

A decline in our appearance came next. Claire's own hair had come to look like a wig, as if her body might reject it all at once. Her hands had the dimpled plastic cast of a mannequin, a body painted with something fake, then cooked. She had never worn much makeup before, but now she was pasting her face with it and she shuffled through the house with the clownish features an undertaker smears on his bodies.

I smiled her way, a little too wide, because the display concerned me. I produced superlatives and praise, in chivalrous phrases that sounded like a foreign language, but I couldn't get the tone right. I couldn't scrub my voice of worry. If she returned my look she did so defiantly, daring me to say what I was really thinking. But I had already stopped doing that.

A death mask aesthetics arose, and it occurred to me that Claire was making herself look worse on purpose. Which the sick will do. One can never be sick enough. Even the stricken can milk it.

Some nights Claire and I pushed through the air as if it were solid, our bodies cleaving into fuzz, and then we came to a halt in it, locked up as if in a thick paste.

"What's wrong with you guys?" Esther snapped one night, looking up from the book she was reading as we drifted through dinner. Those words alone tightened my face and I tried to cloud what I heard so I could breathe again.

Clouding. A good word for the strategic inattention one needed to practice around children.

This was October, before my medical smallwork began, the interventions I conducted to protect myself and Claire. Smallwork, the techniques to keep you alive, at large, prompted from instructions received at our synagogue hut, when it was time to take matters into our own hands.

On our bookshelves we had yet to install the speakers that would pump fine washes of hiss into the room, an acoustical barrier that would mostly fail to cloak Esther's language.

In our town, in the sweet spot of our county, we were like dark lumps of flesh moving through plasma. In a thousand years, perhaps, our descendants might evolve into creatures with a morsel of understanding at their core, some insight to untangle their gnarled dilemma, but for now, at this moment in our unevolved history, we were blessed with no skill for diagnosing our withered, exhausted state.

We groped about, and if there was a harm's way, we plunged into it so deeply that we were smeared up to the neck with the very stuff, the greasy paste, that was slowly killing us.

We were tired, is what we said, which was like saying we were alive. Of course we were tired, who wasn't? Asleep is the new awake, Claire conceded, tossing her hair back to reveal the muddled watercolor lady she'd made of herself. We weren't worried yet. Don't let your children see you worry: a rule we pursued, because in our hands a public show of feelings was not sporting. Claire and I had a way of smiling gamely at each other, which meant an admission of illness would be seized upon and punished. We would summon great blame. Our marriage, among its other features, had blacklisted claims of weakness.

"I'm sorry, Sweetie," I said to Esther. "We're fine. We should go to bed early tonight, that's all."

Issued as a gentle command from one ashen father to his family.

Esther had turned back to her book by then, reading with the glaring superiority that suggested that this adventure story, or whatever she happened to be reading, was so far beneath her, she could hardly see it, idiot language engraved into paper by morons. And then when our food was already wilted and cold, after the conversation had expired, we heard the barest muttering from her. "If we go to bed any earlier, we might as well not get up."

. . .

The symptoms worsened. Someone from Forsythe, one of the medical research labs, called it a virus, menacing to the old, the weak. Menacing to the living, he might as well have said. Claire and I looked dipped in ash. Claire smelled sour, and given the distance she kept from me, I must not have smelled so fine myself.

Something streamed down my legs when I coughed, when I breathed too hard. Something as warm and slow as blood.

Soon we had to work at the basic behavior. It was work to walk. It was work to get dressed. To get undressed was work. To pee, to drink, to groom, forget it.

With no official diagnosis forthcoming, we troubleshot at home, white-boarding the safer explanations first. Maybe this wasn't a sickness so much as us getting older. Who knew what we were supposed to be feeling, anyway? We assessed our self-care and charted our intake. On principle we ate the better foods. Was one meant to be perfect at nutrition, otherwise be sickened? At first for dinners we had nuts and greens and the healthy oils. Plates of firm white fish crusted up in a glowing pan, shards of salt littered on top. A handful of salad on the side. For dessert a flavored ice or some crisp, cool fruit.

Not anymore. The food burst into rotten morsels in my mouth when I ate. I thought I was chewing on skin, maybe my own. Frequently I spat sad things back onto my plate, and if I ate at all, I waited until Claire and Esther were asleep, snuck into the kitchen, and sucked on a rag soaked in apple juice, which offered cold relief.

Our weekly trips to synagogue, trekking to the woods each Thursday, were robotic, if we even went. Until October we heard only the usual services, Rabbi Burke's sermons lightened by occasional broadcasts of Aesop's tales. At synagogue we sat in stunned exhaustion, taking in nothing, and we barely got ourselves through the woods back home again before collapsing.

Claire and I started making way for each other, the small courtesies one shows a sick person. Wide berths in the hallway and boundaries observed in bed. We slept in lanes, did not visit each other in the night, even for the sexless embrace, to extinguish each other's insecurities, to see what comfort there wasn't in someone else's cold frame. Skills arise to suit this sort of work. I could turn over without breaching Claire's side of the bed. A person wants his space when he feels like that. Even our functional kisses—good night and, less happily, good morning—were drily offered at a distance, faces braving the infected space, bodies angled away as if leaning into a terrible wind. Separately we showered and bathed and soaked in salts, we rinsed with astringents, dutifully pursuing what hygiene we could manage, but something wasn't washing out, and I was versed enough in rotting, spoiling, putrefaction—we all have our specialties—to know that these odors of ours were not the oils of the skin or the tolerable foulness of sweat.

If Esther banged on the bathroom door and so much as shouted "Hurry!" that word alone tightened my throat. I'd go to my knees, the wind knocked out of me.

The evidence was mounting, but I seemed to have a pact against insight, a refusal to name my poison. Esther had no such inhibition. Esther knew, in the precocious way of nearly everyone but us. She might have thought it was what she said that hurt us: the actual words in their scathing specifics, as if meaning itself ever had that kind of power. But she could have been singing us love songs, cooing little melodies of affection, and the effect would have been the same. By now, or maybe always, the meaning failed to matter.

I required Esther's total silence. When I looked at her—a young girl dipped in a shell of unkillable health—it was with pure, scientific ambition. I had a technical, professional need, and it wasn't personal, or of course it fucking was. I needed my daughter to disappear from my sight. If I could have had a wish, I would have wished her away.

Dr. Moriphe, when we returned to her, did the blood work, metabolic panels, thyroid function tests, an ESR and a CRP. Claire got spun through a cylinder that whirred and clicked, a picture of deep blue space flickering on the screen, her body rasterized into a galaxy of points and dusky blotches.

Nothing to worry about here, reported the doctor.

Nothing your tiny mind can conceive of, I thought.

I sucked on a swab, spat in a jar, peed in a cup. My bottom was probed and, like a little boy, I giggled. Nothing conclusive came back, just the mortal data, the numbers within range, the levels of little concern.

In the waiting room neighbors stared at their pee-soaked laps, hacked into fistfuls of cloth. Some went shirtless from the pain. Out in the parking lot people shivered in their cars, sometimes didn't get out. The occasional ambulance stopped on our block, stayed too long, drove away finally, too quiet, its lights revolving in funereal silence.

Later Dr. Moriphe was sick herself, but doctors and their entourage employ a different vocabulary for their own physical failings. Each appointment I made was canceled by her office at the last minute. She, too, was not feeling so well. She was never really feeling up to coming to work, they said. Would you like to see someone else? they wanted to know.

I'd seen someone else. Someone else was a moron.

"Does she have children at home?" I asked.

What a gorgeously long pause came back.

They couldn't give out that information. We can pass on a message to her if you like, they offered, in their best professional voice. And I said sure, sure, please do that. Pass on a message.

5

Then came November's stay, a sweetly deluded phase of recovery that we fed with great doses of denial.

But in Wisconsin there were early adopters. A fiendish strain of childless adults who consumed the toxic language on purpose, as a drug, destroying themselves under the flood of child speech. They stormed areas high in children, falling drunk inside cones of sound. They gorged themselves on the fence line of playgrounds where voice clouds blew hard enough to trigger a reaction, sharing exposure sites with each other by code. Later these people were found dried out in parks, on the road, collapsed and hardening in their homes. They were found with the slightly smaller faces we would routinely see on victims in only a few weeks.

Drifts of salt blew in from the west, blew out to sea, leaving bleached streets, trees abraded to pulp. Perhaps just a coincidence. Sometimes the driving was blind, and on the highways blowers mounted to poles kept the roads clear.

But at home Claire woke up one morning and declared us cured.

Esther was away at horse camp, her school's fall trip. They'd gone to Level Falls Farm, a four-figure getaway that promised intimate occasions with horses and the experts who baby them. Blood money paid out to stop the flow of Esther's demands for a few seconds. Money paid to her school, who we already paid, so they could take her away for a while and we could fucking breathe.

Esther was probably riding a horse right now, wearing the black Mary Janes she refused to shed for anyone, even if it was a shit-clotted field she needed to cross. Or she was lugging a saddle to the stable, or standing not-so-patiently as someone overexplained something Esther already knew. At home she fumed when you doled out information she took to be a given. Anything factual went without saying. Esther opposed repetition, opposed the obvious, showed resistance to anything that resembled an instructional phrase, a word of advice, a sentence that carried, however politely, a new piece of information. These were off-limits, or else we would be scorched by her temper. Out in the world I wonder how she concealed it. With strangers a level of control must have been available to Esther that we never got to see. One hoped.

Perhaps while her mother and I were at home believing we might be getting better, Esther sat quietly in her farmhouse room at a mirror adjusting her collar so her head did not look, in her words, "like a tube," which was a great concern of hers that she angrily shared with us and that would never, ever be solved, because it was our fault. We'd made that body of hers, shaped it. We'd done it on purpose, out of spite, to keep her freakish, ensure her difference. Hadn't we? We were, she said, probably *glad* she came out that way. Oh, probably. At home we defeated this tube of Esther's head, daily, with high collars, scarves, turtlenecks. Endless strategies of cloth, sculpted around her neck. Even though we failed to detect the disorder ourselves, we made Esther's head seem rounder by fitting her with wide glasses, prescription-free. This would fool the eye, make her look like something that she was almost certainly not. And sometimes it even calmed her down, allowed her to move on to other troubles, our little girl's great project of faultfinding—with us, with others, with the world—that would never be complete.

With Esther upstate, our days without exposure numbered four by now.

Our health seemed to be flowing back, but there were hidden factors in play. We were ignorant of the illness plateau, the comprehension ratio we'd soon surpass. There were only so many words you could stand before you were done. About the child radius we were naïve. Naïve is too mild a word for what we were. With this illness, signs of recovery were the trickiest symptoms of all. Feeling better was perhaps just a form of stunned disbelief, a shutting down. Maybe this was the quiet before the really fucking quiet.

"I think I feel better," Claire announced, sounding blurry. "I'm definitely kicking this thing."

Said the half-dead person, I thought.

It was remotely possible she was right, which isn't to say Claire wasn't capable of objective diagnostics, but that sometimes she suffered from spells of positive thinking.

To prove her vigor, Claire cornered me, sexually, made a physical trespass. Seeking, it would seem, someone to leak on. But my body, pajama-clad and sweated out, with enough blood to power only part of me, failed to cooperate. Her lips dragged across my back like a rough little claw.

"What do you think?" she said. There was something forced to the way she kept rubbing, as if she wanted to get down to the bone.

Claire's breath soaked into me and she pitched her voice against my neck, speaking so closely to my body that only gibberish came out. This should have felt nice, but something sour hovered.

"Want to?"

"You mean now?" I stalled.

"We could," she said, and her hand dropped, found my coldness, squished it inside her fist.

There was no response. I rolled out of range.

Claire never propositioned me, which on its own would be understandable. Language shouldn't be required for a married couple to toil for their grain of pleasure. But she never actually took off pants, mine or hers, or got the enabling oils or the towel. I guess that was supposed to be a man's work, or maybe only mine. She sent out clues and then waited for me to follow through, but often I did the reverse. Some days I was blind to the clues a little bit on purpose.

In this case I was hoping to wait for Thursday, when we were at synagogue, the two of us in the woods after the broadcast had ended. In the hut, with the cold air pouring in, and the radio crackling in the background, it was easier to surrender to what sometimes, if we were exceptionally lucky, felt unterrible.

Claire furrowed back into me, tugged too hard, and I swallowed some bile. Part of her on the wrong part of me was gritty and rough. There was a terrible smell in the air, most likely my own, and my groin was cold. It seemed as if what she gripped so fiercely might come loose in her hand.

I tried to look at Claire, but her face was too close. "Should we later?" I said, hiding the apology in my voice.

I sold the gambit with the most unbothered look I could manage. It was important that she not feel rejected. I noted, too, that sudden atypical sexual desire, with predatory indicators, was a clear symptom. But of what I still wasn't sure.

"I'm just so happy," Claire said, and her hug turned cozy, safe.

Wasn't I happy, too? she wanted to know. Wasn't I?

We hadn't been outside in days. We hadn't gotten dressed or done more than swish some cold water in our mouths, inhale a little bit of soup, maybe submit to the coarse body brush we treated each other to at bedtime. But bedtime seemed to be all day lately, and since today, *with the contagion absent*, we found ourselves moving faster and suddenly dressed for an outing, we got in the car and took off for a black-blanket picnic in our usual spot, up on Tower Ledge.

The field was quiet when we arrived, thoroughly childless. Some older couples, wrapped in parkas and camp blankets, huddled around their bread and jam. They suffered from the facial smallness; I tried not to stare. But people with shrunken features seemed short on time. It was like they were on their deathbeds. A ventilator chugged along on a carpet, churning liquid in its tank. Beneath a shawl two women shared the mask, passing it back and forth without bothering to wipe it out between turns.

As usual, some families had run extension cords up from their cars to power portable heaters, casting shimmering air over the field. You could walk through pockets of heat, as if they had burst through a hole in the earth.

In the field no one sang, and if there was speech, it was whispered at levels too low to decode. People hummed in secretive tones, giving in to fits of coughing when their breath failed. When Claire and I walked through the grass looking for a dry patch where we might settle, picking our way through collapsed piles of people, we triggered ripples of silence in everyone we passed. No one wished to be overheard.

But I didn't want the secrets of these strangers. I did not think I could bear them.

The picnic tables, usually loaded with serving boats of communal food, were empty except for traces of gauze rolls, some shredded medical supplies. Wrist straps and crumbled yellow tubing sat in the dirt. A fluid had dried and gone dark in streaks over the grass. It looked like the aftermath of an outdoor surgery.

At the shaded end of the field, where the sand run was installed, no little dogs tore back and forth, kicking up blizzards of sand. No dogs to be seen in the whole field. No dogs and no children.

Over on the scorched cement pads no one was shooting off rockets into the woods below. The public fire pit hadn't been cleaned from last time, and last time seemed like long ago. A mound of coals spilled over the rim of the hole, and the spit rod was still filthy with skin, from what might have been the final cookout.

The field was usually so crowded that family blankets met at their edges until the grass was covered in a great rug of black tufted wool. But today our rugs were scattered far apart, too few to ever connect, and we sat in distant rafts from each other, mostly out of earshot.

"I guess it's sort of cold," I offered, by way of a theory.

Claire didn't second me. She must have also known that couldn't be it. We'd come here in weather far worse and the field was packed with families. In the snow last year we rolled our blanket over frozen grass. Someone built a fire inside an old iron lung, which got so hot it glowed. When the sun set in late afternoon some elders launched from a slingshot hardened balls of birdseed, which ripped through the sky and occasionally got intercepted, in dusty explosions, by the bald sparrows that kept watch in the trees and shot out when they saw food.

It was not such a nice day and there was illness in the field, but we decided to stay. We'd come all the way out here and both of us dreaded being home again, where the house smelled of our own spoiled traces. Esther was coming back tonight, so at least today, for a little while in the field, we could spend our recovery out of doors with some people who were almost our own.

The picnics were not strictly for the Jews of our neighborhood and maybe Bayside or Fort Wine, but they'd winnowed down that way. We were a community bound by an agreement to graze in the same field and enjoy the sight of each other, but beyond that it needn't escalate.

We used to bring our kids to these picnics as surrogate social agents and the kids seemed to coagulate in some violent, anonymous way, even if the adults cuddled inside their own force fields and only said hello to one another.

Hello was the perfect word. It began and ended all contact, delivering us into private chambers from which we could enjoy other people in textbook abstraction, without the burden of intimacy.

The kids would devour their food, then run off down the foot trail that dead-ended in a wall of trees. Well, other people's kids. We used to bring Esther to the picnics, but she clung to us and sulked, building out a gloom that she somehow bloodied our own hands with, as if *we* created her moods in a lab and force-fed them to her every day, giving her no choice but to display feelings of our own authorship. The other kids formed a roving pack, moving like one of those clusters of birds that seem to share a single, frantic brain.

Claire and I would scout the kids for Esther, identifying girls her age, potential targets for friendship.

"I like that girl's shoes," I'd say, and Esther wouldn't even look, just tell me that *I* should go talk to her if I liked her shoes so much.

"Is that how you captured Mom? Complimenting her footwear?"

"I didn't *capture* your mother," I said.

"Not yet," smirked Claire.

Kids approached Esther and asked her to play, but she politely declined, citing fatigue. Or she'd say, "No thank you, I never really get to spend time with my parents," putting her head in her mother's lap. Claire accepted the affection, ulterior or not, and petted Esther's hair, careful not to push things too far.

Last year a gaunt, tall girl trespassed our blanket and asked, in the workshopped tones of a second language, if Esther wanted to come see something. The girl smiled conspiratorially, as if to suggest that Esther's idiotic parents could have no idea how brilliant this thing was that she was inviting Esther to see. Parents were creatures with ruined, insensate heads, and how could they ever be expected to appreciate the marvels of the Monastery valley woods? What was it they'd found, a bucket of fresh, oiled genitals? When Esther declined, failing even to look intrigued, the girl ran off and was soon sucked into a cloud of children who plunged down the hill, shrieking.

"Sweetie, I thought she seemed nice," Claire said.

"Because she asked a question? That makes her nice? That's a fairly low standard, Mom."

"Well, because she was inviting you to join in, and that's a nice thing to do. She made an effort to include you."

"So if I try to coerce someone into doing something they don't want to do, then I'll be considered nice also?"

This was Esther logic. It was formidable.

"You guys wouldn't go running off with a pack of strangers," Esther said, "so why should I?"

"It's fun," I ventured, bracing myself for her response.

"Dad, can you name one time in your life when you suddenly ran off with a group of people you didn't know, screaming and laughing, simply because they were your age?"

I looked down, hoping Esther would lower her voice. But it was true, I could not think of a single time.

"I guess it's something you sort of stop doing when you get older," I admitted.

Esther looked at me so hard I couldn't bear it.

"So why can't I follow your example and never get involved in such practices in the first place? I'm not an animal. I don't follow people around simply because their asses smell good to me."

I probably sighed. Certainly I expressed disappointment without speaking. It always surprised me when I didn't just stoop to Esther's level but dug down below it, responding to her killing logic with sub-lingual ordnance. She watched my little performance, the facial codes I sent out to no avail. I saw her straining not to feel sorry for me.

"This picnic would be more successful," said Esther, as if she were honestly trying to troubleshoot what had gone wrong, "if you guys gave up your urge to control me."

"But where's the fun in that?" I said under my breath.

Sometimes Esther appreciated these retorts. Not today.

We were surrounded by other parents on the black rug, some of whom were overdoing their attempts to show they were not listening. Mostly they'd stopped talking, staring into space as if some wind-borne peril had paralyzed them.

"I think it's a perfectly successful picnic," Claire announced. "I'm having a terrific time. I really am."

The word *really* showed up now and then in family conversations like these. We all clung to it. A desperate little adjective.

Claire struggled to trust what she'd said. Perhaps she thought a voice-over would convince our audience. She had the amazing ability to conceal all evidence that she detected our prevailing moods, and if she ignored them maybe those moods would vanish. It is true that Claire's indifference to our despondency sometimes had a medical effect.

Esther looked as if she had been studying our discussion for a class. Her face was blank. She'd fended off another friend and perhaps in her world—with its new-generation accounting—this was a point scored, another success.

Down the ledge an awful blast of laughter rose up from the children, but on our carpet we were quiet.

Without Esther today we tried not to trouble our few neighbors in the field by staring. No one wants to be seen asleep with a blood-cracked mouth. The ventilator chugged and the wind swept waves of dry warmth at us from the heaters. A hairless couple slept loudly on the carpet nearby, the wife's face erased beneath a white hospital mask.

We ate and rested and we talked a little. Claire insisted that she felt fine. I wanted to believe her, but I felt scared deep in my body. This might have meant nothing. I could feel that way at the wrong times, when things were fine, when I slept or even laughed. Surges of fear that I'd learned to ignore. Eventually you stop paying attention to your own feelings when there's nothing to be done about them. I wanted to tell Claire I was frightened, but it seemed like one of those remarks that would lead to trouble.

Claire tucked some cookies in her mouth, moving them around with her tongue as if they had bones.

I would have liked to believe in her recovery, but the evidence was impossible to ignore. On our carpet Claire looked like one of those terminal patients let out of the hospital for a final field trip to her favorite restaurant, a ball game. A pity outing. She was thin and pale and when she smiled something dark shone from her mouth.

I would not oppose what Claire claimed about herself or argue her from her position, so I said nothing of the bruising on her hands, the dried blood crisped over one of her ears. Instead I scooted next to her and felt how little she was, how even through her coat I could feel the long cage of my wife's bones. When I hugged Claire, with sick people strewn in the field, I felt the shallow swell of her breath and she seemed to me like a bellows that I could control, opening and closing her to the air of the world. I thought if I held her I could always be sure she could breathe. I could just squeeze her a little bit, and when I released her the sweet air would rush in to revive her.

From our portable radio came word that studies had returned, pinpointing children as the culprit. The word *carrier* was used. The word *Jew* was not. The discussion was wrapped in the vocabulary of viral infection. There was no reason for alarm because this crisis appeared to be *genetic in nature*, a problem only for *certain people*, whoever they were.

It was probably only contagious within a certain circumference.

Allergy is such a broad word, claimed one of the experts on the news. Of course, to some degree, we are allergic to everything. But we react at different rates, sometimes so slowly that we never show symptoms.

I imagined myself tearing up this man's credentials, burying him in a hole.

As our tools of detection improve, we see more symptoms.

At this point it was not a terrible idea, if you felt you *fit the category*, to bring your child in for testing.

When they started listing counties, I turned off the radio.

The day defaulted with small eruptions of chatter until the air fell cold at the appointed hour. The sun looked ready to falter. Our neighbors drifted off, helping each other from the field in a long, slow shuffle until Claire and I were alone.

This was what we wanted. We usually waited late into the afternoon for everyone to leave so we could have the last bright minutes of the day to ourselves.

At a high southern swell in the field, past the fire pit, a sight line down the ledge into the tangle of evergreens allowed us to see the rough location of our forest synagogue, a little two-person hut hidden in the woods.

If our hut had an antenna, perhaps it would surface through the trees and serve as a landmark. Maybe on a day like this we could look down from the field and see it. But our hut used no antenna, so from the field you could never see the structure itself or even the little trail we took each Thursday up from the creek bed to get there. From above you couldn't see anything but woods. From above you couldn't be sure that our synagogue existed. Sometimes even inside it, while Rabbi Burke's sermon pumped from the strange radio, I felt the same way.

Claire and I held hands as the field darkened and we said nothing. Our silence was a rule of the synagogue, something we swore to when we were first entrusted with membership. We did not discuss what we heard there, nor did we discuss the hut itself. Even just looking at it from this elevation in the field we remained, by mandate, quiet.

But I wouldn't have had it any other way. The enforced silence was a relief. Because all talk was banished we could not disagree, we could not mutually distort what we heard during services. There was nothing to debate, nothing to say, and the experience remained something we could share that would never be spoiled with speech.

On the footpath back to the car, we passed people huddled in the woods, voices warped in dispute. A man wept and a woman seemed to berate him in whispers. Normally when couples fought, Claire and I put our heads down and charged past them, congratulating ourselves later for getting along so well. We'd never fight like that! Out in public! We were better than that!

But this didn't seem like a domestic argument.

Through the trees, in the grass, sat a man and woman I recognized from the picnics. They had two kids I didn't much enjoy, boys who belted each other and fell down so often, they seemed immune to pain and probably the higher feelings as well. But I didn't see the boys now, only the parents.

Standing over them was a large man with red hair, wearing an athletic suit. He was not one of the regulars from the field. I didn't know him.

"Everything okay?" I called into the trees.

The couple didn't respond, just whispered harder.

"We're good," the tall redhead finally answered, and when the man groaned, the redhead seemed to shush him.

Are you speaking for everyone? I didn't ask.

The redhead looked back through the trees, weaving to get an angle on us, but I'm not sure what he could see.

Claire pulled on my arm. "C'mon," she said, "let's go."

It was getting darker and colder and Claire and I were too tired to have been out this long. She tugged on me and leaned downhill, pleading.

"Maybe I should call someone," I whispered to Claire, pulling against her.

But the redhead must have heard me.

"We've already called someone, they're coming. Everything's taken care of."

He didn't look our way. He seemed to be trying to block my view of the other two. If I could have examined them, would I have seen the facial smallness, felt a hardened callus forming under their tongues? Would there have been a yellow stain in their eyes?

Claire started off downhill without me, said she'd meet me at the car.

The redhead went to his knees, folding his huge body over both of them as if he might protect them from a blast. Then a distant, small sound, a kind of high-pitched whine, pierced the air. But it could have been anything, really. It probably was.

I waited and heard nothing, then struck off down the path back to the car.

When I looked back one last time, the redhead had emerged from the woods and stood by himself on the path. He didn't see me, just started heading uphill, back to the field, which was empty by now, and certainly growing dark.

I couldn't think what a man like that would want up at a Jewish picnic field at night.

This was Murphy, walking away from me. I would formally meet him in a week, and not by accident. He was already canvassing Jewish families, probably had been for months, or even longer. *Canvassing* might not be the word for what he was doing. *Cornering*, *manipulating*, *extracting*. There is no precise word for this work. There can't be. In the end our language is no match for what this man did.

6

That evening we got to work on Esther's welcome-home dinner. We cooked in silence. This was us at our best, stew building, salad making, sweating, and braising. We cleaned as we went and we bussed each other's dishes. Maneuvering around each other with polite touches on the arm. Claire and I were suited for joint tasks, parallel play. We were proud of how well we got along in the kitchen, when married couples were supposed to drive each other to violence while assembling a sandwich. Harmony came easily for us, and it was perhaps our most salient statistic, the least problematic of our virtues.

When Esther returned, we didn't know it at first. She slipped quietly into the house and went to her room. The bus must have dropped her off, but we heard no greeting when she came in and our little welcome home ceremony never happened. Claire was putting some laundry away as I was setting the table when I heard her yell, "Oh my god, you're back!"

A blast of one-sided chatter filled the air. Countered by the return fire of Esther's silence. I saw no reason to intrude on their reunion. I waited at the table as Claire's voice muddied into nothing against some part of Esther. This would have indicated the hugging and nuzzling, the probably exaggerated joy. I could picture Esther half squirming away, too embarrassed to openly enjoy the affection of her mother, but not cold enough to flee it entirely. I was bracing for her ambivalence to mature into a more liberal hostility.

"Esther's home!" Claire shouted.

I held my ground.

Esther's allergy to ceremony was predicted by all the guides we'd half read about teenagers. We saw it coming, then put our heads in our own asses. We were warned, but still we insisted on basic politeness as part of some dim instinct we had to remain in control. Esther abhorred all the functional vocal prompts one bleated in order to stabilize the basic encounters, to keep them from capsizing into awkward fits of milling and hovering. Hello and good-bye and thank you to strangers; good morning and how are you. These phrases were insane to her. She would pick the simplest rituals, the most basic behavior that people keep in their back pockets and whip out without a fuss, and wage dark war against them, scorning us mightily for caring about the exchange of niceties.

"What have you learned, *Samuel*, when you've asked me how I am?" she sniped once.

"Maybe I've learned . . . how you are?"

"Right," she nodded. "And you can't tell that by looking at me? Is that really your best way to find out what you need to know?"

"Sweetie, talking to you isn't just about gathering information."

"Apparently not, because you don't remember a single thing I say. Your gathering mechanism is fucked."

Had Esther just said *mechanism*?

She seemed in her element during these conversations, glowing with the power she had over me, as if I should enjoy it, too.

I'd parry with oily fathery lameries. "Doesn't it feel better to say things to people?"

"Feel better? It feels like shit. It feels entirely like the worst kind of shit."

Little did she goddamn know.

"Okay, darling, I'm sorry."

And thus a rhetorical marvel was engineered: I apologized to Esther, regularly, for her refusal to be queried on her well-being. I regularly failed to mount cogent justifications for any of the human practices. They turned out to be indefensible to her. In the end I was a poor spokesman for life among people. Such were the victories of language in the home.

. . .

After they'd snuggled and debriefed, Esther trailed Claire out of her room. Esther looked heavily guarded, as if to say, I have been at horse camp and I have changed considerably, in ways you could never understand, so let's not waste each other's time, you old asshole. Stay away from me, you tiny, silly creatures, for you have not been to horse camp.

Out of consideration for her privacy, I did not strive for eye contact.

Leave the little gal alone, I reminded myself, give her space, even though I wanted to hug the crap out of her and maybe get a smell of those horses I had paid for her to play with.

Such admonitions against trespass kept me afloat with Esther. But she was adorable-looking, which I wasn't allowed to mention, and the one thing I most wanted to do, to hold her and tickle her and just be next to her, was the one thing that was definitively not on the table. Not even near it.

Esther's usual poker face couldn't really hide her suspicion. She had deep energy reserves for uncovering contradiction and hypocrisy. When she smelled it she jumped into action. This new bit of news—Mom and Dad are feeling better—was vulnerable to attack, obviously. Clearly she'd been clued in to our ostensible recovery.

I saw her mind working away at the weakness of everything she'd heard from her mother, the great dismantling project going on not so secretly in the twitches of her face.

"You're better," she announced, unimpressed, as she flipped through the week's worth of catalogs that had come.

This bedside manner would help her one day, no doubt. Rhetorical mode number forty-fucking-five. Death through obviousness, insistence on the literal. I will show you that your basic claims about yourself are insane, simply by repeating them back to you.

Then it graciously changed into a question. "You're feeling better?"

I breathed hard from my nose, as if to say: "According to some," but what came out was a scoff. Sometimes if I took the same sarcastic tone as Esther we'd remain allies for a bit longer, but I always failed when it came to the music of the sarcasm, and even that phrase, "music of the sarcasm," should be a giveaway that I was out of my league. The acoustics changed every year, or more often than that. Usually I produced the sort of tonal errors of speech that made her seem to hate me even more. I was one of those dads who gladly gave up his own identity in order to act like someone Esther might hang out with at school—as if a wet-faced, overweight, middle-aged man with adolescent speech habits that were slightly out of date did not trip any number of warning signs and send up alarms all over the neighborhood. Sometimes my desire to please meant that Esther still ignored me, but without hostility, and these were the spoils I greedily enjoyed in my role as her father.

"Dinner's soon," I said. "If you want to get cleaned up and . . . you know."

Esther looked at me with what seemed like pity.

"Oh, I do know," she said. "You don't even know how much I know."

"Okay," I laughed, even though I had no idea what the hell she was talking about.

7

At dinner we tried to extract the details about Esther's trip, but all she did was eat and mumble. The trick was to make this conversation unlike an interrogation, to conceal our basic curiosity, which is what Esther found to be our most appalling trait. *How dare you care about something? Don't you know what a breach it is?* When we let down our guard and showed interest, Esther's anger flared up.

My tricks of reversal were never any match for her, either. I could say, "It sucked there, I heard," and she would grunt. I could say, "Your mother made love to a horse once," and she would scoff. I could say, "Eloise (the nickname we'd privately given her grandfather) will be surprised to hear how well you've learned to fire a pistol." Nothing, no response, ever.

So we fell into the old cajole. We prodded, she resisted, we sulked and put our own irrelevant feelings in the air, and Esther suddenly, after we had cursed the whole transaction and felt disgusted by the topic, got talkative, after which we tuned out and quietly longed for her to shut up.

The medically definitive moment came with the story of the horse.

Esther had much to say about a horse there named Genghis, a great old roan, a sergeant of the New York grass. This horse, apparently, had shown Esther some exclusive, rare affection. Or so claimed the instructor, who was evidently impressed that Genghis, who did not care for people, had made an exception for Esther. But people are always telling kids that a particular animal likes them. Kids are told that every person likes them, too, when in fact most people do not, or could not be bothered. And yet this horse really, really did like Esther, in some kind of different way, which in the end couldn't but impress Esther, who in her diligent way made a singular effort to distinctly *not* be liked, which made this horse in my view an idiot, and could she maybe get a horse, you know, for real, if she saved her allowance and did what we asked of her and promised not to want anything ever again?

I did not appreciate how easily Esther had been fooled by this sort of thing. Where was the old suspicion, the doubt, the more or less unchecked hatred? Why didn't she mistrust this horse the way she mistrusted, for instance, us?

I said, "Whatever happened to: any horse that likes me isn't worth a damn?"

Claire shot me a look. Slow it down, she didn't need to say. Don't spoil her enthusiasm.

"And who names a horse Genghis?" I continued.

Esther stabbed at her food.

The best part of the trip, she told us, was the last day, because they were allowed to take the horses on some back trails. The kids went off alone, she said. The kids rode unsupervised all day and even got to put the horses away and do stuff the counselors usually did. And then they got to eat whatever they wanted that night because the counselors didn't feel like cooking, supposedly.

Didn't feel like it.

I had to ask, and the counselors, well, they'd come down with something, hadn't they, some really nasty, uh, flu?, and the timing wasn't so good but they'd all gotten pretty sick, so they sort of rested while the kids stayed up late and talked and it was the best night ever.

Dinner provided the first localized site of language exposure since Esther had returned from her trip, and what happened to our bodies would prove to be textbook.

We did not know it yet, but LeBov had already issued guidance that the toxicity was perceptibly worse after you've broken exposure from it, the reaction far more visceral. From Esther's mouth came something that was causing a chemical disruption, like a mist borne on the climate. That's the only way to explain it, and this was when any notion of a toxicity not connected to Esther's language seemed instantly absurd. This wasn't her hair or clothing or rural dander. This was nothing that could be washed off. The evidence was pouring right out of her face and we were bathing in it. There was a soiled quality to her words, something oily that made them, literally, hard to hear.

Later philosophers of the crisis, like Sernier, would mock the poetics of all this. He'd decry the absence of facts, the vague and personalized anecdotes that inevitably pollute the possibility for real understanding. Personal stories, Sernier would say, are the most powerful impediment to any true understanding of this crisis. As soon as we litter our insights with pronouns, they spoil. Ideas and people do not mix.

I would agree with everything Sernier says. But I'll point out that bugs crawl from his mouth now, and there's no one left to read what he wrote.

I looked over at Claire, who had been awfully quiet. Usually she stayed quiet on purpose, in retaliation, to allow Esther, as she put it, to discover herself out loud. To Claire, I was the obstacle as we battled for a foothold as parents. She would say that I offered so many listening prompts to Esther, such eager receptivity and sentence finishing, that I obliterated our daughter's conversational flow and actually caused her reticence. One can be adversarial, apparently, through aggressive attention. My signs of interest, and their vocal accompaniment, claimed Claire, were the problem.

I looked over at Claire after Esther's monologue, and she had vanished into herself, ghosted out with her long stare. Her hand covered her mouth, seemed to want to disappear inside it. In her eyes I saw nothing. They had gone to glaze.

There's our answer, I thought.

Welcome to the relapse, I wanted to say, but Claire lurched from her chair, mumbling, "Excuse me," and Esther and I looked away from each other as we heard confirmation from the bathroom, the sound of someone we loved trying mightily to breathe.

I produced some elementary noise interference with my utensils on the plate, but my food, some kind of porridgy loaf that was supposed to be a risotto, oozing over my plate like the inner mush of an animal, was bringing up my own small swell of nausea.

I cleaved into it, breaking its gluey shell, and a thread of steam released over my face.

Esther broke the silence first, her mother heaving in the background. "Wow," she said. "Glad to hear you guys are on the mend. I was beginning to worry."

"Well, we wouldn't want that," I said, and I pushed back from the table.

In the closet I grabbed a towel and went in to help Claire. I dampened the towel in the sink, knelt behind her at the toilet, held back her hair, which felt dry and breakable in my hands, and I brought my body down softly against her, feeling each of her shaking spasms deep inside me.

When Esther approached the bathroom I pushed the door closed, and Claire and I stayed in there until her footsteps retreated.

Even then we waited, catching our breath, which didn't come back so well. For what felt like hours we sat together on the bathroom floor with the faucet in full thunder, until outside the streetlights sizzled out and we could be sure that Esther had finally gone to her room for the night and closed the door. Only then was it safe to come out.

8

At noon each Thursday, before the illness began to deter our worship, Claire and I collected religious transmissions from the utility hut on the county's northern back acre.

As Reconstructionist Jews following a program modified by Mordecai Kaplan, indebted to Ira Eisenstein's idea of private religious observation, *an entirely covert method of devotion*, Claire and I held synagogue inside a small hut in the woods that received radio transmissions through underground cabling.

The practice derived from Schachter-Shalomi's notion of basements linked between homes, passageways connecting entire neighborhoods. But our sunken network existed solely as a radio system, feeding Rabbi Burke's services to his dispersed, silent community. Tunnels throughout the Northeast, stretching as far as Denver, surfacing in hundreds of discrete sites. Mostly holes covered by huts like ours, where two members of the faith—the smallest possible *chavurah*, highly motivated to worship without the *pollutions of comprehension* of a community—could privately gather to receive a broadcast.

Our hut stands where Montrier Valley dips below sea level into a bleached, bird-littered marshland, and the soil rests under a rank film of water. If we took a direct path from home we could be listening to Rabbi Burke in under an hour. But monthly we had to change our route to the hut, switch approaches, delay arrival. Sometimes we spent half a day on detours so elaborate that even we became lost on our way to the woods.

Such huts were the common Reconstructionist camouflage of the time, erected over the gash in the ground, huts with gouged-out floors and a fixture called a listener to welcome the transmission cables and convert the signal sent from Buffalo, Chicago, Albany into decipherable speech.

Huts could be anywhere, disguised in the woods, hidden in plain sight. Yards would host these huts. Sometimes a field. Huts were marked with a star that only glowed with soil rubbed on it, affixed with a surveillance camera. To repel the curious, its walls might be armored in dung.

Generations ago, on Long Island and elsewhere, holes like ours were lined with stone, made to pass for wells. Mock pulleys and bucket systems were propped over them, every manner of concealment employed. The holes were guarded by boys, protected by a wolf, filled in with sand, prettied up with gravestones. Tradition tells different stories about how our predecessors channeled the rabbi's word and none of them much matter. In any case, I don't care so much for stories.

Our hut was assigned to us early in our marriage by Rabbi Bauman, and it was ours alone. If other Jews gathered there to worship, then we never saw them in that sector of woods. The rules of the hut were few but they were final. Claire and I were only to go together. We could neither of us attend this synagogue alone. The experience would not be rendered in speech, you could not repeat what you heard, or even that you heard anything. Bauman was firm on this, said our access would be revoked if we breached. You would not know who else received worship in this manner, neighbors or otherwise. Children were not allowed access to the hut. Their relation to you alone did not automatically qualify them. They must be approached separately, assigned their own coordinates. Curiosity about how others worshipped, even others in your family, *even Esther*, was not genuine curiosity; it was jealousy, weakness. Burke called it a ploy against our own relationship to uncertainty. You can know nothing of another's worship, *even when they try to tell you*. To desire that information is to fear a limitation to your own devotion.

There were rules of appearance as well. A hut could not look maintained. We tended the grounds, kept the landscape looking unvisited.

In the fall I cleansed the surveillance camera, its lens gummed up by summer, by steaming heat and the moths that melted into slurry against the glass.

Build nothing of splendor over the hole, was the rule. If it were not for hostile visits, a naked hole would be ideal, a hole not hidden by any hut.

Rabbi Ira no doubt envisioned a hut-free world, where anyone could stop at a hole, crouch down, and avail himself of a sermon flowing up from the earth. The religion would be *on* all the time, would pour from the earth. But the world didn't accommodate this ideal. Disguises were required.

The technology of the hut was a glowbug setup. The hut covered a hole and the hole was stuffed with wire. From our own hole came bright orange ropes of cabling, the whole mess of it reeking of sewage, of something dead beneath the earth. This wiring was grappled to the listener, and the listener, called a Moses Mouth by Bauman, even while we were instructed to never refer to it, was draped over the radio module. I'm understating the complexity of this. But on a good day, it just worked.

Transmissions flowed into the hut on Thursdays, usually at noon. Sometimes no messages came, or they arrived in broken notes from the radio and we suffered through services in languages too foreign to know. Our gear was faulty and old. The glowbug had one dry little input that always needed grease. In the winter it cinched shut and I'd have to stretch it back open with my finger.

Sometimes it was not word that we received at the hut, but a hissing silence, months of it, even as we waited for guidance, freezing in the hut under a pile of rotted blankets, groping beneath each other's clothing to dispatch little moments of pleasure.

We did what we could, within the bounds of the rules, to make the hut cozy. We filled a wooden crate with extra hats, sweaters, mittens, then painted on it, instead of our names, the word *Us*.

Each time we visited the hut we brought a pink rubber ball to feed into the hole. We took turns dropping it in, listening for the distant, wet bounce. We wondered how many balls it would take, how old we'd be, when the balls piled up so high in the hole that they overflowed into the hut.

If we missed a visit sometimes we could coax a summary from the archive, my private term for the expired messages festering in the wire. But the summaries, if I released them, were skeletal, in bones of language that often could not be joined for sense. Such messages were often hammered flat, their meaning ripped out, as if the rabbi's mouth when he spoke had been filled with glue. Transmissions expired into garbled tones if we did not enter the hut in time. But if we squatted in the hut and waited, if we slept there or overstayed, the transmissions receded, failed to issue in language we could understand.

From Buffalo the connection could be severed at any time, when tampering or illegitimate listening was attempted, and of course it was attempted all the time. Which meant that if the line was dead for too long, someone was out there trying to hack into Rabbi Burke's broadcast.

The secrecy surrounding the huts was justified. The true Jewish teaching is not for wide consumption, is not for groups, is not to be polluted by even a single gesture of communication. Spreading messages dilutes them. Even *understanding* them is a compromise. The language kills itself, expires inside its host. Language acts as an acid over its message. If you no longer care about an idea or feeling, then put it into language. That will certainly be the last of it, a fitting end. Language is another name for coffin. Bauman told us the only thing we should worry about regarding the sermons was if we understood them too well. When such a day came, then something was surely wrong.

At the hut a few days after Esther's return from camp, when there could no longer be any doubt about what was sickening us, Claire scooped grease from the tub in the bin, then lubed the orifice in the floor by plunging her entire hand inside. I crouched behind her and when her hand popped out, I draped the listener over the fixture.

The listener, a warm bag filled with conductive gel, stripped away the hiss to reveal the underlying speech. Ours was scissored for us by Bauman from a larger bolt, and he gave us a quick course in its care. A small box of maintenance tools was entrusted to us, but I'd never needed it. I'd stashed it in my bedroom dresser, a box with a chisel, a thimble, some rubber clips, and clear sheets of what looked like gelatin.

The listener could not endure sunlight, nor could we risk hiding it in the hut, so we kept it buried in an unmarked grave that rotated according to season, and we retrieved and cleaned it for each visit.

Today the listener gripped the fixture as it siphoned out a broadcast, sputtering sound into the hut. On the steps we waited as the system hissed to life. Claire huddled inside her parka, stiffening when I touched her.

Burke's service, when finally it crackled on, centered on blame and how we might distinguish ourselves through its broader adoption. But first we had to listen to songs, Burke's melodies distorted through copper wire. From the radio came warbled noisings filtered through miles of earth. It is possible that in person Burke possessed a beautiful singing voice that transformed the dull language of song lyrics into transcendent moans. Transmitted all the way to our hut, Burke's incantations only made us feel that we were listening to the death throes of an old man in bed, someone uttering his last.

When the service began, Burke held forth on the opportunity called blame. In blame is a chance to step into responsibility, to make of our bodies absorbent parcels for the accusations of others. Burke discussed how we might extinguish doubt in our neighbors, make their fears small. He insisted that blame can have no literal meaning; there really is no such thing when you love the Name, our term for Hashem. Blame exists only in our desire to bestow cause locally, and there is no such thing. *No such thing*. When people seek to place blame, it means they have nothing left to give. It reflects their inability to appreciate the inscrutability, the all-knowingness of the Name. Taking blame is then a service, and now we are called upon to offer this service again.

"A tremendous opportunity has arisen," Burke said. "We have the chance to take the blame for something extraordinary, an incomprehensible affliction."

Claire and I sat together on the cold floor of the hut. I could feel her listening next to me. She had tightened with attention.

Burke started shouting, the higher registers of his voice distorting the speaker.

"We can take this blame as a curse, and rage against it, crying out about unfairness. How can my child be blamed for anyone's sorrow? My child is innocent! Innocent! Or we can receive this blame as a gift to us, which is what it is. So much of what we must do today is sculpt our understanding to accommodate what we cannot bear. Now we must help people who do not understand, even if we are lost ourselves. This is our role. And we do this by stepping forward, saying, *I*, it was *I* who did this. *I* did this to you. Not my child. *I did it*."

Claire sounded like she'd been struck in the chest.

"Understanding itself is beside the point," Burke said, more calmly. "Do not make of it a fetish, for it pays back nothing. That habit must be broken. Understanding puts us to sleep. The dark and undesired sleep. Questions like these are not meant to be resolved. We must never believe we know our roles. We must always wonder what the moment calls for."

Rabbi Burke did not officially exist in public. There was no such person. Our system of worship was likewise kept secret, which means that our practice at the hut suffered its share of misinformation and rumor. The more we concealed it, the more it troubled people, so they invented actions for us, ascribed false powers to the radio. It was guessed to be a hole in some secret location that speaks only to Jews. From the hole came bits of data: sound, word, and pulse, that Jews alone could decode, using their oily gear, their hacked electronics.

We endured lurid speculation on what we might be doing in the woods. We were called forest Jews and in newspapers cartoons depicted what awful work we'd undertaken. The Jew, in these images, sits on a jet of steam that charges him with special knowledge. God's air, heated to a vapor, is blown over the mystic. The Jew fits his sticky red mouth over the nozzle and sucks. Into a vein in the Jew's leg comes the cold, clear liquid.

And then the speculation on the dark electronics of such messaging, how a system like this could even work. A radio console with a flesh underside is postulated. Modules sheathed in gauze, lubricants siphoned from children, injected to flow through custom gears.

In our defense spoke only those who said we did not exist. We'd been invented by our enemies to give them something to tear apart with their teeth. How convenient, a Jew with important secrets. How self-serving to you, they said. These were our defenders, but to them we were a fiction. It was not clear that we owed them gratitude.

The Jewish person who has not received an assignment at a hole, and the Gentile who has only heard rumors about the gear that governs the hole's ritual, have missed the elemental purpose of these transmission sites: *the Jewish transaction is a necessarily private one.* I am thinking of people like Murphy who would plunge his fists into it, believing he could extract some perfect remedy for the speech fever.

The topic was a common one in the broadcasts. Burke returned to it often. What others, with no information, might make of us.

Let such errors stand, he always said. Their mistakes put good miles between us. There is no better blessing for us than to be unknown.

If a knowledge is to be made public, went the saying, it should erect a shell around our secret. Such is true of the Torah, the Talmud, the Halakha we appear to follow. When we communicate, we do so to throw them off our scent.

Claire and I had done our part. Said nothing. Never indicated for a moment that we were members of this faith.

"To be a Jew is to let them be wrong about you," said Burke today. "If we cannot allow this, then nothing is possible."

He always lowered his voice when he was nearly finished, an emphatic whisper he used to hammer home his final point.

"There is nothing like being profoundly misunderstood. Let others expose their secrets, advertise their identities, neutralize their mysteries with imprecise language. A Jew must project behavior distant from his aim, must cast up a puppet world for those who are watching. Puppets made of real flesh. Puppets who weep, bleed, die."

We had, it seemed to me, succeeded perfectly at being misunderstood. Again and again our huts were surveilled, seized, burned, for fear that the Jew was drinking something too important out of these holes, drinking directly from God's mind, eating a pure alphabet that he alone could stomach. These were the fearful rumors. Such an apparatus, if true, was too good for Jews alone. It must be breached, overturned, made to work for the others. The holes must be explored, chased to their source, fucked dry for their secrets.

And they were.

When a hut above a loaded hole is found, a hole that is hot with language, the hut is overturned. If the listener is buried elsewhere, *as it must be*, then no reception is possible. Even when the exposed cables are jammed into every kind of translating console by engineers, without a listener nothing but burnt tones are ever heard, and even these are confused for last year's wind, swept underground now and dying.

Without the listener draped over the radio module hugging that fucker until it releases its broadcast, these are the spoils the intruder will hear, these at most, and he will soon cease to care. Not least because such washes of sound render the inexperienced vandal docile, listless, apathetic.

After all their violating labors, what is extracted from these holes by intruders is never anything coherent enough to be called a language, and the public curiosity whispers down into nothing again.

Foolish Jews worshipping in the mud, goes the claim. Let them have their holes, their ancient language of clicks and whistles and yells.

And have them we damn well do.

The radio fell silent when Burke finished. Before he signed off he promised that a brief message from Rabbi Thompson would follow. Until then there'd be a low rumble from the module, remote voices chopped into pieces too small to understand.

Claire curled up on the hut floor and I pulled a blanket from the bin.

"If you get up I can put this under us," I said.

With a show of labor, her body in pain, Claire pulled herself up and stepped from the hut. I rolled out the blanket and brought Claire back in, lowering her down again. Without removing her shoes she shucked her leggings to her knees, then turned on her stomach.

"Okay" was all she said, not even looking up at me. She was ready.

I did not yet know if I was aroused.

Claire was quiet today, but sometimes our best intimacy occurred after the most difficult sermons. We could not speak of them and I don't think either of us was even tempted. Our minds worked away in private at what we heard, but our bodies sometimes wanted the busywork of a cold joining of parts.

Burke's sermons reminded me of what I did not know, could hardly ever honestly feel. "You come here because of what is missing," he always said. To listen to Burke was to believe I could be curious about something. In theory I felt a great awe for what could not be explained, but in practice I felt too alone. Always I worried that I lacked the great appetite for uncertainty that Burke demanded. What if uncertainty held no appeal for me?

A distant hissing reported from the radio, the searching work of the listener, divining the wire for a signal. Before I dropped down over Claire for our intimacy, I put my coat over the radio. Sometimes vestigial sound poured out, accidents in the broadcast, and we preferred these stifled so we could concentrate.

Claire stretched long and I covered her. Beneath me, even clothed, she felt bony. I worried my weight was too much for her, so I held myself up with my arms, letting my face settle in her hair.

We worked the messy connection by shifting clothing, Claire's leggings in a ruffle around her knees. The moment of insertion was abrasive, but soon a moist warmth engulfed us, and we settled into a dutiful pursuit of pleasure, sharing the labor as equally as we could. Fairness always, even in these grisly animal matters. When Claire took the lead from underneath, I held my breath so I could feel her against me. When it was my turn to provide the motion, I shut my eyes and put all my weight, it would seem, on my face, which pressed into the filth of the blanket.

It was here, one guesses, that our toxic Esther was conceived. Certainly it was here.

We coupled under the hiss of the module until Thompson's broadcast kicked on, and we missed the first part of it, heard only the coat-muffled drone of Burke's second rabbi, a rabbi with more technical, practical concerns.

My completion, when it came, did so without my full knowledge. I noticed it drooling across my leg when I looked down, felt myself shrink and go cold.

"I'll be outside," Claire said, before I'd even gotten off her.

We kissed and I helped her up. She never seemed interested in Thompson's information, so she'd wait in the yard, stretch her legs, get some sun, if she could find a spot not too shielded by trees. I don't really know what she did out there while I stayed inside and cleaned up. But Thompson often provided more concrete information and I always wanted to hear him out.

Thompson spoke in warnings today. Warnings and guidance. Usually he followed Burke and simply reaffirmed the need for secrecy, urging us to a deeper privacy, reminding us of the levels of disclosure we succumb to every day without even knowing. Disclosures in the face and eyes. Disclosures in our bearing, our dress. Disclosures through omission, everything we fail to say and do. The Name is the only one who does not disclose. When we find no evidence of the Name, that is when we can be most sure of him. But we, we wake up and reveal ourselves until everything special vanishes. Our privacy drains from us no matter what, said Thompson.

And now that weakness merited ever more vigilance. We would be queried on our affiliation, he said. That is not new. We might be followed. A threat I never took seriously. It seemed so grandiose to believe anyone cared how Claire and I spent our Thursday lunch hour. But Thompson said our hut visits should only be conducted with special watchfulness.

Then it was doctors who received his scorn, doctors and experts of any kind. We were to take matters into our own hands. The doctors are scared. Of course they are. From doctors we would receive no insight. If we could gather our own statistics, we would be better prepared. Thompson fell into a list of technical details and materials, read quickly in a desperate voice, the transmission flickering in and out.

There was, it seemed, smallwork to be done now, and this was how to do it.

Sometimes when Thompson spoke I had to touch the wet belly of the listener to ground the signal. Otherwise it shorted, fell mute. This rarely happened with Burke's sermons. I used the back of my hand against the listener's cool, slick exterior, pushed up into the softness until I felt resistance, as if deep inside the listener, if you gouged enough jelly from it, was a long, flat bone.

Thompson provided the details that would inform my first round of smallwork, the tests and procedures I might perform, *taking matters into my own hands*, to keep Esther close to us.

When the service finished I unseated the listener and wrapped it in plastic before burying it behind the hut. Back inside I stuffed the cables into the hole and covered up the hole with a floorboard.

Claire and I made no sign to each other outside, only stared at the yardless plot of dirt that circled our hut. It was our right to ignore what we heard. Burke always said there was no true reaction to the service, no single response. "Bafflement is the most productive reaction," he said. "This is when the mind is at its best. This is all we are in the face of the Name's mystery."

We walked the perimeter of the hut and finally groped our way into a conversation about the brush, beating it back, knowing that we'd never do it so long as the rules were in place. But we indulged these conversations about gardening anyway, let them fill the air so we could use our voices again, which always sounded so loud and wrong in the air outside the hut, after so much of our own silence. We thought it'd be nice to plant some grass here one day, and we'd better do it soon, hadn't we, before the grotesque wall of trees crowded in too close. Before the trees grew into the hut itself.

This would almost make a kind of home for us, wouldn't it? Just in case? We could do some work on the land, build an addition onto the hut. It would not be terrible. Couldn't we live here someday if we needed to, if it came to that?

You weren't supposed to, but who would know? How could that be bad, to make this place prettier and livable? There is no possible way that could be bad. Making a place nicer was a good thing to do. No one could argue with that. No one would have to know.

9

LeBov, by radio—broadcasting from a secluded location *for his own protection*—brought his diagnosis public, called out the toxic Jewish child. A disease seeping beyond its circumference, radiating from the head, the face, the mind.

There are particulars I do not wish to share, said LeBov. A secrecy that made his claim seem more true.

It was hard to disagree, but everyone did. They protested out of conviction or denial or fear or real scientific understanding. The diagnostic debate played out with proponents and detractors firing evidence back and forth across the massive pit of confusion we all swam in.

The culprits, the carriers, the agents of infection, were Jewish children, all children, not just children, some adults, all of us.

The culprits were infirm only, or maybe just the healthy, or maybe only those who'd eaten dirt, or not eaten enough of it. An autopsy was called on the whole living planet. The expertise in each case was minor and romantic and you could hitch your fate to any of it, so long as you didn't mind being wrong.

To challenge matters, a child-free settlement in Arizona produced victims with identical symptoms: facial smallness, lethargy, a hardening under the tongue that defeated attempts at speech. No exposure to a child, let alone a Jewish one.

LeBov wasn't bothered. "I'm speaking of the cause," he said, "and this cause spread fast a long time ago. Our forest Jews know what I mean. *Just ask them.*"

When the affliction crystallized on a map, colors coding the victim radius, the image was pretty, a golden yellow core radiating out of inner Wisconsin. Whatever was happening seemed to happen there first. But there were flares of activity everywhere, and every day they changed, the whole map strobing over time into one blinding sphere.

Activity was the word for people finally hardening in their beds for good, sewn up in frozen limbs from speech and its offshoots. *Activity* was the diplomatic word for its reverse.

Whatever anyone knew, they knew it with desperate force and you were crazy not to believe them. But when you melded the various insights to forge a collective wisdom, you had total venom pouring from every speaking creature. The common thread among the theories was that whoever was to blame, children alone were resistant.

It was a piece of evidence not lost on the children.

At home, in the weeks after Esther's return from camp, I traversed the dirty five-mile wedge of boulevard that insulated our house from the woods, chasing the question of the Esther perimeter. Basic smallwork prompted by Thompson's sermon. How far away from our daughter did we need to remove ourselves to experience an abatement of symptoms or even, one hoped, the ability to breathe enough air to stay functional and conscious?

On my evening walks, initially to Culpin Boulevard on the north end, or to Blister Field and its adjacent parks just south of the synagogue prison, where the narrow, tree-clotted streets give way to plantless swaths of gravel, I tracked the distance that would be required from Esther for the sickness to retreat.

Men my own age wandered by, smothered in winter wear, their eyes locked to the footpath. From their mouths curled thin ribbons of steam. Women with the same gray face as Claire's wheezed under the cover of trees. One of them offered a shy wave I chose not to return. Or perhaps her raised arm was meant to ward me off.

Nothing much lived in the air. The occasional sickly bird chugged past overhead, its body translucent. These birds were so undefended, so slow and stupid at flight, I felt I could grab them from the air.

When it was children I saw, particularly the older ones who roved together and glowed with obscene health, I changed my direction. Slowly, though. Careful to disguise my caution.

In our neighborhood, anyway, these children were not just Jewish. This was a mixed, feral pack, drawing from vast bloodlines. And together, when they spoke in unison on their nighttime tours, their weapon was worse.

Sometimes it was hard work, the air too rough with sleet, my body unfit for hiking so far afield. My equipment was awkward and heavy, like carrying a squirming person against my chest, and I would forget to turn it on. Or the battery pack overheated, burned through the shielding, raising welts on my skin beneath the warm metal plate.

I stopped to rest on benches, in the grass, against the knee wall at Boltwood Park, and then hours later I struggled to my feet and hoped I recognized my surroundings well enough to return home. Not that home was where I wanted to be. Sometimes I suffered shallow sleep on a bench until it was dark and then woke to wet, frozen pants at my crotch and a shard of drool solidifying into ice at the corner of my mouth.

On such nights I was critically chilled and scraped absolutely raw from such contorted sleep, but I walked home under streetlights and felt so lucid, so glaringly vital, that it scared me to open the door to my house again and fight back through the awful air to my room, where I would fail to sleep in noxious proximity to something my body could no longer endure.

On days of minimal exposure to Esther, I conducted perimeter and fence line ambient air quality tests and sent in the results for analysis. Sediments of speech, airborne now, might indicate different toxicity thresholds throughout the area.

The numbers that returned offered no insight I could use.

I utilized a real-time aerosol monitor with data logging, purchased secondhand from Science Exchange. Collecting air samples was straightforward, and I looked like any citizen out for a night of hobby work, gathering bugs in a jar, not that anyone ever stopped to question me.

This after administering a full broad-spectrum heavy-metals panel, inconclusive on us both.

This after following the standard collection protocol for poisoning, testing our blood, hair, saliva, and nails.

Such samples I scraped from Claire when she slept. Humors for a futile investigation.

You'll gain no satisfaction through tests of the air or water, was a sentence making the rounds.

Point the testing wand into the child's mouth, was another favorite.

Or, fill the child's mouth with sand.

The walks each evening were my prescribed escapes from the home, and they became a necessary after-dinner regimen. I performed smallwork with salts, knowing little of how to modify my tonic, knowing nothing of a delivery system through poultice applications on the sweeter nerves inside of my arms, the so-called Worthen site, proceeding only with some unmodified antiseizure agents as a foundational syrup.

Laughably amateur modifications, yet ones I hardly understood. I needed to believe Thompson that my own understanding played no role. I could execute a procedure without knowing why. I had to believe, per Burke, that my own insights, if I even had them, were an impediment to survival.

At our home, since Esther's return from camp, little household habits emerged that soon were absorbed into our schedule. A scattering after dinner, improvised medicine injected into the fatty softness of the leg from a Windsor needle, then flight outdoors. We practiced, with full complicity, an avoidance altogether of family time.

For once, Esther's disgust for us was mutually convenient. An altogether necessary disgust. We exploited it, allowed her to think we were keeping our distance at her request. But we saw her sometimes looking in at us from doorways, without her scowl, her body free of its habitual disdain. She stood in her pajamas and watched us, radiating something very close to concern.

Most nights Claire disappeared into the crafts room, or had never come out of it in the morning. Technically no crafts emerged from this part of the house. We named it once with the hope that someone, sometime—a future child of ours, perhaps—would go in there and be productive, make something pretty or useful or interesting. Such were our speculations for the children we might have. They would fashion objects that glowed or spoke, and we would sit in wonder as we held their tremendous work in our hands. This was, apparently, one reason to bear children. It would guarantee some future astonishment, restore to us our sense of surprise. Our children would solve some fundamental boredom we could not escape, and it would happen here. We could not wait to feel proud of something like that.

Now the room contained a guest cot and an unplumbed sink, with one window painted shut. Some tub buckets and a little footlocker and a fridge lined the floor. The linoleum was buckled in the corner, beneath a baseboard that had grown so sodden and soft that I finally pushed a night table against it to block it from my sight.

The occasional brownish rag came out of Claire's room and a stack of clean rags went in.

10

On the night I met Murphy, dinner was abandoned. Perhaps it had never been attempted. Esther slipped into her room, where gelatinous bird sounds flowed out, half-words and astringent syllables that produced a low-grade menace.

I'd braved a conversation with her, counting on her angry silence, which she delivered with force. I asked her, nervously, to limit her speech, with every expectation of getting shouted down, of getting mocked by our skilled and vicious little mistress. She smirked off, sparing me any response, and in the following days she launched a campaign of sonorous gibberish whenever she thought we were in earshot, and that earshot was something harder and harder to escape.

Earshot. Such a very true word.

My plan was to track my symptoms without appearing too conspicuous. Beneath my coat I buckled my DRE Axis 4 portable vital signs monitor. The tubing had gone yellow, and cabling was exposed through the insulation, but the device held a steady charge for my outings and collected reliable data.

At the corner of Hospring and Woods, where the evergreens hung skeletal and brown, with sick branches that looked burnt by wind, I stopped for a one-mile readout.

A row of privets concealed the single-level houses that ran south along Hospring, and there in the unweeded mulch bed at the roots I saw, for the second time, the strange man from the picnic trail, the redhead who'd threatened the Jews. He was retching into the weeds, giving it his all.

He had seemed daunting when I first saw him off the trail, hulking over the Jewish couple as if he might carve into their backs and eat them. Now he was ill, on his knees.

I recalled a sermon Burke had delivered months ago, when everything from the Jew hole was still safely abstract, wisdom I could enjoy in the unactionable pit of my mind. They will sniff at your legs, went Burke's sermon. They will wish they were you. Beware the man on his knees, the display of weakness. But the sermon had not passed through the radio coherently that day; static cloaked the transmission. Every other word was *weakness*, as if the broadcast were looping by mistake. We were to fear weakness not in oneself, where it should be cherished, but in others. Or not fear it, but mistrust it. We too easily believe in the trouble of others, erect a machinery of caring. Look through the story at the teller's need, was the caution. Share not your full story, went the warning.

I stood closer to the hedge, tried to see the redhead's face, thinking that at least he'd hear scuffling and turn to acknowledge me.

When I approached him, a pale cylinder of liquid birthed from his mouth, his lips stretched to allow its passage. A faint hiss followed, almost pretty, like crickets in the trees at night, but then a sour smell filled the air.

He was decorous in his expulsion and it appeared to come at no visible cost to his body. I reasoned that he must vomit with some regularity. He made it look natural, as if his face occasionally needed to void itself.

I turned away as he finished and asked if he needed any help.

The retching stopped.

"Oh, goodness," he said. "I didn't see you there." He coughed, swallowed, arranged his appearance.

This was Murphy's first lie.

I frisked myself for a tissue I didn't have.

He brought out a handkerchief, touched it to his mouth, as if he were dabbing a drop of soup from his lips.

"Sorry about that. I thought I was alone. Give me a second."

He opened a tiny bottle, swished a mouthful, then spit a black mess into the bushes. From a small tin he scooped a grease with his finger, then smeared it inside his mouth, running it around with his tongue. Some flavoring to mask the bile, maybe. I wasn't sure.

With a spoon he scraped some dirt over his pool of sickness and then stood to kick more mulch over the area.

"It's actually good for the plants," he said, and he stuck out his hand.

I managed a laugh.

"Murphy," he said, and we shook hands.

He didn't seem to recognize me from the hiking trail.

I gave him a name for myself—*share not your full story*—and we stood there in the cold, looking everywhere but at each other. I needed to get at my gear for a measurement, or else this whole cycle was blown, but I couldn't perform a half-mile reading in front of him and he failed to produce the body language that would allow us to go our separate ways.

"You're sure you're all right?" I finally asked.

He laughed. "Not even close. But at least I'm out of the house."

He seemed pleased with this answer, but then he noticed the bulge under my coat.

"You're not all right, are you?"

Murphy smiled at me with believable concern.

"I'm fine."

"Uh-huh. Well, how many miles out are you?" he asked.

He tapped the machine beneath my coat, which he could not have known was there.

"From what?"

"Your kids."

"I have just one." As I said that I pictured an oversize Esther, towering above Claire and me, bending down to crush us.

"One will do it," he said.

I'd not discussed the toxicity with a stranger, but the information was too rampant now to pretend I didn't know what he meant. *Everything is a disclosure.*

Murphy did nothing to disguise his curiosity at my silence. *Curiosity* might be too kind a word.

"Okay, how about this?" he asked.

Murphy opened his coat and flashed some corroded metal, a vital signs kit not unlike my own, strapped to his chest like a bomb. There was something brown and wet on his, though, glistening as if smeared in paste, but I didn't get a careful look at it before he closed up his coat.

In return I did not similarly open my own coat. I hugged it closer instead.

"I'll do us a favor then and go first," he said. "I have four kids. Try to multiply your bullshit into that. I am two miles out. That's my minimum. Less than that and I'm sure we could bond over some symptoms. Want to?"

I didn't answer, but I gave him to understand, through a controlled smile, that he was not wrong to confide in me. Perhaps there was something to be learned here.

Listen for a change, Claire's old admonition, suddenly seemed useful. She would say it as a joke, mocking the folk wisdom, emphasizing the phrase's secondary meaning—*if you desire change then first you must listen*—but I think Claire actually believed it. Wisdom would come from outside ourselves. We must keep an ear to the ground.

If that was true, then it was the deep listeners among us, consuming so much more of the venom, who would die first. My indifference to others might end up buying me a little more time.

Murphy and I walked together and I lost track of our direction. He boasted of the insulation he'd installed in his home. The soundproof barriers with R-values above twenty, the speech-blocking baffles, some sediment collectors that were yielding a *not uninteresting powder*, even if the use of this powder was still beyond him.

For some reason it kept falsely testing as salt.

His kids were younger than Esther, and, to hear him tell it, they were compliant to his wishes. Little eager subjects who sat for every experiment he could devise. This whole thing *excited* them, he said, even though it's hell on us, and I didn't ask who the rest of the us was.

"If you think about it," said Murphy, "our kids are the first generation. They are the first with this power. We're seeing an incredible transition."

Transition to what, I didn't ask.

In his house quiet time was nearly all the time, but Murphy said it had stopped mattering and they were worried. He and—I forget his wife's name, if there really ever was a wife—were beginning to question if there wasn't something else going on, an undetermined allergy radiating from persons beyond his children, as if the toxin were replicating, and his testing had gone in what he called a very different direction.

Why, for instance, would the sickness endure even if the children were silent?

"Have you given any thought to that, that it isn't just them?" he wanted to know.

I *had* given thought to that, so much that I'd exhausted myself. To Murphy, in response, I offered the obvious idea that there was no way to reconcile why children's language should be toxic while the language of adults was not. The acoustics were the same, child, adult, machine. If you taught a chimp to speak, that speech should sicken you, too. How could the source matter? It doesn't make sense. None of it makes any *sense*.

Murphy scoffed.

"I'm fascinated by people who pout when they can't find sense and logic, as if it's not fair when something in na obvious pattern. It's a fucking epidemic, and the l That's how it *succeeds*, by being inconsistent and u is for toddlers in a goddamn sandbox. No one wants to admit that our machine of understanding is inferior."

"I'll admit that, but it's not malicious to try to understand what's happening," I said.

"No, maybe not. But understanding takes its toll. It's a fucking disease in its own right.

Murphy brough he inside of his mouth with another jam.

He held it out for me to try.

"If we're going to keep talking, you're going to want some of this. For protection."

"What is it?"

"This? It's child's play. Some basic shielding. It's been around for a while. It's pretty much lost its effectiveness for me, but I don't want to take any chances. You could rub some on your throat first."

I thanked him but declined.

"Still waiting for an official solution? Don't you think it's time we took matters into our own hands? The doctors are scared, right? Aren't the doctors scared? That's what I'm hearing."

I looked at him, determined to show no sign I'd heard those words before, not so long ago, from Thompson.

"I don't think we'll get any insights from them, that's all," Murphy said.

More of Thompson's exact language.

He smiled at me, waited. It was like he was watching me open a present, excited to see my reaction.

Murphy wasn't Jewish. There was no way he'd have access to a feed from a hole. Except this was certainty based on nothing I could name, a certainty I found I had come to specialize in. I caught myself feeling curiosity about another person's faith and tried to shut it down. Whatever Murphy believed should not concern me. It would dilute my own ideas, even if presently I had none. I was not supposed to care. I knew that. I knew it.

I just wish that I could have felt it, too.

At the intersection where Nearing dead-ends into the synagogue prison wall, Murphy directed me out of the streetlight and we walked down the unlit causeway toward Blister Field and the electrical tower.

"Are you reading LeBov?" Murphy asked.

"Not so much," I said. "Which books would be good?"

Murphy looked confused. "LeBov doesn't write books. Books expire. Books get hacked. No one wants to leave that kind of evidence."

It seemed important to reveal a kernel of the dilemma, in good faith, to discover Murphy's strategy. I took my time and tried to fill him in on my fledgling perimeter work, the respite during Esther's trip to camp. I drew a distinction between the genders, because it seemed obvious to worry about how resistance differed. Claire was always sicker than I was, *always*. And I floated the Jewish question, since the news had already spit out this idea of a chosen affliction, something related to genetics and faith and whether or not your distant relatives thousands of years ago were covered in shit-clotted fur and prone to kill everything in sight.

I suggested, in counterargument to LeBov, that Murphy's children were not Jewish, were they, and yet apparently they carried the toxic language as well.

Murphy nodded, perhaps too slowly.

"LeBov isn't *blaming* Jewish children," he said, carefully. "This isn't about *blame*. He has profound respect for them. How can you not appreciate that kind of power? His diagnosis is medical, not political. How can we not be curious about where this thing started?"

"I thought you were suggesting that curiosity was pointless."

"Well, maybe LeBov has a reason. Sometimes you say something unbelievable in order to promote a new idea. You build authority that way, and possibly it's better to be doubted than believed. It is more productive to be doubted. What good is it when people believe you?"

Reading LeBov would catch me up on things, explained Murphy, but I had to be careful not to be misled. There was too much conflicting information, too many doctored broadsides attributed to him, loaded with unverified ideas. The speech cautions making the rounds, for instance, against *I* statements, against certain rhetoric deemed to be more toxic, *attack sentences*, that sort of thing, were probably *not* LeBov's cautions. Even if it was possible, said Murphy, that an ultra-restricted language, operating according to a new grammar, might finally be our way out of this.

Which meant, what, that the vague worries and rules of someone who might not exist were now being called further into question?

It didn't help that no one knew much about who LeBov really was.

Or maybe, Murphy speculated, it did help, and that was precisely the point. Maybe the best leaders are the ones we cannot really know. The misinformation coming out of Rochester wasn't exactly an accident, he felt, but a fairly advanced strategy. They knew exactly what they were doing up there at Forsythe.

"In some ways, misinformation can be more useful at a time like this."

I could not follow this reasoning.

Word on LeBov, said Murphy, as a for instance, was that he was childless. He was a woman. He was a teenager. Anthony LeBov was two people, a father and son. LeBov had made himself forget the English language, he self-induced aphasia through high dosages of Semantiril, or he took scheduled breaks from listening, reading, all comprehension.

Nothing was verified, but Rochester was certain, if you wanted to know where the good thinking was getting done. This was news coming out of Rochester. Forget Rochester. Rochester didn't mean what you thought it did, said Murphy. It was said that LeBov participated in the Minnesota trials, the lab work in Denver, some study in Dunkirk of which he alone survived.

LeBov, went the story, had a chamber upstate. LeBov did cryptography. Most of the work now was in the wilted alphabet, which wasn't even its real name. I was sure I had misheard this, but I didn't want to interrupt. Until the world's vocabulary got pumped through a kit, and no one could even agree on which kit to use, we wouldn't know anything.

"The solution is in scripts, don't you think?" he asked. It wasn't a question for me. "Visual codes. Except not the ones we know. The ones we know are already causing problems. Reading is next. It's not even next. It's now."

We had to prepare for a time, said Murphy, when communication was impossible. This thing started with children, but you were a fool to think it would stop there. Some of us were fools anyway.

"You've heard of the flame alphabet, of course," said Murphy. "I'm sure I don't need to tell *you*."

Again this look of his, as if he'd reached into my head with a dowser, monitoring my reaction to see if he'd struck water.

I nodded.

I wouldn't show him. Perhaps he was kidding, or, worse, testing me. But this was something straight from the hut, a seasonal topic of Burke's, when he adopted tones of high caution, warnings so spectacular you could not entertain them as remotely true. If you expected to go on living, that is.

Murphy held forth on the flame alphabet as though he'd been in the hut with us. The name as deceivin[illegible]de. Nothing called by its accurate title. We've traffi[illegible]t language that must be translated anew. N[illegible]d. Rebuilt. The call for a new code, n[illegible] messages that would bypass the toxic alph[illegible]ally foul speech we now used.

Some of [illegible]rphy's rant was unfamiliar, strayed into craziness. Nothing from the hut. But other phrases seemed lifted exactly from Burke, as if he'd recorded and memorized the sermons.

The problem was that I had disregarded a lot of these sermons because—I should be honest here, and there is no one left whom I wish to deceive—these ideas bored me. Maybe I failed to understand them. Burke agonized over speechblood, an engine ripped from the language so the language would fail, and I took it for granted as the higher registers of a religion that did not always move me. The flame alphabet was the word of God, written in fire, obliterating to behold. The so-called Torah. This was public domain Jewish information, easy for Murphy to obtain. We could not say God's true name, nor could we, if we were devoted, speak of God at all. This was basic stuff. But it was the midrashic spin on the flame alphabet that was more exclusive, spoken of only, as far as I knew, by Rabbi Burke in our hut. Since the entire alphabet comprises God's name, Burke asserted, since it is written in every arrangement of letters, then all words reference God, do they not? *That's what words are*. They are variations on his name. No matter the language. Whatever we say, we say God. This excited Burke to shouting. Therefore the language itself was, by definition, off-limits. Every single word of it. We were best to be done with it. Our time with it is nearly through. The logic was hard to deny. You could not do it.

Of course somehow I had found a way. And Rabbi Burke must have found a way, too, because he went on using language and in the end seemed stronger for it. What was Burke but disembodied speech? He showed no signs of walling himself up in silence any time soon.

If Murphy did have his own hut, it didn't seem possible he was breaking protocol in the worst way. Speaking freely of the secrets, sharing them at length with a stranger. And if he had no hut of his own, then somehow he'd gained access to the transmissions, to *our* transmissions, and this he wanted me to know.

Murphy said that someone under LeBov was a troubleshooter, apparently, did speech tests, was favorable to lists. Lists were all the talk at Forsythe. Blacklists, safe lists, green lists, healing lists. There were words to fill all of them. But the healing lists, these were short, and no one was saying for sure what words were on them, not until they were tested, tested *very thoroughly*.

These were highly guarded lists. A small group of people would be entrusted with them, hone them in Rochester, test for toxicity only on themselves.

"Words you'd recite for medicinal purposes? Some kind of healing acoustics?" I asked.

Murphy tilted his head, grimaced, suggesting maybe, maybe not. Suggesting an idiocy he couldn't meet halfway.

I said something about Babel. It was the easiest myth to invoke, queued up for renewed scrutiny, and it was getting batted around by anyone who believed our oldest stories still mattered. What I said was probably nothing. Maybe I only said the word *Babel*, let it hang out there as if that's all that was required.

Murphy wasn't impressed. "That topic is exhausted. Mythology is the lowest temptation. You want to talk about first causes, I'd go back before the Jewish child and cite mythology, the most sickening specimens of speech. We subscribe to these supposedly important stories, religious stories, and we ignore their inanity, how moronic and impractical they are. Can we prove the stories don't make us sick? Because they happened long before we were born, we somehow decide they are extraordinarily important and we shut our brains down, we turn into imbeciles, we let the past start thinking for us. *That's sickness*. Talk about a fucking precursor."

"I don't think those things actually happened," I said. "As in really happened. If we're still talking about Babel."

He'd gotten himself pretty worked up. A halo of spit ringed his mouth, his eyes flaring.

"And you're an authority on what has and hasn't happened? Where'd you do your training?"

"It's a parable," I said. "You believe that, right? You don't think it's a true story?"

"Forget it," he said.

I had no interest in speaking about Babel, a heavy-handed narrative from a world that wasn't mine. Those obvious myths from the Old Testament—*decoy, decoy*—bored me anyway. I'd brought it up because of how harmless it seemed, drowning in easy connotations. But part of me couldn't resist the topic.

"So you're saying," I began, as if [illegible] understand what he was saying, "you're sayin[illegible]hich God strikes down his people wi[illegible]ory about losing our power of speech?"

"That's exactly wh[illegible]ying," said Murphy, quietly. "Sometimes it serves a larger interest to keep people from communicating. The sharing of information hasn't always been a good thing. Sometimes it is a very terrible thing. Perhaps always. God behaved appropriately in that situation."

"You don't think people will write books about this very topic, linking this speech poison, or whatever it is, to something biblical?"

"On the contrary," said Murphy, "that's exactly what I think. As always, people will court the gravest misunderstandings. People are driven to be wrong in the most spectacular ways. There's fame in it. We are in a high season of error. But don't fool yourself. There aren't going to be too many more books. We're not going to see a lot of documented analysis or any kind of analysis. This crisis is different. It will be met with muteness. There's no time for a last word. The last word's already been had, and it wasn't by us. Civilization's first epidemic to defy a public exchange of language. This is a plague among cavemen, and soon we'll only be grunting to each other about it. You can't exactly describe a poison with more of itself, write about how poisonous writing is. And pretty soon the causes won't really seem to matter. The whole fucking idea of cause."

Murphy fell silent and we walked through the cold streets back into my neighborhood. It would be morning soon and I wanted to get to sleep before Esther woke up. My gear was heavy and hot on my body and I was tired.

"I guess this is me," I said, stopping short at a buckled brick path.

It wasn't my house we stood in front of, but I didn't want Murphy to know where I lived. I pictured him the other day in the woods, harassing the Jewish couple, and I hadn't seen them or their violent boys again. I figured I could say good night, walk around and hit the alley, then cut back over to my house.

"Here we are, huh?" Murphy looked at the house and then back at me with a grin.

I had picked a difficult house to lie about. There was a windowless store with a side entrance dormered onto the residence. The sign said it sold ribbons, cartridges, adhesives. A portion of the roof was exposed, with blue Tyvek badly nailed over a hole. It would be too cold to live there. Whatever construction that was under way must have been abandoned for the winter.

"All right, uh, *Bill*, or whoever you are," said Murphy.

The name I'd given him was Steven. He was testing me. I let it go. *Manage your disclosures*. The problem was that, by lying, I'd made him more curious. I needed him to feel he had picked me clean.

"You should come to the Oliver's. That's where we've been meeting. But you'd better get right with meds, and soon, no matter what you believe. You need to start dosing. Have you been to the Oliver's?"

I stalled. "Sure." I pictured myself in a long, beige room trying to climb over a wall.

"Obviously you haven't, but that's all right."

Murphy seemed less amused, rubbed his face so hard it hurt to watch. From his pocket he took out the grease again, pushed a tuft of it into the roof of his mouth, smacked his lips.

"Bill, I'm not the devil. I'm not evil," he said. "You're not alone is all. It's perfectly all right to work together on this thing. But I think I understand. Privacy and all that. You have your little hut, I presume? Your forest worship? Maybe you're one of those? People are wondering if there's some, *you know*, in those locations."

Some, you know, *what*?

Murphy paused, waited for me to roll over on my back with my legs in the air, begging him to take me.

"It would seem that secret channels of insight are obliged right now to open up, reveal their wares. This is definitely not the time for secrecy."

Oh, but yes it is, I thought. I gave him nothing.

"I hope it works out for you," he added.

This was bait I would not take. I smiled, lacking all the required skills for this conversation. My lies were glaring, but Murphy remained polite.

"Here," said Murphy. "Here's the address, and my number."

I looked at the script on the card and my eyes watered, lost focus.

Murphy nodded up at the house that wasn't mine.

"You'd be lucky if you really lived here," he said.

I stared at the house without really seeing it.

"Check your vitals," said Murphy. "No children in there that I can tell. I bet your heart is thriving right now. I wish to fuck that I lived here."

He was wrong. My heart wasn't thriving. It felt tight and cold, strangling inside my rib cage. I needed to get out of there.

We stared at this house as if we were tourists looking up at a great cathedral.

"Anyway," Murphy finally said, "don't court too much blame out there. You know, *blame is interesting*, but be careful. It's a dangerous strategy."

Blame. I'd said nothing to him about it.

"I'm sure we'll see each other again."

Not if I can help it, I didn't say, whoever you fucking are.

11

It was early November. The Forsythe drug trials sped through testing, and the basic anti-speech agents were released for free to the public, dumped into empty newspaper bins on corners.

The drugs were a medical slush short on real medicine, soggy little tonics desperate for vast strengthening. It was the wrong time for placebos, for liquid vials of nothing. When we injected them, they only stupefied us until we sputtered awake in a different room. Instead of healing us, this medicine seemed only to bring on spells of afternoon death. A rehearsal, maybe. A warm-up.

In the days after my run-in with Murphy I rigged a lab in the kitchen, following Thompson's orders. On my conscious nights I milled speculative medicines designed to keep us healthy enough to hold our ground at home. Such nights were coming less often, but when I was able to crawl from the rug in my home office, where I had erected a person-size humidor in which to test the inhalers, and when the evening was cleansed of potential encounters with Esther, I started boiling down drugs.

From the kitchen's single crusted naval port window, as I waited for my solutions to cool, I watched the emergency vans cruise down Wilderleigh at night, sampling the air with roof-mounted saucers and testing wands that spoiled from their bumpers like fins.

No such vans roamed the streets in daylight. A medical truck might have parked on the corner, but I suspect this was for the personal use of a neighbor, the private removal of a loved one who'd just fallen to the toll. A yellow hearse roamed the neighborhood, opening its doors to sheet-covered gurneys. And the occasional diesel helicopter pitched north of us through the upper Montrier Valley, taking aerial surveys, but it was a skeletal effort that could not have yielded much useful information. If officials wanted data on the predicament, they gathered it at night from the vans, and this I knew because nighttime was best for lab work. If there was medical forensics being practiced in our neighborhood, I'd see it through the window.

Esther was no threat at night. At night she slept, or she left the house, teaming up with the other underage weapons in the neighborhood.

The lab was piecemeal, outfitted with equipment I swapped for at the Science Exchange. On the kitchen counter I looped tubes between a trio of beakers, and I flipped the circuit to the furnace so I could plug in the micro finer, which pulverized whatever organic matter I required as ballast, without causing a brownout. Working with no furnace made for cold nights so I repurposed our silverware drawer to hold a stash of sweaters and socks. Hats and whatever else I kept in a wire basket in the pantry. I had a separate handmade Valona machine for fats.

With an induction burner I reduced solutions of saline, blended anti-inflammatory tablets, atomized powder from non-drowsy time-release allergy vials, and milled an arsenal of water-charged vitamins, particularly from the B group, along with binding agents and hardened shavings of an herb dust I'd crushed in the mortar. The salted protein sheets, rolled out from bulk supplies of medical gelatin, I stretched on the dish rack until they resolved as clear as glass, and once they'd hardened I cut them into batons and hollowed out their middles so they could be injected with medicine.

With a cold-reduction process I isolated lead—quivering, gangly worms of it—which served as a jacket around the pills I fed poor Claire. These weren't time release so much as time capsule. Health bombs to go off only when the exposure was intense. Or so they were designed. I planted secret weapons in my wife and she swallowed them down without a fuss. My logging was steady now. All these trials and procedures are documented.

We told ourselves, when we spoke at all, that it was helping.

. . .

I mentioned this work to Murphy the next time I saw him. I didn't want there to be a next time, I never did, but there always was. He admitted there was a small chance, statistically insignificant, that it could help. Medical shielding, a chemical serum. It wasn't *technically impossible*.

We'd run into each other by accident a few nights after our first meeting—I had little reason to think otherwise—in the bitter early morning hours down near Esther's school. I wasn't even checking my vitals. There really was no need anymore.

He found me resting on a bench, as if he happened to be walking by, and I filled him in on my kitchen lab work. He seemed sympathetic at first. Sat down with me and really listened.

"Failures have their place in our work," he admitted, after hearing me out. "I've had my flirtations with failure. There is a small allure there. I commend you for seeking out failure so aggressively. But this idea people have of failing on purpose, *failing better*? Look at who says that. Just look at them. Look at them very carefully."

I tried to picture the people who said that, but saw only my own head, mounted on a stick.

"They talk about failure all the time," said Murphy. "They're obsessed with it. Really what they're doing is consoling themselves for being ordinary, boasting about it, even. They've turned their incompetence into a strange kind of glory. They have entered the business of consoling themselves."

And you think that's what I'm doing? I didn't ask.

It was a cold, awful night, and my only consolation, solitude, was gone for the moment.

"You're testing on two people, and you'll probably be dead before your work will help anyone. You need a much, much broader test population for your studies to lead anywhere. You know that, right? It's not as if you want *only* you and your wife to survive, right? You're doing this work because you want to stop the epidemic, right?"

Right, I thought. Right. I think.

Murphy repeated his invitation to the Oliver's. Or Forsythe. I wasn't really clear about the naming. I didn't care.

What *wasn't* failure? I wanted to know. Was there something that was working?

Murphy spoke of a vaccine derived from *children*. When he said that word he grew quiet, looked around as if we were being observed. He didn't like to believe this, he didn't *want* to believe this, but if *the children* harbored the poison, then they no doubt contained the antidote to it as well. *No doubt*. It stood to reason. He mumbled on about blood, marrow, building tolerance, immunity, controlling the circumstances. This was a favorite word of his. *Circumstances*. It sounded so odd when he said it, one of those words designed to make me forget other words, the whole language.

Murphy felt that we should be drawing blood from our own kids, informally, gently, of course. Everyone will soon come over to this approach. It needn't cause any trouble. In the spirit of science.

"Don't tell me you haven't thought about drawing some of, what's your daughter's name again? Her blood?"

I had not told him Esther's name, had not even told him I had a daughter. Just called her my kid. If I had thought of drawing her blood, a nighttime withdrawal while the girl slept, I would not reveal that to Murphy.

"You have the source of the disease living in your house and you're not even curious what her blood might reveal under a microscope?"

Profoundly incurious, I thought. Deeply, hugely indifferent. I looked down and smiled as if he were being hypothetical.

Murphy waved the question away, letting me off the hook, repeating that if I'd only come down to the Oliver's, I could see what was being done.

I pictured children linked by medical tubing to one of those vast, overhead syringes. I pictured a wolf climbing a slippery wall, on top of which sat some glistening piece of meat.

I thanked him and said good night. Had to be getting back. Work to do. Pretty tired now. But Murphy didn't respond, didn't move.

Among other things, Murphy excelled at a refusal to release me from our encounters. It was a strange power of his, to pretend a conversation had not ended.

"Wait," he said, his head cocked, listening.

I wanted to go home, get away from him, but I stopped, quieting my breath. You could hear the engines running the neighborhood homes. Furnaces and water heaters droning on. Above us came a hum from the telephone lines.

Murphy gripped my shoulder, raised his other hand in concentration, his eyes closed. And then I heard it, too.

A din rose out of the north field beyond the school, and as the sound bloomed it grew piercing, wretchedly clear, borne so quickly on the wind, we shuddered when it hit. Voice-like, childlike, a cluster of speech blaring out of the field. The sound crushed out my air. Behind the noise ran a pack of kids, so shadowed and small at that distance, they looked like animals sprinting across the field. Coming right toward us.

In front of them came a wall of speech so foul I felt myself burning.

Murphy scrambled, grabbed me, and we ran for cover. In the bushes I felt his cold hand in my mouth, a greasy paste spreading against my gums, his fingers reaching so far into me, they touched the back of my throat.

I gagged over his hand, fought to breathe. Murphy wanted to reach all the way into my lungs. I tried to relax my mouth, my throat, but I could feel my lips stretching, starting to tear. Murphy's weight was on me, his own scared breath against my neck.

I gave in, exhaled, letting the man cover me, spread his medicine deep in my mouth. Then finally Murphy pulled out his hand, wiped it on the grass next to my face. The release from this agony felt sweet, and I could breathe again.

The kids cleared the field, ran past us, their voices sounding—I wasn't sure how—harmless to me now, as if I'd only imagined the effect before. The awful wave had passed through and now I felt no acid in their speech. Just kids' voices squeezed against the higher registers. Sharp and annoying, maybe, but safe. I had a fruity taste in my mouth and I had to keep swallowing. The paste triggered a gush of saliva that I did not want to give up. I drank what released in my mouth and watched. Everything out on the street under the lamp seemed gorgeous and clear.

One of the kids stopped on the sidewalk across the street from us. He'd caught someone and now he was going to attack. He crouched, his hands cupped over his mouth, and he started shouting. A series of single word cries, projected through his hands, as if he were launching ammunition from his face.

But this was no abstract show of force, this was an attack on someone who hadn't found cover in time.

Sprawled on the street beneath the boy was someone who wasn't moving, and the boy made sure of that with repeated volleys launched right over the body, a relentless flow as the body twitched on the asphalt each time the kid spoke, as if a cattle prod shot electricity from his mouth.

Then the body stopped twitching and the boy relented.

When the boy stood up we saw his face in the streetlight, so long and solemn and awful to behold.

Except the kid wasn't a boy. It was my Esther. Her hair was wild and she wore an outfit I didn't recognize, some long coat that was too big on her.

From our hiding place in the grass we watched her.

"Be careful of that one," whispered Murphy into my neck.

I tightened at the warning. *That one.* That one was my one and only.

Esther looked down at the person at her feet, seemed to whisper something. Then she ran to catch up with her friends, dwarfed by her coat. On the street that body still didn't move.

Murphy climbed off me, sat back in the grass.

"That one is trouble," Murphy said. "I'd like to see a sample of *her* blood, wouldn't you?"

In my mouth I felt that I had eaten a piece of terrible meat.

"What did you give me?" I asked.

"A gift." Murphy handed me a tissue.

I didn't thank him. I wanted to be sick.

Murphy crawled up to me, held my face tight.

I felt that I should go after Esther, if slowly, carefully, but I was afraid to move.

"Now say thank you," Murphy said. "Or have you forgotten your manners?"

His hand gripped my face so hard, I could barely form the words, but I did it, I thanked him, and he released me.

Murphy relaxed, sat back.

"Well, you're welcome," he said. "It was really my pleasure. But now I'm curious about something."

The man on the street groaned, rolled over. I couldn't be sure, but it seemed to disappoint Murphy that the man was not dead.

"I'm curious," he said. "I've done something for you. Now how do you propose paying me back?"

12

The next day I struck out for the hut alone, Claire too ill to join me. I offered to drive right up to the trailhead for her, perhaps all the way down past Boltwood, if we could get the gate open and sneak our car through. For Claire I would even drive down to the northern foot of the stream where it ponds and there's a small turnout. From there I could strap her to a sled and drag her up the embankment. It'd be bumpy but we could line the sled with pillows. She would hardly have to walk. I'd carry her that last leg, if she wanted. We could bring extra blankets, a thermos of soup. It would be good to go to the hut today. Good for us. It might help.

I wasn't sure I believed this, but I needed to sound hopeful for Claire.

It didn't matter, because she declined the invitation. She didn't even decline, just failed to answer, staring with dread focus at her own little finger, as if she could will me from the room by exercising that top knuckle back and forth, back and forth.

Without Claire I took the cautious route, down Sedgling to 38 for one exit's worth of highway, only to return to town from the north, dropping into the valley from the old Balden Road, which is so steep that no matter how slow you take it, riding your brake the whole way, you fairly skid along the sand to the bottom, where the Montrier electrical tower sits planted inside a guarded park.

Even here I doubled back along the dark wall of the Monastery, in case I was being followed, because Murphy seemed too easily to find me. Even though I'd driven this time, driven not just the long way but the entirely incorrect way, a route that made no navigational sense, I could not risk running into him today. I would follow Thompson's rules to the letter.

Behind the hut I extracted the listener from its shit-caked bag. At the rusted orifice in the hut floor I squeezed the hole until I could pull on the fitting, but the hole was stiff. Today I could hardly force it open. After a finger-mincing effort, it ripped wider with what sounded like an animal cry and heat spread into the hut as the listener shriveled in my hands. Soon the bag stoppering the hole swelled with air, inflating gently as if a sick person lay beneath it, breathing his last. Now, at least, a transmission might be possible.

I found the labor dispiriting. It was too much effort to get to Rabbi Burke. You should have been able to plug in our radio and turn it on. But Burke had indicated once, while praising us for our adherence to protocol, that sentences pertaining to the Jewish project must come in certain lengths, precise strings of language, stripped of acoustical excess. Otherwise they were invalid, not technically a part of the authentic language, which required endless honing, pruning. The listener enabled this, in ways I would never understand. The requirements we upheld at our hut would fill a whole other report until it burst into rags. As with any religion, one supposes.

Perhaps other options might present themselves here, I hoped. Burke, or even Thompson, would have to consider more concrete guidance now, particularly since LeBov was saying we *knew something*. Everything had changed. One's faith was meant to yield actionable material at times like this, I always thought, when one's own imagination had failed, when nothing seemed possible. Wasn't this why we accommodated an otherwise highly irrational set of beliefs?

I had not done this hut work alone before. Solitude was not authorized. And this was no Thursday, which doubled my violation. I half thought I'd see some other Jew in the woods toting his own blood-slick listener.

Tuesdays are mine, he'd snarl, heaving his hot listener over the console.

I would guess that my visit took place on a Tuesday, but days were not easy to track. It was hard to believe that it should matter, that access to our faith would be blocked on some days, regulated according to some inscrutable limitation in, of all things, forest electronics, radio science.

Lately there were days I wished I could walk into a real synagogue, *a real one*, sit down, and listen to a live person, a person I could then follow home with questions.

When the listener was sealed to the bag and my tests for leaks yielded only a mild stream of wind from the hole, I ran the orange cable into the console and sat down to listen. I waited there in the cold hut and I squeezed out all other noise, freezing on the wood floor.

Nothing happened. Hours later I'd only gathered hisses and blips, a language ripped apart, turned into flesh and then shredded. At one point I discovered that with my face pressed against the listener, more voices flowed through the radio, a tumble of speech from a man whose voice was far lower than Rabbi Burke's. A different man entirely, speaking in what sounded like Old English. The harder I pressed my face against the listener, smashing it into the wet flesh, the clearer this man's voice became, but it seemed I'd have to hurt myself to make his words audible. I'd need to break my skin, fracture my jaw, taking the listener inside my own face, and I could not bring myself to do it.

Instead I retreated, went back to the standard procedures. But the module could build nothing else from whatever weak signal trickled through. Yesterday's signal, the vestiges of a message that might have once mattered, but by now had been hacked into nonsense by exposure in the hole. A sermon built only from wind, a wind that had been buried for years, only to spill from the earth now with no force or meaning.

The listener could not even pull a fairy tale from the cable for me, which it sometimes did, after Burke's sermon had been discharged, sometimes instead of Burke's sermon, instead of Thompson's typical aftermath.

Claire and I always got excited that we might hear a story instead of a sermon. The line would crackle, seem to die, and then, with no preamble, a broadcast surged on that played the old stories, one after another. Scratchy-voiced recitations of Aesop's, or the story of the dry well, which we very much loved, no matter how many times it played. Even "Rothschild's Shoes" was not terrible. We did not find it a terrible story at all. We never complained if we got to hear it from the radio in our hut.

And these stories, unaffiliated as we guessed they were, unrelated to our religious practice, these we could talk about together. These we could share out loud, which made us like them even more.

Our favorite line was, *Then what does he do when it rains?*, asked about Rothschild of the golden shoes. We used to ask this of each other on the way home from the hut, and we asked it solemnly, sometimes holding each other's faces, trying not to laugh. We came to say it of nearly anyone we saw who seemed too good to be true, happy and attractive and successful. Yes, Claire would say later, when we were home in bed and debriefing on this person, trying not to show how threatened we were, *But what does he do when it rains?*

Now in the hut when I looked at this sad apparatus, the crumbled rubber, the flannel insulation from some other time, the felted "skin" lining the orange cable that I could not touch without gagging, I felt queasy about how it all worked, how these parts, useless and absurd on their own, were meant to accomplish anything, least of all connect me to rabbinical guidance pumped in from an elsewhere I couldn't name.

Burke was gone today, Thompson was off. Nothing flowed from the radio. I was alone out there, and any channel of insight would have to be one I manufactured myself. This I did not know how to do.

Cold as it was, I stripped off my clothes, then wrapped my body over the listener, hugging it so tightly that a broadcast finally surged into the hut. If I held still and squeezed the listener for dear life, I could now hear Rabbi Thompson, even though he sounded old and tired, as if he were transmitting from late in his life. In his sermon were medical instructions, more of the technical work we might pursue, and I took in as much as I could before my body failed and I fell from the listener, freezing.

Without Claire the hut felt small and false, the childish architecture of some hack inventor, someone who *didn't believe enough* that this location would actually be inhabited by real people one day.

Claire and I were proud—I'm speaking for her because she couldn't hide how she felt—that we had something private like this that was our own, and that it gave us something to listen to, to think about, to rail against, to love. But there were times when I wondered why it had to be so difficult, so dependent on questionable equipment.

Sitting there as the day grew dark, the listener perspired on me, and one part of it, a fin canting from its rear that seemed encased by a soft wood, was so hot that I felt sick when I touched it.

It was time to go. Given the extra distance I had to travel to get home, I was in a hurry. I rushed to the woods and took the northern trail down into the valley again and up the other side to where the car was, jogging the whole way so I would not have to walk those woods in the dark.

In my haste I believe I left the listener there on the floor of the hut, or perhaps I dropped it on the porch, the shining limb.

I cannot understate the error of such an action.

I failed to bury the listener when I was done.

With Claire this never would have happened. She was fastidious, held us to protocol each time, and together we checked and balanced our tasks, dispersing whatever ritual worry we might have until the worry turned small.

No, I left the listener there, exposed for anyone to find, to try to use, because I'd broken code and gone alone to the hut. Because I thought I could do something like this by myself.

13

In late November documents crowded my mailbox. Printouts sealed in manila lacking address or postage. This was my first view of *The Proofs*, a medical broadside of LeBov's that Murphy called required reading. It resembled a university newspaper, except blown strange, its histories slurred, its facts effaced.

The text was pale blue, like a writing erupted under skin. The illustrations—illness maps, perimeter lines for the epidemic, and module schematics—were drawn by a palsied hand. In these drawings germs were people or beasts, and viruses looked like the world seen from miles away. Speech from the faces of children was rendered in ugly rushes of color, with each color coded on a wheel to some kind of distress.

On the back page Murphy had written: *I've entrusted you with something, now it's your turn.*

He'd found my house, then. Which meant he had followed me. I pictured him striding in the shadows down Wilderleigh on a cold wellness walk, his children barking at home while his wife moaned in the corner. If there *was* a wife. He was waiting for his moment, watching my house from down the street.

I concealed *The Proofs* and looked at the issues alone in bed. But with each delivery I put everything back in my mailbox as I'd found it, creeping out in the dark of morning so Murphy could not know for certain I had received what he sent.

Inside *The Proofs* I found historical precedent for the language toxicity. A kind of medical foreshadowing from earliest history. Signs from the past that this would happen, or that it had happened before and been snuffed out, forgotten. Hippocrates, Avicenna, a long list of experts who knew without really knowing that our strongest pollution was verbal.

The master dissector Gabriele Falloppio, forerunner of the modern autopsy, found what he termed curious *erosions* in the brain from multilingual patients. Or more notably Boerhaave, who registered speech aversions in the infirm and began to use small doses of speech as homeopathic treatments. Boerhaave saw only one way this could go, hoped to trigger immunity through controlled exposure. Hoped to, but didn't.

Throughout *The Proofs* were phrases lifted from as far back as the medical spookeries of Laennec and Auenbrugger, sometimes misattributed, sometimes attributed to medical scientists I'd never heard of, because, I suspected, they had not actually lived.

Theories of exposure, but more than that. A grammar detected in breath, in wheezing. A new rationale for listlessness. Epidemics like cholera reimagined as speech-driven, miasmatic cyclones, an airborne disturbance, to be sure, but one that fed on the denser pockets of speech, grew stronger in such places, dying out in regions of controlled silence.

The finer print offered no attribution. No masthead, no bylines. Just the name *LeBov* raised in a sickly script. You almost needed night vision to see his name. With a computer one might have mocked this up alone and run off copies at the supermarket.

A list of speech rules filled the inside cover. A caution to ration one's *I* statements, suppress reference to oneself, closing off a small arsenal of the language. The various speech quotas scientists were proposing now, even if they didn't believe it would matter. Grammatical amputations. A list of rules so knotted that to follow them would be to say nearly nothing, to never render one's interior life, to eschew abstraction and discharge a grammar that merely positioned nouns in descending orders of desire.

Presumably if you wanted nothing, you'd have no occasion to speak.

In a section of historical anecdotes I read that in 1825, Jacob Gallerus, a chemist, was sickened by his family. A letter to the medical dean of some Dublin college, written by him, asking for outside verification, which was not granted. He recorded symptoms of nausea and dizziness while in their company, determined the sickness occurred only when they spoke to him. Troubleshooting not listed, diagnostics similarly absent. A form of inbreeding, he called it, to listen to his family. There is congress in speech, he wrote. It is illicit from them. It is obscene. A sentence from *The Proofs* I will always recall: *I am not similarly ill with strangers*. In his cellar Gallerus built a soundproof room to recuperate and to purge himself—these were his words—from the exposure to his wife and children. To what end it isn't said. Of what he finally died neither.

Alongside the historical anecdotes were medical recommendations, refutations, preventative treatments.

If a child was deemed viral, he was salted. This by the Jews, I read. What kind of Jews, it was not clear. Circa sometime that was not mentioned. Salted in the deepest sense. A cake of it rubbed over the limbs, salt poured down their mouths, into their cavities.

It is possible, I thought, that these were stories. Fancies. But if so, they were not good ones or even whole ones, but facts made wrong, broken open and remolded into lies. Someone reaching back into history and rearranging the parts, but with a filthy hand. Which would be to what end? The urge to falsify such details was without any purpose I could name. There was too much, additionally, that I knew to be true.

In a section related to *materials* I read of pariahs and salt, lepers and salt, the use of salt when it comes to lunatics. Salt as a detoxifier. From Jews comes the idea of salt as the residue of an ancient language, which I'd heard at the hut. Such salts were dissolved in water and dispensed to mutes, to the deaf, to infants on the threshold of speech. Acoustical decomposition, the powder left over from sounds. What this proved went unsaid.

In *The Proofs* a pattern of cryptic evasions became clear, of failing to deduce.

From recorded language, broadcast in a controlled environment and subjected to freezing temperatures, is collected trace amounts of salt. Whorf and Sapir perform this work with some graduate students. A salt deficiency lowers language comprehension in children.

The practice of language smoking originates in Bolivia but quickly travels north. In Mexico City it is perfected. Words and sentences tested by a *delegate* in a smoke-filled tube, at the end of which is stationed a sacrificial listener called, for unknown reasons, *the bell*.

The bell's brain, when he dies, is pulled and separated into loaves. The loaves are tagged and named. Only drawings survive.

More instances of rot in the brain from those who have exceeded the threshold of listening.

In 1834 a family of five in Rotterdam are discovered expired in their home, parents and children blanketed in hives. That same year, farther north, a series of rashes observed in children, rashes with what is inexplicably called "a tonal element." Rashes, hives, welts: of inordinate concern in *The Proofs*. *And the connection is*, I wondered.

In the island of Port Barre the citizens employed expired animals for soundproofing. Walls of pelts on stilts over fault lines. The typical strategy of shielding with organic matter. Usage of animals for such purposes not being the point, apparently, but rather the unanswered question, from what were they soundproofing? What was so loud that needed quieting? Autopsies show a nonmedical diagnosis. Blackened cortex, they call it.

Perkins refers to the "person allergy," a toxicity to others. Uses the phrase as if it's an accepted disorder. He fails at developing any effective shielding. Scoffs at the use of animals for such work. Meat is in fact an amplifier, he will say.

The young Albert Kugler has a superstition against the utterance of certain words. Proper names are volatile, likewise imperatives.

A section, mostly inscrutable, written perhaps in code, or in an eroded language, on which words are volatile. A volatility index?

None of them not, the conclusion?

A tribe from Bolivia rations their use of spoken language by appointing a delegate. Again this term, *delegate*, who uses language so others don't have to. A language martyr. These tribe members speak and write on behalf of the entire community. They die young, their hands bloated, hearts enlarged, goes the claim. No asterisk, no footnote. How the others die goes unmentioned.

Hiram of Monterby calls language the great curse. Esther of the Fire, in her almanac, decries the pollutions of the mouth. It will burn in your mind, says Pliny, of a speech he hears an unknown traveler deliver at the roadside at Thebes.

If I could only speak such words at my enemy, would say Pliny. What weaponry I would have.

I knew my Pliny pretty well and I was fairly sure this was wrong, hadn't happened to Pliny. Or anyone. Yet the tone was assured, hardened in the rhetoric of fact.

The brain of Albert Dewonce, whose job it was to listen to troubles. Of whom nothing is given, but one can guess at the kind of job. Heard more words than anyone alive, was the claim, this Dewonce. His brain, they said, when he died, was decayed at the core, a lather of cells that could not possibly have received any information. Says the coroner. The cortex, blackened. Says his wife, he was sick each night from what he heard.

A brain that had been rendered to slush from speech, then.

Stories of this sort all throughout. Did any of it stand to reason? The profound cost on the brain itself. Its limited resilience in the face of, what, *language*?

A person's language age can be measured through a test of his Broca's area, such test to be performed with a tool whose name is defaced, unreadable. Unattributed drawings near the text are perhaps this tool. Language age, a phrase used throughout *The Proofs*. Language death, when the body is saturated. At the cusp of adulthood. A drowning of cells, is the phrase. The time of quota, when the threshold is tripped, at or near the age of eighteen.

Giving Esther four more years, I noted.

Another section, a test, called *How Do You Feel When You Read This?* Then some words slung together without logic.

The reading did not harm me. I scanned through what was written but felt nothing. Sometimes numbness took me, working like a vacuum to siphon off what I knew, but it did not feel connected to *reading*. It felt like a headache that had grown cold, pulled long, a headache on the move through parts of me I never knew felt pain.

In future issues of *The Proofs*, a final theory of rashes was pledged. We'd see working drawings of the Perkins Mouth Guard. The thirty-word language would be revealed, the least toxic words in our lexicon, but these words would primarily be place-names.

The Proofs was conspicuous for its absence of conclusions. One was not sure it was not simply the stitchery of Murphy, whose motives were somehow other. Deeply other. Unguessable. If *The Proofs* was advocating something, it did not say. It was not for sale. How many copies there were, I didn't know.

Before folding up my evening reading and stuffing it back in its envelope, I saw in smaller print, bound by a box, a paragraph of text with the title *Take Heart!*

What a thing to do, and how very much I wished I could.

14

The red busses of Rochester pulled in that week, parked outside the school to collect their cargo. They came from Forsythe, a universal *F* scratched into their hoods. These were not busses so much as engorged medical waste canisters, motorized and fitted with tires, dipped in brilliant red paint. The medical waste being our children.

The cockpits of the busses, *should passengers become vocal*, were wood-boxed, soundproofed, blackened, double-locked.

An *optional alleviation*, these busses were called. Your children, went the pledge, would not be subjected to medical tests. Nothing invasive. They would be kept safe, held for you, in order for local recoveries to flourish. Medical babysitting.

Segregation was the strategy. *Divide and conquer*. But this was more like divide and collapse, divide and weep.

Minnesota was a destination, a low-activity coordinate. The toxicity couldn't linger with those thermals. You wanted to be where the wind was. A certain species of it. Some kind of grassland facility in Pennsylvania was listed as well, where a new form of ventilation was being attempted.

A picture of the destination floated around, an empty field with a horse trotting through. The imaginary landscape of a travel brochure. We were meant to envision a clean, new settlement, a territory free of peril. *Your children will be safe*. Maps for the evacuation were taped to lampposts, peeling away to litter the street. *Track your child*. You'd see one of the sad fathers standing alone in the road, examining one of these maps, which depicted a future that did not include him.

The busses filled with children. Some orphans—mothers and dads fled already—mounted the stairs alone, taking a snack from the basket in the aisle. When parents appeared, they held their kids' hands. Their faces showed something no one could decode, mouths stretched into grins. They delivered their children into the hushed busses, then bent down to the cargo bays to stuff in a suitcase. Children with labels stitched across their coats, their names rendered in scrawls of yarn, as if they weren't already lost. Walking toxics, before we fully understood the poison of scripts: the slower, awful burn of writing when you saw it. Children should be neither seen nor heard, especially if they carried names on their clothing. Then together or alone the parents returned to their cars and drove home.

And the busses roared from the neighborhood. Headed elsewhere, carrying part of the problem away from us. For now.

Because this exodus was optional, some children still remained. Including Esther and her friends. But was *friends* really the word for that group, who lorded over the neighborhood in our final days, creating barriers of speech so putrid you could not cross them?

Per Thompson, I escalated my smallwork in the kitchen lab from solid medicines to smoke. Even if this succeeded to numb our faculties and kill off input, it would be the mildest sort of stopgap. At best I was buying us dark minutes, prolonging the stupor. At worst I was rushing us closer toward some highly unspectacular form of demise. If we were dying I wanted us to die differently.

Otherwise we'd be found in sweat-stained pajamas leaning against the toilet. We'd be found on the low bench we'd installed in the closet under the stairs, for hiding, Claire's face stuck to my hair. We'd be found deep under our blankets in whatever bed we'd made for ourselves that night. Or we'd not be found, because one of us would have wandered into the yard and then the woods, confused, only to collapse in a ravine.

In those last weeks at home Claire sometimes shuffled into the kitchen and surveyed my lab work. She pulled up a stool and sat at the counter as I fed our medicine through the bottle-size smoker.

Claire watched while I freebased for her one of the mineral trials, using a kitchen apron draped over her head for a vapor hood.

She endured the exposure without coughing and I detected gratitude in her eyes. I could tell even without looking that she was smiling at me while I worked, content to be together in the evening.

The medicinal smoke was bitter and I swept it from her face when she finished a dose. She looked at me so gently, and when I held her for a neck injection her skull felt small and cold in my hands. When I needed Claire's vitals she accommodated the kit over her ribs, opening her robe for me without complaint. She even did so without my having to ask.

Every few days, it seemed, she graduated to the next belt buckle on the kit, her body losing size, her face retreating on her head, taking on that awful smallness.

I wanted only to provide Claire with some medicine that might help her sit near Esther, to endure her company without symptoms. After precisely timed doses, she dragged herself through the house and tried to visit with her daughter, if by chance her daughter was home. A narrowing of her motives had led to this small desire, but it remained difficult, and Esther had little patience for a chilled and sick mother who only wanted to cuddle.

One night I heard Esther yell, "You're disgusting," and walked in to find Claire sprawled on her back, smiling up at me. She'd gotten what she needed. She'd hugged her daughter, and the retaliation had been worth it.

Esther, inside her large coat, headed out the door.

If the smoke from whatever powders I'd scorched was thick enough to hang in place, I captured it in bags, to create smoke purses, little sacklets of fumes that could be punctured by a juice box straw if I required a small dose.

In the spice cabinet I kept wicker baskets filled with these smoke purses, labeled in black marker. If I had data relating to Claire's response to the inhalation, I noted it on the back of the purses. I wrote things like *no change*. I wrote *muteness*. I wrote *talkative*, *erratic*, *nervous*. I wrote *giddy*. I wrote, and this I wrote most, *no data*. Or I wrote nothing at all. The writing was strange to my hand. Sometimes before writing on the pillowy bags I had to practice on paper, and I could not always recognize the script.

I suspected that if I wrote the wrong thing, the wrong way, the lettering would harm me. I'd excite some new sensitivity in my perception, and I would collapse.

Those were quiet nights. Claire and I took breaks outside, bathing our faces in the cold November air. Our neighborhood was chilled and flat and all green growth was gone. I loved it so stripped down and frozen. There was something sculpted to the shapes, as though our streets had been carved from ice, colored with pale dyes squirted from a dropper. I loved the frost on the cars at night and the steam that flowered in marble-smooth shapes from the yards, like perfect gray ghosts made of balloon material. To be outside without our coats in such cold raw air was exquisite. Sometimes puffs of breath rose from a porch down the street and we heard the muted voices of our last neighbors. But usually no one was out, and if there were lights it was the blue glow of the streetlamps. These lamps only sharpened the darkness, radiating a pure blue smolder that made the night feel stronger. A final absence of light that would take hours of sunshine to boil off.

When the vans drove through, they did so quickly, with so little noise, their engines seemed swaddled in silencers. Or perhaps they had no engines and glided past our house on a perfect slick of air.

It was Claire one night who offered that perhaps we didn't need the medicine we'd just finished scalding our lungs with. She seemed to be suggesting a change of strategy.

"It's so good of you, Darling, the work you're doing," she said, staring at the street.

We sat bundled in a shared blanket on the steps. The cold air felt intense in my chest. I knew how wrong it was to feel happy, but I could not help it.

I didn't look at her. *Work* was a wishful word for my failures in the lab. Nothing was good of me. Claire's compliment was only necessary because of how obvious the failure was. Whatever I was brewing and pumping into her was nothing I should be thanked for.

"I know you've probably thought of this," Claire said, her words slurred, "but maybe it's not the best thing for Essie with us taking all this new medicine, in terms of how it might make her feel."

"It's not for *her*. It's for us."

I knew I was missing the point, but I couldn't tiptoe around the euphemism. Esther's well-being had become a distant concern, like worrying about the flesh wound of a god.

"Is there something, or are we . . ." Claire started.

I waited, but the sentence never finished. It dug a little hole in the air between us, and the hole throbbed, until I realized it was there for me to fill.

"The busses," I said, giving it my worst guess. There was a chance Claire wanted me to finish her sentence this way, didn't have the heart to do it herself. Maybe I was the one who had to say it out loud.

"We could bring her down there and see," I continued. "That would remove her from anything unpleasant at home, and then we wouldn't need to interrupt our work. Best of both worlds, maybe."

"Best of both worlds?" asked Claire. "Really."

She shook her head, wouldn't look at me.

We could, I thought. Esther would not even need to know why we were going. *A field trip, a vacation, with horses certainly. I'm sure there will be horses! Just look at this picture*. We could pretend Esther didn't know what these red busses were, and it would join that larger field of perceptions, insights, and facts I also pretended Esther did not possess.

The logistics of getting Esther strapped in a bus seat evaded me, led me into thoughts and plans I did not wish to have.

Was I not meant to think the unthinkable? Hadn't our hut training led exactly to this, courting unbearable circumstances as a matter of principle?

Claire sighed, but in such a kind, noncombative way that it disarmed me. It made me sad to think that she'd been rehearsing this conversation for days, probably, hoping to sound kind and wise and open-minded. She wanted off the medicine. I think she wanted off more than that.

"Esther's not going anywhere, Sam. You don't get to make that decision, and I'll never agree to it."

It was always awkward to hear my own name in her voice. We never did that. Never. We openly discussed that we never did that. It was somehow unbearably intimate and deeply hostile at the same time.

I nuzzled up against her. "I know. I'm just saying."

Which wasn't true. I wasn't saying anything. What I particularly wasn't saying was that I could never send Esther on a bus, either, but by taking that position I could keep Claire sympathetic to the medical trials. She'd see it as an either-or situation. I saw no other way for us to stay at home.

"I don't think medicine is the answer anymore," she said. "I think there is no answer. I just want to be with Esther when it happens."

When it happens? I didn't want to ask.

"Will you let me?" she said. "Could you arrange it?"

I squeezed her hand and she squeezed back, which once meant that things were fine between us, a language of anxious grips that we exchanged to rescue ourselves from disagreement. Now, it was code for nothing. You translated it and it yielded speech vacuumed of meaning.

"I promise you it's not going to happen."

"You *can't,* though. You can't promise me anything."

Claire's breathing changed and I felt her sobs in my body before I heard them.

I tried to stop what was coming by saying her name, but this only triggered it harder.

"This is my fault," said Claire, shaking. She gestured at the street, as if she were taking responsibility for the whole world outside our house: the people, the trees, the weather. She'd done this.

I reached for her but she pulled away, repeated her claim. It was her fault. All of it. The entire thing. It was all her fault.

"Please, Claire."

"I am to blame." She raised her voice, shouted into the street. "*I* did this!"

I ducked, as if I needed to show my embarrassment to any invisible person watching us from the dark exteriors of the neighborhood.

I told her it wasn't true. I reasoned with her, asked for evidence. There was no evidence.

"Yes, but he told me it was my fault. He told me! What kind of person does that? He must have a reason. If the rabbi is not right, then I will never forgive him."

I said, "We shouldn't even be talking about this. We can't be talking about this. You know that."

"Why?" she shouted. "Why the fuck not? How can we *not* talk about it? How do they expect us to do that? It's impossible."

"The rules," I whispered. Instantly I hated how this sounded.

"The rules? From Bauman? How do we even know who that old man was? He was *no one*. A fucking weirdo. He's gone. We've never seen him again. We haven't seen anyone! There's no one to see."

"But there doesn't need to be," I said. "What would that even do? It's a distraction."

"Speak for yourself, you bastard."

Claire cried hard into her hands. Hoarding, monstrously, this unknowable thing all to herself.

I said, "I won't discuss this with you, Claire. I can't. This is a conversation you have to have with yourself. We keep our own counsel."

"Talking to myself is not a conversation! I have no counsel to keep. I'm *alone*. You are, too. How can you stand it?"

"You're upset. Let's get you inside and maybe try a different dose. I think I know what I did wrong."

"Oh, you have no idea what you've done wrong. No idea. You've done enough. Just keep that fucking medicine away from me."

I stood, tried to walk it off, but it didn't come off. I couldn't shake it.

"So this is your fault?" I said. "You really believe that?" I asked her. "Fine, let's fucking talk about it."

Claire nodded up at me. "It's the first thing that's made sense out there for me in years. It's the first thing I heard that felt true and real."

The first thing? In *years?*

"It wasn't *true* and *real*. It was a sermon. You're not meant to believe it like that."

"Oh? Then how the fuck am I supposed to believe it? If I don't believe it, then why are we going out there? Is it a joke?"

I didn't know what I was saying now, but I kept talking.

"The lessons are abstract, something to think about."

She scoffed. "Maybe to you they are. If you want to escape all responsibility, that's your business, Sam. Do that. If that's what you call keeping your own counsel."

"Well, if it's your fault, *if you actually believe that*, then fix it," I said.

Claire seemed confused.

"Make it better," I shouted down at her. "Make this go away, *Claire*. Undo it. I'm going to fucking wait here until you do.

"You see?" I said. "It's meaningless. Your claim is fucking meaningless. It's the most selfish thing of all for you to take the blame, as if you had anything to do with this."

She looked at me in high disbelief.

"Selfish?" she asked.

"I'm serious," I yelled, and she flinched.

"If it's your fault, do something about it, *Claire*. Otherwise shut up and never say that again. Never open your mouth about this again."

This stopped the crying. I watched my wife draw in her forces, sealing herself off from not just what I said, but from *me* as well, from the evening, from the days that had passed. A project of wall building, face hardening, secret fortifying of everything that mattered to her. All done without moving, an inner construction project Claire seemed to command until she was, in all the ways that matter, gone. Sitting on the steps Claire receded, drifting farther and farther away from me until she looked up at me with the stare reserved for a stranger, all intimacy erased.

"It's not your decision," I said to her, softer. "You can't break faith because it also breaks mine. I can't go out there without you. *You know that*. It doesn't work. I already tried it. We have to go together, to believe in it together."

She laughed. "But we *don't* have to, Sam. We actually don't. Find someone else to believe in nothing with. I'm done."

"It's not your choice," I whispered.

"Oh, I think it is. And, anyway, it's for the best. I have it on good faith that if I stop going, Esther will be safe. Someone's made a promise to me, and, unlike you, I think he can keep it."

"Someone?"

"Yes, Sam. Someone. You don't know him."

"Claire, please," I said. "This person."

"Forget it."

"He came to the house?"

"I said forget it."

"One question."

"No. No questions. No questions and no answers."

"Claire. Did this man call himself *Murphy*? Does he have red hair?"

My wife did not respond, but she gave me such a queer, searching look, and then it was a long time before she looked at me again.

Together we sat staring out at the street, the final exhausts of Claire's sobs gasping out. She slid to the far end of the steps, kept to herself for the rest of the night. She was perhaps too weak to bring herself inside.

Salt blasts had streaked into the neighborhood. You couldn't see them at night, or even so well in the day. Mostly it was the pellucid salt already washed clear by the wind. But you felt it crunching under your feet, some living thing recently crushed into grain.

I looked east toward the man-shaped silhouette between two

houses where the sun would appear in a few hours, but there was nothing there to suggest a sun could ever heave itself into the sky again. I would never get used to that.

I could not ignore how that space looked forever immune from any illumination. Places give no warning that they might soon be erased by light. There is never a single thing to suggest that some grotesque change is coming that will reveal all, and soon.

A language solely of place-names. What would we possibly say to each other?

Sitting with my wife, whose disgust pulsed over me, I laughed to myself over these assessments, thoughts of a final or irresolvable darkness. There was textbook wisdom surfacing a little too easily. Sentimentality was no doubt a side effect of the speech fever, compounded by the side effects of all our failed medicine. The side effects of fighting, the side effects of knowing nothing, the side effects of being done with it and somehow, for no reason I could detect, still alive. One uses one's deathbed energy to project meaning where none can be found. How does the species possibly benefit from such an action?

Your feelings will matter to you and to you alone, would say LeBov. You will surge with emotion over situations that have no bearing on the crisis. It's a tactic. A trick. Believe in it at your peril. Better to bury yourself alive than give these ideas any due.

LeBov's wisdom, like anyone's, most fitting for those who wished to live, who had tasks in mind they still hoped to complete. For the others, like us two on the steps that night, wisdom is a high-handed scold, a reminder of what you're not capable of thinking, some bit of behavior you can't even reach for. Whether or not LeBov would prove to be right would remain to be seen. That night I wanted to expire on those steps, breathing in the perfect, cold air.

In many ways, that would have been a preferred outcome.

It still seems important, given all that's happened, to report that across the street from my house, there was a hidden piece of the deadest air. No glow whatsoever, even from the streetlamps. I felt I could shine a lamp into it and the light would be extinguished. Just a swollen patch of darkness that seemed to throb the more I stared.

15

By early December we huddled at home, speechless. If we spoke it was through faces gripped in early rigor mortis. Our neighborhood had gone blank, killed down by winter. It was too cold even for the remaining children to do much hunting.

I don't know how else to refer to their work, but sometimes they swarmed the block, flooding houses with speech until the adults were repulsed to the woods.

You'd see a neighbor with a rifle and you'd hear that rifle go off.

The trees stood bloodless, barely holding on in the wind. We sat against the window and waited, spying out at the children when they roved through. The children—they should have been called something else—barking toxic vocals through megaphones as they held hands in the street.

I hoped they wouldn't turn and see us in the window, come to the door. I hoped they wouldn't walk up the lawn and push their megaphones against the glass. And always I hoped not to see our Esther in these crowds, but too often there she was in the pack, one of the tallest, bouncing in the winter nighttime fog, breathing into her hands to keep warm. She'd finally found a group of kids to run off with.

If there was an escape to engineer we failed to do so, even while some neighbors loaded cars, smuggling from town when they'd had enough. The quarantine hadn't been declared, but in our area they weren't letting children through checkpoints, except by bus. Basic containment. If you wanted to leave, you left alone.

Even so, bulky rugs were thrust into trunks. Items that required two people to carry. Usually wrapped in cloth, sometimes squirming of their own accord, a child's foot poking out. A clumsy game of hide-and-seek, children sprawled out in cargo carriers, children disguised as something else, so parents could spend a few more minutes with what ailed them.

Claire retired as my test subject. She stopped appearing in the kitchen for night treatments, declined the new smoke. When I served infused milk she fastened her mouth shut. If she accepted medicine from me she did so unwittingly, asleep, whimpering when the needle went in.

I couldn't blame her, falling away like that, embracing the shroud of illness. But I did. I conducted nightly campaigns of blame and accusation, silently, in the monstrous internal speech that is only half sounded out, a kind of cave speech one reserves for private airing. In these broadsides Claire spun on a low podium and absorbed every accusation.

If I prepared a bowl of steamed grain and left it on the table for her, salted as she liked it, pooling in the black syrup, she passed her spoon through it, held up a specimen for study, and could not, just never could, finally slide it in her mouth. For Claire I cut cubes of meat loaf, and at best she tucked one or two in her mouth, where she could suck on them until they shriveled to husks.

Claire no longer slept in her bed and she seemed too listless even to maneuver to the crafts room, to the guest room, to anywhere she might be able to fall unconscious in private.

I was always trying to offer her shield, a modesty curtain, so she could come undone alone and unseen. She shouldn't have to collapse in hallways. If necessary I helped her along, at least to a corner, where I could erect a temporary blind.

Once I found her asleep in the bathroom, one eye stuck open, leaking a speckled fluid. I crouched down and closed the eye, blotted it with my shirt. It opened again and she whispered at me.

"Hi there."

I looked down at her and she blinked, perfectly alert.

Claire must have thought she was smiling, but that was so far from a smile. With my fingers I tried to change the feeling, to reshape her mouth. I couldn't have her looking at me like that.

Her lips were cold and they would not stay where I arranged them. Her face had the weight of clay.

"Go back to sleep" was all I could think to say, and I draped a bath towel over her, leaving her to rest on the cold tiles.

At home I took charge of what remained of our dwindling domestic project, the blending of food into shakes, the cleaning of all our gray traces. I formed a packing plan, a strategy with regard to the luggage, mapped a route to outskirt lodging. Our pajamas, robes, towels, dishrags, these I washed every day, closing myself in the laundry room where the hot engine of the machine drowned out noise and thought. Against the hum of the washer I was, for a little while, nobody much, and this was how I preferred it.

I left Esther's warm, folded clothes in her bedroom. Often they went untouched. Or later, after Esther had plowed through the house before returning to her gang, I'd find the pile toppled onto the floor, a heap of black crumbs, like someone's ashes, dumped over it.

Claire's robe went mostly unwashed, because she didn't like to take it off, and if I ever found her half asleep and staring into nowhere from her resting place, she wouldn't respond when I asked if I could do any laundry for her, she'd just smack her lips to indicate thirst.

"It'd be nice to have fresh clothes, right? I could clean these and have them right back to you."

I tugged at her robe and she pulled away from me, threw an arm over her face.

"Your robe will be nice and warm out of the dryer. We could get you covered in extra blankets in the meantime. It'll be nice to be clean. You'll feel better."

I spoke to Claire as if she understood me, but she only stared. I spoke to her through a stiff, heavy face that seemed fitted on my head solely to block me from speaking. I sounded like a man underwater.

As our tolerance departed for the speech of children, so, too, did our ability to speak. Language in or out, we heard, produced, or received. A problem any which way.

To keep Claire hydrated I'd have to peel back her hospital mask, prop her upright, and press the sippy cup straw through the gluey seal of her lips.

I lowered the mask when she was done and flowery welts of orange juice soaked through the fabric.

When it was time to clean her, I filled a bowl with warm water, settled it over a towel at her bedside. With a washcloth I soaped her neck and face. She lifted her chin, gathered her hair out of the way. I squeezed little pools of water over her throat. I placed another towel under her feet, then lifted and washed each leg, rubbing as softly as I could, watching the little streaks of redness follow my cloth.

Claire's legs rose too easily in my hands, as though they'd been relieved of their bones.

With the last of the water I reached into Claire's robe and washed her stomach, the skin that once held her breasts. I peeled her from the bed so I could wash her back, pushing the washcloth under the robe, feeling each hollow between her ribs, a sponginess I did not want to explore. Then I settled her back down again, pulled up her covers, lifted the mask from her mouth so I could replace it with a clean one.

She forced a smile, but a shadow had spread under her gums, a darkness inside her mouth.

When I brought her soup, warmed the long bread she loved, or offered Claire some of the candies that usually she could never refuse—baby amber globes with a cube of salted caramel inside—at most she would roll over, heave, pull the quilt above her head.

It was only when the front door swung open and Esther came in the house sweating, crazed, in clothing I'd never seen, that Claire sat up, drawing on some last reserve of power. She always wanted to catch sight of Esther, to watch her from a doorway, so she followed her from room to room, keeping her distance, and Esther tolerated the stalking. You could see in her whole body the effort she made to endure this attention she loathed.

Esther had changed. Her face was older, harder. Filthy from her outings, but spectacularly beautiful. Of course I must think this, I'm her father. Fathers do not easily succumb to assessments of ugliness where their children are concerned. Esther had never been a cute child, but she'd grown threateningly stunning in the last few months. She let her mother watch from a safe perimeter and she was considerate enough not to turn on her with speech, to stop and speak until Claire fell. Esther saw her mother in doorways, looked away, said nothing. It was her greatest kindness to us, that silence. I will always appreciate the restraint she showed in those last days.

16

Esther's birthday fell on a Sunday. Claire was oblivious, wheezing beneath the medicated linen I'd dipped for her. I realized what the day was late in the afternoon after crawling on the floor of the shower, the water softening my face.

What was called LeBov's Mark had grown in fast, a hardened lump under my tongue, anchoring it down. The shower seemed to help. On the tiled floor I could tilt my face into the spray, let the heat loosen my throat. In the bathroom I exercised my voice so that it would not flow from me in shapeless moans.

Last year, when Esther turned fourteen, she'd wanted no party, just money and privacy. She used those words exactly, then said: "Why would you even ask me what I want if you have no intention of delivering on it?"

Delivering on it was her phrase. To which Claire and I could only shrug, agree, say *Okay, sure, we can give you that, Honey*. And then we wondered, *How much?* How much money, how much privacy does she want?

Esther wanted us to promise that we'd not talk about the birthday, not mention her age, absolutely not remark on how she'd grown up or changed or stayed the same, not reference what she was *supposedly like* as a baby, since *why would I want to know*, she'd asked, *what you think you used to think of me?* She claimed such a detail was an obscure statistic, a piece of information that *future corpses*—her phrase—stored in their bodies as a charm.

Esther reasoned that, in any case, we never felt fondly toward her *at the time*, that we loved her best in hindsight.

It was true. Our family suffered from issues of calibration.

"Even now," she said. "It's happening right now. Years from now you will have distorted this moment, which is an awful moment, into something nice, and you'll badger me with that memory until I agree, which I'll only do to make you stop talking. You are professional distorters, incapable of simply seeing a situation for what it is."

Years from now. The things we will do. In the end Esther really did underestimate us.

Memories of any kind, for Esther, were similarly off-limits. Shed the skin and burn it, apparently. Memories that asked Esther to picture herself doing something she no longer recalled, like skating in a rope chain of children, when she was seven, down the traffic lines of an iced-over Wilderleigh Street. This was the week the elm fell to lightning and we built a snow fort circling the trunk. Or climbing a ladder stretched flat on the grass and pretending it was vertical, so that each time she let go of it she fake-tumbled to the bottom.

Such images were an attack. They caused physical pain, and why did we insist on hurting her? Why did it seem that we were instinctually driven to cause her pain? It was not right to hurt her on her birthday. Especially on her birthday. What kinds of parents were we, after all?

We'd grown so accustomed to hiding our feelings around Esther that it seemed easier to just not have those feelings in the first place.

You people and your memories, she'd said through a sneer.

Esther requested that her birthday not serve as an occasion for us to pretend that we were closer than we really were, since why should that random date, *a date based on the most flawed and sentimental calendar*, make us suddenly tell lies about how we really felt?

"Sweetie," I countered.

"See, like that," she said. "There's a lie right there. You think that a generic endearment will somehow show how you feel toward me, *talk me out of how I actually feel*. One word is going to do that, a word used for pets? How many people use that exact word to hide what they feel? It's like you're throwing up on me, actually. I feel like you just threw up on me."

But in the years before these revelations and rules, before she was overwhelmed by insights she felt compelled to share with us, we'd had birthday parties. We staved off tantrums and avalanches of greed, accommodated in our home the children who seemed to function—if barely—as Esther's friends. Along with these preteen colleagues we welcomed skulking parents, who would invariably let one of their babies—babies had not been invited, but there they were, there they always were—go off on a shelf-clearing campaign. Then a parent would quietly retreat, without the baby, to the off-limits master bathroom and take a toilet-wrecking shit that could never be flushed, only to emerge with the blissful look of someone whose own home is not being destroyed at this very moment, stepping half-apologetically, but really with relief, with genuinely visible relief and perhaps even a kind of lurid joy—*this party is really fun!*—over dumped cupcakes, grinding them further into the rug we should have pulled up before the party, but did not, because in the end we always failed to imagine how savage these people could become.

"*There* you are," the parent would scold the baby, as if it was the baby who had disappeared. The baby would crawl over, try to stand, hold up its arms in supplication to be carried, then topple over.

Depending on the baby, it would either sob, laugh, or be gorgeously oblivious to all mortal proceedings. One of those three behavioral paths.

"Come smell the shit I took," the parents never said.

Instead the one-sided, rhetorical, patronizing dialogue would commence: "What did you do? Huh? What did you do?" the parent would interrogate the baby, picking it up and seeming to study it for evidence.

A theater of mock blame the parent should have been directing to the mirror.

"Why not ask someone who can actually answer you?" I wouldn't say to them. "I'll tell you exactly what your baby did. Would you really like to know? Can you handle a conversation with a real, live adult?"

I stood and stared at these people and they serially failed to read my mind.

Instead they would be locked in some kind of airborne mouth-tickling activity with the baby—holding it aloft and, to all appearances, trying to eat it—a baby who by now, so many years later, as a seven- or eight-year-old, I'd guess, was probably shouting that same parent into a corner, turning the parent pale, speaking with so much force that the parent was husking, shelling, dying in a house somewhere probably not so far away.

Had those parents built a locker beneath the stairs, as we did? Cut in a peephole, lined the little room with pillows? Had they shielded themselves from the speech of their offspring, effaced their hearing, or damaged the little ones themselves, stopped the reeking language at its source? Were they pumping white noise from the old slab radio, and did it not fully hide the child's speech? Or perhaps the parents had already fled upstate. If they were smart. If they knew how to shut down their attachment apparatus and see their children for what they really, most essentially, were. Agents of such terrible mouth sounds that, relation or not, one hoped never to see them again.

On Esther's final birthday in our house I went to the kitchen to get to work on the cake. There wasn't much food left in the cupboard, just some pancake mix and a blend of baking powders I'd dumped into a bag. From the meaty, mineral smell I figured this would give a lift to the cake, at least if I got the batter down to room temperature and shocked it into a hot oven so it might have some spring.

For liquids I had an egg and some buttermilk, the custardy sludge from the bottom of the carton.

I could boil the buttermilk to kill off bacteria, then flash freeze it before dumping it into the batter. The egg, too, would need flame, because it was likely spoiled by now.

I broke it into a pan, stifled a gag, then whisked it over a simmer until it frothed up, sputtered, and grew clear again. Mostly it did not congeal. The hardened parts were easy to flick out. When the pan cooled I slid it into the freezer, went to work on sifting the powders.

For sugar I reduced the last of the orange juice until it thickened into a syrup, then whipped in a thread of honey. This would have to do, because I needed the last of the sugar for frosting. I liked to feather it on lightly, then comb it up while hardening it with the medical cold blower, as if the cake had a fright wig.

The frosting I colored silver with a bead of food-grade aluminum.

When she was younger, Esther preferred black frosting on Fez cakes, and she liked these cakes tethered by rope candy. Or, if not rope candy, then string, dipped in food coloring and pan-seared inside a thin jacket of sugar. When she was ten we'd cooked, cooled, and braided her own rope candy, but left it clear.

"Color is vulgar," she said, quoting somebody.

Once we'd built trails with jelly beans, linking the baby cakes by candy cobblestone. Esther discovered that the jelly beans could be cut smaller and arranged so densely, it seemed the entire gathering of cakes rested on a pebbled surface.

Instead of a candle Esther would have me soak the perimeter of the cake with a squirt of kerosene, which flamed a perfect halo. When she was nine we strung a wick between two pieces of wire that bordered the cake. The laundry line, we called it. We lit the wick from both ends while singing "Happy Birthday" and watched it fall into the frosting. The two little balls of flame found each other in the center of the cake, burned out, and left a dark, charred circle.

"The burnt part is the best," declared Esther. "I get the burnt part!"

Today I had no candle, no sweets. I did have a placebo smoke purse, which I'd billowed with safe vapors early in my experiments with Claire. The purse had cured—the plastic must have been tainted—yielding a reddish smoke inside.

I rolled an egg of wax, scooped it hollow, then linked it by drinking straw to the red smoke purse.

The smoke drained from the purse through the straw, filled the ball of wax, clouding the inside of it, turning it dark.

I removed the straw and quickly sealed the ball of wax. With a potato peeler I set about shaving the ball, thinning its surface to transparency. Then Esther could see the red smoke trapped inside. Perhaps she'd pierce the ball with her teeth, let the smoke release into her mouth.

A birthday smoke should be red. It's the prettiest color for smoke.

When I was done I placed the wax ball on top of the cake. It sank slightly into the silver frosting, and that was that. It didn't symbolize anything. This was the point. It was interesting to look at and I thought that Esther might have fun holding it up to the light, wondering how the dark red smoke got in there.

I found Claire beneath her linen shield and helped her into the hiding place under the stairs. Her body was light in my hands these days, but if I pulled the comforter she was resting on, I could drag her as on a sled from room to room, interrupted only by the thresholds, which offered a small obstacle Claire didn't seem to mind.

I did not speak, did not tell her where we were going, but she'd want to see this, her daughter's birthday. Together we could watch safely through the hole in the door our own little girl. It would be safe. Esther would come home and have some cake and we could watch her together.

I left a trail of Post-its that would lead Esther to the cake, which I'd positioned on a pedestal table within view of the peephole. We'd bored a hole into the crawl space door and now this was our little shelter beneath the staircase.

Next to the table I pulled up the children's chair she used when she was younger. Surely she could still fit into it. And at this height she'd be right in our line of view, provided she didn't move the chair and turn her back on us.

Inside our heads Claire and I could sing "Happy Birthday." No one would have to hear. Esther wouldn't even know we were there. She could enjoy her cake and it would be nice to be together again.

I pushed Claire into our cave beneath the stairway, tucked her all the way back, then crawled in myself. Claire did not rouse herself or show much interest. When the time came, when Esther returned, walked through the house, and then found the cake, I would wake Claire and help her see.

We settled onto our cushions, pulled shut the door, and waited. Claire leaned against me, seemed to whisper something, but I think she was speaking to herself.

From where I sat I could see perfectly through the peephole. That was a pretty cake on the pedestal, its little wax ball starting to sweat from the smoke. I was just fine to wait here.

It was dark and late when I woke beneath Claire's damp body. Someone was in the house. I pressed my face to the peephole.

The footsteps shook the floor. Esther must have been wearing boots. She clomped through the house as if she were old and slow. I could hear every move as she walked near to us, then far. All I saw through the hole was the little silver cake on the table.

The steps drew closer, and then a voice called hello. A man's voice.

Hello and hello and hello. He called out the name *Steven*? Steven as a question. He asked if Steven was there. Walked through, opened and closed doors. Was Steven home? Anybody?

"Hello?"

It was Murphy.

I held my breath.

He was bundled for the cold. He stood huge in our little house. The room was doll-size with him in it.

He stopped next to the cake, let a finger drag through the frosting. He turned and looked at the door that sheltered Claire and me.

I stared at him through the peephole and did not move.

The wet rattle of Claire's breath seemed suddenly loud. I could not shush her. Even placing my hand over her mouth would not work. The sound didn't come from her mouth, but from her chest, her whole body. Our hiding place vibrated with Claire's gasps.

Murphy walked off, resumed calling out *hello*, but in a lifeless, obligatory way, as if he couldn't turn off his voice.

I waited for Murphy to leave, but he took his time. He went upstairs, came down, went back up. At one point it seemed that he pulled up a chair, sat for a while, before scooting out again.

In our bedroom Murphy seemed to move some furniture.

Finally the front door closed and his steps retreated.

I kept on waiting, pictured Murphy walking to his car, opening it, getting in, and driving away. Then I pictured the same routine again, over and over, until I could be sure that he was far away.

Except I could never be sure of that.

Claire's weight was stifling, a wet pressure. I pushed her off me and climbed out of the crawl space to survey the damage.

All throughout the house everything seemed as it was, except upstairs I discovered that the hut repair box was missing from my drawer. The little tools meant to fix the listener at the Jewish hole, tools I'd never needed to use. This box was all that was missing. For all of Murphy's raucous rummaging he hadn't taken much.

But the cake had been disturbed. Not eaten, but violated, the ball of wax collapsed, smokeless. Something had been dropped on the cake, then removed. I made a fist, held it above the ruined cake. This was too large.

The size of the crater was just right for Esther's hand, I reasoned. Balled up, punching down.

I couldn't believe she would destroy her own cake. Certainly the cake had collapsed because I had baked it poorly, failed to follow a recipe. It was stupid to think I could go in the kitchen and improvise like that.

Perhaps Esther was not hungry. Perhaps she came in and saw the cake and decided she might have a slice later on. Only not now. After dinner, maybe.

I'd put it in the refrigerator, is what I would do. The cake would be there for her when she was hungry. Perhaps when I was feeling better I would have a piece, too. Maybe Esther and I could sit quietly together over a piece of cake. I'd skin back my frosting for her, because she liked extra. There'd be no reason to speak. We could enjoy each other's company in silence, in the kitchen, on her birthday. If I could find a candle, an old-fashioned one, we'd light it up. It'd be nice to sit together, listening to our forks click on the plates. We'd be sure to save a piece for her mother.

17

LeBov died that week. A feature ran on the news, a final piece of television. He was sixty-two. Or he was sixty-eight. An assistant found him at home, where he lived alone. Two of his many children apparently lived nearby. I missed the picture they flashed of him, but then a photo of one of LeBov's sons, cast up on the screen, showed a suntanned, elderly fellow with a white ponytail. *LeBov's son*. There was no mention of a wife. LeBov had been taken to a private facility in Denver where he later expired. This was the language used by the newscaster. *Expired.*

There would be no funeral.

According to the news, LeBov was perhaps the first researcher, certainly the most outspoken, to identify the threat of language.

All the good it's done, I sat there thinking.

The editorial assessment of the news program was that LeBov's death was particularly distressing at this time, given our current situation.

A toxicologist by training, they called LeBov. He had lived mostly in Canada, spent the early years of his career developing his theory of a primary allergen, allergy zero.

Later in his career LeBov focused on the toxic properties of language. Most recently, *until his passing*, he had been the director of a private research lab in Rochester called Forsythe. He was working closely with health officials on the problem of the viral child.

"Claire!" I called out into the cold house.

LeBov was known for disseminating his views in underground publications. Designed, some said, deliberately to mislead. Filled with false information and historical inaccuracies invented to bolster his theories.

A montage spun together clips of other scientists appraising LeBov's contributions. He merited scorn, derision, from a pedigreed cohort, doctors, scientists, linguists. But these were old clips, exhumed from an archive somewhere, stitched together to form a portrait. All the footage was from well before his death, before his recent lunge into credibility. These men and women, pronouncing on the now dead LeBov, projected a vital cheer quite terrible in hindsight—sitting in offices or newsrooms while off-loading their expensive opinions about someone they could safely dislike in public.

These scientists had yet to live in these times. Today, yesterday, the past few months. Their short-term futures were going to hurt, and they had no idea. Where were these fine people now? I wondered. Were they hiding yet?

Have you found shelter? Is it finally quiet and safe where you are? I wanted to ask them.

Not a person alive could be made to talk like that now, look so healthy, using language as if it did not break something in us.

Even the newscaster, broadcasting live, wore a bloodless mask, staring, one supposed, at the words on the teleprompter. Eating the vile material for his very employment, each word producing the crushing. You could tell. He seemed to weaken by the second. They'd done him up in television paint. One could see that this man did not have long. For some reason I recall his name. Jim Adelle.

Jim Adelle's *News Hour*. *A Special Report* with Jim Adelle.

I wonder how many more days he had to live.

The feature continued. I settled in to listen as LeBov's colleagues detailed his work, decried his methods, his results, his person.

"Claire!" I called again. She couldn't still be asleep. I knew she'd be interested in this.

LeBov's theory of allergy did not assist his career. One of the desert universities finally offered him a silo, but they kept him away from students. Later he distanced himself from the theory, then finally renounced the idea as dangerous.

Not really a rebuttal, I noted, to call your own idea dangerous. More of a sensationalizing gesture to increase attention.

This would turn out to be a signature method throughout LeBov's career. He advanced an idea, often a problematic one, beat its drum until everyone was revolted, then turned on himself, often through pseudonym, and attacked his own work. He staged battles in the academic journals between two different versions of himself, argument and refutation coming from the same man.

At conferences LeBov sent imposters to the podium in his place. No one knew what he looked like, apparently. Then he sat hectoring his stand-in from the audience, protesting every idea, sometimes storming out in disgust. He accused himself of fraudulence, plagiarism. In at least some cases it would seem that he was correct.

LeBov's signature work, in the end, addressed the trouble with language, the word *trouble* being, in his view, an understatement. He argued for most of his professional life that language should be best understood, aside from its *marginal utility* as a communication technology—*can we honestly say it works?*—as an impurity.

Language happens to be a toxin we are very good at producing, but not so good at absorbing, LeBov said. We could, per LeBov, in our lifetimes, not expect to process very much of it.

In answer to his detractors, LeBov asked what it was that *ever* suggested speech would not be toxic.

"Let us reverse the terms and assume that language, like nearly everything else, is poisonous when consumed to excess. Why not assault the folly that led to such widespread use of something so intense, so strong, as language, in the first place?"

Where was the regulatory body? LeBov wanted to know. Where was the marshaling instinct for speech, for language itself?

It causes the most unbearable strain on our systems, LeBov would say. It is not very different from a long, slow venom.

This idea was never granted legitimacy, evidenced by the battalion of naysayers. He simply had no proof. Witness after witness remarked on LeBov's lack of evidence, and the word *evidence* came to indicate something significant that LeBov was missing, like an eye, a limb.

They had some audio for this, a response of sorts. *More than anyone else in the world, I wish that I was wrong*, answered LeBov, in a voice I felt I had heard before. *What a relief that would be, to me, and also to my family.*

"Claire," I called out again, softer. I listened into the house to hear some sign of her. "Come sit with me."

LeBov had written something, a screed, on the Tower of Babel, apparently, but retracted it before it could go to press. The other version of the story is that LeBov wrote in and protested to his own publisher, demanded they pulp the book. The book was a dangerous speculation, an assault on reality.

"Claire, Honey?" I called.

The Babel document came up a few times in the news interviews, though no one, it seemed, had read it. LeBov had an obsession with this myth. More than that, a bone to pick. He felt that it was a misleading, dangerous myth. It had, he supposedly argued, been copied out incorrectly, transmitted from generation to generation with a serious degree of error. Now the myth as we knew it presented a terrible impediment. I saw where Murphy had gotten the idea.

Claire appeared in the doorway, fully dressed, brushing the last of her hair.

"Why do you keep yelling my name?" she asked.

"I wanted you to see something," I said. "This show I'm watching. On this guy who died."

"Well, you could have said that. I wish you wouldn't yell my name. I really can't stand it."

I apologized to her.

"It's fine," she said, leaving the room. "But I can't stand it. Please don't do that anymore."

"I'm sorry," I said again, feeling less sorry.

"And I said *it's fine*," she yelled from another room. "Stop apologizing."

Sorry, I said to myself, wondering how many times in my marriage I'd said that, how many times I'd meant it, how many times Claire had actually believed it, and, most important, how many times the utterance had any impact whatsoever on our dispute. What a lovely chart one could draw of this word *Sorry*.

A linguist from Banff scorned LeBov's idea of a toxic language.

"This idea implies a physical component to language. Some material antigen," she said. "What exactly is the substance, in chemical terms, that is causing this allergy he speaks of?" asked the linguist. "Language is the scapegoat here. If there is a problem—and I highly doubt there is, I cannot imagine such a thing—it is one for the immunologists."

Was the Banff linguist, I wondered, simply part of LeBov's long plan, designed to control the flow of the argument?

The linguist held forth, smugly dismissing an idea that had recently come into its own. It interested me that the linguist's inability to imagine something constituted a sound rejection of its possibility.

I cannot imagine such a thing.

If only that kept it from coming true.

You had simply to look out the window to see the missing evidence she was calling for, watch the neighbors drive off and not return.

Actually you had only to look at Claire, if you could even bear to. I certainly tried to avoid sight of her, even dressed up, even with her hair, falling out as it was, brushed back over her small face. That sort of witness bearing did no one any favors.

LeBov was dead, so enemies could alert the world to how unimportant the old man really was, before irony would come along to smother them alive.

I thought of Murphy and wondered to what authority figure he would answer now. Was he trembling in his room at home now that his master had died?

The final segment of the news focused on LeBov's Jewish problem. LeBov exhibited, admitted one commenter in rather shy tones, an unreasonable interest in the private activities of members of *a certain religious faith*.

LeBov often stoked, our expert remarked, the long-standing rumor of a segment of the Jewish population who worship privately, sharing wisdom through an underground signaling mechanism.

Of course we have found no basis for these rumors, the expert assured us.

Of course, I thought.

These rumors show a profound disrespect for people of diverse faiths.

Yes, yes. A profound disrespect.

When a scientist, *particularly* a scientist, the expert warned, buys into superstition, into lore, and uses them as *paradigms of insight*, our entire method of knowing is threatened. LeBov shows no respect by fanning the flames of a dangerous rumor, a rumor that only seeks to further isolate those among us who *do* practice authentic religious observance. To people of genuine faith, LeBov's antics are a disgrace.

LeBov had apparently called for the forest Jews to come forward, to quit hoarding their fucking treasure.

From what I could tell, LeBov knew little of our practice. He bathed in the standard misinformation, took wild swings, threw out a stinking bait that, I was sure, none of us would take.

Wisdom, he argued, was meant to be shared. Particularly wisdom that offers *precise guidance on our crisis*. A crisis like this, he said, requires assets. We must develop assets that will assist us in our change, and we can never ignore the source of a poison, *the source of it*, when we look to soothe its symptoms.

The source of it. He was talking about children.

Which had what to do with our religion? I wondered.

A closing thought on LeBov from our expert. I do not recall the man's name or title, just that he wore a collar and a dark robe, and that his thoughts seemed to come so slowly that they caused him pain.

"LeBov's idea that science cannot help us, but faith can—this is an idea that resonates deeply for me. Deeply."

He attempted an important pause.

"But when the faith to which he is referring *does not exist*, I can only be profoundly troubled. It desecrates the real, authentic Jew to imagine a false and private one, and to accord that imaginary Jew with secret powers channeled against the interests of the world at large. It's a desecration."

The feature on LeBov ended and Jim Adelle seemed caught by surprise, swaying in his chair behind the big news table. He put his finger to his ear, listened to his producer, winced. Perhaps, instead of a verbal message, they'd sent a knifelike frequency into his head. In the end, I bet Jim Adelle would have preferred that to words.

He looked up but his focus couldn't quite meet the camera. He seemed to be staring at something inside his own eyes. With a mechanical face he repeated the news. LeBov was dead.

I got up to continue my apology to Claire, if I could find her. It was going to take a little bit more work.

Then they showed LeBov's picture again.

Except on the screen where there should have been a picture of a man I've never seen, whose voice I'd hardly heard on the radio, they showed a picture of Murphy. It was unmistakable. The same red hair, the same immortal skin. A recent photo of Murphy.

I crouched into the blue funnel of the television to get a good look.

So. This was LeBov.

Do not let him confuse or mislead you, Murphy had said. Or was it LeBov who said this to me?

Are you reading LeBov? That will catch you up on things.

If he was still alive, and I had a terrible feeling that he was, I was pretty sure I knew where I could find him.

18

News of the quarantine issued through the car radio on my way down to the Oliver's. It would be temporary. The neighborhood would be restricted to children, protected, necessities provided. Details were given about the gate, the fence line, the use of dogs. It was time for everyone else to go.

A diversion would be created for the children. Something involving the school. Or was it the prison?

They were giving us a day, a day and a half, to pack our things and leave.

Some suggested destinations followed. Shelters, towns, mostly fanning to the south. Wheeling, Marion, Danville, the quad county district, Albert Farm. Towns with undeveloped space, meadowland. Counties with soil still soft enough for digging, where the salt was naturally repelled by the winter air systems. The list was not long.

The way I heard this was: *Do not go to Wheeling, Marion, Danville. Avoid the quad counties and Albert Farm.*

I pictured Claire under blankets in the backseat of the car as I drove all night, wondering where to stop. She was not ready to travel, especially with no destination, no promise of comfort or safety when we arrived.

Wherever we ended up, we would need to be separated from our volatile fellows. The toxicity had spread beyond children. Not everywhere, not fully, but that was the trend. Everyone would make everyone sick, with children the lone immuners. We should not, according to the report, even be together, unless we could refrain from speech, take a pact of silence.

We urge you to travel alone. Consider this an allergy to people.

I was as bad for Claire as Esther, or would be soon. Earlier today, when I found Claire after the report on LeBov and subjected her to my lengthy, defensive apology and watched her shrink into the bed while I spoke, it wasn't only because she had grown sick of the sight of me. It was my language as well. It was that I had spoken at all.

If we traveled together we had better hold our goddamn tongues.

The radio report followed in robotic tones, with cautions, locations to avoid, roads that were closed. Rivers and bridges, the Sheldrake, Wickers Creek, the Menands Bridge. Something about the airspace of Elmira and a marine warning near the Mourner's Sound. A different station was given for the full, updated list of closures, but I did not switch over. I could wait to hear the names of places I should not go.

At a stop sign I heard a sharp noise and something hit my car. A whimper floated up, perhaps from my own mouth. The streets were dark, boiling circles of light spreading from the streetlamps. A pack of children tore across a yard, fled from sight. I locked my doors. Then a soft thing fell into the car and the car lifted, as if someone were out there, trying to push the car over.

I stepped on the gas, revved it hard, but the car was blocked by something. It whinnied forward, the engine straining, and seemed to elevate in the back.

One of them pressed his little face into the driver's side window, so close. He smiled, his lips moving, as if he were singing. With his finger he tapped on the glass, made a twirling motion for me to roll down the window. His hands formed a posture of prayer under his chin and I believe he mimed the word *please.*

He wanted to talk.

I hammered down on the gas again and the car whined, lifted, then released with a squeal over whatever had been blocking it and I sped away.

In my rearview mirror a few of them crouched over something, not even looking my way. They formed a circle, went to their knees, and that was all I saw.

It was just kids, out in the street after suppertime. That's all it was. Kids playing in the road.

In the Oliver's parking lot I sat in the car to listen to the rest of the broadcast.

The emergency report was delivered in clipped tones, the voice of a woman who seemed unable to hear herself, as if she were reading a foreign language phonetically.

An escalation in the toxicity had been observed in places like Harrisburg, Fremont, with more reports coming in. Something had happened in Wisconsin. Wisconsin had experienced an incident. There was, according to reports, a complete absence of speech originating from Wisconsin. This was no longer a poison from children. In Wisconsin all language, no matter the source, was toxic. The children alone were immune.

> The Wisconsin area has unfortunately been a reliable precursor. We believe that what happens there will soon, we do not know when, happen here.
>
> Health officials counsel seclusion, even from loved ones.
>
> We unfortunately have to expect this escalation to spread. Even if you now find that exposure to speech sources other than children—including this broadcast—does not cause a disturbance, we cannot advise you that this will be the case for very much longer.
>
> This station, as of tonight, will be suspending reports. We are working on a method to stay in touch. We will find a way to reach you. Please do stand by.
>
> In good conscience we cannot continue. We wish you safety in your homes tonight.

The station faded to static. I spun through the pre-sets and found nothing else, just sharper or lower-toned hissing, from one end of the dial to the next.

The parking lot of the Oliver's was crowded with vans. From one of them came a fat tunnel of hosing. Little wisps of smoke spilled from its papery surface as the hosing curled away from the van, dropping down a fenced-in manhole.

The smoke smelled clean, fruity. Whatever work was going on was soundless.

A man wearing a clear vest stood by the manhole with a clipboard. After vigorously massaging my face to prepare it for speech, I asked him what was going on.

He smiled, shook his head, pointed to his ear.

This meant, what, he was deaf?

I pointed at the manhole, shrugged, and mouthed: "What is it?"

The man shook his head in the negative again.

A worker climbed from the hole as I walked away. He picked clumps of a wet cheese from his face. Tethered to his waist was an orange cable as thick as a man's leg, and he dragged it from the hole where they pinned it in place on a specimen table. I'd seen that cabling before. The man with the clipboard grabbed his radio and, instead of speaking into it, held it out at the cable, as if whoever was on the other end of the radio needed to hear this.

But then I heard it, too, and it was unmistakable. From that orange cable, with no listener attached, came the voice of Rabbi Burke, singing one of his songs. A song I'd heard before.

In the lobby of the Oliver's I looked for Murphy.

People hurried around breaking things down, packing boxes. A stack of crates sat at the door, waiting to be loaded into the vans. The crates had breathing holes drilled into them, arrows painted on their sides, pointing up. The sweet, gamey smell of a zoo was in the air.

A young man in coveralls sat at a table up front, seeming official. When I asked him if Murphy was here, he could only repeat the name back to me, as if I'd issued a math problem he was not expected to solve.

I explained that Murphy had invited me down here. Spitting image of LeBov, I didn't say. *Rest his soul.*

It was hard to understand him through his respirator, a steamed-over mask covering his mouth.

"Invitations aren't required," I think he said, pointing at the open door.

An elderly couple swept into the lobby. They clung to each other, looking at us as if we were wild animals. The woman cried out, fell. From nowhere rushed two guards with blankets. They covered up the couple and dragged them away.

"We're open to everyone," said the young man.

He pushed his respirator to the side, wiped his mouth, then carefully fit it back on. With a handheld mirror he checked the straps that cut across his cheeks.

"I know," I said, even though I didn't. "But Murphy thought my research might benefit, or that, what I mean is, people here might benefit from the work I'm doing."

The man returned the sort of smile professionals are trained to give no matter what you've said. I could have threatened his life, my own. I could have asked for the bathroom. I'd get the same lunatic smile.

He leaned in close, placed his finger over my mouth.

He wanted me silent. I supposed I understood, so I didn't reply, only nodded, looked away.

From a box he retrieved a white choke collar, mimed for me to put it on. It was smeared in what smelled like Murphy's grease, cold on my neck. My face relaxed when I fastened it on.

He said Murphy's name aloud, as if that might jar his memory. Finally he said, "I'm sorry. I'm not very good with names."

I wanted to say: Red hair, large face. Excels at ambush. Perhaps immune to the problem we're all here to solve. Not who he seems to be? That Murphy?

I couldn't say *LeBov. It's LeBov I'm looking for, because I have reason to believe that he's still alive, operating under a different name. Murphy. But you probably know all of that, don't you?*

"Is there someone else I could talk to?" I asked.

And say what? And do what?

"I'm afraid the time for that is over."

Literal language was useless for what I'd come to do. This man was refusing to read between the lines, acknowledge any subtext, and thus we were locked in a prison of exact meaning, impossible to shed.

It would turn out that LeBov's language protocols, as practiced by his staff, prohibited nuance, inference. They were nearly moot now anyway.

He stood up, gathered some papers, among them what I took to be a copy of *The Proofs*.

I pointed at it. "Where'd you get that?" I asked.

He pointed at a pile of them sitting on another table.

Right. He would victimize me with facts, fail to elaborate, force me to excavate an ultra-specific set of questions to which he would then show his dumb, blank face. *Quiet uncertainty is perhaps the most medicinal mode.* I was not going to like this new form of speech.

He pushed a pamphlet at me. "You might want to look at these protocols. Some things to keep in mind when you speak, if you really must speak. You've mentioned yourself a few times, and it's probably worth avoiding. It's not personal. Or I guess actually that it is. It's really personal. It's just that the studies are pretty conclusive about this stuff."

"The studies?" I asked. "Is that what you've been doing here?"

A low growl issued from one of the crates, triggering a chorus of animal cries throughout the lobby.

"Or talk all you want," he said, bored. "But do it somewhere else."

His smile had a little bit of clear shit in it. I could smell it.

I took the pamphlet, stared at it without focus. The text was slightly darker than the white paper it was printed on. My hands were unsteady and the text wobbled, as if it hadn't been fastened to the paper. I felt sick, a tightness in my chest.

"It only *seems* harder to read," he smirked. "It's much, much easier on the . . . you know," and he tapped his head. "We're probably going to see a lot more of that soon."

I pictured seeing more of something you could hardly see to begin with. That great unused resource, the invisible air. We'd fill it with text, the nearly translucent kind. That would solve everything.

"Sorry to run but you'll have to excuse me," he said. "We're closing up. This Forsythe is probably not going to meet again. Maybe that guy you're looking for, *Murray*? Maybe he's in Rochester?"

Murray of Rochester. In my mind I hacked at him with a long knife.

It was dark outside and the Oliver's staff had finished loading their vans. They drifted out of the lobby into the parking lot. I guess they would go home and pack now, maybe get an early start and hit the road later tonight, before the sun came up. Beat the traffic.

It's hard to describe people who are silent as a matter of life and death, who move through the world in fear of speech. You can hear the swishing of their limbs, the music of their breath. None of them spoke.

They left the building with small waves of the hand to each other, faces down, and walked out into the night.

As the man in coveralls walked off I asked him if he'd had any news, if he knew anything. I tried to raise my voice but the white collar on my neck seemed to limit my volume.

"Go home, stay inside," he said, over his shoulder. "Do not talk to anyone."

"Right," I said. "But do you know what's actually happening?"

"We're telling people, just to be safe, to say their good-byes."

I watched him leave. He embraced an older, well-dressed woman on the way out. She was crying. He kissed her cheek, then disappeared into the throng of vans.

19

There was one place left to try. It would involve parking the car at Blister Field, ducking under the fence, and trekking through the woods until I reached the stream. The stream would be dry now, maybe iced over, and I'd have to traverse the bank in darkness, groping on hands and knees until I found the half-rotted footbridge that would bring me across.

Then the far bank would need to be climbed and tonight it would certainly be slippery. Slippery and sharp, with stones pushed up from the frost heaves, the bitter ends of tree roots bulging out to collect heat from the air.

I never went to the hut at night. But tonight would seem to be an exception to the rule. These last months were an exception, if one wanted to be strict about it. It was hard not to feel that the codes of access at our hut were written for unexceptional times. All the guidance I knew was written for unexceptional times.

I climbed the last of the riverbank and bushwhacked through low, dry branches until finally I reached the little footpath that would lead me along the southern approach to the hut.

Before I even arrived I saw the wild glare of a flashlight. An oily glow zoomed through the woods and I ducked down to watch. The hut had no window, just a framed hole long relieved of its glass.

On warm days Claire sometimes sat in the empty window frame while I readied the transmission.

Now inside our hut a man crouched and shook, peered out at the forest. Parts of him were all I could see. I stayed hidden in the trees, watching that smooth, preserved face, the orange hair boiling on the head.

LeBov was alive and he was Murphy.

He looked from the window hole with the light under his face, showing himself to the dark woods.

I circled quietly, keeping my distance. From behind a tree I watched as he went in and out of the hut, sweeping his flashlight in small arcs of discovery.

Occasionally the flashlight settled on something and he dilated the lens. He'd stoop over, pick something up, examine it in the light, then, invariably, he'd toss it to the ground and resume his search.

LeBov circled behind the hut, dragged over a crate, and climbed up on the roof. From there he crouched, seemed to pick at the shingles, and then slid down and disappeared, the glare from his flashlight strobing in the high branches.

I dug in against the embankment. LeBov's flashlight retreated into the far woods behind the hut, and then I heard nothing, saw no more light.

I sat back to rest. I'd give it a little bit more time.

I should have gone home. At home there was still so much to do. We had to pack, ready the house. Claire would need help. Perhaps I could lift her into the bath, let her soak. More than that, she might need persuading. I had to think about how I would explain our next move, how to remove all choice from my presentation.

She'd want to stay. Beg to stay. But I couldn't let her.

Staying wasn't staying. They'd find you and wouldn't have stayed at all.

Beyond that were my medical supplies, just a bare minimum, and where to put them. The key gear, and then at least a suitcase's worth of medicine. I'd want to resume my work as soon as we relocated. To lose momentum now would be a mistake.

But I didn't go home. The woods were fully quiet now, the light was gone. LeBov had no doubt finished with his defilement and moved on to other fine projects. I'd missed my chance to confront him and I will admit that I was relieved.

I groped into the darkness toward the hut. In front of me I could not even see my hand. With each step I braced myself for a collision, something sharp to strike my face.

I'd spent so many days here, thoroughly explored the grounds, dug shallow holes each time I buried the listener. Claire and I had walked home thoughtlessly, paying no attention to our surroundings, and we'd never been lost, never felt scared by unexplained sounds in the woods.

Now in the darkness, hours before we would leave town for good, I was completely helpless just steps from the hut. I wish to remark on the darkness of this place without resorting to hyperbole, but I do not think that is possible.

I reached out my arms, leaned, then fell into the dirt.

It was easier from there to move on hands and knees, but I needed to keep one arm up to guard my head. I crawled through frozen mud, butted into a tree stump, then corrected my attack and crept forward. Finally I struck the wall of the hut, and from there I guided myself until I collided with the staircase.

When I opened the door, a flashlight switched on. LeBov had wedged himself into the floor, his legs dangling down the hole.

"There you are," he said.

Across the hut floor he slid the grease tin, and I scooped some of it into my mouth.

He gestured to his neck, so I spread some there as well, pasting the white collar tighter on my skin.

It took hold in my face, softening my mouth, and my vision sharpened. When the tightness in my throat released, I found I could speak more easily, even if the ability brought nausea along with it.

"This is private property," I said quietly.

"Oh? I'd love to see your deed."

I stepped inside, leaned against the doorway.

"Maybe first you could let me know to whom I am speaking," I said.

"You're not the only one who can use a fake name."

"Apparently not."

His legs seemed trapped in the hole.

"Can I help you?" I asked.

I wanted him to be aware that I could take two steps up to him and deliver a sweet kick to his face. He would not be able to get away from me in time.

"No, thanks," he said, oblivious that I was sparing him. "I have everything I need."

He reached across the floor and grabbed a duffel bag, which clanged as he dragged it.

"I was saddened to hear of your death," I said. "It's a great loss. For all of us."

"Thank you. You sound sad."

"Yes, actually. I am sad. I'm sad that you're here where you do not belong. It's private, and there's nothing here for you."

"Nothing," he said. "I wouldn't call this nothing."

He held up my listener. It was ripped down the middle, coated on its underside with something shiny. The bottom pouch was leaking and the gel had spread over LeBov's hands.

"Okay, good for you. You must be so pleased."

"I am fairly pleased," he said. "I thought that I might need your help, but I don't. Now I need to get myself down this hole."

He screwed himself farther in, squeezing his hips past the floorboards.

I'd never gotten in that far, but I'd never had to.

"That's not how it works," I said. "There's nothing down there. You're missing the point."

LeBov was submerged to the shoulders now, holding his bag above his head as if he were about to wade across a stream. He was trying to vanish down the little hole in the floor that normally housed our transmission cables.

"Believe me," he said. "I am not missing the point. I think that you're the one who has missed the point."

Something was wrong. LeBov was straining, turning red. He couldn't force himself through, so he squirmed out of the hole and retrieved a saw from his bag. From a position on his stomach he reached into the hole and started sawing, stopping to examine his work with the flashlight. When he finished sawing, he sat up and raised a finger as if we were meant to listen for something.

We heard the clatter of wood falling away from us, but we did not hear it land.

Probably the rubber balls at the bottom of the hole absorbed the impact.

"Maybe now," he said.

. . .

I told LeBov that I felt obliged to ask him some questions.

"That sounds like a burden. Unburden yourself. By all means. You have about forty-five seconds. If that's how you'd like to use your remaining time, feel free."

"Okay. Why did you do it?"

LeBov didn't even take a minute to think. It was as though I'd asked him a question he'd rehearsed all his life. From LeBov I merited the canned response, deflection delivered with a hint of superiority. I hated people who could answer questions like these. Any kind of questions, maybe.

"There are certain boundaries that I'd prefer not to observe when it comes to my own identity," LeBov said. "There's a lot of behavior that I want to accomplish, but I don't need all of it, or really any of it, attributed to me. Attribution is a burden. In that sense I'm less like a person, a person as you might think of one, and more like an organization. There's also behavior that I need to undo, to take away, and this is often best accomplished by others, people who can erase action, alter ideas. I have a staff who work for me, of course. It's always startled me that people are so cautious when it comes to who exactly they are. It's almost the only thing we actually get to control. What a missed opportunity, really. For instance, you don't even know that I'm the real LeBov. But it's hard to grieve the choices made, or not made, by uninspired people. The sympathy allotment doesn't extend that far."

"So you change your name, fake your death."

"Look, that's nothing. That's cosmetic. Not even cosmetic. I moved around some grains of sand. Or not even that. I can't invent a small enough metaphor for what I've done. It's that insignificant. It adds some maneuverability, that's all. Some spaces open up. Everyone's presumed dead now anyway, as of tonight, after the radio darkness. Today was the last chance to die and have it reported. I hit the last news cycle. My death was the last story before the blackout. The world's last obituary. You should be congratulating me."

I looked at this redhead squeezing through the floor of my synagogue.

"Congratulations. And if in the process of this important work you hurt someone?"

"Then, uh, they feel pain? Is that a trick question? Is that really what's at issue right now, your hurt feelings? Could your perspective be any smaller?"

"You spoke to my wife."

"Someone had to. At least she actually listened. So much for your unified front."

LeBov reached into his coat and removed a long darning needle.

"Here," he said, rolling it over. "If you don't jam it in too hard, you won't do any permanent damage."

"To myself?"

"To *anyone*. Jesus, you are so self-centered. Thousands of years of Judaism, topped off by exclusive, secret access at your hole, for ultra-rare religious guidance, and this is all your people have come to?"

He gestured at our surroundings as if I, too, was meant to examine them.

"I'm sorry," he said, "but this place is sad. I examined your, what do you call it, your Moses Mouth? Your enabler? You all have different silly words for it."

He was referring to the slashed-up listener in his bag.

"Listener," I whispered to him. I don't think I'd ever said it out loud.

"You examined it?" I asked.

"And you didn't even bleed the withers, or whatever that fucking extra skin is called. It's completely engorged. You only used it to tap into Burke. That's insane. I've never seen such a rudimentary listener, and I have a good collection of them now. Anyone can listen to Burke, because *there is no Burke*. You don't even need a fucking listener. I can drop a copper wire into any conductive soil and pick up that signal. Probably with my landline telephone I could dial it up. It's completely unsecured. Public domain. Probably ham radio. I bet people get it in their houses. I bet you could pick it up off a filling in your molar. You spent all this time out here with this amazing device and you never wondered if you were hearing the *right* broadcast? The deepest feed? Instead you fucked on the floor like animals. Honestly, sometimes I had to look away. You didn't care and you fucked in a pile of musty sweaters. I'm kind of astounded. The Burke sermons were recorded years ago and play on a loop."

"Right. And you'd know that how?"

"Uh, because I've memorized them? Because they repeat? Burke's sermons are decoys for people like me who hack into the transmission, to appease us, to make us stop looking. *They're not real.* They're bait, you fucking kike. You're supposed to *activate* your listener to pick up the real transmissions. Even the morons down in Fort Wine figured that out. What do you think that box is for that I got from your house? You didn't even slide in the *glass*. Those tools were untouched."

"It was never broken," I whispered.

"But it fucking hell was! It was dead. How could you not have noticed?"

LeBov was ready to go, his tools packed, his bag strapped to his chest.

"You still have time on the clock," he said. "Any more questions?"

I stared at this man filling the hole in my hut.

"No?" he said. "I have a question, then. I'll use your remaining seconds. We'll say that I owe you. My question is, for whose benefit is it?"

"Is what?"

"Your complete inability to understand what's going on."

"I don't see that it benefits anyone," I admitted.

"Oh. I was just curious. That strategy is really unfamiliar to me. It kept me fairly interested in you. I figured you had a deeper play. I thought that perhaps I was missing out on the angle and I wanted to see what you'd do, but then you didn't do *anything*. I guess that's your play?"

LeBov gave some genuine reflection to this idea.

"You have a novel way with confusion. In another world inertia might have helped you, might have seemed genius. But even this thing with Thompson. I mean, you really believed that, that he was a *rabbi*? You didn't recognize my voice?"

"You want me to believe that you were Thompson, too?"

"No, not particularly. It's more interesting when you don't believe deeply obvious facts. That's far more fascinating to me. I like to surround myself with mistaken people. I draw strength from it. It increases my own chances for success."

"Agreement is a poison, right?"

"That's part of it."

"So the medical approach Thompson prescribed," I started.

"I needed it done and there you were, needing to do it. It occupied you, didn't it? It took your eye off the ball. I didn't think you'd take it all so seriously, but thank you for obliging."

"And your promise to my wife?"

"I'm proud of that. You don't often find someone so ripe for turning. She's a wonderful lady. I enjoyed her company tremendously. Reverse conversion, talking people down from their beliefs. Pretty standard. Anyone can feed a doubt. I gave her hope, which is more than you were doing for her. You treated her like a lab rat and now if you even speak to her she's going to die."

"She's not going to die."

LeBov laughed.

"At least your denial is consistent."

Then LeBov dropped down into the hole and disappeared.

I crept over, ducked down to see, but there was nothing, just the smell that seemed to follow me around, the sour fume of sleeplessness and decay.

From the depths of the hole I heard LeBov's voice.

"Listen," he called up. "I'd invite you to Forsythe, but there's that wife of yours. You realize that you're hurting her, right? Every time you talk to her? You probably think you have her best interests in mind, but believe me you don't know what they are. Her best interests don't involve you. Her best interests require your absence. Until death do us part, though? I hope that works out. But if you change your mind, we could use your help."

It turns out that I did have a last question for him, one that I was still trying to form. I whispered it down the hole, afraid, for some reason, to raise my voice too loudly.

I asked—certain that LeBov was still down there, plotting his course beneath us—about the Jewish children. Early in the epidemic, those reports that the Jewish children were the only toxic ones? I needed to know if that was true, if the epidemic really emerged that way. Was Esther among the first? Or had he, had LeBov, influenced that information? I whispered this down the hole.

"Did you make that up, too? Did you spread misinformation?"

I waited for his response, jets of cold air from the Jewish hole rushing over my face. But LeBov didn't answer.

He was already gone.

20

At home that night Claire fell asleep in Esther's bed. Not the sleep that people can easily be roused from, but the leaden hibernation that resists all signaling, raising a carapace on the shell of the sleeper that cannot be pierced by mere shouting. The heart rate slows, the hands grow cold, and life inside the body begins to spoil. Once the vigilant waking person has succumbed, the body consumes itself. A fume rises from the torso as it molders.

It happened sometimes, the little death when Claire slept. Perhaps it happened more now that Esther was spending most nights out of the home. Her bed became one more resting ground for Claire, who toured our rooms in the night looking for the bed that would be the best staging ground for her nightly disappearance.

Her daughter's bed, one must allow, had become her favorite site for this project.

But tonight Esther came home to be alone, missing her pretty little room, and there was trouble. I'm pretending to know what drove her. I do not know. The exercise of guessing at Esther's actions, her thoughts, is an advanced one, requiring skills I do not have. But wherever she was and whatever she was thinking or feeling tonight, she came home, and when she did, she encountered something that caused her to give liberal voice to her feelings, to use a voice that for many weeks had been bottled up in our home.

Maybe when Esther came home she crawled into bed, only to find her mother's dry body under the sheets. The rank-smelling hair, the bruised neck. Perhaps the mouth guard that her mother used to keep her from gnashing into the exposed nerve pulp of her teeth, perhaps this mouth guard had come unseated and was hanging from her mother's lips like a piece of meat.

It caused her to climb up on her mother and assume a feral crouch, opening her throat for the pure injury to pour out.

By the time I arrived Claire was facedown, holding the pillow over her head. She had woken up only to swoon again. It looked at first like a posture of defense she had struck, but when I checked her she was far from seeing or knowing me.

Claire's blackout was stubborn. I felt as if I were hacking away at the sleep that covered her. It did not help that Esther was in full tirade, producing a language so rank that I failed to breathe, lost control of my hands.

The air was clogged with speech and I fell from the bed. It was coming from everywhere, a wall of sound bearing down on my hips—the pressure seemed to be coming from inside me, something trying to force itself out—and I crumpled, started to retch.

I couldn't block the sound with my hands, and I felt myself blacking out.

I remembered LeBov's needle and grabbed it from my pocket. I jammed it into an ear, but missed the hole, piercing the cartilage on the outer ear. I tried again, slower, letting the tip of the needle fill the ear hole, then, when I was sure of my aim, jamming in the needle until it passed through the thinnest part of the inner ear, which presented no more resistance than a tissue.

I did this without thinking, with no sense of how much pressure was required.

If you do it right, you'll cloud your hearing for about an hour, maybe longer, LeBov had said.

He didn't elaborate. I didn't ask. An hour earlier, sitting with LeBov in the hut, I didn't think I'd drive a needle into my head so that I could deafly handle the vocal cloud of a child.

The pain was deep. For a moment I heard distant crying. A person, a bird, a siren. Warm liquid filled my ear, poured down my face.

I touched it, expecting to draw back bloody fingers, but the liquid was clear. Clear and warm.

LeBov's needle didn't work. I could hear perfectly from the punctured ear. I only hollowly contemplated approaching the other ear with the needle, ramming it in to balance the pain.

Esther had stopped speaking by then anyway. My activities with the needle had rendered her mute. She stood watching me, a mostly convincing look of fear on her face. An effective display of crying, soft crying that she seemed to want to suppress, came next. She performed her grief for my benefit, but I had other things to do. The house was calm now. The only sounds were from our Claire, who mumbled something from the bed, rolled deeper into her covers.

These were such reassuring sounds to me, the sounds of Claire not yet gone.

Esther crouched next to me, her finger crossing her lips to show she would not speak. A sign I once might have trusted. She brought her shirttail up to dab at my ear, to wipe free some of the discharge, and it seemed for a moment that she was intent on hugging me, but I pulled her hand away. I pulled it away, stood up myself, and walked strongly with my daughter out of her room, dragging her with me, through our house and out the front door, where I left her alone in the yard.

I would like to say that love shows itself in strange ways, but that would not be true in this case. Sometimes love refuses to show itself at all. It remains perfectly hidden. One spends a lifetime concealing it. There is an art to this. To conceal love is, in its way, the most sophisticated kind of smallwork there is.

Esther stood outside our house with her head down, shoulders small.

I rushed her again, moved my daughter yet farther into the yard, and she slumped over me, let herself be carried. At the sidewalk I dropped her and with my hands I made the most terrible gesture I could.

It was the most fluent I'd ever been without speech.

Stay, stay there. Do not come in this house again. You are forbidden from here. We do not know you.

Esther looked up at me and nodded. With her little finger she crossed her heart.

I would not be fooled by her ministrations, such conspicuous acts of tenderness designed to fool us into letting down our guard. She should have known better. Maybe now she would.

Tonight I needed to protect my home and that meant keeping people like her—blood relation or not—well clear of it. If Esther tried to return I would be ready for her. I would meet her with everything I had.

21

We drove out the next morning. Our breath was scarce and we were bruising in dark pools beneath the skin. A small wound on my leg failed to bleed. It opened like the mouth of a baby. From the gash came the faintest wheeze of sound. I flinched when I heard it, braced for it to sicken me, too.

People swarmed the street. I could not see their faces. Our evacuation was orderly and our denial so final, we were spared overt displays of grief. The day was hot, there was weeping down the hill, some other person's weeping, and in our own yard, under the fractured shade of the oldest tree on our block, such a clutter of moths bothered the air. These were the slow, bird-size moths, so awkward they may as well have been tagged and numbered.

My face felt so heavy, I thought I could remove it, step on it until it composted. I coupled my hip bag of adrenaline with boiled-down Semantiril to queer any speech sounds I might hear. I needed speech estranged into grunts and huffs. Even these could command people into action. I required speech submerged in fluid, warbled, buried in the ground. The Semantiril got me close. It brought foam into the holes, filling in whatever silence was left inside a word. What I heard were solid blocks of tone, like the test sounds from an emergency broadcast.

Throughout the day I paused while loading the car to huff these vapors from an oily lunch bag.

The last signs of life flickered inside Claire. That much and no more. When she looked at me I felt the high disgrace of being known for what I am.

Outside the house was a whiteout of silence, the sound of a whole neighborhood holding its breath. I kept my head down, vowed not to see. If I did not regard others in their shame, their haste, perhaps they would spare me from seeing mine.

Once I had Claire in the car, I noticed she was clutching the letter she'd written to Esther. Somehow she'd found the strength to sit down and write a final message. It was sealed and I was not to read it or ask about it. Fairly simple parameters to follow. The envelope was wrinkled with sweat, with whatever leaked freely from Claire.

I wrote no such letter myself. There was something blackening to the act of writing words, like carving into flesh. My hand felt foreign. It would not cooperate. And if I did write anything, it looked like a drawing dismantled into too many pieces. I could make the parts but I could not put the parts together.

Decipherment of words on a page was too difficult. When I managed it, I was never sure what had happened, who'd been killed by whom. It was becoming clear to me that reading would be something I would avoid. The very thought of it sent a wave of fear through my chest.

When I finally sat down with a voice recorder the night before, I produced only excuses. The rhetoric of a whitewasher. Nothing passed for tender in what I said, which meant that I had already communicated all I could on the topic. Everything else, like most of my parenting to Esther, would have to go without saying, without doing. But when I listened back to the recording, to check the quality of the sound, I heard the sounds of a man with cloth stuffed in his mouth. In the end this was what I left for Esther. There was no larger wisdom I could impart.

Here, my final words to you, just nothing. It is all that I know.

In the car I pulled Claire's nightgown from where it was bunched under her legs. I straightened her coat. Beneath the seat I clicked the lever and shifted her back. Her legs released into the freed-up space and she relaxed.

I did not want to hurt her so I did not speak. I held her face and mouthed, "How's that?"

She stared straight through me.

I looked at this stoic, long-suffering woman, who really should have died weeks ago. What an insult this all was to her. She did not want me breathing in her space, leaning my weight against her. She did not want me getting close. In Shippington, in Lobe Arbor, in one of the fields that ran flush to West Hollows, Claire could be alone all she liked.

If there was a plan, it was that we'd head down Route 4, but take the splinter trail that cuts beneath the Monastery, following the tracks until the trail dovetails with 41. In Shippington or Lobe Arbor we'd book a motel, monitor the situation from there.

I'd called ahead this morning, gotten nothing, not even an unanswered ring.

When I thought of Esther alone in the house, without us, I pictured her being waited on by . . . us. Facsimiles of us. Robot usses. Father and mother us, hovering over Esther with bowls of berries, with the special dinner of steamed greens, the de-meated slab of protein and sautéed bread she liked. Her own baby bowl of salt, hooked onto her dinner plate like a sidecar. I couldn't see her, Esther didn't exist, without a satellite of us orbiting by, although I'm sure Esther had no problem imagining her solitude. We'd always cooked and cleaned for her, served her food, done her laundry, put away her things. Standard-issue caretaking. There was no way to distill these tasks into words and leave her with any clear sense of how to take care of things herself. But I flattered myself when I thought that what Esther needed was instructions regarding the house, a set of operational strategies to keep her afloat inside the family home. That is not what Esther needed.

When Esther was finally old enough to walk to school by herself, she still wanted approval for things that were too basic to be considered talents. Eating an apple. Standing on one leg. Soon she'd want to be congratulated for waking up, leaving a room. Once she sat on our windowsill—she must have been eight or nine already. She was very pleased with herself, swinging her legs back and forth.

Do you know, Dad, that I can do a trick?
Oh yeah?
Yeah!
I can make my legs go this way and that, that way and this!
I see that.

Do you see?
I do.
You're not looking. Why aren't you looking?
I'm looking. I see it.
You're not, though. You're not.

I should have congratulated her. Who was I to say this wasn't extraordinary? What did I really know about extraordinary things?

At the car I crouched down next to Claire to administer her travel dose. When we got to the motel I would bathe her, let her sleep, and go out and get us some food, if I could find any. Perhaps she would sleep for days. I would let no children into the room. Would I hurt the children if they approached? I had not decided. I would refrain from speaking. The television and radio and phone would be unplugged. Claire would enjoy total silence. She could rest and eat and rest and bathe and eat and sleep until this was over and she recovered.

I had recuperative medicines in mind for this next phase. Claire needed a few weeks of quiet.

Perhaps we'd find the moans that were safe to exchange, and into them we'd spread enough meaning to get by.

I pushed Claire's gown up her legs and grabbed a handful of skin.

She didn't flinch when I jammed in the needle.

A clear bead of serum gathered on her thigh, clung to a fine hair.

Despite the precaution against speech, I spoke to Claire, and I wish I could remember what I said, if only to seal off this memory and never consider it again. I have not found my doubt to be useful. It is a distraction to live so long with uncertainty.

What I said to Claire may have been an estimate of our departure. Probably that sort of chatter, whatever was coming next. We were minutes away—*Let me check the trunk. Are you thirsty?*—or it may have been an endearment I offered. Did I say that I loved her? Nothing but wishful thinking would suggest that I did. Such a phrase would have sounded awful on that day. Certainly ill-timed, certainly self-serving. A phrase designed purely to trigger an equivalent response. But wishful thinking has had its way with me. It has hounded me. In all of this silence it is my primary voice.

Did I say that I loved her?

The question is immaterial. It's the last piece of speech I gave my wife, and it matters to no one but me.

The car was packed, but before we could leave I had my own injection to administer. I'd doctored my blend with a trace of Aphaseril, which curled into the serum in a dark ribbon that settled at the bottom of the vial. For privacy I crouched down against the rear wheel of the car.

"Here's how," I said to no one, and fed the needle into my loneliest vein. A coldness overtook me as the needle found purchase, chilling my groin, rising up my stomach. I clung to the car as my heart surged. Such a sweet ache rushed in to cover the nausea. It was what I needed to make the final push out of here.

2

22

When the departure horn tore open the New York air, and the cars started their slow crawl from town, Claire opened the passenger door and stumbled into the grass. At first I thought she forgot something in the house, so I let her stagger away.

My wife in her nightgown on a strangely warm December day, running not so well from the car.

Go ahead, I thought. If we couldn't have Esther, we could have more of her stuff. Grab the baby teeth stashed in the foot of an old onesie, the self-portrait Esther took with her long face overlit in the lens, the blanket stitched from Esther's stuffed animals that might make this easier. We have *no* more time, Sweetheart, we really don't, but go ahead. They're motioning us to leave now, so please hurry.

It was true. The officials of the quarantine had initiated a semaphore that left no room for doubt. People so disfigured in padding they looked like technicians from a bomb squad, waving bright yellow traffic rods, firing a jolt at those few of us who were seeking to stay put. Men and women doubling over in the road from lightning shot into their torsos. It was time to go.

But Claire didn't go to the house. She crossed into the field, entered the high growth, and before she even reached the meadow she faltered.

I raced after her but by the time I reached her she was fallen, her eyes already cold. She couldn't even make it to the tree line. By the time

I reached Claire the men of the quarantine dropped down on me, dragging me back to the car.

I left Claire on her back in the grass, staring through me, at something no one else could see. She looked finally gone.

From the woods trotted a pack of dogs, like old men in animal suits, barking with human voices. Behind them trudged a human chain of jumpsuited rescuers, arms linked so they'd miss no one. They were flushing stragglers from the woods, kicking the bushes for shapes.

And there were some stragglers. They thought they could wait out the evacuation, then return to their homes until this blew over. But nothing was blowing over. We kept believing it couldn't get any worse, as if our imaginations held sway in the natural world. We should have known that whatever we couldn't imagine was exactly what was coming next.

The technicians of the quarantine carried me over their heads in grips so fierce I couldn't move.

I caught one last sight of Claire. She seemed confused. No one told her she'd come up short in the field and collapsed. No one told her she had not escaped.

They stuffed me in my car, shut the door, then banged a hand on the roof to tell me it was okay to go now. Join the procession out of here. Get going. *Without her*.

But it was very much not okay. I scrambled across the seats out the other side of the car, made a break for the field to get my wife—even dead, she should be coming with me, even if I had to drive up to Fort Wine to bury her—but they grabbed me again, pushed me back in, this time guarding the doors with their cushioned bodies.

When I kicked on the doors they were blocked from the outside. It was like my car was underwater and I could not get out. Underwater, with padded men hovering over me like . . . like nothing else I've ever seen.

From inside the car I watched them take Claire to their truck and then the truck's cargo door slid down and the truck's lights flashed once, before the truck pulled out and took, not the street, because the street was clogged with cars, but the field that stretched out beyond our houses. And if the truck stopped as it cruised through the grass, it was only to collect another straggler, some local citizen who had lost the strength to leave and would now join my wife and the stunned others inside that dark vehicle, headed slowly out of sight like the rest of us.

23

I drove from home through a gridwork of shadow, the car cold and dark. When I cleared the town line I hugged the access road along the wooden boulevard until it converted into open asphalt at Meriwether. A shudder of speed bumps shook the car, launching me onto the highway.

A siren from town erupted in deep, low tones. It blew nearly too low to hear, but I felt the rumble of it deep in my hips, and it took miles of driving before the vibration released.

The quarantine with its poisonous children was behind me.

In my rearview mirror no cars followed, nobody traveling north. Everyone else fleeing town had peeled off west, south, and I had the road to myself. The view was mostly washed out by the winter air, but outside of Van Buren a trail of smoke ripped through the sky. Somebody's flare from some road somewhere, maybe.

I drove until I slumped exhausted against the steering wheel and the car crunched to a stop in a gravel swell. I awoke with salty, warm blood in my mouth and drove on, sometimes following roads that were so broad, so ill defined, it seemed I was traveling through a vast parking lot.

This was far from home already, along the northern vein toward Albany. In my life I had not driven this far north. This must be what birds feel when they look down on the world and find the entire landscape new. Suddenly they've flown into a strange place where even the wind is foreign on their bodies, a wind so thick it's like a person. He's mauling you and you can't move. Everything is different. The buildings, the earth below, the wires bisecting streets into broken pieces of stone.

My maps were old, drawn for a louder world, and it sickened me to even consider them.

The road grew over the curb, threatened the grass. As I gained distance north, the road leaked into the woods, spreading over hills, a blanketing of asphalt. I could not leave the highway. The rumors about this region were true. Even the hills were made of road. I pulled over, but found only more road to clear, and no matter how far I pulled over I only entered new parts of highway, which spilled in every direction. It was not safe to slow down. More cars joined me now, humming past in reckless vectors, a traffic without lanes, drivers staring at the hardened space ahead.

I held fast to what seemed a straight line and did my best to focus.

By noon the road eased into a slushy grass, and I drove faster, the wet soil like a wake of water beneath me. I crossed Allamuchy, where trees enclosed the roadway in a dark tunnel, violated by shards of light so blinding they seemed to throw white rocks in my path on the highway.

A fine green grass covered the countryside here, blown flush to the soil by the volley of speeding cars. Whole meadows leaned over at once as if some great airplane roared overhead. Outside of Corning a thin geyser of mud shot from the earth, whining into the air before stalling at its peak of flight, then falling in streaks to the ground. I do not know for how long I pushed forward. With my windows sealed the world passed by in silence, and such conditions made it almost impossible to mark the passing of time.

At intersections the stop signs had been effaced, caked in metallic red paint. Road signs and city distances had likewise been distorted. Most public writing, issuing basic commands to drivers, had been camouflaged. The bright, hammered slabs of road signs still hung from their posts, but they were wordless blocks of color that commanded no action.

Wherever the epidemic stood north of town, no one was taking any chances. If there had been any language in the countryside, it had now been systematically erased.

I saw no real writing for hours. Such conditions suited me fine.

At a county border marked by a heap of rope, a man on a ladder disguised a road sign, adding marks to the letters until they flowered out of meaning. The word looked to have once been *Rochester*.

That such a word once meant something seemed now only to be an accident.

I drove on. Before checkpoints I slowed. With one of Claire's hospital masks I wiped the warm leakage from my eyes. No one questioned me.

Somebody wept inside a clouded booth, where a line had formed. I saw the colorful body bags of Albany. A woman outside a medical tent sprayed a mist on what looked to be an antenna, the dark rod quivering in her hands. Possibly it was only a braided metal cable, feeding into a mound of dust at her feet, but I did not stop. Her ears were packed with mud.

I could stick a wire into any piece of soil and listen to Burke, LeBov had said.

At most during these checkpoint stops a man peered into the car, smelled the air. My trunk was opened and probed. For children, no doubt, they searched. For something I did not have.

I held still and watched through the rearview mirror as they picked through my gear, holding utensils up to the last light of day, smelling deeply into my duffel. My toolkit was discovered, spilled out into the road. Someone ran a finger into the neck of a beaker, gathered a residue, licked it. A smoke purse was tossed onto a vented snuffing mat and stamped out. It burst with a wet noise, its smoke spilling downward into the vent, as if someone was employed in a cave to inhale the fumes of our world. Nothing but the smell of burnt dough drifted to me up front in the car.

The younger officials were clothed alike in the full-body suiting, but the older ones had not managed to assemble a uniform. Some still wore their household robes, medical gowns, pajamas under coats.

The jumpsuits of the youth were blue and seemed to be fashioned of wool ticking. These inspectors lacked even the discipline necessary to tyrannize anyone, to cause paralysis and fear, and it seemed that soon they would drift away from their posts into the hills and sit down in the grass and collapse.

The great effort of eager amateurs was everywhere. There were none of us who were not amateurs now. The experts had been demoted. The experts were wrong. The experts had perished. Or perhaps the experts had simply been misnamed all along.

24

It must have been Woodleigh where I was waved to the side after my car was searched.

I pulled over near a standing coffin, but no one approached. I waited as other cars were waved through. Blue sedans swept past, passengers hidden behind viral masks.

The man who finally approached had a small face that rode too high on his head. He beckoned down my window and reached in for me. With his thumb he probed under my arm, burrowing into a spot that was suddenly raw. He directed a penlight into my eyes, studied my face, positioned it in different angles. I returned calm expressions to him and did not spoil the encounter with speech. He, too, was silent, and if there was any noise it was only my own breathing.

Before I was waved through, he handed me a sheet of paper embossed with a crazed freckling of Braille. He placed my hand over the sheet, running my fingers along the bumps, which felt like Claire's skin. He passed my fingers back and forth over the Braille message and I could only smile at him and shrug. If this was reading, it was the kind that left me cold. Had I *read* it? I couldn't be sure. I had no reaction, but that could be true of other things I read. Perhaps that was the intent of such a message and I had read it correctly. With a sneer he snatched the paper from me and walked off.

I drove on, passing a stretch of small, wooden prisons dug into the hillside, marked by symbols too strange to read. I must have been near one of the Dunkirks, at the broken radial that once linked them in a breezeway leading down to the sea.

Outside of Palmyra a tent hung from a tree. A crowd of people had formed, lined up to get inside. What did these people want outside of a tent? A field of fresh-dug holes spread out behind the tent, mounds of dirt in cemetery formation, ready to be shoveled back in when the holes were filled. Graves so soon, I thought.

Humps of earth reared up in meadows, not just hills and natural elevations, but architecturally engineered redoubts. Mounds and swells and bunkers, as if air was bubbling up from underground, creating shelters under skins of soil. Every manner of door was cut into these dwellings. Wood, glass, fencing, cloth. Some were free of any visible means of entry, the sealed homes of people who did not mean to come out again.

No exit left the freeway to reach these shelters. If people roamed out there, they were too perfectly camouflaged against the landscape. The sun was abstracted on the horizon, merely a placeholder. I kept the threat of it on my driver's side periphery, figuring at this pace I'd land at my destination right after nightfall.

When there were no houses and the road was free of cars, I stopped and climbed into the long grass of the embankment, stretched my body. Beneath a canopy of trees I gave in to what seemed to need to come out of me, pouring so much hard sound from my person I thought it would not stop and I would never get my breath back.

I wept out all my air. I wept a little bit of something darker. I wept until my voice grew hoarse, then failed, and I kept weeping until I fell to the grass, finished.

My chest felt like it would break. I clutched the grass so hard that my hands, each finger, felt broken. My face was too tight on me. I wanted to cut it off.

If indeed I was only crying, it was like no crying I had ever done before.

In a world where speech was lethal, I could not share with anyone what happened when Claire collapsed in the grass and I failed to help her.

I would never be able to lie out loud about what happened the day I left my wife and daughter behind, driving north alone.

At least I had that one, small thing all to myself. My shame would be safely contained inside what was left of me. Barring some miracle, I'd never be able to tell this story. It could die with me. Very soon, I hoped, it would.

Back in the car, night seemed impossibly far off. I was ready for darkness. I knew that difficult thoughts and feelings awaited me, but still they had yet to arrive. I wanted to be more tired, to have some better reason to find a turnout and shelter my car until morning. But I couldn't stop now.

When the sun went down, slipping behind the hills, the road thinned into a single lane and started to climb.

On a bird-strewn incline I came upon women pulling a cart up a footpath. The tarp thrown over their cart so clearly covered the bulges of people. They were fooling no one. I pressed the gas pedal to the floor, but the incline was so great I could hardly pull ahead of them, so we climbed in parallel up the southern ledge that ringed the city of Rochester.

At the summit the trees grew rumpled and dense, as if they had been forced to mature under dark glass. Cars on the road below moved in orderly lanes into a single checkpoint, a wooden low-rise with well-dressed guards. In this traffic streamed a caravan of red busses, windows blacked out. The lights of Rochester were only mildly brighter than the darkness, small pale stains oiling the air. If you stared into the light, it retreated until the whole city seemed covered in dark grease.

I pointed my car down the hill and headed into town.

25

In the Forsythe parking lot I fell from my car and crawled over hot asphalt, circling an endless fleet of red busses, looking for an entrance to the building.

Forsythe was not a government structure with its typical transparent woods, or one of those low, glass laboratory compounds where clear smoke worked like a lens, sharpening the air over the roof. Forsythe was, instead, just a high school, a research lab embedded within the old educational structure that still had the mascot carved in its face. A game cat whose teeth jutted out from the facade. The name of the school was covered now in a swipe of rust.

Some men were waiting at my open car when I realized I had crawled full circle, gone nowhere. They fell on me softly, lifted me into the air as if they'd throw me into the sky and discard me.

Someone grabbed my keys and the taillights of my car squirreled through the nighttime air, then disappeared around a building.

There went everything I owned.

My helper spoke through a plastic mouth fitted over his face, but what he said was so foreign and airless that I cannot here transcribe it.

The message traveled so fast into me that I felt torn open. The phrase, whatever it meant, was like an act of sudden surgery, the kind that cuts the rotted thing from your body, leaving you empty, healed, exquisitely released from pain. That's all I remember.

. . .

I woke inside a light-scorched hallway. A salted object filled my mouth. Someone shoved it deeper, his fist jammed into my face, as if he was trying to hide his whole arm in my body. I breathed through my nose and tried to keep up, but my mouth was too full with the gag of salt.

My escorts held me close and I let their bodies guide me. We moved from hallways to small rooms, waited at doors, then passed through tight corridors until we mounted a steep, narrow staircase and came up on the floor where I would be staying.

I tried to keep my sense of direction throughout this interior maneuvering, but the compass I conjured in my mind had only a single direction, the needle in a palsy over a symbol I didn't recognize.

A man in a lab coat removed the salt object from my mouth and something tore as he pulled it out.

I felt hands on me, sharp pieces of bodies that stank. Someone with a practiced touch lifted my arms, removed my shirt. He'd done this to many people, I could tell. Disrobed them while they slumped over in a stupor, readied them for some miracle.

I was held in place while something pinched under my arm, deep against the bone. It is hard to know if I made any show of my feelings. I looked down as a syringe pulled from a perforation under my arm, the skin hugging the needle as it retreated.

This was no medicine I had tried before. It brought my eyes halfway shut and I could do nothing to open them again.

The man spoke in that foreign, airless language, his breath oily in my mouth, and this time his phrasings made me cry. I cried in the most childish, open-faced way.

I let myself fall into his arms.

With a thumb jammed between my shoulder blades, he worked a finger from his other hand deep under the bone of my sternum. He had a hand on each side of me and he crouched, readied himself in preparation.

I draped over him, unable to stand.

When my lungs were empty, he squeezed, as if his thumb and finger might meet inside my body. I believe he succeeded.

The sensation came too quickly for me to cry out. My face tightened, a blast of pressure leaking from my eye. He slipped out from under me and I fell.

He left me in a heap on the floor.

. . .

The medical procedures at Forsythe, at least those I received in the parking lot and outer hallways of the recovery wing, belonged to no speech fever treatment I knew. Hebraic phrases delivered through a prosthetic mouth, triggering ecstasy, promoting unconsciousness. Perhaps these were the healing phrases Murphy—LeBov, I should say—had mentioned. Then there was the profoundly painful bodywork, the deep-tissue manipulation and extreme compression. Crushing. These practices had not been discussed publicly.

Against the cold wall of my room, in clothes that reeked of my travels, I spoke for a time with Claire. I spoke to her in private tones, words dismantled into grunts, because Claire did not need anything spelled or even sounded out for her, she never did.

Sometimes I could summon my wife's voice, no matter where she was. Sometimes she would talk back, even if it was only me willing it so.

I found myself arguing for the family, trying to make a case that we needed to stick together, and as I did that, I could see Claire's face, a stricken look of disbelief on it, a really appalled look that I would even begin to suggest she did not *also* want that, which of course I agreed to as fully as I could, but I could tell from her face that it was too late, I had cast myself as the one who wanted unity, I had excluded her from this desire, and how dare I do such a thing?

Stick together? She didn't need to ask. *This from the man who drove off without us?*

What's important now, I started to say to her. What's important now . . . What's important is that we . . .

I pictured Claire waiting for me to say, waiting for me to actually *know* what was important now. She stood over me.

Dig yourself out of this, she didn't need to say. *Go ahead. Get down on your knees and start digging your way out of this. I'd like to see how far you get. I'll be right here, watching you disappear into the earth.*

26

My days in this northern hole of Rochester were speechless and dark. I saw no sun, never felt the sky darken. No authentic sky prevailed in the Forsythe recovery wing, no windows through which the light might fail.

Ruptured mattresses littered the floor, sleeping bags with the bottoms kicked through. A brittle pillow bore the facial welt of the last patient who slept here.

A man's work shirt had been chewed, swallowed, spit up in a glaze of bile.

Mesh baggies of hair hung from the ceiling, repelling flies. Possibly the hair attracted them instead.

Most rooms were furnished with wooden chairs, seats scarred by fire. Rope railings hung from the corridor walls. The blind could pull themselves to the bathroom without falling. The blind, the sick, the tired.

These quarters so far I occupied alone, with the exception of a man left too long to spoil in what I came to think of as Room 4. His face was so white, it seemed painted.

It was early December. Year of the sewn-up mouth. The last December of speech. If you were not a child, safely blanketed in quarantine, bleating poison from your little red mouth, you were one of us. But to be one of us was to be something so small and quiet, you may as well have been nothing. If we had last messages, we'd crafted them already, stuffed them in bottles, shoes, shot them out to sea. Words written for no one, never to be read. When pressed for something significant to say, most of us said so little we seemed shy, could not speak the language. We wrote down our names, our dates, the names of our mothers and fathers, the towns we lived in. On notebook paper we sketched pictures. Our last words weren't even real words.

Claire was wherever they took people like her, still blinking and breathing, camouflaged against a hillside of salt.

Esther was thriving in the world she must have always craved, where the washed-out idiots of preceding generations had finally been banished, rags crammed down their throats. I worried for her without a world of older people to loathe. Now she lived with a population of her own kind, where self-hatred meant you gnashed at whomever you saw. And they you. How much time did Esther have before her own face was *touched*, before her tongue hardened and grew cold in her mouth?

Oh, of course I did not know where Claire was. I did not know where Esther was. Even as to where *I* was, I was hardly sure. But my ignorance did not slow my mind from its suspicions, and these held a vivid persuasion all their own.

At Forsythe my sleep was not patterned enough to signal the hour. With no smallwork to perform, the time of day failed to matter. What did matter was so far beyond me, I sometimes could not even see it. But still it hovered out there in dark shapes, however much I wished it gone.

LeBov would find me. He'd hear of my arrival, come get me, bring me into some important fold, if there was a fold. LeBov needed me, if only to practice those black tasks no one else could carry out. I'd let him use me again. Better that than having no use at all.

Rabbi Burke never used the word *devil*. The universal coinage was worthless, in his view. Words that mask what we don't know. But he spoke about dangerous people who orbited the moral world, building speed around us, rendering themselves so blurred, they looked gorgeous. Burke spoke of refusing dizziness, latching on to these satellite monsters, of which one must count LeBov, so we could travel at their velocity, see them for what they were.

For now I slept in my sweaty room, ate the briny lobes stuck to my hallway food stand, rested wide awake, venturing into the carpeted hallway only when I needed to pee.

Outside my door stood a wire magazine rack filled with a stash of refreshments, unlabeled glass cylinders of water, cloudy pouches of juice. Whatever I drank was so heavily salted, my mouth became scoured. At the urinal I peed a heavy, white pudding. But I lacked the strength to discharge all of it. Sometimes it sat low in me, an anchoring sediment, as if I were meant to carry this slow water forever.

The bathroom was dank and its lone faucet, protruding from the wall, blew debris-laden air from its nozzle. If liquid rode in this stream, it clung to the sand that blasted out. I held my hands under the nozzle, beneath a wind that scarcely moistened my fingers. I bent to it and swallowed jets of wind so fierce, they knocked me against the back wall of the bathroom.

The air sped through me with such turbine force, I sensed a bird's violation when its beak opens, wind penetrating every last space inside its body.

When I pictured Claire, she crouched in the woods, caked in mud so the dogs couldn't smell her. In my wishful thinking, which amounted to all my thinking, Claire had fled the truck, scattered to the tree line, then vanished into the woods. From there she watched our house. In her gown she strained to get a safe look at Esther. She strained and failed. When I pictured this, Esther remained hidden from Claire, would not show herself, and her mother did not relent, crawling through the woods for every advantage of perspective.

No matter how much I wanted to, I could not get Claire to see Esther, even though I should have been in charge of my own imagination. It should have been child's play to picture these events, but somehow this imagery was blacked out in me. When I moved Esther and Claire together in my mind, a darkness fell and they turned into distant, weak shapes. Even if I could collide these shapes, at that point they were not even people, just blocks of cold darkness that looked nothing like my wife and daughter.

Early in my stay, I discovered a way to access Rabbi Burke, but the method had difficulties.

At some point I woke up to an engine shrieking overhead. It was day, it was night, it was early, it was late. The time was best judged, if it needed to be judged, by how thirsty I was, and now my tongue was as dry as a sock in my mouth.

Above me, jets of smoke poured from a ceiling fixture. I reasoned it to be *intentional smoke*, a smoke meant for me, *the patient*, as opposed to exhaust fumes from an accident elsewhere at Forsythe.

Finally they were medicating me so I could get out of there. A nozzle in the ceiling pumping vapors into the recovery wing.

The flow was loud and cold. No matter where I huddled in my room it reached me, pouring cloudy fumes over my face. In the hallway it pumped. In the other rooms, even Room 4, covering in fog the man on the floor.

Sometimes the machinery behind the spout whined and the smoke spewed faster from its hole. When I tried to stop it, thinking perhaps the spigot could be dialed down, I discovered that the cork ceiling panel it protruded from was unusually soft. Soft and easy to remove.

I stood on my chair, ducking the putrid smoke, rotten and icy at its source, and pushed aside the panel. The drop ceiling disguised a tangle of plumbing ducts and power lines, but something else snaked through that space as well: a bright orange cable such as the one that pulsed up from our Jew hole. *A shining orange piece of conduit*. I'd recognize it anywhere.

I wanted to think that this cable could have been anything. It probably was a coincidence. Plastic orange insulation could not be exclusive to the forest Jews who deployed a Jewish radio. But when I gripped the cable it warmed in my hands, pulsing as if fated with a heartbeat. It gave off the same heat, the same nauseating smell, as the cable of our hut.

To be sure, I checked the other rooms, the hallway. I dragged my chair throughout the recovery wing, pushed aside ceiling panels, and found the orange cable wherever I looked. In Room 4 I stood over the fallen man and found the orange cable buried in his ceiling as well.

When I traced the cable out of the recovery wing, I struck a concrete wall and could follow it no farther. The cable flowed up from somewhere and retreated, never revealing itself from the recovery wing ceiling. It was tucked away. It was traveling elsewhere. To some other Jew's hut, perhaps. Why it detoured through Forsythe, a building that was once a high school, and not even a Jewish one, was beyond me. Clearly it wasn't meant to be found.

But I *had* found it, and now I wanted to listen in. If LeBov could intercept the feed without a listener, then so could I. I'd worked my own orange cable for years, learned a thing or two about the secret Jewish radio.

The wire magazine rack was easy to dismantle. I straightened the curved frame, rotating a small length of wire like the hand of a clock until it snapped off. With this short wire I climbed back on the chair, grabbed the warm meat of the cable, and pierced the shielding until the wire penetrated the cable's core. A sudden antenna.

On the chair I braced myself, thinking I was bringing together two powerful forces that might knock me to the ground.

But nothing happened. No transmission, no sound.

I'm not sure why I thought there would be. I'd bridged no signal, simply pierced the cable and possibly deferred one channel of the transmission into the air of my room, where it died out inaudibly.

It's true that the medical smoke briefly faltered in my room when I pierced the orange cable, sputtering from the nozzle, but that might have been a coincidence.

What I needed to do was extend the wire from the orange cable to a grounded point of metal conduction, then parlay the transmission into something that could pass for an audio speaker. Then I'd be able to hear the feed. If there *was* a feed. If this was a Jewish transmission at all.

From the straightened coils of the magazine rack I snapped off a clutch of longer wires, crimping them onto the short piece that pierced the cable, and in this way I wove a necklace of wire from the ceiling cable to the electrical outlet in the baseboard.

From here I used the final length of wire to bridge the signal into the best point of conductivity I could think of, the most natural audio speaker there is, at least when you have no other radio equipment on hand: the flesh inside of one's own mouth.

I coiled a tight nest of wire using the last scraps of the magazine rack and stashed it under my tongue. This was elementary antenna work. When I was ready I would feed the wire from the electrical outlet to the nest in my mouth, consummating the transmission. Perhaps then Burke would speak. Burke would make himself known through my mouth. My rabbi could be heard again.

My face was cold, as rough as an animal's back. LeBov's ointment last week had bought me some time, softened my palate enough for me to speak in ways I didn't understand. But that had worn off by now and my face had the buzzing, numb feeling of a sleeping limb. It therefore did not concern me that I was delivering the Jewish voltage to my mouth. My mouth was probably the safest place to test this bit of smallwork.

I sat down on the floor with the conducting wire, gripping the chair leg for support. At this point I should have taken stock, given some last thought to my Esther in the quarantine, Claire barely alive. I should have paid my respects to what little was left of the world I knew. But instead I touched the wire to the metal nest inside my mouth and fell at once into a tremble.

My vision blistered, blackened, and a seizure surged through my body. A darkness came over me, and in a great rush of sound, the Jewish transmission gushing from my face at a shattering volume, I blacked out.

27

Blessed are they who keep his testimonies quiet, who share them not even with themselves.
They make no crime in the air; they walk in the ways.
How does a person cleanse his way?
By saying nothing of your word.
Let me never announce the thought. Let me not corrupt it with sound.
Your word I have buried in my heart.
My heart I have buried in the woods.
These woods you have hidden from me in darkness.
You have commanded us not to know you and we have obeyed. When we have known you we have looked away, put blacklings in our eyes.
If my ways are directed to keep your promise, then I will not be ashamed. If my ways are directed to keep your promise and I am rendered alone, then I will not be ashamed.

This is the prayer that flowed through my mouth in the Forsythe recovery wing. It repeated day and night, even if I slept through it, even if I shut my mouth. It streamed at such a volume that it shook the room. When I sealed my lips the sound of the prayer beat against the backs of my teeth, fought its way out, the wire so alive with the transmission, you could still hear it resonating inside me.

I was scared to move, afraid to disrupt the transmission as it shook through my person, the nest of wire so hot in my mouth, it burned.

But for however many days I hosted the transmission, this prayer was all I could get from the cable, all that played, and the person behind it did not sound like Burke.

I adjusted the wire, shifted the nest in my mouth. To no avail.

I came to know the prayer with the greatest intimacy.

Your word I have buried in my heart.

I grew so alert to its obvious meanings that they sickened me, leading me to secondary, ironic intentions, disguises of rhetoric I would not normally notice. But soon these, too, felt fraudulent and then I returned to the literal meanings, which had gained more force now that I'd spurned them. That, however, did not last, and by the end the words had shucked their meaning entirely and evolved into a language of groaning, beyond interpretation. Or susceptible to the most obvious interpretation of all.

I wish I could report that the prayer flowed from my mouth in the broken, transfixing voice of Rabbi Burke, a voice I longed to hear again. But it did not. A prayer repeated by Burke would be one I could endure, could grow to love, even blasting through my face so hard I couldn't see.

But this prayer came from my lips in a horrible voice other than Burke's. The tones of it were weak and scared. It was a thin voice: *my own*. The voice I used back in the days of speech. The voice that had never worked very well or much and that sometimes repulsed me, even before it sickened anyone else.

Around the burning wire I spoke this prayer in my own voice, and even though it came from me, sounded like me, seemed in fact to be *my very own prayer*, I could do nothing to make it stop.

I removed the wire. I spit out the nest. I climbed back on the chair and severed the transmission from the wire to the orange cable, replacing the cork panel in the ceiling so the cable could no longer be seen.

But it didn't matter. The prayer came harder out of my face, even when I hid in the bathroom, even when I nuzzled up to the fallen old man of Room 4. I'd triggered it myself and now this prayer wouldn't stop for anything.

28

On a warm day in what turned out to be April, I departed the recovery wing of Forsythe Labs. I was woken gently that morning and from a steel door at the bottom step of my lodgings, goggled men helped me inside a light-soaked tunnel.

My guides did not seek to communicate. They maneuvered me with their hands, herding me to the other side.

Above me holes pierced the arched roof, where harsh portions of sky shone through.

When we cleared the tunnel we entered a tube-framed dome, its roof covered by plastic clear enough to give a view of the area. Outside the dome, the broad trees of Rochester hung over us. From the branches grew leaves so fat, they dripped a green fluid onto the roof.

Leaves already in full bloom, grotesque with life. Temperate air and the sun stalking a route impossibly high for the winter months.

I performed some calculations. The season was spring. Spring was well along now. When I arrived here it was December. I had served over four months in recovery, by myself. It was difficult to factor how the time had passed.

The prayer had finally died out in my mouth, I think. But in some ways I never stopped hearing it. Perhaps I'd simply learned to relegate it to the background.

. . .

The morning of my release into the research wing was reserved for procedural matters, decontamination. A truck drove through and sprayed me with an air hose so forceful, I clutched into a ball on the dirt until it passed.

A clump of black fur was pressed to my neck with a forceps, and when I buckled with dizziness I seemed to have passed the test.

A man used a tweezers to extract a piece of paper from a medical waste bag. I squirmed away from it, some deep instinct repelling me from reading. From behind me someone gripped my face and again the paper was dangled, twisting in the breeze.

My handlers averted their eyes.

The paper tilted, caught the perfect plane, and for a moment I saw it clearly. It had words on it, the sort I knew and would never forget, and I was forced to look at them. Yet more papers were tweezed from the bag and held before me, one after another. I was out of practice, but I knew I could estrange myself from language, should I encounter it. I could squint away the particulars, fuzz them into nothing.

But part of me was curious. Perhaps this was their only way of telling me something. Perhaps these notes held a message for me.

My interest appeared too late. The last page was retracted, the bag sealed, and then a handler stepped forward, gripping a short needle in his work glove, and jabbed me with it. I looked away as he drew from my thigh the blood they apparently required.

The other tests were routine and I submitted to them patiently. The goggles worn by my handlers were curious: the light was not bright enough to call for them. I realized then that they did not wear goggles to shield their eyes from the sun, but rather to keep themselves from being seen, to hide their eyes. I had seen no other unadorned faces, made no eye contact, heard no speech. The silence of everyone and everything felt pressurized, achieved at some cost I couldn't calculate.

When my examination was done, someone nudged me from the filthy yurt into a clearing, the Forsythe courtyard.

On top of a perfect circle of grass, a table stood loaded with bread, toasted seeds, a bowl of jam. The rolls were still warm. When I tore one open the steam bathed my face, and in my mouth it was soft and salty, so lovely to taste I nearly wept. On my second roll I spread some of the pale yellow jam and scattered the blackened seeds over it, stuffed the hot mass into my mouth, then looked for something to drink.

Nothing else had been laid out. When a handler passed me I grabbed his arm and made a drinking gesture, but he ducked away. The nimble way he evaded me, not hostile, just effortless and fast, as if he were executing a precisely timed dance move, suggested he had practiced this kind of avoidance before.

I waited while my work order was finalized, shifting along the courtyard every so often to keep the shade, which was terribly cold, from overcoming me. There were others, apparently dragged from a recovery tank somewhere also, likewise encased in oversize pajamas, huddled against themselves inside the great open courtyard. We looked like prisoners staggered in precise intervals so someone, stationed in a high tower, could practice his rifle skills.

In buildings as formidable and cold as this, one expects to look up from a courtyard at cruelly small windows, and see desperate faces pressed to the glass, the urgent signals of people held against their will. Instead the facility wall that gave onto the courtyard below featured broad sheets of transom glass, allowing more sunshine than a building as featureless and leaden as Forsythe would seem to be able to tolerate.

No ashen prisoners crowded behind the glass, only lab-coated observers, standing in full view. The glass shielded an indoor deck of some kind, allowing people to stand and study the doings below.

Before I was taken to my new room, I glimpsed what must have been capturing the interest of those people up in the observation booth: a man under a clear dome in the courtyard, his head encased by bright yellow earphones. A crowd of lab-coated observers stood outside the dome with clipboards, while above them their supervisors surveyed the spectacle.

The man tugged at the earphones, righted himself, and shook his head, trying to tear them free, but they were fastened tight. The observers, near enough to enter the dome and help him, showed no reaction.

With those lemon yellow headphones and his black suiting, the subject looked like a bee trapped in a jar. From his gestures one might conclude that the headgear was burning his ears.

He was the first of many I would see. I would never learn what they called them, since naming of this sort had no application anymore, and anyway could not be shared.

Volunteer, *test subject*, *language martyr*: tasked out for experiments to test the toxicity of the languages being devised by people like me.

By the time I was ushered inside, he whimpered silently under the glass, having given up on removing his headphones, which one supposed were transmitting language his body could not bear.

Oh, one supposed this all right. A froth of bubbles clouded from his mouth.

I did not look at his face very carefully, but I would see him again. And again. And again. Within weeks, once I took up my new role, this man's agony would be my responsibility alone. The voice pumping poison into his body may as well have been my own.

29

On my first day of work in the research wing, in a private office with a view that gave out onto the rock face I would think of as Blank Mountain, I checked the lockers for medical equipment.

I had no access to my car, and no one would retrieve my gear, my samples. My mimed requests were ignored. Or a blanket was tossed over my hands and someone bowed before me, head averted, and squeezed my wrists so tightly I fell.

I got the message. Sign language was restricted unless new forms of it were being tested under controlled circumstances. If you forgot this and brought your hands into gestural action you were subdued. They came out of nowhere and they did not look at you but if you tried out a language, even a silent one, they put a stop to it fast.

In my new office I believed I could resume my work with chemicals, with vapors and mists and smokes, with augmented medicines. Even if LeBov had been Thompson, it didn't mean that the medical work was a dead end. I'd given some thought to this. LeBov trafficked in long displays of falsity, perfecting his untruths, and I'd been listening to Rabbi Thompson speak from the Jew hole for years. If there was identity subterfuge at work, it did not automatically negate the recommendations of Thompson, whoever he really was.

Other mysteries remained. I had yet to determine what went into LeBov's speech-enabling grease. I was also unclear about the white collar at the Oliver's.

But in the low cupboards and drawers, in the cabinets mounted above a faded slate counter, I found no beakers, tubes, or burners. The raw materials for a chemical kit were absent. There were no raw materials for anything, no bulk drugs, no running water or salt bag. The medicine cabinet was empty of medicine, the refrigerator was tilted open, rimed with mold, gutted. Its power line curved around the back, with no sign of an outlet.

A drafting desk stood at the window, and in its drawers I found paper and the makings of a lettering kit. Rubber stamps, ink pads in different colors, and a set of baby sawtooth knives. Alongside these were a clutch of chrome pens, bottles of ink, an engraver's kit, a set of reference books labeled with a poison symbol, and, most interestingly, a scroll of self-disguising paper—paper with small windows factored in that could be enlarged with a dial—that allowed you to see only the script character you were presently reading, and nothing else, not even the word it belonged to. It broke the act of reading into its littlest parts, keeping understanding at bay.

Smallwork.

Unless you dialed open the window at your peril, this device revealed only part of a letter at a time, and even of that part it revealed so little that you might never guess that this mark on a page was participating in the larger design of an entire letter, which itself joined others in a set of interlocking designs called words, that would coalesce on the page to *mean* something, and thus bring a reader to his knees. This paper let you forget all that.

I sat down and fiddled with the apparatus, trying it out on whatever text I could find. Such redactions would keep my own work from poisoning me. If I desired, with the self-disguising paper, I could write with the perfect impassive remove that would keep me detached from the very thing I was writing. I'd have full deniability.

Elsewhere in the desk were some retired alphabetical designs, produced perhaps by my predecessor.

I pictured a man with blackened limbs, sitting on the high stool with his stylus. Of course he died of his own work. One day he lets down his guard, forgets his language shield, starts looking through his alphabets, and they poison him.

The work he left behind came stuffed in a binder. Had any of it mattered to anyone at Forsythe, had it somehow transcended the limitations of our current repulsive alphabet, I figure I would have known—it would not be here, we would not be here—so this was failed work. But since it was failed work, I wanted at least not to repeat it, which meant I needed to study it, to understand what went wrong. And that struck me as problematic. Such work would take me days with the self-disguising paper, as if I needed to go thread by thread through a pair of trousers in order to determine that they were wearable.

To examine my predecessor's work I customized the pinhole device, scissoring a thumbprint-size divot from a page of cardboard, then running that cardboard over the materials inside the binder. And with that I toured through his written work, studying dissected parts, the spatter of letters, drops of what must have been his own blood mottled into the page.

Much of my time in those early days at the script design desk was spent creating inhibitors that would keep me from seeing what I was doing.

After some hours of scrutiny I concluded there was nothing here of any use, just examples from our own alphabet, fattened here and there, rendered so erratic that they looked like the lines of an EKG.

My predecessor was poor at his job. He seemed to have looked at our existing alphabet, decided that nothing was wrong with it, and, in fact, if only its parts were emphasized, bolded, the *A*s fattened, blackened, perhaps, and so on, then all of the sick fakers might finally fall at his feet and praise him.

Or perhaps my predecessor enjoyed sending obviously fatal scripts to the testing grounds. He could watch from his glassed-in perch as the English language quietly picked off test subjects one by one, eating away at everything crucial inside their heads until there was nothing left but mush.

That first day, after studying the examples left to me, I realized what I was meant to do here in my office with no trace of medical equipment: I was meant to test letters, alphabets, possibly engineer a script. I was meant to string together symbols that might be used as code, a new language to outwit the toxicity.

The solution is in scripts, don't you think?

Visual codes? Except not the ones we know?

Of course LeBov, then Murphy, had said this to me for a reason. And maybe this was it.

. . .

Outside, hordes of people sought entrance into Forsythe. A mob of bodies swelled before the gate as if suspended in emulsion. Some had covered their heads. The ones with kerchiefs looked like mummies floating at sea. Others were fitted with masks, dark scarves, some kind of putty that filled their eye sockets.

At the very back of the crowd, keeping their distance from the others, stood a group who had fashioned homemade tackle to defeat language sounds from penetrating their defenses. Headphones reinforced by wood, by metal disk, spread with a cream.

Elsewhere stood those who had dressed for the weather, as if waiting for the train to take them to work. Perhaps for them such defenses were futile, too much bother, an assault on their pride. They were born to language, to speak and to listen and to share what they felt and thought. If such activities would kill them, then so be it. They'd not debase themselves by wearing equipment that didn't even work.

These people, whose worlds had been suddenly sealed up by a sickness from language, who had been forced to cease all communication with their loved ones, their friends, strangers, and who now stood patiently outside hoping some answer was being devised in here: What might they say to each other if they were suddenly given a language that worked again?

30

At my desk each day I chased the notion that the alphabet as we knew it was too complex, soaked in meaning, stimulating the brain to produce a chemical that was obviously fatal. In its parts, in combination, our lettering system triggered a nasty reaction. If the alphabet could be thinned out, shaved down, to trick the brain somehow, perhaps we could still deploy this new set of symbols, or even a single symbol, the kind you hold in your hand and reshape for different meanings, for modest, emergency-only communications.

I decided to go all the way back to the first scripts. I had to rule out cuneiform, hieroglyphs, wedge writing. From the Egyptian I had to exclude the hieratic and demotic writings. It was impossible to be thorough, so I took shortcuts. Of the cuneiform I surveyed and dismissed were the Hurrian, Urartian, the Sumerian.

Each of these I re-created with meticulous examples and each of these was retrieved from my office by a technician, who came to my research floor in the afternoons with his medical bag to collect whatever specimens I had, all of which I created under cover from myself, in working conditions I thought of as *controlled ignorance*.

From my office the specimens were brought downstairs and readied for testing against people, people already shattered and near death, overexposed to the very thing I made more of every day.

And so my work began, ruling out approaches, touring through the history of letters and alphabets, borrowing liberally from incompatible scripts, inventing new ones, correcting mistakes burned into the old ones.

What the Pollard script could not do, neither could the script of Fraser. When I blended them it was worse, and when I crammed in the lettering from elsewhere—as with the Bamum script and the script from Alaska, whose characters I sought to flatten, because a central bone could be amputated from these scripts and they would collapse into rumpled shapes—the mixture was likewise noxious.

Did the language itself matter? Was ours exhausted and did an ancient one need to be revived, or were we bound to invent a new one, avoiding the perils of every language that has heretofore existed, I wondered.

Or was it the way that language was rendered, drawn, projected, *seen*. Had we tried everything possible in this realm? Was the delivery system the problem?

To test this I created white text on white paper, gray on gray, froze water into text-like shapes and allowed it to melt on select surfaces—slate, wood, felt—which it scarred so gently, you'd need a magnifying glass to spot the writing.

I tried pointillizing type, whitening or darkening it, making a scattered dust of it on the page, then blowing that dust free with a bellows until it could only be read under blue light. I tried copying it on the machine until the duplication rendered it ghosted and pale. The usual distortions, obvious, of course, and all failures.

If we hid the text too much, it could not be seen. If we revealed it so it could be seen, it burned out the mind. No matter what. To see writing was to suffer.

Strictly to rule out surface as a factor, I wrote on clay, I squeezed water onto wood using a dropper. Onto foam I poured channels of fluid, then hardened that foam with hot air. The paper I used was baked, bleached, soaked in lye. I ordered paper made not just from cotton and linen, but wool, the wool shorn from whatever was still out there, the world I was now protected from inside Forsythe.

From my window I saw no animals. I had a pair of binoculars, and when I was tired of the detached work of language creation I zoomed in on the hills of Rochester, hoping to see something.

Oh, I saw nature during this surveillance, obscene degrees of it. The binoculars magnified the catastrophe. I saw indecent splurges of beauty as summer tore open huge holes in the earth, from which came forth a sickening march of every kind of plant, as if the suddenly stifled world of people left more room for nature to fill, which it fucking well was going to do.

A paper of silver was produced for me, upon which letters were raised only through application of a light wand. A birch paper dipped in copper appeared in my materials box. Across its face I rubbed some salt. I scripted with salt on black felt, sprinkled salt over a twisting wooden model of block text, mounted on a wire like a nursery mobile, upon which the salt pooled in hills, creating the ephemeral shape of letters.

With stones I rubbed text away from paper, with sticks and clay bark and pastel markers I tested how much I could cover text without fully hiding it, and whether the covering mattered, being sure our test subjects would be shown plain blocks of color alongside shades that hid writing beneath.

I shaped letters with yarn, hieroglyphs with yarn, arranged yarn in the minimal spatter of contemporary shorthand. With a tweezers I laid down a vertical script of yarn, hung yarn from wire so it draped just so, and with jets of air blew the yarn into letter shapes as it swayed. Or so I surmised, for I did not look at the device myself. With yarn I wrote full sentences in the Coptic alphabet, the Indus script, Linear A and B, all proven toxic already, all capable, in blocks and paragraphs, to generate sickness—micro coma, paralysis—in the reader, but then I tugged each end of the yarn on these sentences until the words pulled long. I tugged on the yarn and documented each stage until the yarn was pulled so taut, it stood out in a straight line and could never be mistaken for language.

The results you already know. We took this work to our subjects, then stood to watch from the observation deck. If it was indoor work, the work of reading, we assembled the material in sealed-off rooms, into which a subject was brought, shown a chair, left alone.

The materials were bound, sealed in foil.

To be thorough, we tested on men and women alike, young and old, sick and well. There was a healthy supply of subjects on hand. People lined up for this work. They volunteered, fought to be first, scratched at each other without mercy, as if they'd been profoundly misled about what waited for them inside Forsythe.

Which of course, well, they had.

From my window I saw them, and from the observation booth I saw them, and sometimes I didn't need to see them at all. I could stay at my desk and picture the sad readers being led into the testing area, strapped to the medical monitors. I could picture exactly how they would react. The work was foregone. To see it, to confirm it, was only a waste of time. I would know if something actually worked. The news would come fast. Or perhaps, if I ever did develop a script that could be read without sickness, restoring language to our fine species, I wouldn't be so quick to share it with the good people of Forsythe.

Perhaps such an invention, kept private, was just what I needed to find my leverage.

31

At Forsythe one worked, one ate, one rested, and on occasion one consensually fucked a stranger, an arrangement that produced merely a pinhole of joy. Beyond that entertainment was limited, at least for my class of researchers, since our appetites were highly regulated. We were under shield. Our health was a priority.

Health. Perhaps that wasn't what people with stiff, shadowed faces really had, whose tongues had atrophied. People unable to look at each other. Out of shame or fear or maybe finally a true loss of interest. If we looked away from each other in the halls, it was mostly because we'd seen enough. Other faces were just uglier parts of the landscape inside of Forsythe. And people might have hurried past you, but soon they seemed transparent.

When I wanted to see children I watched old television shows, the comedies.

A recreation room near the observation deck was furnished with a low couch, and if the room was empty I sat down when the workday ended and enjoyed the shows. They were edited now, the contamination sucked out of them. I could watch without fear. Oh, mercy. The cleanser at Forsythe had swept through these shows and smeared over the faces of the actors with his blurring tool. I pictured a man waving a wet, foaming broom, spewing a clear lather over people's heads, since feature recognition was generating too much toxicity in our volunteers. But even with their smoothed-over faces you could still see the young people tear around the artificial interiors of the TV studios, and in place of the dialogue these children hurled at each other, and the voice-overs that must have once straitjacketed the action, the technicians had looped in a sonorous, low-toned music, which sometimes made it seem that the little blond-headed children spoke a language not of words but of some intricate beeping songbook, a sonar for animals.

I relaxed with a bowl of clear soup, settled deep into the cushions, and for those hours I could almost feel like I was home with my family enjoying a night of television. Each evening over soup the television children—their faces swept into drain-like puckers of flesh—performed the archetypal behaviors. They danced, drove cars, dug a terrific, wet hole in a yard, accompanied an artificial wolf on a perilous adventure, or stood in place and probably said funny things to each other. They gathered in their smart outfits, the crisp white shirts and ties, holding stubby, flesh-colored canes, sometimes raising them as weapons, cocking their heads at each other. This kind of thing sometimes amounted to an entire episode of a comedy, a milling crowd of young people doing things with their faces and heads.

I soon tired of this style of entertainment. It began to stand in for the memories I had of home, and I did not want those disturbed. Instead of Esther at the state fair holding a barbecued turkey leg that she could neither eat nor surrender to me, since she was so proud to be in possession of such a gigantic animal part, I now pictured a television actor licking an ice-cream cone so roughly that the ice cream plopped on the ground, whereupon a legless elf riding in a low cart zoomed in, scooped up the half-melted ball of ice cream, and raced away. Even the elf's face was muddied at the features, spackled smooth. Instead of the laugh track one presumed would accompany such an accident, droning notes would pour out, a blizzard of dissonance. I lacked the discipline to refuse these images as they appeared to me alone in my bed, hours later. I allowed them to hijack my mental space and hardly fought them off. It was easier to let them play on, endlessly, and such was the material that frequently sent me into spells of anxious, restless sleep.

But in bed at night, rarely, these television images expired and a mental vacancy settled. Suddenly there was nothing to think of, nothing to see, nothing to feel, as if the reception had failed. There was room for me to will my own thought, my own memory, and I would hurriedly try to call up something unique about Esther.

A vacuumed space would appear at first, a howling little hole, but if I strained and brought all of my resources to bear on the matter, I could piece together a fractured puzzle, a child's drawing she had made of herself, a photo collage scissored apart and glued back with the prismatics of a ransom note. It was always shards. If I managed to conjure what mattered to me, what she genuinely looked like, I could only ever picture Esther with that awful blurred face of the television children, the sharp green speckling of her eyes wiped in streaks, the flushed color of her lips leaking upward from her mouth through her cheeks and forehead, a swirl of colors clouding her face. If I was lucky enough to picture her face, it smudged in my mind, as if, even in the past, *even when I knew her*, she wore a stocking over her head and I never once saw my daughter's face for what it really was.

32

After television I cast around for a sexual partner and these were usually available at the coffee station.

I had a favorite, although I don't care to admit it. In my mind I called her Marta. Sometimes, when I thought about her during working hours, I spelled her name phonetically, in Chinese, using the Soothill Syllabary. Some of the dummy texts I wrote in the Phags-pa script were addressed to Marta or documented some pleasing feature of hers.

Marta was wiry, severe. Beneath her skin was the faintest grid work of blue-colored veins that fell short of forming a picture of something I could never quite name.

In bed Marta and I were each impassive and facially bland in the extreme, as if we were competing with each other in the washing of windows. It took effort to control one's face so totally while fucking, to disable one's gestures and reactions, and it was not long before I was put in mind of the dead, just dead people, people who had died but who somehow had managed to start fucking each other, not because they still lived, but because this is what the dead did. This is what it was like with Marta. She had died, and then I had died, and then the two of us, in our dead world, had found a way to join parts, a grim and dutiful task, a collaboration of the dead on becoming slightly more dead with each other, this to be achieved only by deadly fucking until we turned blue and gasped with exhaustion, careful not ever to look at each other's dead faces.

Marta and I collaborated on rapid-fire release, a sprinting frenzy of goal-oriented sex. We chose not to kiss, but sometimes we held hands. Not for tenderness, I don't think, but for balance. That's why we sometimes needed to connect our nonsexual parts.

Sometimes it wasn't Marta whose shoulder I tapped at the coffee station, and I had to make do. I'd walk off with whoever it was and then see Marta not noticing or not caring as she did the same. I could always rely on her to project no response about an encounter. Sometimes it was Emily, or Andrea, or Linda I tapped, and off I went with them, and once it was Tim. I didn't care. It wasn't making love, it was making do. And I made do as a matter of course, often toward the end of the week, after a fit of the faceless television in the lounge. It didn't matter. In private quarters we dropped our robes and transacted with legal precision, as if we were performing light surgery on each other's genitals, the most delicate cuts, masturbating against the sweaty obstacle of another person, hoping to raise the difficulty of self-release.

We may as well have withdrawn my emission by syringe. The glow of orgasm was so vague, I experienced it as a theoretical warmth in the adjacent wall, as something atmospheric nearby that I could appreciate, but that I myself barely noticed. When I reached climax with Marta, I felt the material vacate my body, which counted for something, but the accompanying gush had departed, relocating off-site. It might as well have been happening to someone else. Perhaps it was.

But as detached as the Marta sessions were, I did prefer them to the solo work. Alone I raised no boner, even when I wanted release before sleep, when a cold, leaky emission was what I craved in order to break my seal with the day and let me think that something different was waiting for me tomorrow. I thought too much of home, and home was not a thought that carried with it the slightest erotic possibility. In fact, it only served to repel it. Home provided a sound defeat of the erotic, a complete and final stifling of it. In bed, alone, I may have approached myself with seductive touch, but it seemed only to trigger a rush of vivid imagery, imagery I myself had lived through, which may as well be called memory, the vilest stuff. The result was that I fell asleep holding my cold penis, missing my wife and daughter.

33

At Forsythe there was little news of the outside world, because the outside world had slowed to a freeze. Most of what happened elsewhere happened silently, underground, far enough out of sight that unless you saw it for yourself, it probably happened in your imagination.

What there was to know could be seen on surveillance monitors throughout the suite of leisure byways on the Forsythe laboratory mezzanine.

Footage came in of some settlements overseas. A cinema of the perished. From Denver also came film. Grown men locked under glass in a bleached field. On some rocky coast a houseboat of old people tied off to a dock, hoping they wouldn't be noticed, shouted into the cold water. The film out of Florida was so finally blackened, no shapes bled through.

On the monitors you could see children on horseback in the Catskills, dragging audio sleds. Faces brilliant and large, the happy people we once were. By now I'd gotten used to the button mouths on grown men, eyes crowded in close as if for warmth. It was too much to see a face so large, a child with feelings that could not be concealed. I preferred the new smallness that better hid the insides of people. Insignificant faces that bore no message. Another house with the lights out.

The strategies of the speechless were obvious. There was the strategy out to sea. The strategy in the mountains. Overseas the strategy was similar, but fire seemed more frequently involved. Films from there were burnt or films were blank or the films only showed water in looping reels that never seemed to end. If this was a catastrophe, many parts of the world stubbornly showed no sign of it.

A project was under way in Montana, copied in the Dakotas, in a sandy stretch of what looked like Utah. Corridors of speech ignited by children would block the passage of the older weaklings. Telephone poles and electrical towers were pressed into service to keep the vocal weapon in play. Speech was routed out loud from every kind of vertical structure, pinged across wilderness coordinates so no space was left silent.

Beneath these channels of speech were the most vicious accumulations of salt.

Too often the footage revealed some badly swaddled survivor caught out in the language. If you watched all night you could see him starve.

Sometimes after working hours a small-faced scientist stood staring up at one of these news monitors, so riveted in his vigil that you had to step around him on your way to the coffee cart.

Finally among the speechless there was the strategy of the tents. In every location tents in circus colors had been erected over the ground, strung up from trees. In line at th[illegible]cloth doorways of these tents stood the speechless, and one at a [illegible]ntered. Five minutes, ten minutes inside, sometimes longer. Y[illegible]t to see their throes, their fits of expiration. They departed on [illegible] covered in a sheet. Sometimes uncovered. A team of voluntee[illegible]tretchers to a field and rolled them over a hole until the stretc[illegible]ght again.

These were the mercy tents. [illegible]le heard some last song, whatever they chose to dial up, a[illegible]wn they went to those sounds. A strategy of acoustical expir[illegible]de by language. Mercy was right. The tents were clearly a kind[illegible]e who remained. No one was forced in. On the contrary, pe[illegible]ought to get inside first. And when a funeral field had filled, the mercy tents were struck and dragged away. Audio equipment pulled alongside by wagon. A jukebox of words to die to.

I had to believe that LeBov, if he was even here, wanted us to see what had become of our peers in the world outside.

If I were in line at a mercy tent, it would be Rabbi Burke I'd most want to hear. Burke or something closer to home. A final message from

Claire or Esther, if I had any recordings. I would have liked to have heard their voices again.

Of the footage shared with us in the corridor, one only rarely saw evidence of the child quarantines where our children lived. The quarantines had evolved into defended settlements, but it didn't take much to keep us out. Loudspeakers on poles, broadcasting the famous old speeches, the fairy tales, radio serenades. It was a hissing wash of poison to traverse, and unless you'd rendered yourself deaf, you didn't get far inside such sound. You stumbled, fell, and probably could not even crawl away. Speech at that volume flashes out deep into the woods, a murmur line. The new maps would be blackened with them.

Some lonesome fathers and mothers tried to penetrate the quarantines, shielding their soaked faces, burrowing in. Individual missions, no doubt. Projects of intimacy. Every so often a dark shape streaked across a field, pierced the sound barrier that blasted an impermeable language to prevent intrusions by the speechless, and disappeared into the darkness of a quarantined neighborhood. What these people did when they got through was not available. How they survived was not available.

Even a camera had not lasted in one of these places for long. Recording devices were discovered and smashed, but that was only a matter of time. Cameras were too obvious. They needed to send not a device inside, but a *person*, one of their own, and that person would be very young, well trained, and entirely hostile to the locals.

Somewhere at Forsythe, *if they knew what they were doing*, if this place was being run by someone who was thinking clearly, working to outsmart the dilemma, they were raising their own children. It sounds like a fictional conceit, the idle imaginings of a culture unimpressed by its own reality, but it would have been one of the first ideas to try. And once, as they say, *the asset had matured*, the asset would be released into the world loaded with enough misinformation to be dangerous. First stop, the quarantines. Project, fucking overthrow. Project *coup*. This work was a given. Perhaps that seems far-fetched. It actually is far-fetched. Which, in my mind, made it all the more likely. As of last December, the far-fetched had pretty much come nigh.

Children, after all, were the ultimate asset.

This would turn out to be true in ways I could never have predicted.

. . .

On the last monitor of the corridor, a lone black-and-white unit that hung at face level, one could sometimes find footage taken from inside the quarantines. When it flickered on it attracted the interest of most of the loitering scientists, who would crowd the set and try to see.

One's first assumption of a child-run community, supervision-free, calls up wolflike youngsters crawling through dirty hallways, eating each other's torsos with lazy relish. But the evidence I reviewed presented a subdued crowd. The children, in the footage we had, their faces turned bland by the editor, had set a long table with plates. They raced across a room, bringing supplies to this table, then sat down to eat. But with their features smoothed over they seemed to be spooning food into the blurry holes of their necks.

In an outdoor scene, captured from what seemed to be an upstairs window of a house, a formation of children moved on the street in the regimented patterns of an old-fashioned dance.

At times the children clustered so closely together, it was as if they'd become one body, swaying over the floor. Why they kept huddling so close together was unclear to me. To the unspoken dismay of my colleagues, I would get right up to the monitor so the heat of it bathed my face, and I'd wish I could clear away the fog from the children to see what it was they were feeling as they clustered against each other like that.

Without sound, celebration and grief look nearly the same.

The background of this imagery had been scrubbed, censored. Instead of the hills and trees that loomed behind them, or even the other houses, the scenery had been pixilated. Someone didn't want us to know where this was, and the children were meant to be shown playing or dancing in the street as though that street was suspended in space. But something gave away their location, and I stopped often when this scene was playing to confirm my suspicion.

On the asphalt, in a pattern at the feet of the children, were the cold mesh bars of shadow that could only have come from a signature electrical tower anchored to a slope not so far away from our old Jewish hole.

I think I knew exactly where those children were, and it was just blocks from my old house.

Even so, what did this mean? It meant nothing. I could not share it, I could not go there, and after watching this loop too many times it began to bore me, even as I sometimes thought the loop kept changing. I knew there was a quarantine in Montrier, because it was forming when I left, and our little town, with its valley on one side and the great hill behind it, offered natural protection. But this footage, from the looks of it, might have been taken years ago.

I wanted to pass it by, duck the dull high monitors, ignore the face-level screen, even if the crowd of scientists suggested there might be new footage streaming through. I wanted to ignore these diversions and move directly to the coffee cart, where the relief and comfort and, if necessary, savagery, were far easier to regulate.

If I got to the coffee cart early enough, I could tap Marta, retreat to one of our rooms for a transaction, then be back at the cart before the last person had been tapped, and there I could tap again and retreat to my room for a second round of intimacy, to wipe up any needs I'd not soothed the first time out.

But on harder days in my office, after watching from the observation deck as my work was placed before some crowd of subjects, who at once fell to fits on the floor, who did not recover even when the offensive material was removed, and who continued in mute throes of agony as I returned to my desk and picked up on yet another dead-end script that was sure to fail, I had needs that sex with Marta only antagonized when the working shift finished. On those evenings, when I passed this corridor through the spotlights shed by the high monitors, and then that white cone of face-level light at the end, I did feel compelled to study this imagery for a familiar landmark, some sign of home, or, and this I hoped for most stupidly, and most desperately, evidence that Esther, older now, meaner, stronger, nicer, I did not *know*, might have lodged herself among these strange, faceless children and might have decided to place herself in front of the camera, so her father, wherever he was now, might see her and might, if he was any kind of human person, do whatever he possibly could to get her out of there.

34

Weeks passed like this. If LeBov was here, I did not see him.

I did my work and fed the material to the technicians, who came to my office with a bucket to collect what I'd done. That's what the work I gave them amounted to: slops. In the courtyard men and women fell unconscious, turned into gazeless creatures. Some of them were sick because of alphabets I made. I raised a sparse beard on my face and I learned to stare between the people I saw.

At work I bent yet harder to the task, determined to rule out anything, however archaic or difficult or obscure, that had once let people connect.

Rebus writing, rune writing, pictograms, they all failed.

Administrative script, scripts of love, the scripts used to conceal secrets and deflect attention. All of the specialty languages I tried. I tried the languages of complaint, of apology and denial. I wrote out simple sentences, hiding my own words with the self-disguising paper. By design I wrote sentences filled with errors, sentences afflicted with inconsistencies of tense and tone. Sentences of poor taste, good taste, no conspicuous taste at all. Grammatical rules, rules of usage, rules governing rhythm and silence, these I broke hard. I used a conventional Roman alphabet but spelled everything wrong. Would it matter? I tweezed letters from words, obliterated vowels, used only vowels, repurposed a single vowel, *O*, to stand in for all of them, to give air to the words, a universal breathiness from a single source. Let them all drink from the fat *O*. And when *O* didn't work I tried the others, to be thorough, but just as *O* failed, of course the others failed, too. *Of course* is the operative term here. Not once did I believe that through lettering alone we'd reach people without harm.

Through lettering alone. Good fucking luck.

I tried everything but the Hebrew alphabet. I knew it was poison, too, but I didn't want this script to cause pain. *Lift not the language into the service of bloodshed*, Burke had said. Or, *these words will open up holes in men*. I would not be the person to pass scripts of these symbols into the courtyard, where seizures would occur. But though I never sent down work that explored the Hebrew possibility, I did make latex letters in the Hebrew script that inflated, once I'd sewn up the sutures, into fat, black clouds. Little floating tumors that were language-free, hovering over my desk until I pierced them. And when I did that, they fell into shredded piles and I swept them into a drawer.

Of course I tried codes. In modern Roman letters I encrypted a suicide note, some gentleman's last words, with the Caesar cipher. From there I re-created what I could remember from historical texts—the Gettysburg Address was one—and fed them into simple substitution ciphers, homophonic coding, and a modified Vigenère cipher. If this worked, it would mean that our own scripts were too obvious and needed to be concealed, encrypted. But it didn't work.

To readers not versed in the code, this presented like pulp. No sense could be had unless the subjects sat down with a Caesar wheel to decipher what I'd done, and we allowed our martyrs no equipment, let alone enough time to drag meaning out of the ultra-cloaked messages before them.

But it didn't matter. *Sense* wasn't what was getting them, the immediate impact of comprehension in the brain. It may have been meaningless, but they were sick regardless, even sicker than before.

The progression of our shared disability defied the going modes of understanding.

So I tried different colored papers, clear papers, walls, cloth, skin. I ran troubleshooting on backgrounds, which interested me, the visual phenomena that stood behind the text in question, to determine how the backgrounds to our written language either support or defeat the toxicity. What kind of air masks a language, and does that air matter?

We lacked the equipment for a smoke machine that might be fitted with a text filter, through which legible typefaces could float out and dissipate in time. A self-eroding writing, a writing that dissolved when it was seen. But I didn't need to make skywriting to know how we would react to it. With cotton balls I tufted up letters, glued them to cork. I acquired an LED board, rigged it to scroll words, to blink the scripts that I commanded.

These light boards not only failed, they brought on new symptoms, triggering a palsy in our subjects, sometimes rendering them moribund, twitching on the testing-room floor until we unplugged the board.

A writing might be made of air alone, I reasoned, colored air, the brittle air in zero-humidity climates, fur or animal hair that's been pulverized by mortar or woven into strands, any kind of cloth, any kind of object, or ink alone, ink on paper, ink delivered by means of stylus. It was worrisome how bottomless my project was. For a stylus I defaulted to reed. But I also used pens, pencils, knives, my own finger dipped in pigment, and a lead nail for scratching over glass. The ancient tools were there for me, dragged from some useless museum, no doubt—*everything at your disposal, sir*, the technicians never said—and I used them, but to use them convinced me further that this direction was doomed.

After every failure I returned to my desk more certain that scripts were finished. No matter how I ornamented them, in the courtyard the result was the same. Months of this confirmation took place, played out against a range of test subjects. The work that I produced, the letters and codes and then the aggregates and compilations of these, sometimes brought to further order and logic by the Forsythe technicians, was nothing but a weapon.

When I looked from the window at the crowd outside Forsythe, clamoring without a sound to be let in, I felt wildly blank, unresponsive. They were desperate for admission but too cautious to riot, too scared, because it'd be so easy to douse them all with speech, to drive them away with a steady broadcast of the simplest words. In days, maybe weeks, they'd be processed through the system, and they'd sit before something I had written, and all I would have to say to them, after all of the effort they went through, was *The quick brown fox jumps over the lazy dog.*

What was compelling them to come here in droves like that, to lay themselves open to such rank poison? What on earth, I wondered, was misleading all of these language martyrs into thinking there was something inside of Forsythe that would deliver them?

35

In his early writings, Thoreau called the alphabet the saddest song. Later in life he would renounce this position and say it produced only dissonant music.

Letters, Montaigne said, are a necessary evil.

But are they? asked Blake, years later. I shall write of the world without them.

I would grow mold on the language, said Pasteur. Except nothing can grow on that cold, dead surface.

Of words Teresa of Avila said, I did not live to erase them all.

They make me sick, said Luther. Yours and yours and yours. Even sometimes my own.

If it can be said, then I am not interested, wrote Schopenhauer.

When told to explain himself, a criminal in Arthur's court simply pointed at the large embroidered alphabet that hung above the king.

Poets need a new instrument, said Shelley.

If I could take something from the world, said Nietzsche, and take with it even the memory of that thing, so that the world might carry on ever forward with not even the possibility that thing could exist again, it would be the language that sits rotting inside my mouth.

I am a writer, said Picasso. I make my own letters.

Shall I destroy this now, or shall I wait for you to leave the room, said his patron to Kadmos, the reputed inventor of the alphabet.

Kadmos is a fraud, said Wheaton. Said Nestor. Said William James.

Do not read this, warned Plutarch.

Do not read this, warned Cicero.

Do not read this, begged Ovid.

If you value your life.

Bleed a man, and with that vile release spell out his name in the sand, prescribed Hippocrates.

No alphabet but in things, said Williams.

Correction. *No alphabet at all.*

36

Sometimes an assembly was called, heralded by a long, dissonant bell.

Here the researchers, scientists, administrators, and the animal handlers who worked their tests in the walled-off southern wing could settle into the surgical theater and view the latest work on display, the experiments with comprehension, the medical tests.

Usually I sat through these assemblies inside a deep facial paralysis. The gatherings had a grueling familiarity to them, and to me they smelled of sport and torture.

Onstage we'd see language spoken through every kind of contraption on the mouth: filters, dampeners, horn-shaped protrusions that must have addressed an acoustical toxicity and turned subjects into ragged, costumed clowns, although by the results witnessed at assembly, they did not soothe the acoustical toxicity, but inflamed it instead.

We observed the testing of a whistle language, delivered through the gashed-open faces of mannequins. Subjects could tolerate, and moderately comprehend, the signals, but when they were forced to whistle, employing a rigorous system of codes, they declined rapidly, showing clear signs of toxicity.

Gesture was tested, mostly on the sick, to see how rapidly they would expire if exposed to unceasing and explicit mime.

Again a mannequin was commanded by remote control to produce the behavior.

We saw every kind of semaphore, like a silent and benighted exercise class conducted by the dead, from the arm-waving style, to be viewed at a great distance, to the single finger-sign languages developed on the middle north wing of the lab.

We watched through perforated masks, distributed upon arrival, lest some of the sickening stuff leak into our senses. Of what we saw, we saw as little of it as we could, which was more than enough for me.

With bloody persistence researchers tested how complex a language of touch could really be. Technicians sat with test subjects and, wearing gloves tipped in abrasives, tapped out rudimentary communications, of distress, of commerce, of desire.

The subjects, reclining in their wheeled hospital beds on the dark, oak stage of the theater, generally endured this work, but only at first. And when they did not endure it, when they made profound protests to the material that was clearly undoing them in every significant way, we were marched from our seats, led from the hall, and corralled as usual back to our offices.

Everything I'd seen so far had prepared me to pay as little notice as I might during these mandatory sessions. And this is right about when a new paradigm was presented to us at assembly, and everything changed.

It was late in my stay in the research wing, when I had already ruled out the efficacy of ancient scripts, had sent reams of alphabets downstairs for toxicity testing, only to have them return in the sleeves reserved for failed research, and I had moved on to the equally unpromising grotesqueries of modern script.

It was a morning around that time when the long bell sounded and we took our seats in the surgery. The lights dimmed. Onto the stage came an old man, his head draped in testicle skin. When he rubbed it and blinked into the lights I saw it was merely his face, beset with a terrible, taffy-like droop. I did not want to reflect what sort of experiments, or what sort of life, had led to possessing a face like that. Behind him wheeled a creaky IV cart.

It was pushed by a child, who was tethered to the thing itself.

I would say that a hush fell at the sight of this man, or more correctly at the *uncommon* sight of a child, especially one who did not seem to be under guard, but a hush had already fallen. We were steeped in hush, drowning in it. The room was sickeningly quiet. I knew nothing of my colleagues, saw almost nothing of their robed and lab-coated bodies, and could detect little from their impassive, gestureless faces. The lack of speech, the absence of language to build us into full people, had turned us into a kind of emotive cattle. Perhaps a raucous inner life produced shattering notes inside us, but with no extraction tool, no language to pry it free and publicize it, even if it was moronic, one sensed that the whole enterprise of consciousness had suddenly lost its way. Without a way to say it, there was no reason to even think it.

Our faces, without the exercise of speech, had atrophied into slack, piggish masks.

Some of us, I would guess, had not spoken in months, more.

That morning a sheet of glass descended from ropes over the stage, walling off the man and the child.

Once they were enclosed, the man looked up, having apparently heard sounds. He studied the ceiling and then, to what seemed like his own astonishment, he began to speak.

There was nothing to hear. All sounds were sealed from us. On the whole it was an unremarkable spectacle, except for when it came to how this feat of nontoxic language exchange was being achieved.

Our jaws were supposed to drop in amazement that an old man could speak. A year ago none of us would have cared. We would have run screaming from what this man had to say. No doubt he'd have trafficked in platitudes, the most killing forms of banality. He'd use speech to tyrannically reaffirm what we all already knew and we'd only be tortured when he spoke. At the very least we'd have been deaf to his message, and even if he lay bleeding at our feet we'd have stepped over him on the way to our group picnic, where we'd feed each other sweaty cubes of honey rolled in salt. Now we sat in our important seats and were meant to marvel over this reinvention of the wheel. Not even the whole wheel, but only a lug nut of it.

And I'll admit that it was impressive. He spoke with no apparent agony, without the clenched pain and contortions every single one of us expected to see. Put him in a tuxedo, I thought, and he's *almost* a gentleman.

On a side-mounted video monitor, the spectacle unfolded in close-up, but what the camera seemed most interested in was not the man or the child, but the apparatus that held the transparent business that I had thought was the man's IV bag.

Indeed it was a bag of *fluid*, but it dangled from the little neck of the child, puckering from his skin into the tube.

From this it flowed directly into the man.

Allowing him to speak, one presumed.

A fluid drawn directly from the child.

Like most important solutions throughout history, this one seemed inevitable. Our own dear children, immune to the malady that is killing us all, must have within them a resistance that, *with a long enough needle*, our best scientists should be able to extract. Finding such a solution was just a matter of time.

Everyone will soon come over to this approach, LeBov had said to me that freezing night back in the neighborhood.

It needn't cause any trouble. In the spirit of science.

After the assembly, the glass sheet lifted and the man shuffled from the stage. Were we meant to applaud or weep for him? We did neither.

The child had to be carried off, but first they threw a sheet over him. The tube that joined them was severed by one of the technicians. It was too far away for me to determine if this liquid was clear or dark. But it hung in a clump from the severed tube, suggesting viscosity. Working quickly, they squeezed the remaining stuff into a vial. Whatever it was they'd withdrawn from this child, they didn't want to waste it.

Assemblies after that featured similar spectacles, and this fluid factored as the golden constant. Whenever it appeared, frequently under guard, always sourced by some oddly well-dressed child who seemed styled for his first music recital, we were supposed to leap from our chairs and rush the stage in order to drink the slimy dregs of it from the tube. The child was never the same one, though sometimes the man was. He was a tired specimen and his face, as I've said, hung badly off his head. But as we moved into summer and the uncirculated air of Forsythe began to stink of blackened medicines, this man, who early on seemed to have been thieved from the morgue and filled with a last-ditch animating dose of adrenaline, began to look functionally dead, dead in all the measurable ways. When the serum was pumped into him he bled freely from his ear. They began to plan for this in advance, packing gauze on the bad side of his head. But even that darkened quickly and slid sometimes down his face during the presentations.

I suppose it wasn't so terrible to become a guinea pig during your last days.

It wasn't hard to piece together what they were showing us. The assemblies never featured text, we were never addressed. If there was sound, it was the kind of dissonant code music that was precisely designed to evoke nothing.

In most of the presentations the subjects were plugged into something, a child, a bag, or a machine offstage, perhaps, suggested by the medical tubes snaking under the curtain.

They clobbered us with the obvious. Okay, I get it, I wanted to say. You've struck gold in those kids. But until they released this fluid into our own labs, until they even *gave* us a fucking operational lab with actual equipment, what were we supposed to do about it, and how impressed was I supposed to be that you needed to be fed by a live connection to a living human child in order to cough out a few unimportant words?

Unplug one of these motherfuckers, I thought. Unplug him from the child and let him run around barking his silly words. Then maybe I'll be impressed.

37

It happened pretty soon after that.

I had finished work early and was on my way to the entertainment suite. Perhaps I'd stare blankly at some faceless television until the coffee cart opened, at which point I'd drop a tap on my partner. On days like this, Marta offered the most reliable respite from a sense of futility, and with Marta I'd never experience the shame of having confessed frustration or despair, or having confessed a single thing, because we did not speak.

Nothing had come of my projects today, as usual. More slogging, more obviously failed scripts, more redundant work that was doomed in advance. Yet I sat there and wrote the deathly language until my eyes watered with exhaustion and my back ached and I wanted only to tap Marta, then try not to drag her to the consort room, where we'd have our angry physical exchange and she'd stare with admiration, with admiration and awe, at something just beyond my face that I would never understand.

But none of that was to be tonight.

I took my usual route from the office to the mezzanine, following the brown hallways that had been scrubbed of every directional marker and now featured only windowless, oval doors every so often, behind which I never heard anything.

I must have been rounding a corner when a team of technicians walked out of one such room, quietly fell on me, covered my head with something hot, which was tied tightly at my neck, and dragged me into a room.

I was thrust into a darkness made swamp-like by my own breath, which steamed up over my face inside of what seemed like a woolen blanket.

Something heavy was dragged across the room, scraped the floor so violently it shrieked, and then I heard the clicks and manipulations of a machine. A fan switched on and a chill settled through the room.

Inside my hood I pitched my breath down over my chin to keep it from reeking up my space. Whoever the technicians were, they were breathing hard, and I registered a worrisome silence until one of them pressed his weight against me, removed some piece of my clothing, and brought a cool solution that felt like alcohol over my skin.

A sleeve was cut free of my shirt and I felt the tickle of a razor shaving the hairs of my forearm.

They were prepping me to receive an injection, and I waited for the sharp insult of a needle, but it never came.

Throughout my captivity I did not struggle. I went limp, tried to comply. But it was hard to comply when I didn't know what they wanted me to do.

And so I settled into the dark, felted cocoon they'd made for me, wondering why I'd been singled out for this molestation, and what kind of procedure was in store.

Nothing I'd done seemed to warrant the attention of anyone powerful. Most of my morning had been spent in futile paroxysms of invention, itself too strong a word. The work was a chore, but I forced myself to do it. After a quick breakfast of peaches at my desk, I'd looked into yet more defunct writing, undeciphered and disappeared scripts, scripts that had failed or been abused or misused or just gravely misunderstood.

I moved from Olmec to Meroitic. In Rongorongo I burned letters onto wood. Always throughout the testing of defunct scripts, I paired Roman samples as a control.

Then I stepped away from the visual side of scripting and began to wonder how content figured into the revulsion. Was our aversion to language based on what we said to each other: the cryptic things, the direct things, the disappointing things, the neutral ones? Was it because of what we didn't say? Had we failed to say or write something that would ensure our survival, and now this failure had grown too massive, become irreversible?

These questions I dodged. They were too big, too hard.

But more came. Was language rich in information, filled with verifiable detail and data, worse than language that lied? Which diction made us sicker? Could abstract language, the kind that skirted anything visual and posited ideas and qualifications over the concrete, be less harmful? Were expressions of love safer than threats?

Everything I produced and sent down to the yard for testing suggested that it was comprehension itself that we could no longer bear.

The days of understanding were over. The question I could not even formulate was this: What was it we were now supposed to do if it was medically impossible to even understand each other without a rapid, ugly sickness taking hold? This was not a disease of language anymore, it was a disease of insight, understanding, *knowing*.

I thought about all of this as I sat in a Forsythe room with a blanket over my head.

My captors pursued a soundless agenda. The room was chilly and smelled of nothing, and I had a sickening fear that whatever aggression they might have planned against me would be nothing compared to simply being abandoned there to expire under a blanket in a side room no one ever visited.

I resolved to make myself as quiet as possible, to silence my movements and breath in order to determine what was going on. I would *listen* my way out of this dilemma.

Then someone cleared his throat, unwrapped my hood.

Standing over me, holding the dark blanket, was the redhead LeBov. It looked like someone had vacuumed the extra flesh from his head and body. He didn't seem older so much as deflated. He smiled, as if our wonderful meeting had been scheduled long ago and now it had finally arrived.

LeBov helped me to a chair, slid me in, then took himself to the other side.

"You're looking . . . not so well," he said.

He was not supposed to be able to speak, and I was not supposed to be able to hear it. We were long past that. My face wasn't hardened so much as lifeless now, a phantom face where my real face once was.

I cringed as a reflex, at the sight of LeBov's mouth moving, waiting to feel the hot speech pour over me, tighten me into crippling spasms. I gripped my chair, braced as if a car was about to hit me.

But something else happened instead. Nothing. Like the night in the bushes when Esther marauded through, and LeBov filled my mouth with grease. I still felt the muscled roughness of speech, almost like a smoke too thick to inhale. But instead of a toxicity, it was cold and oily in the air.

I coughed, tried to swallow.

"You'll get used to it," LeBov said, bored. "Just keep listening. Let it take hold. It's fucking weird at first."

LeBov was right. As he spoke, his speech felt solid in the air. It seemed like I was trying to breathe underwater, and with concentration I could *barely* do it. I could allow his speech in and it would pose no danger.

I looked at my naked arm, which felt heavy and weak. They must have injected me after all. I wanted to say: But I never felt a needle go in.

"It's impressive, right?" said LeBov, noticing my amazement. "Those guys are good."

On my arm a cold bead of blood crawled out of the puncture. I stared at it as if it were a jewel. They'd shot me with something, and now I could speak, could listen again.

My first spoken words in months came out in a cracked whisper.

I said, "Can I ask to what do we owe this conversation?"

LeBov sat back in his chair, looked at me without disguising his excitement.

I found I knew the answer without his help.

"It's that stuff, right? The stuff you gave the old man up onstage?"

LeBov chuckled. "Yeah. We call it 'that stuff.' How do you like it?"

My voice came out weak. It did not sound like me. "So children are fueling this conversation?"

"This very one. Better make it count."

On the table LeBov had gathered some of my work, a stack of scripts, some of the 3-D models, slabs of stone. He made a show of looking through it, scowling at the sheaths of letters, squinting to communicate his displeasure. He passed through it so rapidly, and with such disdain, he could not possibly have given it the attention it deserved.

"What are you doing with this stuff?" he said. "It's ridiculous."

I'd never seen my work exposed like that, cut free of the self-disguising paper. It stunned me that we could spread it out on the table and not retch with illness. My technique was messier than I expected, incoherent in places, letters dropping off pages, failing to come together, breaking into pieces. Imperfections everywhere. I felt ashamed to see it unclothed like that. And yet I wanted to grab the materials from LeBov and rush back to my office. If I could take it all in, if I could *actually fucking look at my own work*, I might be able to really do something effective.

LeBov flipped through more of it and then pushed it all aside. "Are you serious? Do you honestly believe we haven't thought of this already? You're sitting here creating fucking *alphabets*? How small exactly is your mind?"

I tried not to look at him too closely. His teeth had the quality of fossils.

When I spoke my voice was quieter than his, less convincing.

"It's the work you seemed to want," I offered. "There's no equipment here, nothing. So I'm creating scripts, alphabets. You said yourself that the solution was in scripts, visual codes. *You* said that."

"Correction. *Murphy* said that. Slightly different person. Dead to me now, in any case. Along with his so-called *ideas*, thank god."

"Well, how would I know?" I said. "There's not exactly an open channel of communication. If I could get my gear, I think I could get back to some of the medical stuff."

"We have real doctors for that. We have people who actually know what they're doing. Your little purses of smoke, I popped them over my children's heads to make them laugh. Kids love their own little mushroom cloud. They're tchotchkes, and they stink. Seriously. They smell awful. That's probably why your house is still abandoned."

He checked his watch.

I wasn't sure how much more I wanted to say. This was the first conversation I'd had in months, and the muscles of my face had gone soft.

"Maybe I should give you a tour of the real research wing," said LeBov. "We should have 'Bring a Naïve Pretender to Work Day,' and then I'll let you check out the pros."

I did not respond. The antagonistic foreplay had lost its appeal. In my limbs, in my head, I felt the heaviness of what they'd shot me with. It was rough, unrefined, but I wished I could get my hands on it.

I had questions, too. How long did a dosage last? What were the side effects? What exactly *was* the fucking stuff, and . . . I didn't even want to think through this last question, but at what cost comes this serum? What does the extraction do to its . . . host?

LeBov held up one of my finer pages of cuneiform, some Presargonic panels I'd written about a poisoned body of water in the netherworld. Experimenting with one of my Aesop's templates.

"Has it occurred to you that these things are useless if people can't decipher them? You've given cuneiform to people who barely read English?"

"Yeah, that did occur to me. Right around the time that you were drawing fluid out of children's bodies."

"But you did it anyway? See it through to the end even if it's obvious?"

"Well, have you stopped to wonder why that very script, which you say they can't understand, is still making them sick? Isn't that a little bit curious to you?"

LeBov checked his watch again. He closed his eyes in some exaggerated show of irritation.

"Do you have any confirmation that we're even *showing* them your stupid alphabets? Have you verified that?"

I thought of my time on the observation deck, watching the subjects spoil in the heat, get carted off. Wagons of paper were brought to them, unloaded, shoved in front of their eyes, and they pored over it like dutiful patients, scrutinizing it until their vitals flared and someone called a code. This *was* my work that sickened them, even if I could not see it precisely. It must have been my work they saw. But I knew that I was never on-site confirming that, never actually down there to be sure. Such vigilance hadn't occurred to me.

It should have been a relief to discover, to even consider, that I had not caused more pain for all of those people.

But I somehow did not feel relieved.

. . .

LeBov stood up, pushed my alphabets into the trash. "C'mon," he said. "We're going for a walk."

He helped me up. I didn't realize I needed it, but I was unsteady, a bit nauseous once I got out of my chair. His hands under my arms felt like metal tongs. We'd be back soon and I'd feel better, LeBov assured me. There was something small he wanted to show me, something he thought might be of interest.

Into the halls of Forsythe we went. We climbed the ramp and came upon the assembly area, but this usually hectic space was empty. Everything was quiet.

We took the stairs to my wing. On the landing we stepped through the side door that brought us to the observation deck, where I'd only ever stood with crowds of other scientists, looking down at the testing below.

Again I saw no one, just the decontamination procedures outside in the courtyard, a man curled up under the harsh ministrations of a hose.

Here I tried to take a step that wasn't there and I stumbled. LeBov reached for me, but I fell, and for some reason I couldn't get my hands up in time.

My face smashed undefended against the floor.

I scrambled back up but wobbled, tipped, and fell again. The walls were spinning. Above me stood LeBov, studying me.

"That's something we're working on." LeBov stuck out his hand for me. "There are some balance things we need to tweak."

I got up without his help but as we walked to the observation deck I held his arm in case I fell again.

We were still alone. Since I'd left that room with LeBov we'd seen not a single person.

"Where is everyone?"

"I don't care for this place outside of lockdown. The bustle and whatnot. The human contact. I find it distracting. It's rather nice not to be seen, don't you think?"

It didn't really feel nice.

A trickle of blood fell from LeBov's nose and he caught it with a tissue. Then the tissue blackened, started to drip.

He laughed, his head tipped up to stop the blood, which ran from the tissue in a trail down his wrist, right under his shirtsleeve.

"C'mon," he said, through a bloody hand, "I want to show you something."

LeBov's hands and wrists, I noticed, had been badly burned. That would have been the gel from the listener he stole.

We took a hallway that I'd not seen open before, stepped into a side room that featured a narrow spiral staircase, and then descended several flights until the light from above shrank into a star before disappearing, shutting us in darkness. I hugged the railing, took small steps, and kept my eyes down. Something had scrambled my balance and I felt wrong in the head.

At the bottom of the stairs we went through a double door, moved down further hallways that at first I thought were painted brown, but when I came closer I saw that the walls themselves were glass, pressed dead against sheer cliffs of dirt outside. We were underground, in a basement corridor built into hard-packed earth.

LeBov opened a tall door and we stepped into a space that, at first, seemed entirely empty.

"Welcome home," he said, and he gestured me inside.

The room had no finished floor, just soil, with stone walls climbing several stories. In the center, lined with benches and some small generators, was a hole. A perimeter of klieg lights dumped a wretched blast of light down its center, so it looked lit from below. And from the mouth of the hole came the prettiest sight: a bouquet of bright orange cables as if retched up from the center of the earth itself.

I commanded myself to show no reaction.

They'd found themselves a Jewish hole, and it looked like they'd been working it hard.

LeBov said, "So what do you think?"

I moved to the rim of the hole, looked in. They'd roughed out scaffolding down there, reinforcing the crumbled sides of the hole with long, warped two-by-eights. A double-wide ladder, black handprints smeared on the rungs, disappeared deep into the pit, and a braid of extension cords passed the orange transmission lines on their way down.

Was there a hut over this hole once, before it became a high school? I looked over at LeBov, who allowed me my scrutiny. What a curious accident that they'd have one of these down here.

I made a point of showing no interest in the orange cables. I gave them no second look, did not stoop over them to even examine if the outlets had been converted to the Jewish standard. These were thicker than the cable in the ceiling of the recovery wing. Thicker, and there were more of them. As far as I was concerned, the cables were hiding in plain sight and it was perfectly normal for fat cables to pour from the earth from some unknown source very far away.

Under a tarp at our feet wriggled something that seemed to want to get out.

"Is that a balloon?" I asked.

LeBov paused, touched the tarp with his boot. "Not yet," he said.

In the space above the hole they'd carved out a few of the higher floors of the basement, vaulting the room into a huge atrium, but there were no windows.

One wall, however, was devoted to something I was careful not to look at too closely. It was a collection of listeners, perhaps forty of them, nailed to plywood. They differed in size and shape. Some glistened, others were shrunken and dry. They were lobes, or orbs, or limb-like. Most were deep brown in color. A rail at the top of the wall misted some fluid in a cloud that rained down over them, keeping them moist. Beneath each listener trailed a piece of thin, white cabling that joined in a fixture at the bottom of the wall and traveled over to a table covered in a black blanket.

The listeners pulsed generating a low, dark hum. On the top row, in the middle, was my very own listener, shriveled and pale, like an oversize raisin cast in cement.

I turned my back to it.

"Nice hole," I said.

"Right," agreed LeBov. "We think so, too."

I walked back to the door. "Can I return to work now?"

"Well, that's why I brought you here. What would you think about working here instead?"

"No thanks," I said. "I enjoy the view from my office. It's kind of dark in here."

I imagined this massive space filled with listener's gel, LeBov and me swimming around in it, trying to strangle each other before we suffocated and sank. It was like a vast, desiccated aquarium, the sort of space whose bottom surface should not be traversable on foot. And then there were the throbbing, brown listeners, like a collection of human livers. I wanted to get out.

I tried the door, expecting it to be locked, but it opened and we stepped back into the hallway.

LeBov was casual, as if he was asking me to join his softball team. "So will you help us?" he asked. "It could be an interesting project."

"I thought you had what you needed. You said that yourself. What you took from me when you left."

I remembered the punctured listener leaking down his wrists as he tried to wriggle through the hole. Along with his burns, it could have been a cause of the nosebleeds.

"Well, I thought so, too. But I didn't. Your listener has proven stubborn to us. That's why we need your help. The original owner of the thing, certain administrative rights, the ability to modify the property in ways we require. Something about you people is a catalyst."

"Us people. How frustrating for you to have something you don't control. But I'm not sure I understand. Why don't you force me?"

LeBov broke into a fit of coughing.

"That's a really good question," he said, when he'd recovered. "It's a pet topic of mine. Our studies show that coercion has a fairly poor track record. Otherwise, of course, we would."

"Then no, thank you. I do appreciate the offer, though."

"That's not the whole story," said LeBov, and I thought, *Too bad. It never is.*

"We saw what you did with that wire when you first got here, that little act of ventriloquism. That was of enormous interest to us and that's why we pulled you out of isolation. You channeled a prayer none of us had heard before."

"You were watching me?"

"Unfortunately, yes. And we've tried to duplicate your work, connecting wires to the mouths of Jews, to mannequins, to anyone, but no one else is *conductive* like you appear to be. Something about your mouth we'd like to study. And that prayer you were transmitting, that prayer doesn't even . . . exist. We can find no record of it. It's not a *real* prayer, which confirms to us that there's something out there that we need to hear more of. There's a territory of wisdom we don't own, and that's troubling. We need to get you connected in here."

"You want to nail me to your wall and use me as a listener?"

"Well, not if you don't want to."

"Good, because I don't want to."

LeBov checked his watch.

"Whoops. We'd better get you back."

This wasn't the last word on the hole, obviously. LeBov's mildness on the subject was unnerving. But he didn't bring it up again and he seemed in a hurry to get rid of me.

On our way back to the spiral staircase, LeBov stopped at a door and looked in the high window.

"What's in there?" I asked.

"Take a look," he said, standing aside.

Inside were children, seated in rows, like in a classroom, except this wasn't a classroom, it was some kind of hospital ward. The children were drawing, reading. Others stared at a television.

When I saw the medical carts, the tubing, a masked technician bending over one of his subjects, who smiled up at him as the needle was raised, I turned away and walked off. I wanted to get out of there, and I wasn't waiting for LeBov.

LeBov started laughing. A feminine laugh like a cat getting killed.

He fell into step with me, and we made our way back to the staircase.

"Shall I congratulate you?" I asked.

"You shall not, I fear."

LeBov *did* want to be congratulated. He seemed so proud, cheerfully indifferent to my outrage, almost pleased by it.

However they were harvesting their serum should not have mattered to me. But I had questions.

"And the test subjects. Why don't you give them this serum from the children?"

He laughed. "Test subjects? Are you fucking kidding me? Is that what you actually call them? We wouldn't waste it on them. It's too precious, too difficult to, uh, *make*."

LeBov narrowed his eyes.

"Well, why are they here?" I asked. "How do you get them to submit to these tests?"

I thought of the endless crowds, clamoring to be let into Forsythe.

"Your mind has been wasted on small questions. They *want* to be here. It's called choice. They come from all over and beg to be let in. We have a security issue, really. There are too many of them. If they weren't so collectively uninspired, so unspeakably"—he paused, searching for the right word—"*stupid*, they could launch a pretty effective attack on us."

"Right."

"Of course the pictures we've gathered of their *children* don't hurt. A photo of a child is such a strangely powerful tool. Family pictures are funny. Sometimes they are the most boring material on the planet. Literally. There is nothing that causes more agony than someone else's family photo. I weep with boredom at the sight of these things. They could almost be used as a medicine to cause indifference. And yet, if you show one of those very same photos to a parent who has, for the moment, *lost track* of that child, or even voluntarily surrendered that child for medical safekeeping on one of our busses, and you suggest, through mime, because language would fucking kill those miserable, anxious parents, that you might know where that child is, uh, *presently residing*, well then suddenly that photo has turned into what we call here an outstanding piece of leverage. Currency for the mute time. The new money. It's a pretty straightforward economy."

On our way up the staircase LeBov's nose started to bleed again, and as we hurried up the narrow passageway his breath grew wet and ugly. We stopped to rest and he coughed a slurry into his hands, mumbling something. Again I hugged the railing, shutting my eyes against the spinning walls, and followed.

I was released upstairs later that night, disoriented and hungry, as the last protection from the serum fizzed away. I found myself back in the land of the mutes and I was relieved.

Down on the mezzanine I raced to the coffee cart, hoping to find Marta, or anyone. There was no way I would be alone tonight. I would have tapped the old man from the tests if he'd have me. I would have led him to my room, peeled down his robe, and tried whatever I could get away with against his body until he dragged himself from me in exhaustion.

There was no one at the coffee cart. The scientists had paired off already. Tripled off. Gone back to their rooms to nurse their sense of specialness and to marshal every kind of argument for themselves that what they think, what they feel, has any value at all.

I returned to my room, closed the door, and suffered the long, violent seizure of alertness that had come to pass for another night of sleep. Waiting. Thinking. Not sleeping. Never really sleeping.

38

I avoided the observation booth after that. I did not like to join the other scientists for the afternoon stroll, the old thoughtful walk we took with our great brains towering over us, down our serious corridor that ended in glass, where we could watch the good people of Rochester bleed from the mouth, trembling with sobs, while they tried to endure exposure to our work.

Once I knew my scripts were pre-classified as doomed, never even shared in the courtyard, or, if they were, used on the test subjects merely to confirm a *previously held certainty*, a certainty that written language, no matter how inventively conceived or destroyed and then remade, could not safely be read again for very long by people over a certain age, I began to keep some experiments to myself, substituting credible symbol systems and scripts for the technicians to take away, while concealing anything promising—the project that might deliver me from this facility—beneath a pile in my desk drawer.

I even sent down alphabets that had already been tested.

For the decoy work I faked my way to bedtime. When I did not use letters soaked with ink I used objects, mostly bones. These were brought to me in a wire basket, with a set of burnishing tools, abrasives for sanding, some picks, little chisels, a mallet.

This decoy work could not be too amateur. I thought I could go down to the courtyard myself, in person, and use a small hooked knife to slice a divot of skin from myself, then flick that skin over a subject, a language of the body, piece by piece, until I expired at the table.

Or we could perform suicide by fairy tale. Issue a classic tale to each test subject, each technician, which would include the motherfucker LeBov. We could give a fairy tale to every unnamed person of Forsythe, and then on cue, we could commence to read our little tales.

I knew the fairy tale that I would select for my last obliterating language. I knew it inside and out.

Then we could finally bring an end to this thing, a lovely end, death by reading. How many sentences in would we get? Could we get to the part where the wolf is waiting in the grandmother's bed, or would we have collapsed in agony already? Would we miss the best part?

It was a matter of choosing which form of failure to ride out to the spectacular, bloody end.

If I produced the decoy scripts fast enough, and had them available for the technicians when they came, I had enough time to think about my real work, and this, inevitably, had to involve a complete rethinking of the Jewish script.

From my drawer I retrieved the Hebrew balloon shrapnel. The deflated letters had dried and curled over the last few days. Some of them stank of the sea. On a stretching board I revived the pieces, ladled oil into their skin until they were slick, pulled others too long until they tore, and with my molder I formed a new set of dense cubes, like square rubber erasers, with which to build, perhaps, a Hebrew letter heretofore unseen.

With this material I fussed throughout the day, doing mock-ups in ink, laying down string for patterning, making textile samples of this lettering and wrapping the material around different lengths of iron rod.

The script, when I erected it on pins and experimented with small jets of air, looked like the folds of a brain.

I staged it in arrangements that might constitute sensible order, the logic of words, but not the sort of words we'd ever use.

It was foolish, maybe, but I wouldn't be sharing it with just anyone, and if it wasn't harmful, then this was the work I wanted to do, these were the letters I preferred to be near. The Hebrew letter is like a form of nature. In it is the blueprint for some flower whose name I forget, and if this flower doesn't exist yet, it will. It is said that the twenty-two Hebrew letters, if laid flat and joined properly, then submitted to the correct curves on a table stabbed with pins, would describe the cardiovascular plan of the human body. And not only that. That was child's play.

The absolute key was that this letter would, by necessity, need to be orphaned from the flame alphabet, toxic to it and in no way capable of joining its system. No matter what else you could communicate with it, it was imperative that this letter could never indicate the Name, or be part of a word or words that did, however indirectly. It would be the flame alphabet's bastard letter, and I knew who would be the first to receive it.

When the technicians came for my materials, I swept this work aside, passed them Dravidian syntax instead. When I thought they needed something new, I gave them some Foster, one of the more recent, specialized languages, invented solely to promote doubt and uncertainty.

If I deployed the Hebrew script in the predictable ways, using it in words we already knew, it was still too sickening to use. I had tested enough of it on myself to know. But this only suggested to me that standard forms of communication were off-limits.

I hung my secret Hebrew letter on sticks, enlarging the aperture on the pinhole over sample words. These were words that were not even clearly defined and, to my mind, could not possibly exist. Something of their design, the precise way the details of the letters converged when placed together, fused so quickly into the shape of a toxic emblem that I felt an instant chill of comprehension.

But with this comprehension did not come the crushing. My gag reflex was not triggered. I felt a mild revulsion and that is all.

This is what I wanted. It is what our old poisonous alphabet must look like to an animal. Unpromising, of no interest. If it could not be eaten or fucked, what other use could it possibly have? Ambivalence was a starting point. When I studied the letter, looked at it from every angle, I was indifferent, unmoved. I just did not care. This was, if you'll accept the phrase, a breakthrough.

I enlarged the pinhole, allowing more language to fill my field of vision. And every day I—I've never used or even thought this word before—but I fucking *rejoiced*, because when I looked at what might be possible with this alphabet, when I spelled with it by severing it to pieces and using its parts, omitting vowels with it and some crucial consonants, and wrote the safer words with it and then deployed those words into word strings that fell just shy of forming sentences, I was not so fully blinded by sickness that I collapsed unconscious in my chair.

I may have retched, I may have felt the room spin off its moorings as if I'd suddenly been launched from my window over the countryside of Rochester, but foul as these symptoms were, they did not of themselves seem killing, which meant the Hebrew letter had more promise than anything I'd ever seen. I may have been repulsed by the script I made with it, but because it did not finally destroy me, I felt that I had the beginnings of a solution.

With this new Hebrew lettering paradigm I began work on a non-alphabet, a system revolving around one symbol that could never be used in a word, a letter that did not even exist yet, a letter whose existence was merely inferred by the other letters. This letter could fluidly receive or reject ornament, be layered or cloaked, snap open and release, and ultimately be totally disguised, but I had yet to complete the instructions, I had not actually loaned this symbol into a vocabulary, and to one of the test subjects it would look and sound too much like the alphabet that already sickened us. I imagined a single-letter alphabet, one you could hold in your hands. Not that I planned to show this thing to just anyone. This I would be keeping to myself. Myself and maybe one other person.

It would require redundancy and nonsense built in, ligatures that expressed merely noise, to soften the harshness of meaning, extend it, disguise it. I saw it as a foam I needed to add to my system, a cloaking agent. I wondered if it could be built into a person's body, to be activated by touch, by the absence of touch. This, too, must have been tried. We did not precisely understand how to control which symbols were perceived as nonsense, and which ones suddenly came to mean something. In fact, we understood nothing.

When I finished the first prototype, an inflatable letter vacuumed of air so that it looked like a miniature collapsed building, my idea of what had been missing from the Hebrew alphabet all along, I realized that I had inadvertently constructed an artifact that was, in appearance if not in function, very nearly identical to something from our Jewish hut, an item now confiscated. A listener, a Moses Mouth. But smaller. A baby one. New to this life. I'd finally found my smallwork. I could keep something from the motherfuckers who would abuse it.

I put it in my pocket and went out.

39

A few days after my encounter with LeBov, and my first dose of the child chemical that triggered brief fits of speech and illness-free comprehension, I left my office, rounded a corner, and was abruptly ambushed by one of his people. Someone with a covered face hugged me and below my buttock I felt the cold potion flow.

LeBov was waiting for me in the cellar, outside the door to their Jew hole. He was attended by technicians hidden behind goggles, their heads wrapped in flesh-colored rags. *Enough strips of foam insulate to cover a large man.*

On LeBov's neck a stained, brown bandage peeled up over a wound, threatening to fall off.

LeBov wanted to know if I had changed my mind, if I'd consider helping them.

The fluid from the injection activated, shooting through me like a rope of electricity. Immediately I felt that this dose of child fluid was *different*, laced with something harsh, a ballast of amphetamine, a numbing agent. They'd been tampering with it, pushing it through betas.

My speech resources were back. In my face a buzzing commenced, to be relieved only by talking. This medicine didn't seem to just allow for language, it *demanded* it.

I looked through the window to the cold, vaulted space where the hole was.

Something pink was tied off to a pole, floating out of sight. It looked like a person hovering in the air.

LeBov asked, "Are you in?"

"You must have others," I said.

LeBov said, "We do. Nine of them. Foresters. You'll meet them. They're a lovely crowd, and your participation, as they say, would round things out nicely."

Nine of them. And I would make ten. Someone had been doing his reading, a little elementary Jewish procedure, put abroad into the world by our clever elders only to mislead the curious. It astonished me that people expected us to share our holy text, our rules and rituals, with just anyone, or even with each other. *Sharing*. What a tragic mistake. While the other religions begged for joiners, humping against the resisters until they yielded and swore themselves forever to their principles, we set about repelling them, erecting barriers to belief. It was how I preferred it. And LeBov had taken the bait. The so-called quorum of ten Jews required to ignite proper worship. This rule was one of our better decoys. I marveled at how off track he was. Whoever was running Forsythe thought a Jewish tradition, invented in the first place, was going to assist their decipherment of the transmission, a rigorously difficult act not tied to mystical belief whatsoever.

"You think a minyan is going to help you here?"

LeBov coughed with wretched force, while the technicians kept him from falling. His shirt was soaked through with sweat.

"Well, you tell me," he said, heaving. "Enlighten me, please. Tell me what *will* help. I'm at your mercy."

I looked away from him and said, "I wish you were."

LeBov waved aside his technicians, but they didn't leave, only took a step back while continuing to hold him up.

"How about this?" he said to me. "Let's go take a look at something."

I paused. LeBov's show-and-tell had its downside. The last time he'd offered to show me something, it was a room full of children having their essence sucked free into a cup, to be boiled down somewhere into a speech-releasing agent. An essence now forced into my body twice. I didn't get to see what happened to those children after the fluid was withdrawn, and I didn't want to. I wasn't so sure I wanted to see anything new that this man might have to share, but, despite myself, I was already following him.

. . .

We went up one level to a low, ankle-height window. You had to crouch to see out, pressing your face sideways against the cold floor, but this required too much strain for LeBov, so he reclined on the floor with his face at the window and invited me to join him. It was like we were testing a bed together in a department store and the headboard was a window we could see through.

Together we looked into a wet, stone room that held a crowd of people who seemed to be test subjects, potential ones. An endless supply of test subjects seemed to appear at Forsythe, and here was yet another holding tank. This group was no different from those I'd seen, and I was relieved; at least I'd not be shown some gruesome sight today. I knew I should feel pity for these people, but their endless numbers, their compliance, made sympathy difficult. These people today who we saw from the low window apparently had made it through most of the admissions process and were here waiting for their final decontaminating showers.

A jet of water shuddered through the room every so often, and someone stepped up to take his turn, twisting in the spume.

Among this group, huddled against the back wall waiting her turn, was my wife, Claire.

She looked calm, even pleased, as if she was waiting on a bench for the doors to open on a movie she wanted to see.

I tried to animate the months she'd spent since I'd left town, but could not will a picture of the extraordinary narrative that must have unfolded. I could only see her gasping on her back in the woods, trampled by a feral child, or scratching at the door of our house while Esther and her friends barked debilitating language sounds inside. I could not will her image into any functional mode, modes of escape, flight, competence—she had been so *ill*—such as what might have been required for her to first survive, and then to get all the way to Forsythe.

"So," said LeBov. "The plot thickens."

"The plot sucks."

"Well," he replied, as if there were some debate.

"Go on," I said. "This is the part where you spell out the blackmail."

LeBov took that in, said, "That seems tiring, though. Must we really get into that?"

In the stone room Claire had found a friend to huddle against.

He seemed nice, a man with no hair. Not fat now, but probably once fat, because he had too much skin everywhere, skin hanging off him. I guess that meant he'd had trouble finding food. He wore large, women's glasses and I wondered if he walked around expecting to be killed. He had accepted Claire into his arms as if she were a pet, stroking her hair. Maybe he was protecting her.

"What'd you tell her?" I asked LeBov.

"Well, it didn't take much. Actually it took no telling. No wonder she married you. She thinks we have Esther in here. I waved a photo at her. Those family photos again. I'm not even sure it was actually a photo of your daughter. Maybe it's a soft spot for children in general that your wife has?"

I asked, quietly, "And *do* you have Esther here?"

LeBov smiled. "It's amazing what people will believe."

"Would you have us believe nothing?" I said, so softly I hardly heard it myself. I knew I was taking the bait. I couldn't help it.

He paused, gave it some thought. "Well, I do have that also. I have that right now, with some of my workforce, and I quite enjoy it. I have them believe nothing. And then with people like your wife, I have them believe what I require, which is slightly more than nothing. It's not even that impressive. Is there anything more basic than having people believe things? It's an elementary strategy of control, to get people to believe things. There's not even that much artistry required. You should try it."

If someone was operating the faucet in the holding tank where Claire waited, I couldn't see him. One by one the potential test subjects rendered themselves nude before the cold jet of water, brought their speechless bodies into collision with the liquid blast. But it wasn't strictly water, because what collected in the drain had a soapy, black foam in it, a dark brew of bubbles bearding up on the floor.

Soon it was Claire's turn. She shed her coat, stepped from her nightgown, and with self-conscious charm flipped her hair back before submitting to the fierce spray.

She was really quite lovely, my wife.

LeBov seemed transfixed by the shower spectacle. His mouth had gone slack on the window, mist flaring over his face.

So he'd indicated to Claire that they had Esther in here, and now

Claire thought she might just come in and get her? It was hard to think that Claire's stubbornness had persisted over these last few months, had not yielded even slightly to the crush of reality. Esther would be too old for their purposes by now. At Forsythe teenagers were on the brink of illness themselves, but there was no way Claire could know that.

Or there was every way Claire could have known that, and more. I should have reminded myself not to think I had some advantage of perspective here. *What you are most certain of is what will undo you*, had said Rabbi Burke, once long ago. I had scoffed. It sounded like the mantra of a high school teacher who trafficked in homilies that no one believed.

The naked Claire stepped behind a curtain.

"And your plans for her now?"

"She'll serve as an associate tester for us," said LeBov, bored. He motioned his technicians over and they helped him up.

I pretended to know what that meant, and LeBov caught me trying to decipher what he'd said.

"You think we don't rank them?"

"Does it matter what I think?"

"Good point," he admitted.

He went on to explain that her class of test subjects would not die immediately. Claire would be exposed to materials that had not formally been ruled out, scripts, historical speeches delivered in a spectrum of accents, languages laced into ambient room sounds at subvocal thresholds, even though prospects were . . .

LeBov did not finish saying what Claire's prospects were.

"It's possible she'll even get to read one of your funny little alphabets. What a nice reunion that will be. Maybe you should encode a message to her? 'Dear Claire, how are you today? I am fine. This script, by the way, I made it myself! And . . . it will kill you. Love, Sam.'

"Turns out it's not too late to apologize after all. What's the hieroglyph for 'I'm sorry'? In fact, let's arrange that," LeBov said.

He laughed. "Don't you love closure?"

LeBov enjoyed the rhetorical vague. He relished not naming something, in not even talking about something. I felt his pleasure as he refused to say whatever he was obviously thinking. He didn't even really *say* what he was saying. Instead he found some way to make it seem that someone else was saying it, someone he looked down on. He was only the vessel, raped in the mouth and made to channel the words of an invader. This kind of concealment was supposed to create tension, build mystery. We spoke in code, but no one was listening in, and we no longer knew the original language to which our niceties would be translated back. We were trapped in the code now for good. A language twice removed, stepped on, boiled into a paste, and rubbed into an animal's corpse.

We returned to the door outside the Forsythe Jew hole.

I thought of Claire covering herself with the robe they dispense to the subjects, moving into the final processing line, waiting with the others. I thought of her standing there missing her daughter, looking strong and indifferent on the outside, but missing her daughter so hugely that she worried it would show, it would show and then she'd do something wrong, something that would only hurt her chances of seeing Esther again, so she braced herself further, hardened her look, erasing all signs of desire, of interest, of anything. Such erasure of one's appearances, how can it *not* seep into the interior, even a little bit? What treaty is it that finally separates those two territories, the hard resolve of our exteriors and the terrible disaster on our insides?

I pictured Claire going to bed tonight. I didn't even know where the subjects slept, and under what conditions, but that just made it worse. It could not be good, they were not providing comfortable hotel rooms for these people. She'd go to sleep tonight, I thought, and she'd be thinking, *Tomorrow, tomorrow, I'll go to where the children are, and they'll show me to my Esther, and then, and then . . .* And maybe Claire would fall asleep before working out those details, because those details could not be worked out. Maybe she'd not be too hard on herself by realizing how little she knew and how little she'd planned ahead for any of this.

I returned more seriously to LeBov's request that I change work assignments.

"And is one medicated for this work, poking around in that hole?"

LeBov registered this shift in my resistance. I saw the shit in his eyes, the shit that appears when he knows he's getting his way. It filled his eyes and some of it spread onto his face, and even though he had blackened teeth and a festering wound on his neck and his cough seemed like the worst, scariest cough I've ever heard, he beamed with pleasure.

"Sometimes, *in theory*, you'd be given the serum, but it's going to depend on some issues surrounding supply. Supply and priority."

"Well, count me out of these medical trials. I can do my work without speaking."

"But you can't," said LeBov. "Seriously, are these really the conditions that will allow scientific progress, working mutely in a mute room with mute fucks wandering by who can't tell you what the mute loser down the hall is even doing, or even how what you've just done, what you've tried to pass off as adequate research, is more mute loser work that is only a setback for everybody? Don't you find it hard to be productive when you can't communicate with anyone?"

LeBov paused, pretended to think.

"Oh, right. You're not productive at all."

The chemical from the child serum left a taste of berries in my throat.

"I won't be fed this liquid," I said.

"Won't you? Without *this liquid* you wouldn't even be able to tell me you don't care for it. You see the problem, I'm sure."

I remained silent.

About *this liquid*, LeBov remarked that the children were not too pleased to part with it. What resulted, after enough of *this liquid* had been withdrawn—I got no specifics—was a person not quite a child, not quite anything. LeBov said that there might be abilities, or talents, for these children post-procedure, but that these were still, and here he paused, *undiscovered*.

"Maybe you can write stories for them. They can still read. I mean, we don't take away their immunity to language. But their comprehension levels are quite low. What we've found, though, is that people with very low comprehension levels, people who fail to understand things, did not get sick so readily when the toxicity first hit. If your wife got sick faster than you, it means she understood more. Does that ring a bell? Some pretty smart people died instantly. It was nice. It cleared space for lots of less intelligent people to take over."

"Can't you duplicate this liquid in a lab?" I asked. "Make a synthetic version?"

"Have at it," he said. He winced, gently touched the bandage on his neck.

I wished he meant it. Instead, I was having at something they had all agreed was futile. I didn't want that anymore.

I asked who else was using this liquid, what the other side effects were.

"What are you, on the team now? Part of the inner circle? Do you think you can really be a *LeBov*? If you want access, and information that doesn't even fucking *concern* you, then do what I'm asking, fix the motherfucker for me. Get some secrets out of that hole before I rip someone's face off."

The exertion triggered something in LeBov and he fell to the floor, coughing. Around him crowded his technicians, and by wagon one of them dragged in something covered by a blanket. It wriggled under there, groaned. A wet spot soaked up through the wool.

I thought of Claire waking up tomorrow morning thinking *This is the day*, stepping over the badly slept bodies of her cohorts, and then getting led down hallways and corridors and through rooms and out, finally, into the sickening light of the courtyard, where she could finally, she just knew, run to Esther and hug her close, and even if they could not speak, couldn't they be near each other, maybe find a shelter somewhere to enjoy each other's company in silence? Why, after all, would anyone want to keep Esther from her?

But instead there'd be no children greeting her in the courtyard, just a table and chair, and Claire would take a seat as the technicians approached her with a foil envelope.

What would be inside it? she'd wonder, as the faceless technicians opened the seal and removed the contents, page after page, to place before her eyes, retreating quickly to the safety of their shielded rooms.

Now what could this be? Claire might wonder, picking up the materials.

This is when I agreed to help. I would join the crew at the hole, help them fix the transmission, if I could, and leave them to eavesdrop on messages—the old Jewish services that no longer worked—that were none of their business.

It took some time but we worked out the details, polishing LeBov's blackmail until it had a disgusting shine to it.

"I'll need some assurances," I said.

"Of course you will."

"Something I can count on."

"What, Sam, do you want something in writing?"

His smile revealed a slick, black film that had crept all over his teeth.

I didn't, no. I didn't want anything in writing ever again.

We were about to part when I asked LeBov a question, something that had been on my mind.

He sat on the floor, breathing through a respirator. The mask fed into a dark wooden box resting in the wagon.

"When I first met you," I started.

"Memory lane?" LeBov asked, removing his mask. "You want to talk about the old days?" He checked his watch, then signaled to a technician, who appeared to convulse at the signal, folding his body inward as if he'd absorbed a cannonball, like one of those old-fashioned performers.

"When I first met you," I continued, "you were getting sick in the bushes. Vomiting. You were sick."

"Oh, the good times." LeBov took a desperate breath from his mask.

"But were you actually sick? Was that real?"

LeBov dropped the mask, hacked into his towel.

"That's mirroring. I learned it in fucking first grade. You adopt the behavior of your opponent, then escalate it. Saw it on one of those film strips about insects. If he's susceptible, you gain his trust and he thinks he's found an ally for life. *Finally someone who suffers like me! A friend!* Works pretty well on Jews, who usually think they're unique. Maybe even in kindergarten I learned that. With Mrs. Krutz. She was a fucking genius, actually. Mrs. Krutz once . . ."

"You didn't *gain* my trust. I was already suspicious of you. I felt sorry for you. But up at Tower Ledge, that couple you were harassing? What did you want from them? What happened to them?"

"Which couple? There were so many."

I told him which couple. I told him when.

"Oh, I ate them alive, probably. Isn't that what you think? I cooked those bastards in a sauce. Can you picture that? This is ridiculous. Your questions are the questions of a two-year-old."

"Did they have a listener that you wanted?"

"I already had their listener. Spent some time alone with it. Punched it into shape. Have you ever punched one? It's amazing. It's like punching a baby. You know? I mean it's *just* like that. Their listener is nailed to the wall now. A hand-forged copper nail, in case there's any residual current in it. That part was easy. They kept their listener in a cigar box because, believe it or not, they never went out to tie it off on a cable. *Bad* Jews. *Very* bad. They'd stopped going to synagogue. But their *boys*, those were harder to acquire. Negotiations were more . . . demanding."

"Were they your first?"

"My first? My first *what*? Mother was my first, and then Father. And after that my brother Stewart. They were my *first*. Then I went back for seconds. Because I was still *hungry*. Do you think the demon speech began out of nowhere a few months ago and swept through town all of a sudden? A little suburban catastrophe? Is that really what you think? You think I fucking work *alone*? You think there's not a human machine the size of the world that didn't anticipate this *transition*?"

"You know," I said, "rhetorical questions, even with your fucking potion, make me sick to my stomach."

LeBov fell to coughing again, and when he returned the mask to his mouth and continued to cough, the sound of his hacking was rendered hollow, echoing as if from outside the halls of Forsythe, like a secret code in the forest being shared among animals.

40

With LeBov in distress, attended by faceless, hose-weilding technicians, I was released too early back into the facility that afternoon. Before I was escorted away, LeBov started to seize, then yelled something through cupped hands, his hands shaping his cry into a curious acoustical object, as if he'd built a bird from pure sound. I grew suddenly light-headed, and one of the technicians fell to the floor, twitching.

It might have been wiser had they returned me to the holding room and wrapped the blanket over my head until the dosage expired. Instead, I was at large in the halls of Forsythe, where I enjoyed strong minutes of language power before the fluid wore off, a protection that surged into my evening encounter with Marta, which I will relate in a moment. First I hurried back to my office so I could work on the Hebrew letter in full view, without the pinhole device, without the impediment of the self-disguising paper that denied nearly everything of an object. None of those cautions were needed today. These were the working conditions I had craved, and I didn't want them to go to waste.

It was a poor decision.

At my desk, with my language immunity still juicing through me, I surveyed the whole letter, if that's even an accurate way to describe it; this wasn't a letter anymore but a gristled cluster of cells, nearly bone-like, smitten around the rim with hair. It required the moisture and warmth of a hand to activate, at least if I would have my way, and I started to deploy it into communicative service, producing with it a script of a *distinctly personal nature*. As a complete object, liberated from its concealing medical tape and propped against a plywood backdrop, the letter repulsed me, but I took no interest in my own reaction. My own reaction, my own interpretation, my own feelings, for that matter, held little useful meaning for me.

Whoever said that had been right.

Without language my inner life, if such a phrase indicates anything anymore, was merely anecdotal, hearsay. It was not even that. It was the noisings one might detect if a microphone were held against a stone in the woods. Too much effort is required to divine activity within things like persons. There is a reason this subjective material is trapped inside people and cannot be let out. As such, my thoughts, when I bothered to have them, bored me, especially if I could no longer unleash them into the world with my mouth and effect some kind of response from people, so I ignored them and set to work.

I'd never held a shrunken head, but this was what one must be like: a cold, wrinkled organism submitted to a blistering round of dehydration, then crushed down to alphabet size. There were letters based on body parts, activities, feelings, but this was different. This letter, composed of what was missing or inferred in all the other Hebrew letters, was a species unto itself, and while I worked under the bright shield of the child serum, immune to the sluices of resonance, of comprehension that flowed so jarringly into me, my experimental letter gave off the unmistakable stink of organic matter left too long in the sun.

I pierced it with a needle. I pierced it and then squeezed it, examining the hole with a magnifying glass, but no matter how hard I squeezed, no black fluid beaded up. Not even a puff of dark powder.

Several times I gagged on the fumes, which only confirmed to me that it was nearly ready.

The potential was here for a self-disguising object that might be used as languages once were. Even though I could not assess its toxicity today, since I was protected by the serum, I recalled that under no protection, days ago, I had not been durably sickened. Even without the serum this letter had not wounded me. I had to believe the letter would allow for some elementary, nonfatal communication. Serum or not, I had to think this letter would work.

Such was the flawed reasoning I practiced.

As a test I would embed a message Claire would instantly know, something that could only come from me.

What kind of shoes does Rothschild wear?
Probably golden shoes.
Then what does he do when it rains?

My focus felt cold and clear. I did not ask for the serum that made this work possible; I wished it never existed. Yet since it did exist, since someone *had* discovered that a child might be siphoned in order for our speech to resume, I could not now deny its merits.

I pictured the children surrendering it through tubes in an underground room at Forsythe. Not just Forsythe, but elsewhere, at facilities in Wisconsin, Denver. I'd lost track of where the important work was being done.

I pictured myself in charge of this extraction. I lacked discipline when it came to the imagination, and here I was in my own mind leading a team, holding down children, some of whom grew distressed during the procedure, withdrawing the essence that protected them from the toxic speech. Withdrawing it so people who mattered—who had *tangible communicative aims* that they would soon enact, *for the benefit of every living person*—could ingest it and carry on in the world. This was simply about loaning a resource from a surplus site and shuttling it to an area of deficit.

Not everyone needed to speak. We'd have delegates, elected language users. Public servants.

Resource management involved compromise, but the gains could be so glorious.

For reasons totally other than moral, *completely outside of the so-called human implication*, a child-fueled communication system was problematic.

I knew that. And yet when my first dosage wore off I felt a skin peel away, and a skin, and another skin, and it was a great loss, a technical, objective sadness. Not my own, but a sadness belonging to the situation. Unprotected, the air was suddenly a salt on the body, and the overhead lights were a salt, and when I moved too quickly I felt a blast of granular salt at every turn.

An anecdotal observation, meant to illustrate how much protection this serum offered, regardless of its source. It was an exquisite thing, and without it we would be walled off from one another forever.

If the serum was high and burning in my blood right now, I would use its defenses to finally tackle my work with all of my faculties in play.

The first time they'd shot me with enough fluid to endure the session with LeBov, but this last time the antidote lasted longer, and I forgot myself.

I finished work and left my office, testing my power in personal whispers as I went, talking to myself *out loud*. Through the corridors and halls and then on the entertainment byway I walked with a weapon, one that could not hurt me, past my fellow scientists and the technicians and the women in white business attire, some of them dragging bright wagons that carried the same kind of old oak box they used on LeBov.

In the television room the facially distorted children ran as a group into the sea and did not come out.

Out in the hallway nothing was happening on the high monitors. The video feeds of the world offered the same dull exteriors. One feed revealed a man on a scooter whisking down the highway. On another feed a meadow spread out into the distance, disrupted by strange swells. These were shelters, but if people came and went, if people even existed, one saw no evidence of it.

At the child quarantine monitor a small clutch of scientists had gathered, studying the screen. They stood there pretending they were not hoping to catch sight of a child of theirs. They studied the screen as if their interest was merely professional, when in reality they were window-shopping against the glass that held the last possible hope that they might see their children.

I went to the coffee cart and found my sexual partner straightaway, and together we moved quietly back to my quarters, our hands lightly touching.

The ordeals of the day had demanded a trip to the coffee cart. Seeing Claire undergo the shower sequence, prepped to serve inside the facility as a test subject, seeing her endure the decontamination proudly, as if she'd been selected for special service based on her unique abilities, and, further, agreeing to change my work assignment in a few days and begin to help decode the transmissions from the old, abandoned Jewish hole hidden beneath the facility, all of these things led me to the coffee cart, where I felt a sexual engagement was now appropriate.

Tonight with a paralyzed face Marta unzipped my jumpsuit, gathered it up, and placed it folded on the dresser. This was kind of her. I dropped to the bed and watched her undress.

It would have been nice to see Marta undergo the horizontal shower spout where they prep the test subjects, if only because she would handle it gracefully. I felt strongly that it was not a harsh treatment to be sprayed that way, just a forceful one with a specific aim, but it allowed a naked body a particular luminous beauty, absorbing propulsive blasts from the water jets. Marta would have sustained such a treatment nobly, and if I could have watched it facedown against the floor looking through that low window—even if LeBov, wheezing through his blackened teeth, had to join me—I would have gladly done so.

During intercourse with Marta, the last traces of the serum still fizzing in me, I tested the air with a word.

In bed, in the early part of our expressionless exchange, when sexual release seemed so distant as to not even be likely tonight, no matter what techniques were deployed, I spoke by mistake or on purpose, or, more likely, I spoke from a mixed motive that had not been properly examined, and Marta tensed in my arms, tensed and grew cold.

I cannot remember the word I spoke, but I do remember what it felt like to have my hands on Marta when I did it, to feel the violent rejection shake through her body at the release of *a single word*. I was able to hold her body in my hands and speak, and there was no stronger demonstration of how the acoustically delivered word was simply violating. *A disease born straight from the mouth*. How she reacted as if I'd pushed a knife into her ribs and then kept pushing, when it was no longer funny, leaning on her with all my weight.

Marta shot from the bed, rolled against the wall, and came to rest panting. From the chair she grabbed her things and hurried into them. Only then did I start to see what might technically be considered a *feeling* from her. I'd unleashed something, and I wondered, hypothetically, what more words might do, a sentence, several sentences, if I managed to lock the door and bar her exit while I held forth on some topic that might have concerned me, or even addressed the growing bond between us, since we had never once spoken about our relationship.

I had all the power of a child.

As she got dressed and made her way out of my room, Marta looked at me plainly, as if she was curious, in the detached, scientific sense, why I would have any interest in hurting her. I'd seen that face before, and I hadn't realized it was a face that could be shared, used by more than one person, but it had appeared on Claire, and I had always thought that it was hers alone, to use only on those special occasions when I had disappointed her. But apparently this was a face that Marta had access to as well.

Marta's unspoken question—why I had caused her harm—was one I would not have been able to answer. There was a small, decisive advantage to the language toxicity here. One did not have to stand there explaining oneself, inventing motives that might make sense to someone. Explanations of any kind, in fact, were simply extinct.

Among the many rhetorical modes that had perished, it was this one I was not sorry to see go.

41

In the days after that, the serum fully discharged from my system, my immunity depleted, I braced myself for assault. I waited to be ambushed, then hauled off and injected with vile stuff. I didn't just wait for it. I wished for it.

It happened again a few days later.

When my hood came off, a technician was putting drops on LeBov. From a baster he squeezed a pearled fluid over LeBov's face. It smelled of flowers. LeBov clenched in his chair as if the substance burned. The technicians leaned over him, tilting on their toes to press all their weight into holding him down.

The puncture wound on my arm, where the needle had gone in this time, was rimmed already by a shiny black scab.

To LeBov I said, "Was that really necessary? I'd have come to you willingly. I honor my agreements."

He stood up, coughing into a towel, and waved me after him. It was my first night of work at the Jewish hole.

But two things happened the night before that need to be related first. Two things, and then I'll report on my first engagement with the hole.

The night before, I went to the coffee cart and, from behind, tapped Marta, maybe a bit too hard. We'd not been together since I had repelled her from bed with language.

Maybe I struck her on the shoulder. Not a blow to knock Marta down, although it happened to do so, and not a blow to injure her, because that was not a desire I knew about having, even though I had recently caused her pain in pursuit of a broader curiosity, but a firm tap of the sort one delivers to an object to keep it from moving. An anchoring gesture, one might call it. And when I did it Marta buckled to the floor, a surprisingly soft fall, executed with a dancer's grace.

The scientists at the coffee cart looked down at their fallen colleague. We'd all of us developed, in our time at Forsythe, the remotest style of curiosity. We looked at fallen people with the clinical gaze of someone assessing an old painting. *What do have we here?* If my colleagues had any reaction, I was grateful that I would not learn what it was.

Marta was not long for a posture of collapse.

When she stood up to join me, showing no distress at having been knocked down, I saw that it wasn't Marta I had tapped.

It was Claire.

Here was my very own wife in a scientist's disguise on the grounds of Forsythe. LeBov had kept his promise. He'd brought my sweetheart to me and she was safe.

Poor Claire's face was small, her hair too thin. I wanted so much to hold her, to take her to the video feed where I thought I'd seen our old neighborhood. But I had an agreement to honor.

I clutched my wife and together we hurried through the Forsythe hallways. At the door to my room the technicians rushed her with the serum and she did not cry out. She was so brave.

I gripped Claire's hands, forced her to the wall. She couldn't know what we were doing. I would explain later. LeBov had urged this upon me—*when the time comes you must control your wife*—and I had agreed.

The injection would need to penetrate Claire's back. Protocol. I kept her hands from thrashing while the technicians readied the needle. I jammed a knee against her bottom, forcing her to submit.

Poor Claire did not really struggle. She gave me such a trusting look as I restrained her, a shy smile to suggest she would have done anything, anything. And so would I, I tried to silently say back. This was me doing anything right now. *I swear I am doing this for you.*

When the needle went in, Claire sputtered from the throat, tried to summon a voice that had fallen so slack it could not even moan. Only a drowning sound came out of her.

I know, I wanted to say. *I know, Honey. I do. I know.*

Inside my room the technicians plugged in a tape recorder and settled the yellow headphones on the desk. Then from a foil bag I knew too well, they retrieved the toxic tapes, the whole sonic archive I'd stashed in the car. The last record of my daughter. Our own Esther's voice, recorded when I thought that one day I'd need to study her words to figure out why we could not bear them. Oh, one day.

Claire curled up under the sting of the injection, twitched softly on the floor. A technician caught some of the froth that poured out. I stroked her hair, waited for her to open her eyes. *It's all right*, I didn't say.

You could see the child serum start to activate in her, a mineral deficiency erased with one honey-colored syringe, the person brightening again to a world that had been closed to her.

The technicians flashed miniature tools, the instruments of a dentist, a botanist. Fingernail-size mirrors on gleaming, chrome sticks, measuring the moisture in her breath, clamps made of something the color of skin. With a dropper they squirted the same pearled fluid I saw them use on LeBov, but this they squeezed into Claire's mouth. She sucked the dropper like it was a pacifier.

Claire sat up, rubbing her face, and before I could hold her—she seemed confused and scared now—the technicians pulled me into the hallway. They shut me out of my own room and guarded my door. I'd have to sit out here and wait for Claire to be done. I could picture her inside listening to Esther's voice and this would have to be enough.

This was because I'd be getting no dose of my own. Only Claire would get to listen to the Esther tapes. That was the deal. Claire could hear her daughter's voice. Even if her daughter was only reciting lists, Claire could finally listen to her with no ill effects. None. This was all I knew to give her. It was all I had.

The agreement with LeBov was worked out in stages. If things went well with the Jew hole, then my turn was next.

If things went well. What that meant, apparently, was whether or not I could summon LeBov's wall of slick listeners in tandem, because each listener faltered in the presence of another, and the problem was not just electrical. Get the motherfuckers to work together. Braid the orange cables into some kind of sisterhood, then prize them into the dark brown apertures of the listeners. Sneak the conduit into its appropriate cavity, escalating the detection frequency to *x*, to *n*? Put a maximum latch on that cable so Rabbi Zero could be heard, whispering from his Buffalo fortress.

But more important, let them thread any gauge of wire into my mouth. My mouth would no longer be mine. From now on my mouth belonged to them.

We'd hear beyond the rudimentary transmissions of the fraud Rabbi *Burke*. What a *joke*. Beyond the hierarchies of middling low-level so-called *rabbis* on the closer reaches of the radio, into the darker, more exclusive terrain of . . . whom, *whom*?

LeBov wouldn't say.

Because maybe LeBov didn't fucking *know*? Because maybe there was nothing to know. There was no one else out there? No unspeakably wise rabbi, *Rabbi Zero*, issuing guidance beyond the toxicity, advising survivors on some life we are meant to lead after language, since the human sound on our lives had been turned off, and our mouths had been seized, and even our minds, little and dim as they were—I make no argument here—could no longer bear to understand the smallest things?

And if this all *worked*, it wasn't just the tapes of my daughter I'd get to enjoy under the spell of the child serum. Claire and I would be allowed to leave Forsythe. The only solution I saw. The only one. I wanted *nothing* of the feeds or some phantom rabbi, because there was nothing to know. What a fucking joke. Knowing of this kind was only a harm. I would have killed to know less than I did. I wanted to finally be gone from here. Claire and I would be safely escorted somewhere downstate. Maybe they'd put us in one of the red busses, drive us out to the countryside.

Give me four walls of soil and a breathing tube. And a knife. Give me a supply of water. And give me my wife back, you goddamn monsters. Even silent. Return her to me. Then promise you'll leave us alone.

Unless LeBov was deeply full of shit again, sticking his hand into my whole life and squeezing the pieces until they broke. Because that's what people named LeBov *do*. Because restoring the language to a people was only *one small piece* of his work. Child's play, I bet. Smallwork is right. In the end it's too *small*, isn't it? Easy enough to shoot everyone with a fluid so they could shout insults at each other again, launch their campaigns of vocal blame. *Easy*. He would do more than that. LeBov would also erase a belief system, remove love from the air as if it were only an atmospheric contaminant. Love was just a pollutant you could blow clear of a person, right, LeBov? If only you had the proper tools.

I had to believe that LeBov's ambition extended beyond my imagination, into territories yet more awful. I had to believe this, because it kept coming true. I had to start working harder to imagine the worst.

42

When Claire finished her listening session with Esther's voice, the technicians monitored her by console until her language immunity expired. The injection worked for an hour at most. I did not get to see her during this withdrawal, but from the hectic procedures outside my room, I could guess they were deflating their equipment, ensuring that their patient could no longer *hold* a word.

How they test that I don't know, but I hoped they did it without hurting her.

Claire was in my bed when I was permitted back into my room. The technicians would give us a little time to ourselves now.

I would say that Claire looked like she'd been crying, but everyone looks that way. Faces wrecked and wet, eyes red. Everyone always seems to have just wept their hearts out before rounding a corner and forcing out a fake smile for whomever they saw.

I locked my door and went to her. Under my sheets she was cold, still clothed, stiff in my arms.

She looked at me only briefly, then looked away. Claire seemed stunned, tired.

Perhaps it was too much to let her listen to Esther like that. Perhaps she had heard something—our daughter reaching into the future to disturb us—that made her want to be alone now.

What was it Esther even said in those recordings? Numbers and names, I thought, vocal specimens to flesh out the medical picture. A story or two. Could such a listening regimen be so disturbing? I'd never listened to the tapes myself. By that point it was getting to be too late.

When the child serum wears off the face settles back into lockdown and it doesn't feel good. Claire's little face was hard and she looked at me as if I were not her living husband but a frozen exhibit of him that she could study while entertaining an old memory.

It might be easy to presume that, had Claire and I really wanted to that night in my room at Forsythe, we could have spoken. We could have, *had we really wanted to*, weathered the convulsive speech, the air-shredding toxicity that brought us to our knees.

None of that, it could be argued, should have stopped us. Hardened faces, docked tongues, throats stuffed with bloody wood. We had not seen each other in months. Intimacy overpowers such literal impediments, does it not? Haven't the great loves conquered far more than this, surpassed difficulties that made a literal language barrier, such as what we suffered, seem trifling?

Yes, I suppose the great loves have done this.

And ours, that night, did not. Our love that night was minor and it was hard to find. Our love could not overcome the medical dilemma. As the night wore on I became more afraid of what Claire would say to me if she could say anything. The barrier tonight was only a relief. Thank god the language had died between us. Some things should go without saying forever.

In bed we groomed and stroked each other, we rubbed each other's necks. I freed Claire of her clothes and she made of her body a cooperative object.

She was too thin, with a low, sweet bulge in her tummy, the last little part of her to shed fat. Her legs were chalky, dry, as if she'd walked through salt to get here. Should there not have been more evidence of her days and nights, her feelings, the things Claire kept herself from feeling? What was her body for if not to record something so simple as that?

I peeled down my jumpsuit and returned to bed, but Claire took no special notice.

Claire and I had been naked together as a matter of contract for so many years at bedtime that an animal indifference had developed. Perhaps that's a working definition of love. We were fellow creatures who grazed and fed nearby, who tended the same difficult offspring. We opened our faces in complaint to each other when some injustice showered down, frequently by our own hand, and together we linked arms to squeeze out vocal notes of disapproval whenever something struck us as wrong, which only meant we had not thought of it ourselves.

Such a shared habitat allowed ritual nudity to occur at home, a nudity that often heralded nothing but private fits of sleep on top of the same, vast bed.

When Esther switched from needing us to hating us—perhaps the two are not so different—Claire and I stopped being naked together. This is one of the thousands of coincidences that combine to assemble the skeleton of a marriage. After Esther switched off her feelings—after she instituted delay strategies when it came to demonstrations of love—Claire and I undressed and suited up in private instead, removing our nightwear, if the occasion called for it, only after we'd crawled under the blankets and turned out the light.

Just when there was no reason for it, when our history and intimacy made such shyness preposterous, we'd each discovered shreds of modesty with which to build out our evening endgame.

It had thus been longer than usual since we had been under the light and fully nude together. And as lovely as Claire looked, I felt sorry for her tonight, sorry for her and somewhat ashamed of myself for getting us undressed so quickly.

I took Claire's hand and rolled over her. Beneath me her body felt cold and long. I tried to fit myself over her in a way that would trigger something. It would seem that, through touch, through kissing, we might have gouged a worm-size channel through which crucial information could pass, sublingual messages, the kind of pre-verbal intimacy that should flow with thunderous force between the bodies of people so bonded. We should have been able to bypass a mere inability to exchange language.

Everywhere people must have been exploring the alternatives; otherwise they'd be sentenced to solitude. But that night Claire and I showed a mutual failure of the imagination. Without speech we were unskilled mimes locked into alien vernaculars, missing every connection, growing slowly angry that the other person could not decode our thoughts.

I would like to say that without language Claire and I exchanged something. But in fact we did not. We simply looked at each other, at most with forced curiosity. The channel that was meant to dilate between us to allow our feelings and thoughts to flow back and forth, well, it didn't. One witnessed no such channel.

Throughout our endeavors on my bed we remained dutifully mute. We wrestled in much the same way we had when we were erecting the play tent for Esther when she was four, sliding collapsible stilts through a long canvas sleeve, except this time there was no play tent between us, just deflated geometries of air, and we were two old acquaintances grimly determined to extract pleasure from each other. But when our pleasure centers met, they were cold and shielded by brittle walls of hair.

Claire arranged herself on her knees at my side while I settled back and permitted the ministrations that would ready me for our sexual encounter, since that transaction would be the only way to rescue us from our awkward wrestling. Such she did, in rote style, pressing my penis between thumb and forefinger so the top part ballooned angrily and flipped from side to side as she moved her hand.

Her activity was smart, rigorous textbook arousal technique, and she labored with her hand with such determination that her face grew misted in perspiration.

But her manipulations turned my item not toward readiness but to putty. A cold putty that did not stand, but seemed that it would melt into clammy liquid against my leg instead.

When it was clear that her work, tendered so sorrowfully, was not effective and that I would not be able to fulfill my part in the exchange of intimacy, Claire stopped touching me and stared away at the wall.

I was never very good at knowing Claire's feelings, even, unfortunately, after she'd shared them with me. Somehow I still didn't understand. Now, in silence, insights into my wife were out of reach entirely.

For the rest of our time together, we lay on the bed listening to each other breathe. I would like to think that this was nice. A peaceful way to reconnect and feel our bond restoring itself. I would like to think that, but I'm afraid I cannot.

When the technicians knocked I was relieved.

At the door Claire and I exchanged a dry, glanceless kiss. The technicians hovered, faces hidden behind gauze.

Before she left I reached into my workbag, pulled out the Hebrew letter, a cold pelt of hairiness, and pressed it into Claire's hand. My actions I hid from the technicians. I felt like I was handing off a shrunken father. Someone to look after her. The Hebrew letter was the only possession I cared about, and it fit into her hand perfectly. She could hide it there. It would not be discovered.

Perhaps it would read itself to her through her hand as she walked back to her quarters. If my work at the hole went well, we'd be back together soon. Oh, I had no idea how I would activate a wall of listeners I could not understand, especially when, according to LeBov, I had never even properly used my own. Already I was wondering how I could fool the man who seemed to be aware of my thoughts before I even had them.

He'd be ready for any trickery I could devise. He'd have planned for it. He was probably hoping I'd try to deceive him.

I watched Claire's face when she took the Hebrew letter from me.

Thank you for the gift, she didn't say. *I will look at it later.*

And it was only because Claire couldn't speak that she didn't say *I love you.* That was the only reason.

For a moment in the doorway the simple things between us went without saying. You could feel it.

She squeezed the Hebrew letter in her hand and I could almost hear it working. Almost.

What kind of shoes does Rothschild have?
Golden shoes!
Yes, but what does he do when it rains?

He does what we all do, I couldn't say. Doesn't he?

Then Claire was gone.

43

One more thing happened that night, but before it did, I fucked Marta again.

After Claire left my room, the Hebrew letter hot in her hand, speaking only to her the more she clutched it, I went back out and found Marta at the cart, spun her around to be sure it was her this time. I ignored the protocol of tapping and brought her back to my room, my bed still destroyed from the visit with Claire.

Marta could not know that. What happened with Claire happened in a different world. And what was fine about Marta was that she concealed her apparatus for caring. She had an expertise at hiding what mattered most.

In my room I experienced a surge of virility. My area was rigid, but it was also numb. Marta worked calmly at it, ferreting the difficulty, stared past my head and labored to ease the issue.

The room fell quiet and for a moment a trickle of wind intruded our space, as if a whip had been cracked and a sharp rope of air snapped past. It was cold and I thought I could taste it. The flavor of berries trickled down the back of my throat. My vision browned and when the completion came down below, the sudden sweetening, a feeling I could very nearly claim as my own, it flashed through my limbs. Flashed, spoiled, faded.

It was finally clear that I did not need a woman for this, or even a person. I needed a knife.

After she surrendered her hold on me, Marta quietly arranged herself on her side, curled into a ball, because from there she could most easily gain satisfaction, provided I supplied the labor. We could face the same direction, prone in my sweaty bed, as if we were traveling to the countryside, waiting for the piece of perfect scenery to explode before our eyes.

This felt fair, and for a while I spent energy on the project, I put time in. I owed something to Marta. Perhaps this was a way I could repay her.

Marta was silent, and I responded with silence of my own, but still I burrowed away behind her, working through repeated waves of exhaustion to deliver my favor. I kept my hands well free of her neck.

Finally Marta clenched, a wave of coldness overcoming her skin. Or perhaps she coughed and swallowed. In any case she scooted forward and made it known that our activity had ended.

When we finally stood to dress, Marta got herself buttoned up, but before she opened the door she turned to me. This was not part of our routine. She never stopped for an encounter like this, and so I looked down.

It was time for me to be shy. Eye contact with Marta felt like more of a betrayal to Claire than anything. I did not want to be seen seeing her.

This is when Marta struck me in the face.

Had I not been looking down, perhaps I could have protected myself from the blow. Or perhaps, had I seen Marta's fist coming at me, I would have allowed it to travel, just as it did, on its course with my head. Even had I seen it coming, I may have let it through.

I wanted to smile at Marta, and I believe I did, through salty warm blood, but I had fallen to the floor, and she left my room too quickly to notice.

I felt like watching TV before bedtime. My face throbbed. When I touched it, it felt like another man's face entirely. Perhaps in the TV room I'd fill a bowl with broth, maybe find one of the salted cookies for after. I could stretch out in a chair and watch the children follow orders. Maybe they'd try to walk on water, then drop quietly into the sea and the camera would stay fixed to the water until the last bubbles rose and dissolved into the air and the water fell calm again.

A cold, hacking sound track, precisely applied, could leach the moment of all feeling.

But I never arrived at the TV room, never again saw the blur-faced children taking a pet monkey to the grocery store, and only from very far away did I hear the sound track meant to wash this material of meaning, the noises a giant might make from his chest after he's been dealt his deathblow.

One must fairly consider that all music is the sound a body makes as it comes to its pretty end. Is there any sound that cannot be traced back to that?

Usually in the public space of Forsythe I had to wade through mesmerized crowds of scientists, but tonight the entertainment corridor was oddly empty.

Down below, in the hallway outside the assembly, a pack of scientists hovered over something, and from the north hallway sprinted a retinue of technicians, who pushed their way through to what turned out to be a lab-coated body sprawled out on the floor.

There'd been an accident. Someone had fallen and was not moving.

The scientists stepped back to let the technicians work. From a white box came a stethoscope, and this was pressed onto the chest of the downed scientist. The victim was a woman, from what I could tell. She had lovely hair.

As the technicians worked to revive her, the scientists who had gathered started to drift away. They were lost in thought, or maybe just lost. Their minds were hollow and they walked away thinking nothing.

I felt a kinship with their indifference. Someone else's collapse was of no interest to me, either. When you remove the sound from a medical crisis, it feels far less worrisome.

The technicians circled the fallen scientist, lifting her onto a stretcher. With heads down they moved as one and led the woman away. They took their time. The casual pace suggested that their patient hadn't made it.

A reaction seemed optional.

Now I had the face-level monitor to myself, so I checked in with the outside world to see what the children were up to these days, out in their idyllic quarantine where they could hurl language at each other without consequence.

The video revealed the same sunny street as before, a crowd of children circling something, their heads so close together that, with the distortion painted in by the editor, they seemed to belong to a single, blurred cloud. At their feet was the same imprinted shadow, like graph paper tattooed on the road, even while the scenery behind them had been reduced to snow and noise.

The shadow from the Montrier electrical tower again. My old neighborhood.

None of this concerned me, though. None of this held any interest.

I was about to move off and settle in for more entertaining TV when I saw something in the corner of the frame. A girl sat on the steps to a house. She was alone, her hands melted into the blur where her head was, which meant she was hiding her face in her hands. I saw just her body, and it was the bouncing of her legs that interested me. Her knees were together and both legs bounced as one, bounced and then tilted.

This was curious. I'd seen this before.

This way and that. That way and this. This way and that and that way and this.

On the steps, this girl, doing something very particular with her legs.

Do you know, Dad, that I can do a trick?
Oh yeah?
Yeah!
I can make my legs go this way and that, that way and this!

Still, this meant nothing. Still it could have been any kid doing that. Wishful thinking could be vicious. Why should I be impressed? I was not impressed.

Then I saw the shoes: black Mary Janes scuffed to hell, and the sweet little head of hers, even through the blurring, most certainly more *long* than round, very much unmistakably tubelike in dimension, this poor girl, despite the scarf she wrapped around her neck, the square spectacles. Despite everything. The poor thing. She really did have such an unusual head.

My little Esther sitting alone on the steps.

I'm coming for you, Darling, I didn't say. I'm coming to get you.

44

The next morning, after being medically ambushed and stuck with a syringe of the child serum, I descended the ramp with LeBov to the room with the Jewish hole in it, where I'd begin my first day of work.

Behind LeBov trailed a retinue of technicians, faces hidden in foam, which made them look not unlike the children on television, sprung to real life and engraved on the air, reeking of illness. In two wagons the technicians pulled a piece of gear that produced a long, low moan. Through the thin metal bars of one of these things I thought I saw the bright glowing eyes of an animal. Well, perhaps it was a small person. Something looked at me from the cage.

LeBov moved with the careful steps of an old man, but he did so under his own power. Whatever was wrong with him, he seemed proud. I found it to be an interesting strategy. When he stopped, his entourage stopped, hanging behind with their tall foam heads tilted down, as if they were shy.

"We were all sorry to learn about your wife," LeBov wheezed.

"Sorry what?" I said. For some reason I pictured not Claire when he said this, but Esther, sitting on those steps, smoothing down her clothing, as if someone might soon approach and ask her to dance. Her legs swinging back and forth. I so wished Claire had seen this with me last night.

LeBov looked at me. "About what happened. I figured you were there."

I must have been staring at him because he retreated facially, blanked out his features.

"I promised you her safekeeping and I wanted to let you know I didn't do it."

"Do what?" I asked.

"We're not sure what happened. Perhaps it was an allergic reaction to the serum, perhaps she was already sick. Or your daughter's voice penetrated the immunity. This is still happening when the emotional connection is high. We don't know. Or somehow someone broke protocol and rushed her with speech. Whoever it was who spoke to her, it hurt her."

Whoever it was.

I asked, "Hurt her how?"

I pictured Claire leaving my room, the Hebrew letter nearly boiling in her hand, then making it out to the assembly area where something went wrong, and she collapsed.

> *Now what kind of shoes does he wear?*
> *Probably golden shoes.*

The scientists circled her, probably wished they could undress her and cut her open. No one noticed her fist clenched over the Hebrew letter that might have poisoned her. Then came the technicians and their paddle, their dun-colored tools of revival, and the scientists backed away. That was Claire they worked on. While I was upstairs looking at our old neighborhood on the video monitor, catching sight of our shared daughter on the steps.

Was that the word for it? We *shared* a daughter? I'd not thought about it that way before. If we shared a daughter, and something happened to Claire, then I would not have to share Esther with her anymore. I would have Esther to myself.

Only true in a glorious world of hypotheticals. The real truth was that neither of us *had* Esther and in the end we shared nothing.

Outside the door to the Jewish hole, LeBov bent over a wagon, attended to the piece of gear. He rummaged in the wooden box, got his arm in there as far as his shoulder.

Then he fed a length of clear piping into his mouth and spoke, his lips stretched bloodless.

LeBov's words came out watery, leaking around the pipe.

"I'm not going to tell you that she's going to be fine. That I won't do."

I said, "And yet you'll do almost anything else. You've suddenly drawn a line?"

I pictured Claire alone on a hospital bed, ignored by a man who had a cushion for a face. If they confiscated the letter, the corpse of it, there was no question they could track it back to me. If they cared to.

That letter, sucked free of meaning, its story discharged, probably looked exactly like me now. Decayed to resemble its miserable maker. We make the language in our own image and the language repulses us. A damning piece of evidence, as if I'd torn off my face, shrunken it in fire, then sent it out to harm the woman I was supposed to love.

"You're doing everything you can for her, right?" I said. "You're going to tell me that there's nothing you won't do. All the expertise of this shithole is being brought to bear on it, and now you're going to make her better, right?"

A dark froth rose in the pipe that fed into LeBov's mouth. Whether it came from his own nasty interior or the little medical wagon, I wasn't sure, but it filled the pipe and seemed to churn in there.

The chemical reaction did not suit him. LeBov's eyes fluttered, rolled back in his head. He reached for me, to hold on to something, but I stepped back and he fell.

I distanced myself further to allow the technicians access to the man. They'd want to perform their intervention now. Usually they were so quick to come to LeBov's aid. But the technicians hovered and, if anything, pulled farther away, their pillowed faces revealing nothing.

Perhaps they were under other instructions now.

I yelled at them and they tilted, as if they could dodge what I said. Without faces it felt absurd to shout at them, like scolding a stuffed animal. It was clear that they would not be helping their leader.

I crouched over LeBov, pulled the tube from his mouth. It was jammed in there pretty badly and he wheezed when it finally popped free.

Some dark spit clung to his lips, seemed to harden as he breathed on it.

"You should never have taken our listener," I said. "It didn't belong to you. And you shouldn't have pierced it. That was a big mistake. A really big mistake. That's why you're sick. You're not supposed to get that stuff on you. Perhaps you're going to die again."

"That's not it. It's the Child's Play, the side effects."

"Right."

"That's what we call it."

"Who is we?"

"The other LeBovs."

LeBov seemed sad to have admitted this to me. *The other LeBovs.* From the wagon came an animal growl, so throaty and plain it sounded like a person.

"How many of you are there?" I asked.

I pictured a room full of redheads eating from the same animal carcass, licking each other's bloody faces. The LeBovs.

"One too many, maybe."

It worried me to see LeBov so scared, ill.

"I didn't think I'd ever see you feel sorry for yourself."

"There is no *myself.* I bargained out of it."

"In return for what?" I asked.

"Not this," he said. "I definitely didn't think it would be this."

For a moment LeBov couldn't breathe and his eyes bulged with panic. He grabbed his throat and seemed to choke himself, which somehow restored his air.

"Why don't you stop taking the serum if it's making you so sick," I said.

"I don't care for silence. It's not my specialty to keep my mouth shut."

"Then you'll never fit in. I think silence is headed your way."

LeBov endeavored a long blink that did not make things look good for him.

"Don't forget that you've made a commitment," he whispered, eyes still closed.

"That's true."

I palmed his sick face, leaned into it, as if a man had popped through the earth and I was stuffing him back into his hole, where he belonged. If the floor had been soft, I might have pushed LeBov through. His head seemed to give a little as I pressed on it.

LeBov tried to look at me, but his open eye would not obey. His eye followed, with apparent interest, some invisible object in the air. I'd seen such detachment before, when Claire collapsed in the field, a rapturous commitment to an invisible world, and I was starting to covet it.

I said, "I always keep my promises," wondering if I ever had.

Just not to you, I didn't say. Not to you, or your kind. And if you will hijack my body with a chemical in order for us to speak, then I will not be accountable for anything I say. Whatever words I said to you were borrowed. Brought to you by some child lying listless somewhere. One of the siphoned ones. You sponsored what I said. Those words are on you.

I left him there. If LeBov was breathing, it was only mildly. He seemed unsure that breathing would help. On the fence about it. Ready to stop trying, maybe pursue other avenues. Weighing his options. I envied the attitude. At least he was at peace with the coming coldness.

From one of the wagons came a low, soft growl, the unmistakable click of teeth. The technicians bobbed in place like rifle targets.

45

From a hallway beneath Forsythe I entered the room with the broken Jew hole. LeBov sprawled in a black puddle on the floor behind me while his retinue refused to interfere with his collapse. Maybe the other LeBovs needed this one to die. It was hard to blame them. The redhead was too sick to be of further use. Sick from Child's Play. Of course he was. I didn't say good-bye.

Inside the vaulted space the Jewish radio testing was in full swing. This was the large-scale listening task force I was meant to join, siphoning deep rabbi sounds from cabling that I wasn't sure even carried them.

I guess it was my mouth they wanted.

Radio gear glittered along the far dirt wall. An arsenal of antenna wire drooped over a table, in gauges so fine they shone like hair. Some of it, when I touched it, *was* hair. But it was far too long to have come from a person.

On a testing platform Jews spooled wire into the jacked-open faces of mannequins.

The mannequins were pink save for bands of wire necklacing their groin. Boots anchored them to the platform, but a few inflatable mannequins floated overhead, tethered like kites to lightning rods. They looked like little balloon people, in seated postures, hovering upside down in the air. From their mouths spilled an overgrowth of wire as if they were coughing up their insides.

The largest mannequin, on its back with a wire jammed into its torso, wore a copper yarmulke. Around its left arm metal tefillin were strapped.

It was quite a lot to take in. I'd come far from my scripts desk, far from the language-testing courtyard. Here in the dirt vault of the Forsythe Jew hole they weren't creating a new language but listening fiercely for one that might have always been there, however deeply encoded in copper.

The living were conscripted as listeners, too, martyrs seated in docile postures nearby. Citizens of Rochester, Buffalo, Albany. Shirtless men who looked surprised. One of them slowly combed his hair. Antenna wire grew like creepers up their faces. Test subjects with cages for mouths, human antennas. From their faces came nothing but white noise.

Next to the Jew hole itself, under the glare of the klieg lights, some Jewish scientists gathered at a console. Hairless men of my generation shivering inside their gowns.

Disappointment was in the air.

The console they fussed over was one of those moist slab radios fastened by beige elastic to a medical cart, squirting liquid runoff into a scuffed bucket on its underside.

Even I knew this was a questionable device when it came to repairing a transmission from a Jewish feed. It may as well have been a tiny fire in the woods. Perhaps the console radiated heat, and that's why the scientists were drawn so closely to it. They had private reasons for misleading the LeBovs. Surely they knew this piece of tech was a dead end. They knew but were not saying.

Such a phrase might serve as a new motto for our times.

At the feet of the Jewish scientists coiled the bright orange cable, snaking out of sight down the hole. They'd coated it in one of those reception-enhancing jellies. A liquid antenna ointment, rubbed onto the cable, rendering it so sensitive that it quivered in the dirt.

If you listened so intently into nothing, using gear like this, you might hear anything you desired. It made you think we were still being sickened from some language we didn't even know was out there. Inaudible, sub-whispered, mouthed by an enemy from so far away, it could not even be measured. Still it pulsed some toxin on us that made us all crawl on our bellies and choke.

I did not count the scientists, but I could guess there were nine summoned here by LeBov. Nine Jews divining at the quiet hole, to which I'd be the tenth, which would suddenly create the quorum that would ignite the wall of listeners.

Speaking of which, the occasional bird landed on a listener and pecked at it desperately, drilling into the sweet, brown core. No one seemed to mind the vandalism of these birds. Perhaps their work was intentional. Perhaps this was a necessary priming of the listeners. Before they could work in tandem they needed to be mercilessly gouged by a bird's beak.

Beneath the pegboard, there were skins shed by the larger listeners, collecting like shriveled faces in a trough. Next to the trough was a rumpled sack that looked to be filled with cream.

When I looked at the wall of listeners, for the first time I understood why a listener was once referred to as a *Moses Mouth*. Some names are so accurate they are unbearable.

A technician, stationed to monitor the doings of the Jews, gnawed at a sandwich through the tiny opening in his foam mask.

Nobody minded me as I circled the work site collecting what I could carry.

I received blank looks from the Jews. I'm sure I stared back at them the same way. My bruised face may have troubled them. Maybe they'd not even been alerted to my arrival. It looked like they'd not been alerted about anything for a long time.

Here we finally were in the community of Jews none of us had ever wanted. We were machines of indifference with a faintly human appearance. Stonewallers and deadpanners. Unimpressed, even when you pressed on us. Failures in one way or another.

Perhaps that's why we'd all embraced our private style of worship out in secluded huts in the suburban forest. When we came together we felt too much like nothing.

I would not learn what blackmail had driven my forest colleagues into this room. Did LeBov vomit in the bushes for each of these men, months ago in different neighborhoods, laying his trap, or was that a piece of mirroring customized for me alone?

How do you even know that I'm the real LeBov?

As forest Jews, were we supposed to love one another because we drank from the same orange cable, shared the same shade of doubt about the same unknowable deity? I most certainly could not think of the reason. Because love one another we couldn't. It was just a more territorial form of self-loathing to revile people too much like ourselves.

These were men too much like me. If they had a complaint, a disturbance, some kind of undoused anger scorching their interior, one would need a long knife to release it. What's the name of the surgical technique required to draw forth a man's hidden material? Who is it that forges and sells those tools?

We should have all lined up for a leeching procedure, and they could have bottled our private liquid after sucking it free of our concealing shells.

Far above the work site, birds rode thermals inside the Jew hole space of Forsythe. The most gorgeous birds I've ever seen.

When the air grew too crowded with them, a lone bird would plummet, returning to a glass tank in an unlit sector of the Jew hole space. A nude old man sat here, quietly addressing a microphone. When I came closer, to assess his work, I heard a singing voice I knew too well. One I'd never forget.

The old man sang with Rabbi Burke's voice. A perfect imitation. Songs not so beautiful, a warm-up to the sermon to come. No one else could sing in a key that old, on the melodic side of awkward. This was a voice that came from only one man's body in this world. Birds entered his glass tank and careened inside his sounds, as if they could replenish themselves on music. Then they squirmed out through the glass aperture and shot back into the sky.

There was a broadcast bulb above the man's glass tank—the kind you once saw at radio stations—and it glowed white. He was singing *live*, over the airwaves, to whatever world remained.

I stroked the man's hair and he looked up at me with a face I'd always wanted to see. I did not care if his words were from decades ago or today. I did not care if he spoke a decoy service to deceive people like LeBov, whether his sermons were real or fake, because what was the distinction again? It didn't matter to me. He was still mine. And now they'd gotten to him, too, reduced him to a crooning role in this underground work site. Or else he'd always been here, had never left, and it took me this long to find him.

He rested his head against me and I held him close.

So it's you, I didn't need to say.

To which the rabbi offered no answer but a smile so peaceful it was unbearable.

He resumed singing, and the birds circled, waiting their turn in his tank of sounds.

If I were anyone at all, I would have taken the rabbi with me. But I wasn't. It turned out that I was no one, out only for myself, what little of it that remained for saving.

You might protest when I call this man a rabbi. But you didn't see him, did you? You weren't there. You didn't know his voice your whole life the way I did, and if you did, I ask you now to stand down and believe me.

In those final minutes I prowled the work site, hiding my mouth from the scrutiny of those Jews. Were they going to rush me, hold me down, feed me the final wire?

I'd forgotten how to act as if I had an inner life, but it was coming back to me now. The face could be a powerful instrument. I'd make myself look like a creature sent to perform maintenance. Oh, it was the *n*th fucking Jew hole I've had to fix, I tried to suggest, but before I could get to work, before I could let them use my *apparently special mouth* as a reception ground for some unprecedented message to flow through, I needed to gather some equipment.

All the while I inched closer to the hole.

That's not what it's for, I'd once said. *You can't go in there.*

Until I died I'd keep thinking of the things I'd gotten wrong. Like this. Worshipping for years and years over a hole that I'd not once thought of entering.

No one seemed inclined to try to stop me, which suggested that no one sane would ever jump into this hole and climb down into nowhere with any hope of surviving.

Exactly my fucking point.

I crept up to it and from the hole a blast of air hit me, foul and cold, like the rank breath of people who've been buried alive. For all I knew, people *had* been, and they were down there waiting for me.

I'm coming, I didn't say. *I'll be with you soon.*

I grabbed more tools and some cellophane-wrapped lobes of food until my canvas satchel was stuffed.

On a hook beneath the klieg lights hung the quilted coats for a meat locker.

I took one, tested the fit, then layered a larger coat on top of it.

I required a hard shell over my skin. I couldn't be sure what I would encounter down below in the tunnels.

Because that's where I was going. Down the hole and out of there forever.

Above me somewhere, in a bed, plugged into support machines, *or perhaps plugged in no longer*, was Claire.

For the second time now, instead of staying to help my wife, I went the other way.

I looked at no one, then stepped into nothing.

I plunged down the Jewish hole of Forsythe in free fall, the underground wind rushing over me so sweetly it seemed that, perhaps, as I fell, I might have been in bed, too, and if I only rolled over, just rolled over a little bit farther into the darkness, breaching her side of the bed, I could maybe hold my Claire again for a little while, hold her so tight that perhaps it would not hurt so much when together we landed in the world below.

3

46

Yesterday morning I left Esther resting on my cot and walked out into the swale to collect wood. She would not miss me, perhaps not even know I was gone. I chose a southerly trail and jumped through the brush and shittings until I found a nest of felled branches, then took my time striking them into pit-size pieces for burning.

It is late autumn, I think, three years since I dropped down the Jewish hole at Forsythe and made my escape back to the old hut, where the feed has long since snuffed out. The hut makes a small home for me now. The orange cable has gone cold.

I have not kept faith with the calendar. My timekeeping is promiscuous at best. Perhaps it's already winter and the climate is only slow to frost.

I am not so troubled by the season; it's the shrinking of light that gives concern. The darkness of this New York has grown more severe lately, blotting up from the soil before the sun has even withered off for the day. It's a soaking darkness, cold on my body when it comes.

The pretext for my outing yesterday was wood, more fuel to warm our forest hut, but in truth I was looking for something else. Something that will help Esther. What I was seeking is small and it has a face and it breathes so prettily, in little wet gusts of air. Often it comes along willingly. It harbors a medicine inside its delicate chest.

One day, when Esther has healed, when she can sit up and see, when she can tolerate my presence as her caretaker and endure me, if silently, I would like to take her on a tour of this valley in the woods behind her old house.

I can show Esther where I kept watch of the quarantine for so many months, years, the bench I built into the mud, the blind of trees I thickened, branch by braided branch, so I would not be discovered. I can point to where I sat, mime how I looked out across the river until my face ached, hoping to see her behind the town gates.

A more difficult story to reveal to Esther will be how, when I first arrived home—if such a word can apply to our Jewish hut—I contemplated going into the old neighborhood after her. I weighed the risks, keeping her safety in mind, then finally decided against such an incursion. I knew Esther was inside the child barracks and close to a failed immunity—her age was simply no good anymore, and we all grow up to speechlessness now, don't we?—and I knew she'd soon be released without any perilous invasion by me.

What's the mime for such a rationalization? *I would have saved you but I knew I didn't really need to, since you were probably going to be released soon*. My body lacks the finesse for that kind of message. Those contortions are beyond me. Instead I might stare into space and let Esther see—she's a smart young woman—that the issue is pretty fucking complicated.

One might argue that, absent of speech, deprived of all communication, a father dissolves. The title finally expires, and the man probably follows. You don't strip away a father's title and expect the man to live. A former father is just a man who once had a duty to answer. Perhaps he can barely recall what that duty ever was. It nags at him as something he forgot to do, something he did only poorly. Fatherhood is perhaps another name for something done badly.

Perhaps it is better now to liken a father to an animal parent. Certain caretaking is observed, but when the offspring matures, alienation and estrangement set in. Rivalry. The youngster grows preternaturally angry at the father, for some reason angrier at the father than at any other creature, and the father opens a small hole in his chest to accommodate this anger, which flows in rapidly. An emotional ecology is observed, with the energy composted and renewed in the chest of the man. A deep, circular structure is satisfied with the anger returning to its creator, who probably is not equipped to hold it anymore. He must release it through new activities in the world.

It is problematic to father alone. By this I do not mean without a wife. That can actually be simpler, finer. A single authority, a clear chain of command. None of the agonies of partnered power, although I'm confident that Claire will soon join me here at the hut. Instead I mean it is difficult to father without an actual child. How exactly does one father when no child is to be found, and yet the father has not finished his work, has fatherish urges he wishes still to discharge, since he did not do so enough when he had the child on hand? It is a central question.

Now that Esther has returned to me, my fatherhood will be evident to her in even the small touches, and not a word will have to escape my mouth. Esther will come to enjoy the woods behind her old house, find the resources she needs, perhaps one day consider this hut her home. She'd never been allowed at our hut before, couldn't even know about it. Now it is hers. She will appreciate the steps I have taken to ensure her comfort.

We need to get her well first, that's all. This is what I do not, cannot tell her. I know what words do, and I won't subject her to our fatal language. We need to fix her up and get her back on her feet.

Newcomers to muteness are not always pleased. I know this firsthand.

On the cot I have forced open Esther's eyes, stared into them. Her forehead is not just cold to the touch. *Cold* is not the word. The skin of her arms is slack. Her lips vanish into her face. They are paler than her cheeks.

I will admit that there were days when I first had Esther back in the hut, only a few weeks ago, leaving mugs of soup on the stone post for her, putting bread, dusted with salt, near her sleeping face, when I could look at her for the wrong number of minutes, an extended scrutiny that wore down my joy and left me unsure of who it was I had brought home.

It was marginally possible I'd rescued, instead of Esther, a stranger with a different name.

The hair was not really the hair of Esther. It was flat, brown, indoor hair, the kind more often found hidden beneath a person's clothing. Under this girl's tongue I felt the tough, dead skin. LeBov's Mark. We all had it. A tongue fallen too long into stillness, hardening now in the mouth like a bone.

And Esther's body? I did not have pictures to compare this girl to, but I shouldn't have needed them. A picture in the wallet is for others, for boasting, not for the goddamn father himself, who has a picture of his children burned eternally into his mind, correct? Was she shorter than I remembered? Something was wrong. When I recalled Esther, it was now with a smeared face. Where was the smell I could not even describe to you? Life among the worded children had rubbed my daughter in the scent of too many strangers. It gave offense. It did not reach deep enough inside me to trigger my good side. I wanted a sharper dose of recognition. I worried that my paternal instincts would not ignite as long as I suffered this doubt.

While waiting in the blind beneath the ledge for Esther to be released, I recalled the four-year-old perfectionist who flew into rages, the eight-year-old who'd taken modesty to such extremes that she wore a robe over her clothes, the Esther new to her teens who was so disturbingly pretty that her mother and I fell silent when we saw her.

How could a girl so striking tolerate the wretched people her parents had become?

Oh, of course. She couldn't.

While waiting in the blind for Esther's release, what I failed to picture was a gray-faced Esther, as if prepped for entombment, an Esther who was recumbent and dry-lipped with iced-over eyes. I had not planned for such a helpless body, erased of the Esther I knew, much like her own mother when the quarantine was announced. The illness had rendered Esther anonymous, and I found it better not to look too closely.

Still I tended to her. I boiled a broth, filtered it through a cone of flannel. With the residue I made little pills for her to suck. From the larder I flayed a choker of cured meat, and when her fevers surged I worked with cloth to keep her face cool and clean.

Esther did not thrive with me huddled over her, staring, dabbing. If she seemed to see me, it was with a scowl, but scowl does not describe a face that shows disappointment and irritation mixed with something that a father might read as his child's relief. Or maybe he only wants to see relief, and the desire, projected strongly enough, nearly changes the face of the young woman in the bed. I registered the small winces of distaste at my attentions, and, when I was certain Esther was disgusted by my hovering, repelled and annoyed and altogether bothered, I quietly celebrated. When I saw these grimaces I felt more sure that, yes, this was my Esther. *Get away from me*, I could almost hear her say. This was displeasure that I knew. A comfort to see something that I remembered. This was my girl. Finally I grew sure I had brought her home.

After that I draped a woolen wall over the cot, a blanket hanging from a wire, so Esther would not suffer any added distress. No need to punish her with my presence. Esther prefers privacy. I do understand. She deserves what personal space I can provide.

She deserves a little house of her own, too, and maybe when she recovers, and when her mother returns to us, Esther can choose the site herself, so long as it's not too far from this hut. So long as I can get there easily, even in darkness.

47

Not so far off in the sky, the odd bird tours the valley. Birds seem to prefer the speechless world. If you lived here you'd have to be buried alive not to notice the superior joy they demonstrate overhead. Victory laps inscribed in the air. Rubbing it in. Admiring the way their shadows crawl over the salt below. Perhaps you require no convincing. Perhaps such sights are available where you live as well, and you, too, look from your shelter at this airborne gloating.

When I picture you examining this account, dangling each decaying page aloft with a tweezers, I wonder if you are alone, barricaded from someone with whom you once spoke freely. Are you reading this with assistance, an inhibitor cutting into the folds of your mouth? Does some cold, salted tonic sluice through your blood to give you shield, if briefly? Or is your protection something more, shall we say, bitter and problematic, achieved at a greater cost?

Perhaps a little one fell down in a great black swoon after you sucked free his assets, and the transaction has left you, what is the word, *troubled.*

Is there salt where you are, too? Just so much of it everywhere? Can you reckon that it is really the residue of everything we ever said, piled now in soft white mounds? It seems far too pretty to only be our spoils.

I would like to question you on your symptoms, the path you navigated to language, the choices you've faced. But we will never speak, as

I will be dead by the time you read this. We do not get to survey the people of the future, who laugh at how little we knew, how poorly we felt things, how softly we knocked at the door that protected all the best remedies. You are monstrous and unreal to me now, it is important that you know that. You are my reader but I cannot reach into your face and pull out your secrets. Perhaps you live in a time when someone else's harm is not bound up with your pursuit of words and you traffic easily with the acoustical weapon, the clustered scripts. Congratulations, if so. I remember those days, too. It is my true wish that you enjoy yourself.

But enjoyment is not one of the choices we have here today.

Darkness soaks these woods by afternoon, browning in so low. One must be careful in this season not to be caught past noon on too remote an errand in the woods, because after sunset a return home is difficult, even for me, who knows these trails by heart. This darkness is different. It interferes more finally with one's passage through the woods, and one must halt all activity until the sun boils it off, if only partially, in the early morning.

I will admit that I supply some of this darkness myself, through failed eyesight, draining health. My pursuit of language immunity has come with its own dear little cost. A certain serum I use has not agreed with me. Some mornings I discover my yellowed bandages, smitten in dirt and dew, and for a minute I think there is another one like me. I see these bandages strewn around my hut like tufts of rancid snow and think I am not alone until I realize that, *oh, yes,* these bandages are my own, aren't they, and I tore them off last night because they burned. I could not bear the hot wadding on my skin.

As such, I cannot accurately make a statement about some objective loss of light. I have no device to record the expiration of daylight I suspect. I'd not be able to supply evidence for such a decline, my faculties of detection are compromised, and in any case I am not a specialist on the atmosphere.

What errands I have are few. Such freedom to come and go might have been useful back when people spoke, but now it is only a bitter advantage. What an archive of hindsight I've grown fat on, spoiled ideas and second thoughts ripening in my body now for no one, the putrid material. I'd like a more physical way to extract all of it, memories, too, a surgery I could perform to finally release it, burn it down.

It is not clear why the ideas are put in us if we only wish they could be removed again.

Instead of errands to kill the day, I can sit in my hut and wait for my wife's arrival, listening at the old Jew hole for the sounds of her crawling this way.

Oh, don't worry, I am perfectly aware of the fantasy involved here, but what we want is almost never exempt from the impossible. That barrier has very little meaning for me these days. Given what's happened, *the impossible* is just a blind spot that dissolves if we move our heads fast enough. History seems to show that the impossible is probably the most likely thing of all.

But this waiting has its challenges. It is too easy to imagine that one hears a person struggling on her stomach through a narrow tunnel, from Forsythe to here, and the suspense is difficult. When I cannot endure it, I hike up to the vacant town that has stored enough untouched goods to sustain me for years. Some of the food was looted, but only some, as if when people first stormed through, arming their new life of solitude, they found they were not especially hungry.

So for errands there is the gathering of food and tools even as the surplus spoils in my cold locker, plunder spilling down the hillside. Mostly I grab what I already have. I hoard. I stockpile. I do what solitary men in the speechless world must do.

How important that sounds. I mean only to say that the published etiquette for life in these times is slim. A code of conduct for people like me is unavailable, and if it were, it would damage one's body to read it.

What is it called when a dark, hard magnet has been run over one's moral compass so many times that the needle of the compass quivers so badly that it cannot be read?

Machineries of reason, machineries of conduct, machineries of virtue. The machine that regulates instinct, keeps one's hands free of another man's throat, free of one's own. These machines have all, as someone said, gone too long in the elements. Gummed now, rusted, bloodless.

I forget who said it and I no longer care.

I suppose with my time I could farm and hunt and subsist through harvest, but all of those food products on shelves in empty stores off the quiet freeway make such labors unnecessary.

As to hunting, when I consider it now, there is a certain version I have practiced. I had not really named that form of smallwork. *Hunting*. But if hunting means the careful tracking and subsequent acquisition of a living resource, *for whatever reasons*, then, yes, I have hunted.

Just the few times.

48

When I monitor the quarantine across the river, what I see is not so much anymore. The child quarantines here at this final New York—and staggered in settlements up and down the coast, even as the salt rises—have developed an orderly form of dispatch when they need to eject their own, young citizens of eroded immunity, tongues hard in their mouths, newly pained by language.

All of them will age, and all of them will have to leave, and then my town, my house, will be free of their kind, the easy-speaking ones. I cannot fathom another outcome.

Now the little gate opens and out they come, dazed and already ill. No doubt they will not live long, unless they can quickly adapt to the laws of the speechless world.

Hide yourself away, is one of these laws.

And, *If you see someone*, goes another one, *exercise the necessary evasions.*

The laws apply because I am not the only person hidden in these hills watching the exits. I am not the only one with an *interest* in these young people.

There are others like me, but they are not really like me. *Escorts, predators, parents.* So many different words might apply to them.

I've seen them rush to meet the exiles, using a mixed weaponry of kindness and cruelty. A gracious welcome, the offer of a blanket, a comfortable ride in a cart. Or instead a quick capture, a stifling, the enclosure of rope, an abduction. From my distance these transactions play out slowly, without feeling. They suffer from problems of believability.

The rescuers move alone or in groups, faces covered, and most often their lure is food, which our little speakers have had trouble securing. The exiles hardly ever resist. They get so hungry! They are still children, really, and they are sick, but now they are alone. So when the welcome wagon comes, they climb in.

Off they go with their new families to a life without words somewhere west of here. That is how they compass, usually, west, then south. Probably they go to Wheeling, Marion, Danville. I've been too bored to follow them beyond Albert Farm. They almost never drag back this way, into the salt, where nothing is good for anything and nobody would ever think to set up a life.

Perhaps the mute, gazeless family life in underground berms, where even eye contact must be kept in check for its lurches into nuance and meaning, is more pleasant in the sunshine of our warmer towns. Perhaps the salt is finer there, easier to sweep away.

Now that Esther has come to me, or I to her, as the case was, fighting off some rescuer waving sugary hunks of bread at her, then dragging her by spoiled light through the marsh, over the river, and up to the hut, I have little reason to keep watch of the town gate. I've gotten what I came for. My daughter is back in my custody. But sometimes I sit under cover in any case, hills away, watching these exits through binoculars. It's a habit of years.

Over time people either gave up on the children harbored within, or the children came out of their own accord, contrite and quiet. If the parents were lucky, they got to them before anyone else did. But what they did next, where they went and what happened after they arrived, what those people actually did with their days when silence was enforced by the speech fever, that information is not available to me. I refuse to make up stories about such people. To refrain from storytelling is perhaps one of the highest forms of respect we can pay. Those people, with no stories to circle them, can die without being misunderstood.

Too many nights, hiding in the brush, I've lost track of time during my observational work and found it too dark to return to the hut. I've spent sunless hours dug in against some low hillside, forcing from myself an artificial laughter to keep warm. You've heard of laughter in the hills. This is all it is. It's no mystery and nothing is funny. Just a person like me, pulsing sound and breath through his body, trying to stay warm.

I've lived these winters before, speechless, waiting. They bring one too close to the doings of one's own mind, some of which—I finally believe this—must remain unheard, must have their meaning amputated until they're reduced to babble. A careful listener to such interior speech is not rewarded. These winters fail to blot the mind, and what now could the mind even be for, since its fears and lies cannot be shared? Often I have wished that the toxicity, when it came, had reached deeper, into the unspoken speech we stalk and hound ourselves with.

Thinking is the first poison, said someone. One often fails to ask this of a crisis, but why was it not *worse*? Why was the person himself not gutted of thought? Who cares about the word made public, it's the private word that does more lasting damage, person by person. The thinking should have stopped first. *The thinking*. Perhaps it is next in the long, creeping conquest of this toxicity, another basic human activity that will slowly be taken from us.

Oh, I fucking hope so.

49

So yesterday I left Esther asleep on her cot and went out to get wood. I have a chain saw for clearing, but a tool like this is a luxury for someone who wants mostly to sit in his hut and listen carefully at the hole for news that never comes, for a person who is really getting late. I'd settle for a hiss from the wire, just the crackling of static, even, suggesting the orange cable has been plugged in again to Buffalo, to Albany, to I don't care where. Then I might listen to a story from the old days.

They really are the old days. They have aged. They are not pretty to consider.

Why the Jewish feed is so long silent is a question I cannot resolve. Or maybe I should say that I don't know why there's no more bait on the line. Perhaps Rabbi Burke, in the tomb of Forsythe, is mouthing silences on the other end and that's all that is left. Do the birds still bathe in his glass tank, I wonder?

For some years now, since leaving Forsythe by tunnel, I have been alone, and I have worked to leave no evidence of myself in this place. My solitude was corrected by Esther's arrival, an arrival I arranged through years of patience, waiting under cover for her exile to end, hoping that through binoculars I'd see her emerge by horse and cart, by sled, on foot, out of the town gates.

She is my first visitor. Well, that's not accurate. One or two times I brought another person into this hut, three times, a person unknown to me. Maybe we could say this happened five times altogether, persons other than Esther. Is person the right word? In truth I do not care for a tabulation of the activity.

Children, they were. I did not harm them. I fed them soup topped with cut squares of one of my long breads, which I crisped over the cold burner. You'll wonder what these children offered in payment after they'd been fed. This is a natural curiosity. One feeds a stranger and in return, *well.* Soon I will share the details, before my language usage expires here for good.

So yesterday I cut and gathered my wood, then left it piled in its fine pyramid, and stealthed downhill to lie in wait for assets.

Sometimes you see them on the grass ramp that once featured children playing before school. Sometimes they wander right up to you and raise their arms, actually wanting to be picked up. At such times, one obliges. One reaches down and picks them up.

I stayed too long. The light failed. No assets came, just a horse. It was untroubled and calm as it stood eating grass in a field, not even startling when a loud crack shook the sky somewhere to the east.

Ammunition does go off every now and then. It sounded like a house breaking in half.

When I woke it was dark, and I broke my own rule. Esther would be alone all night in the hut if I didn't return. I had to get back, even if that meant hours of blind groping.

Behind the hut I've dug a fire pit, where I cook the occasional brittle lobe, sear a cake of jam, and bring heat by venting into my hut so I can withstand the cold nights. The pit I fill with wood in the mornings, and then again late at night. Sometimes in the middle of the night, when I ache to pee, I wrap up in one of the buntings and stuff more branches in the hole.

Each week I dig out the ash and carry it by wheelbarrow to the softeries, out of sight of our old neighborhood, where the fencing starts, under the shadow of the children's loudspeakers.

It's Aesop's fables they have playing from them now, but the speakers have fallen into terrible repair, warping the speech so badly that it no longer spreads the poison. If anything it sounds pretty, some low-toned singing as if from deep underwater.

Living here is not ideal, no matter how Claire and I used to dream of it. When I was alone I could endure the conditions. With Esther commanding the lone cot now, even my seat at the hole, where years ago I sat with Claire and clutched the orange cable, digging my fingers deep into the flesh of the listener, is too crowded.

Oh, I'm not forgetting that LeBov went down this same hole once. Or maybe sometimes I am.

On windless days I can hear Esther's breath, wheezing from her lungs as if she were straining to inflate a balloon. Sometimes the wheezing stops and it's too quiet in here. I look at the cloth wall that divides us and wonder if this is it. If only one of us gets to breathe, it had better not be me. Suspense left my life a long time ago, but now it has returned. I do not care for it.

It was so dark last night, I could not see my hand in front of my face as I tried to make my way back to Esther. Navigation by starlight was impossible because there were no stars. They were just too far away. Everything was. Had there been stars I could see, it would have meant nothing anyway. Above me would stand the rebuke of an information system I have failed to learn, a map written in one of those languages unsuited to describing anything but itself. Maybe all languages are like this.

I knew I had an incline to gain, but I did not know when to break from it to find the lateral path. Throughout the night I descended and climbed, then traversed along what was not the path. It was never the path. Too often I fetched up in a tangle of trees, probing a clammy flesh beneath the bark. Once my hand worried into what felt like soup, but this was waist-high, and I yanked it free when it started to burn.

I stumbled, fell, sometimes stayed down to rest, breathing in the fine iron smell of the mud, which dried over my face and brought the whole world into silence.

My absence tonight should not matter. Esther preferred me gone from the hut anyway. She'd not even try the soup I'd brew for her, and the bread might only get torn to pieces and scattered to the floor, tossed away angrily as if she were a toddler. Even if I got home before bedtime, when the lamp was snuffed out and the jar of water was replenished on the stone post, I'd be up and down all night anyway, awake on the floor listening to the rough struggle of Esther's breath behind the cloth.

My absence should not matter. I was certain of that. Esther would be fine. Better to stay out here and sleep.

I did not try again that night to push free of my place in the mud.

Nor did I will myself to stop thinking of Esther, alone in the hut all night. The night was warm enough for me to make it where I was. There was no question that she would be all right there by herself. No question at all.

I would wait for daylight, what little of it I had lately been allowed. With daylight I would crawl back to our hut and there I would discover that all was perfectly well with Esther. Of this I was sure.

50

Three years ago I made my escape from Forsythe down the Jewish hole. For months I crept through underground mud on my way home, stopping only to listen for pursuers. The first tunnel I traversed was little wider than the orange cable I followed, and I had to work with whatever digging implements were at hand to gain my passage. At dead ends I did soundings, thumped against the earth until it shaled, and when the wall reported a promising hollowness, I worked with my fingers to bore a cavity.

It was ugly, dark work, and I grew foreign to myself, my skin like a hair-soaked stone, my face too numb to feel.

Others had come and gone before me in some of those passageways. Oh, had they. Their evidence festered along the embankment, muddied, broken, spent. Clothing frozen in dramatic postures, books, papers, shards of once-clear lobes now coated in hair. Luggage stuffed into mud holes. I shed my jumpsuit and clothed myself with the outfits of these pioneers. I found a grooming kit and hacked at the fur on my face, used one of those soft, moldable stones to scrape myself bare.

What a terrible amount of salt was already everywhere, even down below. The first layer of it was burnt. It stuck to your hands.

The books I found remained sealed by glue. Loose pages, scattered like parade scraps, had their text blackened. The broken parts of writing codes were everywhere, handicapped scripts, decipher sheets, etchings in the walls, the local efforts of people to say something to someone, to get a message across.

If people had lived down here in the tunnels, they hadn't done it well, and they hadn't done it for long.

As I burrowed south in the next months I took many trips to the top, whenever ladders appeared in the tunnel or some knotted rope hung down or light wriggled in from above, or, most of all, when the orange cabling, my true mapping device, detoured vertically, usually at a bulging splice in the line. I always followed it. I burst out into fields, butted against concrete slabs, emerged at the bottom of shallow ponds, punching through muck into the air.

Sometimes I even pierced into huts covering the apparent Jew holes of strangers.

Once I came up under a trapdoor that wouldn't fully spring. When I stopped to listen, I heard footsteps, the awful pressure that fills the air when people mute their fear. Someone had rolled a bed over the door I crouched beneath, and when I finally squeezed through, no one was there. It was a damp house that people had left in a hurry. They were outside cowering, probably, petrified by the man who'd broken through their floor. The orange cable I'd followed into this hut divided into a network of the finest little wires, so delicate I could hardly see them. If it weren't for the miniature cups of liquid the wires landed in—brass thimbles scattered over the floor, tendrils of wire dangling into them—I might not have known they were there. Their strategy of conduction was curious to me, but I dropped away and left that place in peace.

Sometimes the orange cable frayed into nothing in my hands. At its pinched-off stump were teeth marks, a black calligraphy of blood where someone had chewed it through. Around me would be nothing familiar. Even the trees had an animal smoothness to their limbs, or there'd be no trees, not even the barest spasms of grass, just pebbled terrain as far as I could see, stones covered by a fine misting of salt.

More and more often, when I climbed through the earth to take a reading, it was night.

I am no reader of the nighttime sky, as I have said. I find its layout obscene. If it was nighttime aboveground, if I was in some kind of featureless lowland and could not safely find shelter, I dropped into the tunnel again, made camp, and waited in the safety of the tunnel for daylight.

Camp was a woolen wall I raised from blankets. With my knife I slashed a vent, then laced a stitching of twine in the seam, so that my window was a scar in the cloth. In daylight I crept out and disguised my hole, performing the obligatory landmark checks that would allow me to find my way back without a problem.

I did surface walks in towns that may have been Dushore or Laporte, the part of New York that seems to absorb so much sunlight it's forever shadowless wherever you look. When I walked through the grass, I'd sometimes step on something hard, panes of glass dusted with dirt, windows to shelters below, installed flush to the soil, easily hidden.

I stopped once to sweep away the grass and dirt of one such window, only to see a small, dark room, where an old man's face looked up at me. This man did not seem afraid. He beckoned. *Aren't you lonely, too*, he didn't need to ask. But I walked on.

In Wilbert, or maybe it was North Sea, smashed radios littered the road. From their severed antennas someone had built a figure of a person, gleaming in chrome, rendered in a posture of contemplation. It sat in a puddle now, starting to rust.

Weeks away from Forsythe, where the tunnel widened into a room-size cavern, I found a stash of jam jars, a cloudy red gelatin tiding inside. The lids pried off with a suck, and into the cavern drifted the bitter smell of skin. I used a pencil to spoon free some of the tinted jelly, which I rolled into logs. When these hardened overnight I subjected them to a long, slow heat.

Such little treats kept me nourished for weeks, and when I lodged one in my mouth, it released such a slow sweetness that for days, it seemed, I needed nothing else, not even water. I eat them still. Whatever's in them is almost all that I need.

There is little else to report of this journey. I surged south, then took exploratory routes away from my path, emerged from underground, calculated coordinates, dipped back into the tunnels, and corrected.

When I saw the Level Falls horse farm stripped of animals, stripped of its barn, just a few troughs remaining that had been turned over and which I did not want to disturb, I knew I was close to home, but judging by the quiet open roads, the unprotected route south into town, I did not want to risk overland passage. I had come this far in the tunnels. Now I would finish my trip underground, where I was unfollowed, unknown, and I could get to my destination in secret.

I lurched east after that. It was trial and error, but mostly it was error, until one morning I shoveled into a crawl space that had no stable bottom, just slimy, flesh-like objects upon which I could not get my footing. These were the pink rubber balls Claire and I had dropped down the hole so long ago, coated now with something cool and slick.

I was below the old hut.

The orange cable elevated. I pictured Claire sitting at the mouth of the hole, waiting for me. She'd have a sandwich ready, a thermos of soup. She'd be laughing, that laugh of anger she delivered whenever someone else's stupidity had been what she was waiting for, the perfect confirmation of all her suspicions. I'd yell up to her that I found the balls, all of them.

They're at the bottom and they're so weird all together, like one of those kid tents with balls in it, except the balls are all bloody. I'll be right there!

I climbed into the corridor. At the top, the mouth of the hole was stuffed with shredded pink insulation.

Perhaps this was what had obstructed LeBov when he made his way out of the hut to Forsythe several Decembers ago.

I picked at the insulation until a sheet of it released past me and slid down the hole. Then I climbed up into the hut.

Everything was mostly as I remembered it. In the corner, undisturbed, was the wooden crate painted with the word *Us*, a tuft of bluish wool hanging out of it.

It was Claire's winter hat, kept on hand for a just-in-case. I crawled over to the crate and put it on, smelling, I told myself, the very last remnant of her.

But the whiff I took returned nothing. It smelled only of smoke.

I walked outside, easily found the old path that dropped down to the creek, and beyond that, growing out of the embankment, was the still-recognizable profile of growth that Claire and I called the Seine.

This was it. I'd arrived. I was home.

Now I just needed to rescue my daughter.

51

Most of the rest you already know. The hut's mechanics were fucked. The orange cable was not just cold but worm-gutted as well. I ignored it for too long, too fearful of town, at first, to trek in and get supplies, letting the wiring blister.

Meanwhile, one of those pink vermin got to it, started eating into the copper, rubbed his bald body against its length until the cable shredded, like bright splinters of candy.

Once, early on, I inserted a copper feeler into the frizzed wiring of the cable, and I wove, from memory, a conductive nest of wire that I slipped under my tongue to complete the facial antenna. When I kissed the wire against the nest, clutching a grounding rod for safety, the old prayer surged on and pushed its way out of my mouth.

You have commanded us not to know you and we have obeyed. When we have known you we have looked away . . .

Whatever this was, it was no real prayer. It sounded like an apology for something that had never happened. I could not bear the sound, particularly in my own voice, and so I put away my wires and did not eavesdrop on this cable again.

I did not give up on my religion. I found only that I no longer required reminders, assertions, repetitions, harangues. Nothing outside myself. Whatever I believed played on inside me with no help from a radio. I'd heard enough for a lifetime. I found I could do without more things to misunderstand.

I spent my first months home determining the safety levels of my new settlement, circling the hut in wider surveys, moving low and quiet, stopping always to listen for pursuers, building my inner map of the place.

Deer froze when I approached, their muzzles frosted and white. I registered no threats of people. In the end I realized that I was well bounded by the murmur line, protected from others, but also captive as well. Unless you were a child, you could only get to where I was by Jew hole. I set up a few alarm lines anyway, some rudimentary triggers that might give me good minutes to vanish if necessary.

I suppose I was really only concerned about LeBov. A new one, maybe, whom I wouldn't recognize. That he was coming after me in the tunnel, would soon punch through the floor of the hut.

I should have filled the hole with dirt, with salt, so no one could come through again. Wheelbarrow after wheelbarrow until the thing was sealed. But I wanted to keep the hole open for Claire. I could not close it down yet. I had to think she would solve the problem the same way I did. I had to.

I'd only been back for a few days when I crept closer to the old neighborhood, heard the tin-voiced stories bleating from the loudspeakers. The broadcast created an effective repellent of sound, the worst choking in the air. If I got too close, I felt the suffocation—an airless panic triggered by an area ripe with language—so I determined early on where the murmur line was, that point on the periphery where I could hear the voice but not understand it. Beyond this I wouldn't go.

Then I marked the trees, some stones. I walked off distances until I found a natural observation point, one of a few that I'd rotate among as I spied on the quarantine, awaiting Esther's release.

There's little else to relate about my early time here. Waste and water were an early focus. Food was never a worry. I collected canned goods from the abandoned town, even if I hardly felt like eating. I must have spent a year without words.

Even in the summer there were cold, clear mornings, and I woke to a silence that only deepened as the day developed, a muteness that felt rich in nutrients, addictive. I was energetic and strong and almost fearfully alive.

On perfect days I braved the wall of trees on the back line of the swale and pushed up the cliff face to Tower Ledge, where we used to picnic. There were no families here now. The old grill cage had tipped over. The dog run was sick with weeds.

I heard nothing and said nothing, read and wrote nothing, and in time my thoughts followed into this hushed hole. I'd never much thought in sentences anyway, but there were always single words, phrases, sometimes lists, and these fell away, until what passed for thoughts were swooshes of sound, hisses whose meanings were clear to me and needed no decoding into language.

It was Claire who benefitted most from this sort of regard. She fit this way of thinking perfectly. When I thought of her while quietly clearing the land, as she'd wanted us to, while running water lines to the back stream, while washing and hanging the woolen skins I used on the walls for insulation, it was in the gentlest sequence of tones. Small, low notes like a lullaby.

I do not mean for this to be a statement of science, or even an experimental theory that the emotional consideration of a person is best undertaken with sounds, and not images or language—how could I prove this?—but I felt closer to Claire that year than ever before. Finally I stopped missing her, because she was with me now. I fell asleep to the sound of Claire, walked out to eat my lunch on the old shrunken rock above Tower Ledge, and all the while listened to sounds that brought my wife fully to my blood, my body. Through sound I felt finally bonded to her, in her company, whether or not she was even alive or, if she was, no matter what she might have felt about me. Her memory had evolved into sound, a perfect refinement. I loved her best that way with all that I had.

I mention this change only because this phase ended when I found the first child and began my project with assets, with person-derived inhibitors. Through medicine I brought myself back to the language and those tones of Claire went, what's the word for it? They were gone. I do not hear them anymore.

For that I blame the craven desire to speak, to write, to be heard.

52

A word about my serum: it is more bitter than water. It is not as cloudy as milk. In the winter it thickens with crystals. It foams into a butter when I squeeze into it, by dropper, a juice of the dark valley salt.

When I need some, I pull it out of little ones. I used it first at Forsythe. The crude kind, the roughly gained immunity, drawn on the priceless account of the child's person. It is the ingestion of this Child's Play, I am sure, that undid LeBov, if he finally did expire.

And it is the ingestion of this that will soon, no doubt, leave me frozen on the forest floor somewhere, blinking in perfect sunlight at a world I can no longer see.

53

I did not assign names to the children I saw in the woods. A remote perspective was best, sheared of sentimentality, which impedes a productive workflow. *Name not that which you intend to cultivate*, was the saying. Maybe it was just my saying. But *cultivate* is such a strong word. They were little ones sometimes sitting alone on a log. Medicine comes at us in so many disguises. It hides in the leaves of plants, grows under tree bark, mulch, sand. Sometimes it stows away in more valuable items, items more resistant to intrusion, and this is where our challenge is fullest. The smallworker addresses these shapes, living or not, and beckons forth that medicine that might benefit the person. But when that medicine resides within the bodies of those entities commonly known as children, the process of extraction grows more, what is the word?

I do not know what the word is.

54

My purpose here is not to detail exactly how I got the Child's Play serum to work, what sorts of failures I suffered along the way. I labored alone with limited tools seized from the half-looted pharmacy in town, made every sort of error, and at first I did not even know what I was looking for.

Blood and skin, perhaps hair, were the likely targets, so I found my way to small samples of these resources, siphoned or scraped them into bottles with little harm. But that got me nowhere close, because what I never saw at Forsythe was how these resources were processed. I knew nothing of the refinements such materials were subjected to, and I had no old man but myself upon which to test my discoveries.

If a little one wept quietly I played music, brought in a soup. Silence was the natural state of my subjects, who rarely probed their surroundings or tested the air with their small words. Perhaps it is because I looked like nothing they could speak to. The years had made me look unfriendly. Or not the years. Blame for my demeanor lies elsewhere. Perhaps the children felt I would be displeased, but if I was displeased it was for reasons that far predated their arrival in my hut. In every way I was a gentle guardian. I provided food and shelter, sometimes sat on the floor with them and played with the little sack of acorns I'd brought in for distraction.

After each round of extractions I tested the results down at the murmur line, walking into the blizzard of Aesop's fables until the crushing took me.

When skin and hair failed, I moved to blood, pricking the child's heel for a drop. I employed coagulants rifled from the hospital in town, seizing the fluid with some salts I'd smuggled out of the pharmacy, salts from *before*. I suspected that blood would be problematic, no easy fix, and in this suspicion I was correct.

Among the many shames was that I focused so much on the interior fluid, overlooking what should have been obvious all along.

The discovery came by accident. One of my subjects, strapped to an old bottled respirator, so large it dwarfed his little face, began the rapid breathing one never likes to see in a small person. Too often it foreshadows the unproductive kind of stillness. At the end of this boy's fit, after I'd removed the respirator and cooled off his head with towels, I noticed, while cleaning up, a residue in the boot of the respirator bottle. A powder.

It was impossible to account for the powder. I'd not medicated the supply of oxygen. It must have come not from me but from the boy, inside him.

I scraped it free with a knife, dumped some into a spoon, and lowered the spoon over my flame.

A clear smoke wobbled over the spoon. It filled the hut, stung my eyes. Into the air came a smell of berries, but within minutes, after my lungs had soaked it in, I collapsed on the cot. Not out of any physical distress. From what I could tell I felt fine. I collapsed because I had suddenly, with the arrival of this child smoke, been hit with a deep, unspeakable gloom.

The hut was colorless, my body in it a burden. The child on the floor looked to be squirming in mechanical postures designed to trigger a reaction.

I noted the repetition of his gyrations, the unimaginative way he thrashed.

I observed my mood, diagnosed it as incidental, then forced myself out to the murmur line. One might as well test the effects of every dosage, even an accidental one like this.

It was a warm day and I was flushed and sweating. Even in the sunshine my mood did not ease. It pulled at my breath, drew my sight into a darkened hole. It was a wordless despair I felt, a final sense of certainty that one's maneuverings were all tethered to some vector of, not even folly, but something far worse. Something much more terrible than folly.

At the shallow row of stones, I crossed the murmur line easily and kept walking into toxic territory. The fairy tales boomed from the speakers with perfect clarity and I did not stop. The recording was crisp and lucid and finally, when I determined that I could listen without detriment, I sat down on the path.

I was fine. The language floated above me, entered my body, and I held my own, swallowing it whole.

The serum was working.

On the path I heard, from the loudspeaker, the old tale of the blindfolded bird who must search for his mother by sound alone. I had not heard this one since I was young. I am no fan of stories, perhaps because they seem more like problems that will never be solved, and this was among my least favorite.

The bird is alone and scared. Because of the blindfold it cannot do the one thing it was made to do: fly. And its mother, though always nearby, learns to keep perfect silence when the little bird is on the verge of finding her. She keeps herself artfully concealed from him, hops away whenever he approaches. All the older birds do, so the little bird thinks he's the last bird left on earth. He calls out and no one answers. The mother holds her breath as her own little bird is so close that he can smell her. He knows it's her, right there. He doesn't need to *see* to sense his mother there. She holds her breath and stands perfectly still, a statue. He circles her, moves in, then finally cries out, at which point she leaps into the air and flies off.

When she returns later that day, laughing, with a lesson to share, he refuses to be comforted, will not acknowledge his mother, will not go near the older birds. He even insists on keeping the blindfold on his little head. Days go by and the bird won't take off the blindfold. He learns to get where he needs to go. He doesn't fly, but he can walk places. He gets around okay. Everyone thinks the little bird is sulking, taking himself so seriously. But it's not true. The bird is in darkness under that blindfold and that is what he has come to prefer. He is not sulking. He is happy. The blindfold becomes a part of him. Even though he will not speak to his mother again, or to anyone else, he is grateful to them. Every day he silently thanks them for their gift.

The story puts it differently, of course. Stories always do.

More stories followed from the great loudspeaker, filling the woods with sound. I spent some of the afternoon enjoying the broadcast of tales down beyond the murmur line. The smoke I'd inhaled was a mostly thorough shield, though with certain words I felt mild convulsions, suggesting a partial immunity, which would need to be addressed.

If the tales themselves did not please me, the voice they arrived in did, and it was this that I wanted to hear more of. I'd not been spoken to in years and the effect was luscious. I had taken this pleasure for granted. The stories were read by a child with a scratchy voice. They'd found a child who herself did not seem to understand the stories, because always at the moment of crisis, of conflict, the child's voice only became sweeter, as if she were entirely innocent of what she was reading. What an enormous gift that would be.

Or else to this girl these terrible moments were the good parts, the ones that gave her a thrill.

Finally my shivers came on more strongly, the stories cutting into my head with a cold pain, and my daylight began to spoil.

I walked home to see how my subject was doing. I'd need more of his breath in order to generate a true inhibitor, and I'd want to diversify beyond this boy. I'd need to establish that this extraction was not a fluke. It was the air of children I wanted, a fine-grained powder that rode out on their breath and offered to us a transformative medicine.

The discovery, in the end, was a simple one. I should have made it months ago. From hyperventilation of a child—ideally, one later learned, a child in agitated fright, surging with adrenaline—comes a residue in the lungs. Coughed up out of fear. And when this residue is refined of impurities, enforced with certain salts, then subjected to heat, it forms the foundation of our immunity. Child's Play. It lets the words back in, if briefly.

Whether such a reversal should be sanctioned is another matter.

55

Once I'd perfected the serum, and could endure without sickness the full range of Aesop's broadcasts below the murmur line, I sat down in the hut with the cherished contraband I'd smuggled from Forsythe: the voice tapes of my daughter, Esther.

A language archive of the girl. Paper and tapes, a broad syllabus of topics, a spectrum of moods. Our viral girl, fourteen years old, singing, laughing, yelling, whispering, arguing, speaking sotto voce, making up words. Reciting letters, numbers, crying out in pain.

I do not tire of these tapes. I will not. I have done the awful math enough times to determine that my inhibitor work is worth it to hear this girl speak. The work of gathering immunity, and the cost of such. Etcetera, fucking etcetera. The exchange, I believe, is fair.

It makes it safe to hear the girl's voice, and for that I would do anything.

I am ready to debate this matter. My arguments are strong. This is the last of my daughter's voice. You will be at a sad disadvantage if you challenge me on this point.

56

Last night I was stranded in darkness, out waiting for a child who never came. If one had appeared, and if I had secured possession, I would have led him to the extraction shed, applied the bottle to his face, and produced, if I could, a scenario that would lead to fright, which would lead to adrenaline, and, if I was lucky, my subject would hyperventilate, in those fast rabbit breaths, enough for me to collect a thimble of his powder.

A fairly standard bit of smallwork. I'd burn it down and bottle the smoke, which I could gust over Esther as she lay prone in the bed. If I'd done my job properly, the smoke would sink over her and she'd have no choice but to breathe it in.

This would be the last use of assets, just for this, so Esther could see something.

If it worked, if Esther sat up and passed the various little tests I could subject her to, to affirm her immunity—the shortest, smallest words I could say, offered in a sequence deliberately free of meaning so as not to disturb her—I would hand her the letter her mother wrote to her.

I've kept the letter safe since the day we left home. It is crushed and filthy, that is true, but I have not opened it. It is not for me. There were many times, under the protection of the serum, that I could have read it, but I didn't. It is for Esther, her mother's words of departure. I would let her read it alone. She could take all day with it in the hut. I would walk out to the clearing to give her time. I would wait as long as she needed me to.

When Esther finished reading the letter she could join me outside, if she wanted to, and I would not ask her what was said. I would never ask her.

But this was not to be. The day ended without a sighting, and my asset supply would have to remain low.

This morning the daylight finally soaked through the woods, forest sounds hissing up as I slept in the mud. Certain creaking reported in the trees, a whisper blew from the sturdier insects, roared over my wet resting place.

I slept well in the soupy muck. I was ready to return to Esther, and not make such a mistake again.

I wished only that I could better see the world in front of me.

A point of light appeared, then throbbed, stretching into a dime-size window, through which I could see just enough to fight my way back to my woodpile, then up the slope north and along that last crumbling ledge to the clearing where my hut stands and everything, from what I could tell, seemed to be exactly as I had left it.

Except that when I went inside the hut Esther was not behind the cloth. Her cot was neatly arranged, the blankets folded as if another houseguest might be coming. She'd made the bed, stacked her dishes on the doorstep, even swept the daily soot from our sill.

At the hammered vent in the wall a fresh blast of heat rushed in, suggesting a newly fed fire outside.

I pictured Esther taking advantage of my absence to tidy the hut, arrange everything neatly, then gather her things and leave. What a hurry she must have been in, thinking that at any minute I'd be home.

She must have stopped to look from the glassless window, hoping I'd not come groping up the path. How relieved she must have been when she could finally leave with no sign of me and night coming on so strong.

I went outside. My field of vision was still limited. Around me hung a brownness, so cloudy I felt I should be able to rub it away. I pitched my head through every contortion to be sure I wasn't overlooking Esther somewhere, slid my vision over the property and yard, because maybe she was bundled under a blanket on a log, enjoying the late morning hum, waiting for me to return so I could brew us some tea.

It was time for her to have healed, bounced out of bed, taking to the air so she could see where she'd been recuperating these last few weeks.

I told myself there was no reason to be concerned, but since when did I believe my own reassurances?

She must have only gone off on a short errand, perhaps a walk to stretch her legs. She would need to return soon, because she was not well, and she was not familiar with these woods. It was unwise for her to hike alone in an area where whole patches of ground can suddenly give way to a lava of salt. She would know that. She would be the first to be aware of how risky it was for her to travel abroad from me when she was so weak like this.

I sat down, held my breath, listened. This silence was for the best. If Esther was nearby, if she could hear me, such a sound, even the pretty sound of her name in the air, would not have been well received. Her name yelled out by me would have hurt her, stopped her progress through the woods. I withheld it from the air.

I heard nobody crawling, walking, running. I heard no one hiding behind a tree, breathing. When I tilted my head, all I could see, very high above me, was a bird. At least I think that's what it was. It was hairless, its face so plain. What troubled me was that I could see the details of its wings too clearly, better than usual, and then I realized it was because the wings weren't flapping, weren't even moving. The bird, far aloft, was perfectly still, falling through the air.

Perhaps it had received a fright, high up in the air. Perhaps it saw something, suffered a shock, lost its powers, and started to fall.

I shut my eyes, waiting for the sound of impact.

57

I spent the morning outside the hut waiting for Esther to return. I could have ventured after her, but there were too many directions she could have taken and it seemed safer to wait, since she would be back soon, I was sure.

When the afternoon dimmed and grew cold, when I heard nothing stumbling out of the woods, I took a pull from my last remaining stash of assets, then risked everything and whispered her name. The word *Esther* was so cold in my mouth. I whispered it, then spoke it, but my mouth was too dry and I'm sure I said it wrong. If Esther was still out there she would have heard only a low moaning, something senseless from far away. Whatever I said was not her name. I should have practiced more. I should have been ready for this.

Now in the advancing darkness I can only wait for Esther to return. One does not simply leave a father when there are still so many terrible uncertainties to master.

I would have served as an escort on her outing. Had Esther desired, I would have even hung back so she would not have needed to see me. I do wish she had availed herself of my experience. It is very possible that I could have helped. Yet I understand that Esther must do things herself, always, on her own terms, and that gains made in my presence, with my help, to her do not look like gains at all. I understand this.

To be Esther's father is to try with all my might not to get caught being her father. I can be that person for her. I will be.

When Esther returns, healthy and strong again, ready to take her place as my daughter, together we can sit at the hole in our hut and listen as one family, the two of us bending together into the old hole that might deliver our missing piece.

We will listen for the footsteps of Esther's mother, who could be here soon. It is a difficult trip, but not impossible. If I could find my way here from Forsythe, groping along the orange cable, then so can Claire. She is stronger, smarter than I ever was, and she can zero in on us even blinded, even ill. She will find us here, it is really just a question of when. When Esther returns to me, we will wait for her mother together, as a family.

It may take days or weeks, but it will not matter, we will wait. And when Claire climbs through the hole, exhausted from her travels, caked in the filth of the tunnels, Esther and I will lead her to the outdoor shower, boil extra water for the cleansing. We'll ready a little mountain of soft towels, and Esther will go inside to choose from the bright new clothes we pulled from the shelves in town.

While Claire showers, Esther and I will smile at each other, look down, draw nonsense signs in the dirt with a stick. We will be excited, but we will wait, give Claire her time.

When my family is together again I will not need to speak, to read, to write. What is there, anyway, to say? The three of us require no speech. We are fine in our silence. This is the world we prefer.

It will be enough to walk out, the three of us, along the high, scary ledge that lords over the creek and cuts up past the shadow of the Monastery into the wide-open field. We will not need to speak. Under our feet will be the vast, shifting salt deposits, just a residue of everything that's ever been said. That's all that's left. We will walk through it into the clearing. We can have a quiet lunch on the rocks, then stretch out to rest in the sun.

I will wait for them here in my hut, and when Claire and Esther return, this is what we'll do, as a family.

ACKNOWLEDGMENTS

For guidance and close reading I am grateful to Marty Asher, Heidi Julavits, Deb Olin Unferth, Sam Lipsyte, Denise Shannon, Andrew Carlson, Michael Chabon, and Jonathan Lethem.

Thanks to Ruchika Tomar and Sunil Yapa for research assistance.

For their generous support I am indebted to the American Academy of Arts and Letters, the Creative Capital Foundation, the Lannan Foundation, and the MacDowell Colony.

ALSO BY BEN MARCUS

NOTABLE AMERICAN WOMEN

On a farm in Ohio, American women led by Jane Dark practice all means of behavior modification in an attempt to attain complete stillness and silence. Witnessing (and subjected to) their cultish actions is one Ben Marcus, whose father, Michael Marcus, may be buried in the back yard, and whose mother, Jane Marcus, enthusiastically condones the use of her son for (generally unsuccessful) breeding purposes, among other things. Inventing his own uses for language, Ben Marcus has written a harrowing, hilarious, strangely moving, altogether engrossing work of fiction that will be read and argued over for years to come.

Fiction/Literature

ALSO AVAILABLE FROM ANCHOR BOOKS

The Anchor Book of New American Short Stories (Editor)